SLAUGHTER at WOLF CREEK

SLAUGHTER at WOLF CREEK

WILLIAM W. JOHNSTONE
AND J.A. JOHNSTONE

P

PINNACLE BOOKS
Kensington Publishing Corp.
www.kensingtonbooks.com

CHAPTER 1

"Buzzard's Bluff," Reese Salter announced as he pulled his horse up before a rough wooden sign bearing the name of the town. The other four in his party of five pulled up around him. Just beyond the sign, they saw a church that had its own sign identifying it as First Baptist Church of Buzzard's Bluff. They took a couple of minutes to look over the main street. From their position short of the church, they could see all the way to the stable at the north end of town.

"It don't look like much of a town," Jack Ramsey felt inspired to comment. "I don't see but two saloons."

"Yonder's the bank," Shorty Cobb said. "At least they got one." He paused a few moments, then said, "They've got a jail, too. So I reckon that means they've got a sheriff."

"Nice lookin' hotel," Paul Porter commented, "fancy name, too—River House Hotel, right across the street from the church."

"Well, let's look it over," Reese said and nudged his horse with his heels. "Then we'll get us something to drink and maybe some dinner." They continued on up the street past the Golden Rail Saloon.

"Maybe I'll just wait right here for you," Hutch joked as

they looked it over. "You fellers oughta be able to go see the dad-blamed bank without me." It was the kind of remark expected from Hutch.

"This'un comin' up next looks more like the one they built for you, Hutch," Shorty said. "The Lost Coyote, they've probably been waitin' for you to show up."

"Well, I don't wanna disappoint 'em," Hutch shot back. "If I don't get a drink of likker pretty soon, I think I might throw a fit."

"If you do," Shorty said, "we'll handle it the same way Porter took care of that ol' hound dog that used to follow him around when it took a fit." His remark brought a chuckle from the gang.

"I'll even do the job for ya, Hutch," Paul Porter cracked. "It wouldn't be as hard for me to do it as it was when I put that ol' hound dog down."

Everyone laughed but Reese, and that was only because his mind was concentrating on the bank as they slow-walked their horses past it. A simple white frame building, it appeared to be an easy nut to crack. From the look of it, he doubted it had a safe with a time lock. By the same token, he would be surprised if the bank kept a great amount of cash on hand. But, while the payday might not be great, it was better than nothing, and the risk involved was minimal. So far, he liked what he had seen. He had never heard of Buzzard's Bluff before they rode in today. He and his gang just happened upon it while following a trail north along the Navasota River. His intention had been to follow it until they reached Wolf Creek, then he was going to head east to Madisonville to spend the night. He figured the fact that he had never heard of Buzzard's Bluff was likely because it was a young town. And if they had a sheriff, he was not likely a highly qualified one, and probably had no help in enforcing the law. When he conveyed those thoughts to Paul Porter, Porter was not sure he agreed with him.

"Look at the buildings on this street," Porter said. "Do they look like new buildings to you?" He didn't wait for Reese's answer. "We just ain't ever heard nothin' about a place named Buzzard's Bluff 'cause we ain't ever operated in this part of Texas. I don't know about you, but I expect it's been eight or ten years since I rode up the Navasota River past Navasota. I just wonder if the bank has change for a dollar. Might not be worth foolin' with."

"They're all worth foolin' with," Reese replied, "'specially if there ain't much risk in it."

When they reached the stable at the top of the street, Reese said, "There was a dinin' room beside that hotel. They oughta still be open for dinner right now. You wanna ride back down there and get somethin' to eat?"

"Won't likely be able to get a drink of likker in there," Hutch replied.

"The food might be better'n what we'd get in a saloon," Jack Ramsey said. "You never know what you're gonna get in a saloon."

"Yeah, but if you drink enough before you start eatin', you don't care that much," Hutch insisted.

"Damn it, Hutch," Ramsey replied, "sounds like you're wantin' to start your drinkin' a might early. We ain't et no dinner yet and we've still got a good piece of ridin' to do before we get to Madisonville."

Reese interrupted their argument. "I'm thinkin' it don't make no sense to ride all the way over to Madisonville when we got a town right here. We might as well stay here tonight."

"Well, that sure makes sense to me," Shorty declared.

"How 'bout it, Reese? You thinkin' about makin' camp by the river, or stayin' in the hotel?"

"I'm thinkin' I'd like to find out a little bit more about that bank," Reese answered. "We mighta just rode into this town outta blind luck. I'd like to find out if it's as easy as it looks. So, I favor gittin' a room in the hotel and leavin' our horses at that stable tonight. We can check out both saloons tonight, and we oughta get a look at the sheriff. If everything looks all right, we can hit that bank in the mornin'." He was already speculating that it would be pretty difficult for the sheriff to mount a posse to go after five outlaws. He would know more about the town after an evening at the saloons.

"I reckon that decides it then," Ramsey said. "Let's go ahead and see if we can get some rooms, and then we'll eat in the dinin' room. I expect we oughta do that first before we take our horses to the stable, in case the dinin' room's fixin' to close."

"I think I feel a fit comin' on," Hutch complained. Reese always talked in terms of what he, personally, was going to do, but it was just his way. There was no questioning his authority. He was the boss, and what he decided to do, every one of the other four followed suit. "I reckon I can hold that fit off a little while longer," Hutch declared when he realized no one was paying any attention to his remarks. With the decision made, they turned their horses around and rode back to the River House and dismounted.

Rob Parker, the hotel desk clerk, looked up in surprise when the five men walked into the lobby. "Can I help you gentlemen?"

"Maybe you can," Reese Salter answered. "That is, if you've got some vacant beds at a reasonable rate. My men and I could use a night sleepin' on a bed for a change, a good meal, and a quiet place to get a drink of whiskey. Can you fix us up with that?"

"Yes, sir, I think I can," Rob replied. "Just for the one night?" Reese said that it was, so Rob said, "I can give you a room rate of a dollar a night, and there's one double bed in each room, but it depends on how many you intend to sleep to a bed."

"That seems reasonable enough," Reese said. "We'll take three rooms." He figured the other four men could sleep double and he'd take a room alone. "That's three dollars, right?"

Rob hesitated a moment before replying. "Well, there's usually an extra charge of twenty-five cents for each additional person in the room, but we've got plenty of empty rooms right now. So three dollars for one night will be all right." He turned the register around for Reese to sign. "You can sign for your party of five, if you like, Mister . . ."

"Hey, Reese," Hutch interrupted. "Ask him if the dinin' room is still open for dinner."

Reese turned to give Hutch a look of disgust for yelling out his name before he turned back to the desk clerk. "Smith," he answered Rob's question, "Reese Smith. Is the dinin' room still open?"

Rob took the three dollars Reese handed him and said, "Yes, sir, Mr. Smith, they don't close for another hour. Like most hotels, we ask that you not wear your guns in the dining room. If you don't want to leave them in your room, there's a table in the dining room where you can leave your weapons while you eat." He reached in the cabinet on the wall behind him and took out three keys and handed them to Reese. "They're the first three rooms at the top of the stairs," Rob said.

Reese held onto the keys until they went back outside

to get their saddlebags to take up to the rooms. Then he put one of the keys in his pocket and casually tossed the other two at the four of them. Like schoolboys, Hutch, Shorty, and Porter scrambled for the keys as if it was a competition. Jack Ramsey, the oldest of the five men, refused to participate in the contest. He was fortunate in that Porter caught one of the keys, so he picked Jack to share his room. Unfortunately for Shorty, Hutch caught the other key. "Looks like it's you and me in my room," Hutch said with a grin.

"I'll be damned," Shorty replied. "I'll go back in there and give that feller another dollar for my own room. I remember that night in Sherman when you threw up all that whiskey in the bed and you was so drunk you didn't know the door was open on your other end, too."

"That was just on account of some bad likker they sold us at that saloon," Hutch insisted. "You know it's bad likker when it gets your bowels in an uproar."

"It didn't affect nobody else that way," Shorty replied.

Reese shook his head impatiently. "You can sleep in my room, Shorty," he said.

"'Preciate it, Reese," Shorty stated sincerely.

They took their saddlebags and rifles up to the rooms, then went back downstairs to the dining room where they were met at the door by Lacy James, the manager. Taking one look at the five rough-looking individuals, Lacy began her speech about the dining room's policy on firearms, but Reese interrupted. "We know," he said and unbuckled his gun belt. The other four men followed suit. "Fellow at the hotel told us you wouldn't feed us if we didn't take 'em off."

"He said you had to start doin' that 'cause the food was so bad that folks was shootin' at the cook," Hutch remarked. "Is there any truth to that?"

His comment caused Lacy to chuckle. Concerned at first sight of the rough-looking crew of strangers, she decided they only looked like trouble. "I'll tell Myrtle what you said. I'm sure she'll take extra care when she loads your plate." She led them to the big table in the center of the room. "You fellows might have a little more room here. Everybody drinkin' coffee?" Everybody was, so she said, "Cindy will be taking care of you. I'll go help her get some coffee out here."

"I'm mighty glad Cindy's gonna take care of us," Hutch responded as Lacy started toward the kitchen. "Maybe we'd better eat something first, though." Lacy pretended she didn't hear him. His companions had long since acquired the habit of ignoring the constant drivel that came out of his mouth, so his effort passed without a comment.

"I'll help you take five coffees out," Lacy said to Cindy when she went into the kitchen. "I think those boys would be better off eating dinner at The Golden Rail."

"Who are they?" Cindy asked and walked to the door to take a look at them.

"I don't know," Lacy answered. "They look like typical saddle tramps. I'm glad Mack is still eating his dinner."

"Well, I hope they don't cause any trouble," Cindy said, "since there's five of 'em."

"Oh, I doubt they'll cause any trouble," Lacy said then, aware that she had caused Cindy some concern. "They just looked like they'd be more at home in the saloon. We'll serve 'em up some good food and get 'em outta here real quick."

The two women took the coffee out and placed it on the table. "We're serving beef stew and cornbread for dinner today," Cindy told them. "If you don't want that, we can give you some biscuits and ham." She looked around the group and all opted for the beef stew. "Myrtle makes pretty good beef stew," she continued. "You can ask the sheriff what he thinks of it." Her remark was met with questioning looks from all five. She nodded toward the kitchen door and the man getting up from the small table next to it.

With a pretty good idea why Cindy had made the unusual statement, Mack Bragg got up from the table, even though he had planned to sit there for another cup of coffee. He walked over to the big table. "Howdy, boys. What brings you fellows into our little town?"

Reese answered him. "Howdy, Sheriff. I saw you sittin' by yourself back in the corner, but I didn't notice the badge till you got up. We're just passin' through on our way to Waco. We decided Buzzard's Bluff looks like a nice little town, so we decided to sleep in the hotel tonight and get a couple of good meals, and maybe visit the saloon tonight. Which one do you recommend?"

"Depends on what you're looking for," Mack told him. "They're both good saloons. The Golden Rail is a little noisier, and the Lost Coyote caters more toward the local folks. They're both run by honest men." He paused and glanced at Lacy. "I should say honest men and woman. Anyway, I hope you have a nice peaceful evenin', and Cindy's right, the food here is mighty good."

"Why, thank you very much, Sheriff," Reese said. "That's right hospitable of you. We plan to have a good time tonight, but we ain't here to cause anybody any trouble. Ain't none of us figurin' on seein' the inside of your jail tonight."

Mack chuckled. "I'm glad to hear that," he said. "I druther not work tonight, myself. Enjoy your dinner." He turned and walked to the outside entrance with Lacy and stopped by the door. "You want me to hang around till they're finished?" He asked, speaking softly.

"I really don't think that's necessary," Lacy replied. "I think we were just over-reacting, judging a book by its cover, I guess."

"Well, you know I ain't very far away," Mack said. "If you step outside the door and holler, I might hear you down at the jail," he joked. "I'll be outside on the street," he said.

Lacy was right in her assessment of the five strangers. They had no intention of causing any trouble in her dining room. They were noisy, but not raucous, content to enjoy a good meal. When they finished, they paid up and compli-mented the cook. Even Cindy was comfortable with their behavior. Outside, they climbed on their horses and rode up to the stable and left their horses with Henry Barnes for the night. "Which one of them saloons you wanna try first?" Hutch asked.

"Might as well try the first one from here," Shorty said. "The one they named after you, Hutch, the Lost Coyote. That all right with the rest of ya?" he asked, but he was looking at Reese for his okay.

"Don't make no difference," Reese said. "Might as well hit the first one we come to."

CHAPTER 2

It was a typically slow day in the Lost Coyote. The small group of regulars who usually ate dinner at the saloon had all finished a plate of Annie Grey's sliced ham with red beans and rice and returned to their regular activities. Only Tuck Tucker and Ham Greeley had remained to have an after-dinner drink. They stood at the end of the bar talking to Tiny Davis, the bartender, and watching Clarice and Ruby help Annie pick up the dinner dishes and clean the tables. "Where's Ben and Rachel?" Tuck asked, since it was customary to see one, or both, of them in the saloon.

"Rachel took Ben back to the office after dinner," Tiny said. "She's tryin' to show him how to do the books, in case she gets sick or something." He chuckled then said, "Ben told her she ain't allowed to get sick. He don't like bookwork."

"Hell," Tuck declared. "There ain't nothin' to learn. I just keep track of my costs and expenses for the harness shop in my head. I don't keep no books."

"Everybody ain't got the head for figures like you do, Tuck," Ham commented and winked at Tiny. "You oughta know that."

The little red-haired man drew himself up to his full

sixty-one-and-a-half inches. "You might think you're japin' me," he said, "but I have found that to be a fact."

"Seems like if you've got such a sharp brain, I wouldn't win so much offa you when we play them two-handed poker games," Ham taunted.

"Shoot," Tuck replied. "If I didn't let you win a few hands, you'd quit playing with me. Ain't that right, Tiny?" Tiny didn't reply. He winked at Clarice instead, knowing she heard Tuck's remark as she and Ruby walked past the bar on their way upstairs after helping Annie. When business was slow, as it was today, the two women usually went to their rooms to rest up for the busy time after supper. They had no sooner disappeared at the top of the steps when Tuck said, "Looks like business is pickin' up, Tiny." Tiny turned to look toward the front door to see what Tuck was referring to. Two men, strangers to him, pushed through the batwing doors, followed by three more a moment later.

Reese paused a few seconds to look the room over. Seeing no one in the saloon but the two men talking to the bartender, he walked over to the bar. "Howdy," he called out as he approached. "Looks to me like you could use some business."

"You got that right," Tiny answered him. "Whaddaya gonna have?"

"Me and my boys have been ridin' for a long time without hittin' a town," Reese replied. "So we're in need of some genuine rye whiskey."

"I can fix you right up," Tiny said. "You want it at the bar, or at a table?"

"We're gonna need a full bottle," Reese answered, "so we'll sit down." He looked around to find his men had already selected a table. Tiny reached under the bar and took out an unopened bottle of rye whiskey. He held it up for Reese to see. "Yeah, that looks like the real stuff," he said. So, Tiny opened the bottle and handed it to him. Then he picked up five glasses and followed Reese over to the table.

"You fellows ever been to Buzzard's Bluff before?" Tiny asked. "I know you ain't ever been in here before."

"Never even knew there was a town called Buzzard's Bluff," Jack answered him.

"That's right," Reese said, "we're just here for the night. Then we'll be on our way to Waco in the mornin'."

"What you goin' to Waco for?" Tuck asked, as was his custom.

"To mind our own business," Hutch said.

"Don't pay him no mind," Reese was quick to say. "He's always japin'. We're going up there to talk to a feller that needs a crew to move a herd of cattle."

"So you're cowhands," Tiny said. "We get some fellows from the Double-D in here right regular. You know any of them boys?"

"Can't say as I do," Reese replied, trying to switch Tiny to some other subject. He saw his opportunity when the door in the back of the saloon opened, and Rachel walked in. "Well, now," he remarked, "the scenery's gittin' better in here for a fact. Does she work here?"

"She's the owner," Tiny said, then corrected himself. "I mean she's half-owner."

"Her and her husband own it?" Reese asked, still eyeing Rachel openly.

"Nah," Tiny told him, "Rachel ain't married. She's in a partnership with Ben Savage, and they make a mighty good team."

"Is that a fact?" He looked back toward the bar where

Tuck had returned, and he and Ham were apparently arguing over something. "One of them two?" Reese asked.

"Lord, no," Tiny replied, chuckling. "Her partner's a retired Texas Ranger. Funny coincidence, the original owner was a retired Texas Ranger, and Rachel managed the saloon for him, fellow by the name of Jim Vickers, but she weren't a partner. Vickers died and left this saloon to Ben Savage. So, Ben retired and went into the saloon business. But he said Rachel was doin' the job of runnin' this saloon, so he made her his partner."

"That's a mighty interesting story," Reese said. He looked behind him at Jack Ramsey, who was leaning in toward him and Tiny. "Are you hearin' any of this?"

"I sure am," Jack answered and nodded to Tiny. "Mighty interestin', I don't reckon you get robbed very often, do ya?"

Tiny laughed and shook his head.

"Does—what'd you say his name is—Savage? Does he ever come into the saloon?" Reese asked.

"Sure," Tiny replied, "every day. He's here now in the office. He don't usually stay in the office much, so he'll most likely be in here before long." He turned then to see Jim Bowden coming in the front door. "I expect I'd best get back to the bar," Tiny said, but paused when Hutch asked a question.

"Why do they call you Tiny?" Hutch joked and stood up beside the huge bartender and waited for the laugh.

Tiny looked down at the smaller man and replied, "Danged if I know," he said. "My name's Gerald." He went back to the bar then to greet the blacksmith. "Howdy, Jim, you drinkin'?"

"Tiny," Jim acknowledged, and nodded to Rachel who

had stopped to visit with Tuck and Ham at the end of the bar. "I wasn't gonna, but I think I could use a little shot of corn whiskey. Maybe it'd help those soup beans I filled my belly with at dinner settle down some. I brought Ben's horse, in case he wants to see if those new shoes are gonna be all right." He looked around the room then, and seeing no sign of Ben, he said, "If Ben ain't here, I'll just take his horse back to the stable."

"Well, he was here," Tiny said, "unless he went out the back door." He turned his head toward the end of the bar. "Rachel, is Ben still here? Jim brought his horse."

"Yes, he's in the office. I'll get him, Jim." She went back out the door and returned in a few moments with Ben following.

"Hey, Jim," Ben greeted him, "you didn't have to bring Cousin down here. You coulda just left him with Henry at the stable."

"Weren't no trouble," Jim replied. "Gave me an excuse to get a drink of likker."

"I'm sure the shoes are fine, just like they were last time," Ben said. "I can tell right away if Cousin likes 'em. Finish your drink and we'll take a look at 'em." He turned to address the five strangers gathered around one of the tables sharing a bottle of rye whiskey. "Welcome to Lost Coyote. Is Tiny takin' care of you fellows all right?"

For once, Hutch had nothing to say. In fact, all five of the outlaws had listened with great interest when Tiny was relating the history of the Lost Coyote. Expecting a tired old man who had at one time been a Texas Ranger, they were all surprised when the formidable figure of Ben Savage walked up to their table. He was definitely not a tired old man. Since Reese was the undisputed leader of the gang, the other four let him do the talking. "Yes, sir, we're enjoyin' a little drink here. Tiny was tellin' us that you and the lady own this place. 'Preciate the welcome."

Since no one seemed anxious to make more conversation, Ben headed toward the front door. "Come on, Jim, and we'll see how Cousin likes his new shoes." Jim tossed his whiskey down and followed after him. Outside, Ben spent a couple of minutes stroking the big dun gelding's face and neck before he took a look at both front hooves. "Looks fine like it always does," he said. Then he untied the reins from the hitching rail and leaped up on Cousin's back. "Seems like a few years ago it was a lot easier to jump on a horse's back."

Jim chuckled. "Maybe I shoulda gone to the stable and put your saddle on him."

"Wait right here and I'll be back to settle up with what I owe ya," Ben said. Then he wheeled Cousin away from the rail and started out toward the south end of the street at a fast lope. When he got to the hotel, he wheeled Cousin around again and galloped back, passing the saloon and stopping at the stable, where he jumped off and turned the horse over to Henry Barnes. "I expect I'd better give him a little exercise," he told Henry. "I'll take him for a ride tomorrow." He had been concerned about the condition of the dun's hooves, so he had let Cousin go barefoot for a couple of months. And when he and Henry inspected the gelding's hooves, they seemed to have gotten healthier, and some of the hoof loss had been recovered.

When he walked back to the Lost Coyote, he found Jim Bowden still standing out front. "Cousin said he likes 'em just fine, but he's gonna miss goin' barefoot." He reached in his pocket and counted out the price of the shoeing and handed it to Jim.

"I owe you for a drink," Jim said.

"That was included in the cost," Ben said. "Actually, I figured it was worth two drinks. Come on back inside and get the other one."

"Thanks, I don't mind if I do," Jim said, and they went back inside. Ben went behind the bar and poured another drink of corn whiskey for Jim.

The party of five got up from the table and Reese paid Tiny for the bottle of rye. "I'll take the rest back to the hotel," Reese said. "We thought when we sat down we'd finish the whole bottle and order another one, but I reckon we ain't the drinkers we thought we were." He smiled at Ben, who was standing beside Tiny. "I don't know about the rest of the boys, but I think I'll walk around your town and clear my head a little bit before it's time for supper."

"Probably not a bad idea," Ben said. "Nice afternoon for a walk, anyway. 'Preciate the business."

When the five strangers walked out of the saloon, Tuck and Ham moved up the bar to talk to Ben and Jim. "There's something that just ain't right about that bunch of drifters," Tuck declared. "I might need to go tell Mack to keep an eye on 'em."

Ham looked at Ben and rolled his eyes up toward the ceiling. Then he said, "Maybe you're right, Tuck. Why don't you go tell the sheriff about 'em? I'll bet he'd appreciate any help you can give him."

"They seemed all right to me," Tiny said, "just a bunch of cowhands on their way to a job up near Waco. What did you think, Ben?"

"Hard for me to say," Ben answered. "I didn't really talk to 'em that long. I saw what Tuck mighta been talking about. They didn't look like typical cowhands if you were to go by the clothes they were wearing. But, hell, they ain't drivin' any cattle now, so I reckon they might wanna wear something else for a change. Who knows? At least they didn't bring any trouble in here, and that's what counts. Right, Rachel?"

"That's right," she answered, "and now that you men have settled that issue, I think I'll go see if there's any coffee left in the pot. Annie may have cleaned it out already. She should be about ready to go home."

Outside on the street, Reese and his gang were also talking about their visit to the Lost Coyote. Porter was the first to express what they had all wondered about. "That damn Ben Savage looks like he could still be ridin' with the Texas Rangers. You reckon he works with the sheriff when it comes to any robberies or killin's in town?"

The others nodded, and Shorty commented. "He's a big son of a gun, ain't he? He was near-bout as big as that bartender. You reckon we oughta think again about robbin' that bank?"

"As long as we're makin' up a posse," Hutch declared, "that blacksmith weren't exactly no runt, neither."

"I swear," Reese interrupted. "I can't believe what I'm hearin'. There ain't no reason to think that Savage would work with the sheriff to catch a bank robber. Why would he want to? He's quit the law business. As long as we ain't robbin' his saloon, he don't care what we do. Even if they was to try to stop us, they'd just be bigger targets to shoot at. I say bring 'em on, and if they did come after us, a couple of shots with a rifle would turn that posse around pretty damn fast."

"I reckon you're right about that," Jack Ramsey spoke up then. "And as long as we behave ourselves tonight, there ain't no reason the sheriff or that ex-ranger should get any idea we're up to somethin'."

"Absolutely right," Reese said then. "Now, I wanna get

a closer look at that bank. Jack, why don't you go with me. The rest of you can go back to the hotel, or whatever you wanna do. We just don't want the five of us to go hang around the bank. We'll just pretend we bumped into each other in front of the bank and stopped to have a conversation."

"We gonna eat supper in the hotel dinin' room tonight?" Porter asked. "That was some pretty good grub we got there today."

"Suits me," Reese replied, "unless you wanna see if that other saloon has a cook." When Shorty and Hutch both immediately spoke up for supper at the hotel, Reese shrugged. "Might as well go with a winner," he agreed. "Matter of fact, we might as well eat breakfast there in the morning, too. We oughta have plenty of time before the bank opens. We can have us a nice breakfast before we make our withdrawal."

"We can visit the Golden Rail after supper," Hutch proposed. "What?" He blurted when everybody looked at him and laughed.

They split up then and started strolling around the little town, looking as casual as a band of outlaws could. Reese and Jack hadn't gotten far when they met Sheriff Mack Bragg walking the street, himself. "Howdy, boys," Mack greeted them. "You decide to stay in town tonight?"

"We sure did," Reese answered. "Like we told you at dinner, we had already decided to stay overnight in your town to see if it's as peaceful as it looks before we even found out that dinin' room was worth spendin' some more time in."

"Glad you're enjoyin' your visit," Mack said.

"We went into the Lost Coyote for a drink after we left

the dinin' room," Reese went on. "Nice quiet little saloon, we met the owners while we was in there. Kinda unusual, a man and a woman business partners, at least in that business. I reckon it makes it mighty handy to have a Texas Ranger right here in town to kinda help out when you have to enforce the law."

"I expect it would," Mack responded, "but Ben is an *ex*-Texas Ranger. So he ain't gettin' paid to help me with my job. And I don't go to the Lost Coyote to help tend the bar when he gets extra busy. He's just half-owner of a saloon." A certain amount of pride dictated Mack's response to Reese's speculation, although Ben had been ready to help on many occasions. "I'll tell you what, though, the Coyote is one saloon I don't have to worry about."

"I reckon not," Reese replied and stepped aside. "We'll take a look at this end of town for ya," he joked. "If anything's wrong, we'll fire a couple of shots in the air, so you can come runnin'."

"That's a good idea," Mack responded, "only it would be better if you had a bow and arrow. We like to keep the noise down, and I'd have to arrest you if you go to shootin' your guns inside the town limits."

Reese and Jack both forced a chuckle in response to the sheriff's attempt at humor, then continued their walk up the street toward the stable. Directly across the street from the bank at that point, there was not much to see. There was no one going in or out at the time, so they couldn't even get a quick look through an open door. "Let's walk on up to the stable and cross the street. I know how we can look that bank over," Reese said. "I wanna see what I'm walkin' into tomorrow morning."

They continued walking up to the end of the street and

crossed over. When they came back down the other side, they stopped at the bank. When Reese stepped up on the little porch, Jack blurted, "What tha . . . ? You goin' in?"

"Hell, yeah," Reese replied. "I told you, I wanna know what we're gonna find in the mornin'. Come on, you need to get a look at the inside, too, so you can help me tell the others."

"You sure?" Jack asked. "I figured we'd just bust in there and take what we could in the mornin'." Reese didn't answer. Instead, he opened the door and walked inside. Jack had little choice but to follow him.

Inside, they found two teller cages on the right side of the lobby. On the other side of the open lobby, there were a couple of doors, both closed. In the center of the back wall there was another door that evidently led to the vault, if they had one. It was a typical setup for a small bank. Standing behind Reese, Jack Ramsey wanted to tell him that the layout was almost exactly as he would have guessed, and there had been no need to come inside to verify it. Reese looked it over for a few moments, then stepped up to the first teller's cage. "Can I help you, sir?" Stanley Townsend asked, having watched with some concern while Reese was looking them over.

"Yes, sir," Reese replied. "Leastways, I hope you can. I'm just passin' through town, so I ain't got no bank account with you. But I would sure appreciate it if you could break this fifty-dollar-bill for me. Seems like every place I go to buy something, they ain't got change for a fifty, and I've almost run out of everything smaller." He reached in his pocket, removed the fifty from a small roll of bills, and laid it on the ledge of the window.

"I think we can do that for you," Townsend said. He

picked up the bill and examined it, then turned it over and examined the other side.

"It's real," Reese assured him.

"Yes, sir, I can see that," Townsend said. "Tens and fives all right?"

Reese said that would be just fine, so Townsend handed the fifty over to Peter Best in the cage next to him and Best examined the bill while Townsend counted out fifty dollars in fives and tens. Best handed the fifty back to Townsend without saying a word, and Townsend pushed the stack of smaller bills under the framework of bars that filled the opening. "What else can I do for you? You might think about opening an account instead of carrying a lot of money around in your pocket."

"I certainly agree with you," Reese replied. "But like I said, I'm just passin' through Buzzard's Bluff. I don't know when I'll be back this way again. 'Preciate it, though." He turned around, almost bumping into Ramsey, who was still staring at the teller. "Come on, partner, we're done here." They casually walked out of the bank.

"You did what?" Hutch exclaimed.

"Went in the bank," Jack repeated. "Me and Reese went into the bank and looked it over. Reese got 'em to break a fifty-dollar-bill he's been rat-holing for I don't know how long."

"Where the hell did you get a fifty-dollar-bill?" Porter wanted to know.

"San Antone," Reese said with a smile, "the last bank we robbed, and I intend to get it back in the mornin'. I didn't see anything to keep us from walkin' right in there and cleanin' out all the cash we can find. I don't know what kind of safe they've got in the back room. We'll just have to see about that in the mornin'."

"How many they got workin' in there?" Shorty asked.

"I don't think there's but three in the whole bank," Reese answered. "Them two tellers ain't gonna be no trouble. Did you think so, Jack?" Ramsey shook his head. "We didn't see the bigshot president or whatever they call him, 'cause his door was closed and he never came out," Reese went on. "So I reckon we'll do it like we did last time. Me and Ramsey and Shorty will go in the bank and get the money. Porter and Hutch will stay outside, take care of the horses, and keep anybody from goin' in the bank. That oughta do it. We've done it before. Ain't no reason why this should be any different. We'll eat us another fine supper and visit that other saloon before we go to bed. Just remember, tomorrow's a workin' day, so take it easy with that likker tonight."

CHAPTER 3

"Well, I see you came back for more," Lacy James greeted them when they showed up at the hotel dining room for supper. "The food must not have been too bad at dinner today."

Never one to miss an opportunity, Hutch responded first. "The food was so bad at dinner that we decided to try you again tonight. We figured it couldn't be as bad as that dinner was."

"Pay him no mind," Reese told her. "It was so good we had to come back tonight, and I expect we might even have breakfast here before we leave town in the morning. What time do you open for breakfast?"

"Six o'clock," Lacy answered as they all started unbuckling their gun belts without being reminded. "Thank you for remembering," she said. "The four of you are welcome to sit where you want." She pointed a finger at Hutch and said, "I haven't decided if I'm going to let you eat inside or out on the back steps." Her quip prompted a wave of guffaws from the four.

"Make him eat outside," Shorty japed.

"I was just funnin'," Hutch pleaded.

"All right," Lacy said, "but if you don't behave, you're gonna have to sit in the corner by yourself." She had to smile at the funny little man. He reminded her of Tuck Tucker. She shook her head when she thought about how concerned she had been when they first came in her dining room. Now, she was happy to see they had come back. They returned to the big table in the center of the room where Cindy was waiting to see if everybody wanted coffee or water.

The five outlaws were already eating the meatloaf Myrtle had prepared for supper when Ben came in the door. "Ben Savage," Hutch sang out when he walked in.

"Howdy, boys," Ben returned. "I see you found the best place for supper."

"We sure did," Reese replied, "and I'm glad we decided to stay here tonight. Does a man good to stop and take a little holiday once in a while. We'll be thinking about Lacy's dinin' room when we're back sleepin' on the ground and cookin' our own grub."

"I know what you mean," Ben said and walked on back to his usual table in the back corner, near the kitchen door.

"Evening, Ben," Cindy greeted him with a cup of coffee. "Meatloaf tonight," she said, "rice and beans and biscuits."

"Sounds good to me," he said, so she went in the kitchen to fetch it. He sat there sipping the hot coffee for only a couple of minutes when Mack Bragg walked in. Ben watched as Mack received a similar welcome to the one he had received from the five strangers at the big table. As he had done, Mack exchanged a few words with the strangers. Then seeing Ben in the back corner, came back to join him.

"Mind if I set with you?" Mack asked.

"Glad to have some company," Ben replied. "'Course, I reckon I coulda sat down at the big table with the five cowhands."

"Yeah, thought about that, myself," Mack said as he pulled a chair back. He sat down, smiled at Cindy when she brought his coffee, and waited until she went back to the kitchen before continuing. "I wanted to talk to you about those cowhands. I had a funny feelin' about those boys, so I went to talk to Rob Parker at the hotel about 'em. He told me they checked into three rooms for the night. I asked him what their names were, and he said the one called Reese wanted to check all three rooms under his name, Reese Smith. Rod said he told him that was fine, but could he just give him the last name of each one of the other four, so he could know who was in which room." He waited then for Cindy to place his plate in front of him. When she left again, he went on. "Two of 'em was named Smith, same as Reese. The other two were named Jones." He paused to wait for Ben's reaction.

"Well, now, that's one helluva coincidence, ain't it?" Ben responded.

Seeing that he had Ben's attention, Mack continued. "This afternoon, I ran into Reese and one of the other men walking up the street. We talked a little bit, then I went on back to the jail. But before I went inside, I stopped and watched those two for a little while longer. They went inside the bank." Once again, he paused to judge Ben's interest in what he was telling him. Satisfied that Ben was interested, he went on. "Later on, I decided to go to the bank to see what they went in there for. I talked to Lawton Grier, and he said he didn't even know those two were in the bank till after they left, and Stanley and Peter told him about it. They said one of 'em had a fifty-dollar-bill and wanted to change it for some smaller bills." He waited for Ben's reaction.

"I can see why you've got a funny feelin' about 'em," Ben said. "Especially since they're reluctant to give anybody their names. Breakin' that fifty sounds like nothing more than an excuse to take a look inside the bank to see what's what, don't it?" He thought about it for a few seconds. "But they've paid for the hotel rooms, and their horses and packs are in the stable. So they're planning to stay here tonight." He took a sip of hot coffee and nodded slowly. "I'd say it might be worth your time to plan a little reception for 'em in the mornin', just in case they're thinkin' about hittin' the bank tomorrow morning."

"I'm glad you agree," Mack said. "I was thinkin' about waitin' in the bank for 'em in the mornin', and I was afraid I might be over-reactin', and I might get Lawton Grier all upset over nothing. I'm gonna go see Lawton after supper and tell him what I need to do. I'll need to get in the bank early, so nobody sees me go in there, and I'll be waitin' for 'em to make their move."

"There's five of 'em, Mack. You're gonna need some help. So, if you ain't got no objection, I'll go with you to talk to Lawton after we eat, and we'll both wait for the Smiths and the Joneses in the bank tomorrow."

Mack had to catch himself to keep from sighing in relief. Ben's offer of help was what he was hoping for, counting on, actually. But he hesitated to come right out and ask for it. "I can't expect you to come to my aid every time an outlaw shows up in town, Ben. I'm the law in Buzzard's Bluff. It's up to me to do the job. I appreciate the offer, though." He waited then for Ben to insist that he wanted to help.

Instead, Ben shrugged and asked, "Are you sayin' you don't want my help? Maybe I'll get in the way of what you've got planned?"

"No, I ain't sayin' I don't want your help," Mack said, swallowing a great chunk of pride. "Matter of fact, I just didn't wanna come right out and ask you for it. You've done your share for the law in Texas. It ain't right to ask you to help protect the town."

"We wouldn't be worth protectin' if we couldn't step up and help in cases like this," Ben declared. "This is our town; we need to help when you're facin' impossible odds. Matter of fact, you and I can handle them that comes inside the bank. We could use some more help outside the bank, though. And I'm thinkin' Jim Bowden is the man for the job. His forge is right next to the bank, and like you and me, he ain't got a family to worry about. If he's willing to lend a hand, I think we can handle all five of 'em. Whadda you think?"

"I think I'm mighty glad I decided to talk to you about this," Mack replied. He paused for a moment then asked, "What if all this is just my imagination, and those boys ride on outta town in the mornin', on their way to go herd some cows?"

"We'll go to the Lost Coyote and have a drink and be glad we didn't have to go to the trouble," Ben said. "I believe Lawton Grier wouldn't complain at all about you bein' ready to protect his bank. We'll go talk to him after we finish supper. Then we can talk to Jim to see if he's willin'. 'Course, you might prefer we talk to Tuck Tucker, instead," he joked.

They waited until the five drifters had finished eating and left the dining room. Hutch saw fit to comment to Lacy as he went out the door. "Looks like there ain't gonna be no danger of you gittin' robbed with them two settin' back there." She laughed good-naturedly and said she'd see them at breakfast in the morning. "Don't tell ol' Ben Savage we're headin' to the Golden Rail to do our drinkin' tonight," Hutch said. "He might come and haul us outta there."

After leaving the dining room, Ben and Mack walked down the side street to Lawton Grier's house, some seventy-five yards from the center of town, only to find Lawton wasn't home yet. His wife, Pauline, said he never left the bank before seven. "He's in his office, doin' something," she said. "If you're going back to the bank, tell him he's gonna get another cold supper if he doesn't show up pretty soon."

They walked back to the bank and rapped on the back door until finally they heard Lawton Grier at the door. "Who is it?" Lawton questioned.

"It's Mack Bragg, Mr. Grier. I've got Ben Savage with me, and we need to talk to you."

Seconds later, they heard the bolt slide and the key turn in the lock, then the door opened. "Mack, why are you knocking on the back door? You're lucky I even heard you back here. Why didn't you just come to the front door?"

They stepped inside the door and Mack explained. "We didn't wanna take a chance on somebody seein' us come in here."

"Is this about those two fellows you came to ask about

before?" Grier asked, at once concerned, especially since Mack had brought Ben Savage with him. "Do you think they might be planning to try to rob the bank?"

"Well, sir," Mack started, "Ben and I have been talkin' it over, and there's a lot of things that just don't add up about those fellers." He went over everything that he and Ben had discussed that seemed to paint a picture of the five strangers as a bit odd. He concluded by saying that he might be like a dog, barking up a tree where there wasn't any coon, but he thought it better to be safe than sorry.

Lawton looked to Ben then. "And you agree with Mack on this?"

"I think he's doin' his job to be suspicious of those five strangers," Ben answered. "I think there's a damn good chance they're figurin' on hittin' your bank in the mornin'. Like you and Mack, I'm hopin' we're wrong, but I'm bettin' we ain't. And if we are wrong, then there's no harm done. Right?"

"Damn," Lawton swore as he rolled the possibility around in his mind. After a moment, he said, "Just tell me what you want to do."

So Ben and Mack walked around the main lobby to decide where they would position themselves for their reception for Reese and his gang. Once they had decided that, they discussed the time they would meet Lawton at the back door of the bank. "If I had to guess," Ben said, "I'd expect them to hit you right at the time the bank opens for business. They'd figure that the tellers had their money in the cages and that you've opened the safe. So we oughta get here way before that, and we can tell your tellers what to do if they show up. Ain't that what you think, Mack?"

"That's what I think," Mack answered. "When do you usually get here in the mornin's, Mr. Grier?"

"Usually around seven-thirty or eight," Lawton replied. "And we open at nine."

"Seven-thirty, then," Mack said. "That oughta give us plenty of time to do what we need to do. All right with you, Ben?" Ben nodded, so Mack said, "Well, I reckon that's all we can do tonight. We'll see you at seven-thirty."

Lawton walked with them to the back door to let them out. "I appreciate your thinking about this. I don't mind admitting that I might have a little trouble sleeping tonight, though."

"I don't know about that," Ben commented, "but your wife said your supper's gonna be cold if you don't get home pretty soon."

Lawton chuckled in spite of his concern for the coming morning. "Don't oversleep in the morning," he called after them as they walked away.

Everything was dark at the blacksmith's shop next door to the bank. But Ben suggested if it was a typical night, they could find Jim Bowden at the Lost Coyote for his usual drink of whiskey. So they headed in that direction to have one with him. They found him there, sitting at a table, listening to Tuck Tucker telling one of his tales of heroism when Ben first came to Buzzard's Bluff, and he accompanied him to Houston to pick up a wagon load of whiskey. When Tuck saw Ben and Mack walk in, he exclaimed, "Here's Ben now, he'll tell you I was right there at that camp ready to back him up."

"Whatever Tuck said," Ben declared, but he walked on past and headed for a table in the back of the saloon. As he walked by, he tapped Jim Bowden on the shoulder and made a slight motion with his head toward the back of the room. Not understanding, Jim just nodded and smiled, so

Ben made a "come here" motion with his index finger. Thinking Ben might have had some complaint about Cousin's new shoes, Jim got up at once and followed him to the table.

"What's up, Ben?" Jim asked when he caught up with them. "Something wrong with Cousin's new shoes?"

"No." Ben chuckled. "If there was something wrong with those shoes, he woulda come to complain himself. Mack and I was just wonderin' if you might be willing to volunteer your services for the protection of our town." He could see that the comment was enough to spark Jim's curiosity. "Sit down there and I'll get us a drink. You like corn I know. What about you, Mack?" Mack said that was all right with him, so Ben went back to the bar and picked up a bottle and three glasses. When he returned to the table, he saw that Mack was already telling Jim what he and Ben were preparing for. So Ben poured the whiskey and let Mack continue.

"Sure, you can count on me to help out," Ben heard Jim declare. "I don't blame you and Ben. I didn't think that bunch looked like they knew one end of a cow from the other. Just tell me what you want me to do."

"Since your shop is right next door to the bank," Mack went on, "we figure they won't notice if you're watchin' the front door of the bank. At least three of 'em will go inside the bank, maybe four, since they'll be wantin' to grab as much cash as they can. But they'll leave at least one of 'em outside to guard the door, keep any early customers from goin' inside. We think you oughta be able to get the jump on who's guardin' the door. I'll officially deputize you, in case you have to use your weapon." Jim nodded solemnly, prompting Mack to ask, "I don't want to put you in any dangerous position, so I don't expect you to take any big chances. But have you got any hang-ups about pullin' the trigger, if you have to?"

"You mean if I tell him to hold his hands up, and he goes for his gun instead, would I shoot him? The answer to that is hell, yes."

Mack looked at Ben and nodded. "That's all we need to know, ain't it, Ben?"

"That's all," Ben replied. "We'll be ready to go at seven-thirty in the mornin'. Even gives us time for breakfast before we go to work." They had a couple more drinks before Mack said that he had had his limit, since he was still responsible for the town that night. When he left, Rachel came over and sat down at the table with Ben and Jim.

She poured herself a drink using Mack's glass. "I don't reckon the sheriff has hoof-and-mouth-disease."

"I think that's gonna do it for me tonight," Jim said. He got up and said, "Thanks for the drink. I'll see you tomorrow."

There was no more conversation for a few long moments, then Rachel asked, "What's going on with you and Mack Bragg, and maybe Jim Bowden?"

"Whaddaya mean?" Ben responded. "What makes you think something's goin' on?"

"Come on, partner," Rachel replied. "I know you. I can tell when there's something going on in your mind. It usually means you're fixing to ride off somewhere and be gone for a long time. You're not going somewhere, are you?"

"You've got too much imagination in that pretty head of yours," he said. "There ain't nothin' goin' on worth talkin' about, and I sure ain't goin' anywhere. I'll tell you all about it tomorrow, all right?"

"If it's all that unimportant, why can't you just say what it is?"

"'Cause it's something that might not even happen, and it ain't even got anything to do with us or the Lost Coyote. I promise, I'll tell you tomorrow."

CHAPTER 4

The five outlaws were spending their evening at the Golden Rail Saloon and finding that establishment more suited to their style of entertainment. Charlene and Bonnie were giving them the attention they expected when they were spending a great deal of cash on whiskey and the occasional trip upstairs. There was no worry about the amount of money spent that night because it would be replenished the next morning, courtesy of The First Bank of Buzzard's Bluff.

"Remember what I said about drinkin' too much of this cactus juice they're callin' whiskey," Reese reminded them as they sat around the two tables they had pushed together to make one.

"Ah, Reese, honey," Bonnie pleaded. "Don't be so hard on 'em. They need some good times to think about when you're all ridin' that trail to Waco tomorrow."

"They'll have plenty to think about, unless they get too drunk to go in the mornin'," Reese told her.

"Well, I'll be go to hell . . ." Jack Ramsey uttered, slammed his whiskey glass down hard on the table, and stared at a tall, rangy stranger who had just walked in the door. "I ain't believin' this." He uttered again and looked right and left to see if anyone else had noticed. When no one seemed to have, he continued to stare at the stranger, who looked the room over briefly before he went to the bar to talk to Mickey Dupree, the bartender.

"What the hell's wrong with you, Jack?" Reese finally asked.

Ramsey turned briefly to look at Reese before turning his head back to stare at the stranger now at the bar. "Don't you see him?"

"Who?" Reese asked.

"At the bar," Ramsey insisted, "talkin' to the bartender, right here in Buzzard's Bluff. This is the last place I'd expect to see him."

"Who, damn it?" Reese blurted, short of patience.

"Lucas Blaine," Ramsey pronounced dramatically, then paused to wait for Reese's reaction. He was certain that Reese knew the name because Lucas Blaine was generally acknowledged as the fastest gun in the territory and had been for several years.

At the mention of the name, Reese sat up straight and craned his neck to try to get a better look at the man talking to Mickey Dupree. After another minute or so of staring at him, Reese still doubted him to be Blaine. "What the hell would Lucas Blaine be doin' in Buzzard's Bluff? What makes you think that's him? That's just some farmer that looks like him."

"That's Lucas Blaine," Ramsey insisted. "I know because I saw him shoot Wendel Lewis down in the Red Dog Saloon, just outside San Antonio. I'm tellin' you, Reese, that's Lucas Blaine. I'll prove it to ya. Hey, Lucas!" He called out, but the stranger at the bar didn't respond. "Too damn noisy in here. He can't hear me." He got up from his chair and walked over to the bar to stand at the stranger's elbow. "How's it goin', Lucas? Been a long time."

The stranger, realizing Ramsey was talking to him, paused in his conversation to Mickey to say, "I think you've got me mixed up with somebody else."

"No, I ain't," Ramsey replied. "You're Lucas Blaine, ain'tcha?"

"Like I said, Mister, you've got me mixed up with somebody else. My name's John Cochran."

His response threw Ramsey for a few seconds. He had been so sure it was Blaine. Finally, he accepted his mistake and said, "Well, if you ever run into him, you'll know why I got you mixed up. You're the spittin' image of Lucas Blaine, maybe a little bit older." He promptly turned around and returned to the table shaking his head in disbelief of the resemblance. By the time he returned to the table, however, he decided he couldn't be wrong, and Blaine just didn't want to be recognized. So that was what he told Reese and the others.

Left to continue his questions, the stranger turned his attention back to Mickey, who had been in the process of answering when Ramsey interrupted. "I'm sorry, Mr. Cochran, I reckon I ain't the one you ought to be askin'. I ain't been here long enough to know everybody around this town. I don't hardly step out from behind this bar, so if they don't come in here to get a drink of likker, I ain't likely to know 'em. And I doubt the lady you're askin' about ever set foot in here. What was her name?"

"Caroline Carter," he answered. "She would have a little boy with her, about five years old. The last word I had of them was that they were goin' to Buzzard's Bluff."

"I wish I could help you," Mickey said. "I reckon you might have better luck if you was to ask some of the other folks when the stores are open again in the morning. Everybody's closed now, except the saloons." A thought occurred to him then. "You might try askin' at the Lost Coyote, though. A woman and an *ex*-Texas Ranger own that saloon together." He took a quick look around to make sure his boss wasn't within earshot before saying, "That's where all the town folks go to do their drinkin', so they might know the lady."

"I'm much obliged, Mickey, I'll stop in there." He turned and went back out the door. And when he did, Ramsey walked back over to the bar.

"Who the hell was that feller?" Ramsey asked Mickey.

"I don't know," Mickey replied. "He ain't never been in here before. I think he's tryin' to track down a woman who ran off on him. Likely beat the hell outta her and she took off."

"He sure looks a lot like a feller named Lucas Blaine, a fast gun outta San Antonio. You heard of him?"

"I've heard of him," Mickey said, "but I ain't never seen him."

Ben and Rachel were still sitting at the table in the back of the room when Lucas Blaine walked into the Lost Coyote. Instead of drinking corn whiskey, however, they had switched to coffee. Their usual customers were drinking and playing cards, and the saloon was filled with a sort of constant mixture of their voices. Rachel called it the Lost Coyote symphony. Ben had to agree that it was a different sound from the busy-time racket at the Golden Rail.

"There's one I've never seen before," Rachel commented when the stranger went over to the bar. "Have you ever seen him?"

"Nope," Ben replied. "He's new to me. Doesn't look like a cowhand, does he?"

"No, he doesn't," Rachel agreed. Curious about any stranger who walked into the Lost Coyote, they watched as he talked to Tiny for a few minutes before Tiny poured a drink for him. They talked some more, then they both turned to look in their direction. "Looks like we're gonna find out what he's about," Rachel said when the stranger tossed his whiskey back, paid Tiny, and started toward them.

"Evenin'," Lucas said as he approached their table. "If you don't mind, I'd appreciate it if I could ask you for some help. Your bartender said you might be able to answer a question for me."

"Sure," Ben responded. "Have a seat. This is Rachel Baskin and I'm Ben Savage. We're the owners of Lost Coyote. How can we help you?"

"Why, thank you, sir, ma'am," Lucas said and pulled a chair back. As a matter of habit, Ben watched the way the man moved, and he noted the Colt single action Army .45 resting in a quick-draw holster. "My name is John Cochran, and I've been trying to locate my sister and her little boy. She's a widow and she used to live in Austin. It's been two years since I last saw her, but when I went to see her, she had left Austin. A lady where she used to live told me she'd gone to live in Buzzard's Bluff. Her name is Caroline Carter, her son's name is Tommy. I thought maybe in a town this small, you would know if someone new moved in."

Neither Ben nor Rachel replied right away, since their natural reaction was one of caution. They both knew who Caroline Carter was, but they were not sure if Caroline wanted to be found by this solemn looking stranger. Understanding their hesitation, he said, "I know you might not be willing to just pass that information out to a stranger who walks into a saloon. Look, I'm gonna check into the hotel tonight. I'm not in any hurry to leave town. If you know where Caroline is, maybe you'd consider tellin' her that John Cochran would like to come see her. If she's willing, then I'll come to wherever she says." He paused while they thought that over. "Would you consider that? If she says she's not interested in seein' me, then that's the end of it, and I'll be on my way."

Rachel answered him. "I may not know where Caroline Carter is, but I might know someone who can tell me." She gave Ben a questioning look, and he nodded. "I won't be able to do it until morning, so why don't you come back here at noon tomorrow and I'll tell you if I was able to find her and what her message to you is, all right?"

"You don't know how much I appreciate your help, Miss Baskin. It's awful important to me to talk to Caroline right now. I've got some money I saved up to give her to help her out on her livin' expenses, too. I expect she's got some with a five-year-old boy."

"I wouldn't be surprised," Rachel said. "Everything costs more these days."

"I won't take up any more of your time," Lucas said. "Thank you again for hearin' me out. I'll see you back here at noon tomorrow." He got up from the table, nodded to Ben, and walked out of the saloon, nodding to Tiny as well when he went past the bar. Outside, he could feel his spirits lifting a little for the first time in quite a long while. He had come directly here from Austin, where a clerk in the post office there remembered Caroline Carter and her young son. The clerk said that Caroline had left Austin and relocated to a little town called Buzzard's Bluff. He was sure Caroline was here! The question now was, would she agree to meet him and hear him out?

"Hey, you're Lucas Blaine!" a thin mustached man announced when Blaine started to step off the boardwalk.

"Nope, you've got the wrong guy. My name's Cochran," Lucas countered.

"Oh, I see," the thin man smiled, nodded his head, and stepped through the doors of the Lost Coyote.

"Well, you really helped a lot there, partner," Rachel said sarcastically. "You didn't open your mouth once."

"Wasn't no need to," Ben replied. "You handled it really well, but I was ready to catch you if you messed up, like tellin' him he oughta go to church and pray he'd find her."

"That's not funny at all," she scolded. She paused then to think about Caroline Carter. She knew, just as Ben and a few others knew, that Caroline had come to Buzzard's Bluff to live with her sister, Marva, and her husband, the Reverend Ronald Gillespie. They knew that Caroline was a widow with a young son. They also knew that she preferred to remain anonymous to the citizens of Buzzard's Bluff, but they didn't know why. Perhaps it was to avoid being found by this solemn and polite stranger. And that was what Rachel would determine tomorrow morning.

Just to change the subject, Ben declared, "Looks like we lost those five cowhands to the Golden Rail tonight. I reckon Lost Coyote ain't lively enough to suit those boys.

Either that, or maybe Tuck put the evil eye on 'em. I think they knew he was a little suspicious when they talked about movin' a big herd of cattle somewhere." Almost as if he heard, the pint-sized redhead sat up straight like a prairie dog perched beside his hole, looked around him, then slapped a card down to beat Ham Greeley's two pair.

The evening wore on, a typical mid-weeknight, with Clarice spending her time visiting with the drinkers, and Ruby entertaining two young Double-D cowhands who had somehow managed to slip into town in the middle of the week. Mack Bragg made one more brief visit before midnight to tell them that the town appeared to be closed up for the night, and he was going to turn in. "See you in the mornin'," he said as he went out the door. The last of the customers filed out just before one o'clock and Ben closed up, Rachel having retired thirty minutes before that. "You promised to tell me what you and Mack have got going on in the morning," she had reminded him.

"I'll tell you tomorrow," he had told her.

"In the morning, you said," she insisted.

"In the mornin'," he agreed, knowing he intended to be long gone by the time she got up.

As usual, Ben woke up the next morning before everyone else sleeping in the Lost Coyote. He struck a match and lit the one small candle he kept on the table beside his bed and checked the time on his Railroad watch. It was five-thirty, just like every other morning. The candle afforded him just enough light to tell him if he was trying to put his shirt on inside out and if his boots were where he had left them the night before. After he strapped on his gun belt, he plopped his hat on his head, not planning to return to his room before leaving the saloon this morning. Ready to go then, he locked his bedroom door and went out the back door into the yard to stand inspecting the new day while he released the coffee he had consumed while sitting and talking to Rachel the night before. From the wood box beside the back door, he loaded one arm with enough pieces of oak for the morning fire. Back inside, he locked the door again with his free hand. Annie would be arriving in about thirty minutes, but she had her own key to the back door of the saloon.

Taking care not to make any noise, especially when he passed Rachel's door, he walked quietly down the hallway to the kitchen. Unless accidentally awakened, she would not get up before seven. Although he got up each morning at least an hour and a half before she did, he was still concerned that she didn't get enough sleep. After he set his armload of wood on top of the stove, he cleaned the ashes out of the belly of it and set new kindling from the kindling box. Then, with only the faint light provided by the window, he arranged his firewood just like he liked it and lit the fire. After he was satisfied that it was going well, he lit the lamp and went to the pump to fill the coffeepot. Annie claimed that his fire always seemed to burn longer and hotter than hers, but he knew she only said that to encourage his habit of cranking up her stove for her in the morning.

By the time she arrived, the coffeepot had finished perking and was settling down on the edge of the stove. She was surprised, however, to find Ben frying some strips of bacon in one of her iron skillets. "You must be extra hungry this morning," she said. "Why don't you sit down and drink your coffee and I'll finish that up for you. Don't you wanna wait till I can roll out some biscuits and cook some grits?"

"I sure would rather," Ben replied. "But I've got to go meet Mack Bragg early this morning, so I thought I'd try to cook a little something and call it breakfast."

Unlike Rachel, Annie didn't ask him what his business with the sheriff was about. "Well, I've got plenty of eggs," she said. "Let me throw three or four of them in that bacon grease. I need to use them up before they get old."

"Three oughta be plenty," he said. He didn't tell her that he was going to meet Mack at the hotel dining room, and he planned to have some coffee and biscuits there. He was afraid it might hurt her feelings, since she always fixed his breakfast and dinner.

She broke four eggs into the pan, anyway. "Big man like you needs more than that to eat. I'll fry more when Tiny gets up. He'll keep us from having to waste any."

He made quick work of the eggs and bacon, since it was nearing seven o'clock and he wanted to make sure he caught Mack before he left the hotel dining room and went to the bank. "Thank you, Annie, I appreciate the trouble you went to. I reckon I'd best get goin'." He started for the door.

She gave him a suspicious look and frowned. "I don't know what you and the sheriff are doin' this mornin', but you be careful."

"Ain't nothin' to worry about," he quickly replied, but he was thinking, *She's having one of her bad feelings. I hope she doesn't tell Rachel about it.* He hurried out the door.

"Well, howdy there, stranger," Lacy James greeted him when he walked in the door of the dining room. "Are you going to have breakfast with us this morning? Aren't you afraid Annie Grey might find out?"

"All right," Ben replied. "You've had your little joke. But it just so happens that I've already had my breakfast. I'm just trying to catch Mack Bragg."

"He's already eating," Lacy said.

"I can see that," Ben said and walked on back to join him. When Mack looked up, a little surprised, Ben said, "I decided I'd just meet you here." He pulled a chair back and sat down. Cindy was standing by waiting to find out if he was eating or not. "Mornin', Cindy, just bring me some coffee and a couple of biscuits." She turned at once to comply. When she was gone, Ben remarked, "I was halfway expectin' to see our bank robbers in here eatin' breakfast. But come to think of it, they've got plenty of time before the bank opens, so I reckon they ain't in no hurry. That is, if they're still in town?"

"They're still here," Mack answered. "I checked with Rob Parker, and as of six o'clock, they hadn't checked out of their rooms. I went down to the stable and Henry said their horses are still there, but they said they wanted to pick 'em up early." He shoved a fork load of fried potatoes in his mouth, then gestured toward Ben with the empty fork. "I don't know, Ben. These fellers are mighty casual about robbin' the bank. I ain't so sure we ain't let our imaginations run loose on us. And we done got Lawton Grier so wound up, he ain't ever gonna take me serious again if they don't try to rob his bank."

"If that's the only thing worryin' you, me and you can hold up the bank if Reese and his boys don't show up," Ben japed him.

"Doggone it, Ben, I'm the one runnin' the risk of

lookin' foolish, if those five saddle tramps ride outta here to take that job in Waco, workin' cattle."

"I expect Grier would be happy we were wrong, but he'd appreciate the fact that you were there to take care of business. Better safe than sorry, he'll say if he's the kind of man I think he is." He smiled at him and said, "We'll always respect your hunches at the Lost Coyote, even if this one is wrong."

At approximately twenty minutes past the hour of seven, Ben and Mack left the dining room and walked up to the north end of town, both carrying rifles and wearing six-guns. When they walked past the blacksmith shop just short of the bank, they saw Jim Bowden firing up his forge. He nodded to them but said nothing. They nodded in return, then walked between his shop and the bank building in order to approach the bank at the back door. Almost immediately after, Lawton Grier and the two tellers arrived at the back door. Stanley Townsend and Peter Best, the tellers, looked at Ben and Mack in total astonishment. Grier had evidently not told them of the activities in store for them that day. Lawton told Ben and Mack that he had decided it best not to tell them beforehand, since he couldn't be sure they'd show up if they knew. So, the first order of business was to enlighten the two tellers on what they expected to be an unusual day at the bank.

"We ain't sure it's gonna happen," Mack told them. "But we're gonna be ready if it does. The main thing is to make sure neither you two nor Mr. Grier gets in the way of a bullet, if there is any shootin'. We're hopin' Ben and I can catch 'em before they get a chance to fire a weapon. So the first thing for you tellers to do when Ben and I spring the trap on 'em is to just drop to the floor behind those cages. That's all you need to remember. Mr. Grier will be in his office, and I'll be in there with him. Ben will be just inside the door to the back room. If things go like we expect, there might not be any call for gunfire."

There was no attempt on the part of either Townsend or Best to disguise their nervousness upon hearing what might be in store for them. "Can't you go ahead and arrest them, if you're sure they're planning to rob the bank?" Peter Best asked.

Mack gave Ben a quick glance and Ben smiled, knowing what he was thinking. "We ain't sure," the sheriff answered him. "Even if we were, I can't arrest 'em for what I think they might do."

"What should we do now?" Stanley Townsend asked.

"What you always do every day, when you're gettin' ready to open for business," Mack told him. "If they show up, it won't be until the bank opens, so you've got plenty of time."

"Right . . . ." Stanley replied slowly, as he considered that.

Plenty of time to think about it, Ben thought. *Be better if there wasn't.* He was glad that Mack was giving all the instructions and answering all the questions. He was, after all, the sheriff, the person with the authority.

CHAPTER 5

With no need to hurry, the five outlaws indulged in one last feeding at the hotel dining room, having now checked out of their rooms. If Lacy James was asked, she would have decided they were in a more carefree mood than at any of their previous meals in her dining room. Had she paid closer attention, she might have noticed they, and Reese in particular, seemed very much aware of the time. And when he mentioned it, the other four abruptly finished up and they all departed. Lacy walked them to the door and invited them to stop in again if ever they were back in this part of Texas.

Carrying their saddlebags on their shoulders and rifles in hand, they walked up to the north end of the street to the stables. When they passed by the blacksmith, they didn't notice the cautious surveillance of their movements by Jim Bowden. Like them, he was also conscious of the time. They continued on past the bank and disappeared inside the stable.

"Good mornin', boys," Henry Barnes greeted them. "Your horses are watered and fed and ready to go, just like you asked."

"Good," Reese replied. "We'll saddle up and load our packhorses, then we'll settle up."

"Fine, lemme know if I can help you with anything else," Henry said.

After the horses were saddled and the packs loaded up on the packhorses, Reese took another look at his watch. Then he compared it to Paul Porter's watch to see if they were close. "Reckon we oughta stroll on over to the bank pretty soon now?" Porter asked Reese.

"I think so," Reese replied. "Let's go settle up." He and Porter went in the back where Henry was mucking out a stall. "Heyo, Mr. Barnes," Reese called out. "Have you got any rope handy?"

"Oughta be a coil of rope hangin' on a peg near the first stall," Henry called back. "You boys about ready to go?"

"Just about," Reese answered. Porter took the coil of rope from the peg, and they went back to the stall where they met Henry coming to meet them. "We'll settle up now," Reese said.

"What tha . . . ?" Henry reacted when he saw Reese's six-gun leveled at his belly. "You son of a . . ." Porter stepped around behind him to grab his wrists and pull them around behind him. Then he tied them together and pulled him down, looped the rope around his boots and tied his feet to his hands.

"You just lay there and take a little rest," Reese told him. "Ought not be for very long before somebody finds you. We're gonna be out front for a little bit. I'll let you know when we've gone. Then you can make all the noise you want, but if you don't wait till we're gone, we're gonna have to silence you. And that ain't gonna be to your likin'."

They left him trussed up in the stall and went into the front part of the barn where their horses were waiting.

"Bank oughta be openin' in about ten minutes," Shorty said.

"Right," Reese replied. "Everybody know what to do?"

"I know what you said to do, but I don't know why," Hutch said. "Why don't we just take the horses on over to the bank right now, so we can just jump on 'em and go as soon as we take the money?"

"I told you why," Reese answered. "If that sheriff sees us with a bunch of horses waitin' right outside for the bank to open, he's gonna come a-runnin'. Your job in this is to keep the horses here outta sight and watch to see when we go inside the bank. Give us about five minutes, then bring the horses." He looked at his watch again and said, "All right, let's go!"

The four of them went out the front door of Henry's barn and walked briskly across the street, then a couple of dozen yards down to the front door of the bank. Once they were in front of the door, they split up, hoping to look like four different individuals waiting for the bank to open. There were no customers there to wait for the bank to open, which Reese figured to make the job easier. In a matter of minutes, the shade went up and they could see Lawton Grier through the glass as he turned the *CLOSED* sign around to *OPEN* and unlocked the door. They might have thought it odd when he didn't open the door and welcome them in. Instead, he did an about face and hurried away to his office across the lobby. But things were going too well to question.

"Keep everybody else out," Reese said to Jack Ramsey, then he opened the door and went inside with Shorty and Porter right behind him. Reese paused a second to turn the sign back to *CLOSED*. He motioned for Shorty to go to Lawton Grier's office while he and Porter squared off in front of the tellers' cages. "This is a holdup!" Reese barked. "Empty them cash drawers into the bags!" He and Porter each shoved an empty pack bag through the slot in the cage window. Both tellers dropped out of sight behind their cages. "What tha . . . ?" Reese blurted and started to run around to the side of the cages.

"Drop it!" Ben commanded as he stepped out of the safe room door, his rifle leveled at Reese. Behind him, he heard Mack step out of Grier's office and order Shorty to drop his weapon. Reese froze, and when he did, Porter was left to make an instant decision. No one had a gun aimed directly at him, so he turned to shoot at Ben. It was a poor decision, for Ben put one round in his chest that dropped him and cranked another cartridge into the Winchester before Reese could pull the trigger. "Don't you make the same mistake," Ben warned Reese. "Drop it." Reese dropped his pistol. Ben walked over and kicked it over against the far wall. That left Shorty alone in defiance.

Outside, Jack Ramsey was just in the process of telling Jim Bowden the bank was closed when they heard the shot fired inside. Not sure what was going on, Ramsey tried to look through the closed door. When he turned back toward Jim, it was to discover a rifle aimed at him. "This here Henry rifle has a hair-trigger, so I suggest you just ease that six-shooter outta that holster with nothin' but your thumb and forefinger of your left hand and toss it aside. Then you can set down with your back against the wall, and we'll wait to see what's going on in there." The husky blacksmith was evidently convincing, for Ramsey saw no percentage in protesting. He tossed his gun a few feet away from him and sat down beside the door, his back against the wall.

Still in a dilemma, Shorty didn't know what to do. He

and Mack were in a standoff, each aiming his weapon at the other, so Ben settled it. "I don't know what you're thinkin', but the only way you're gonna walk out of here alive is if you drop that gun. If you try to shoot the sheriff, I'll kill you. If you try to shoot me, the sheriff will kill you. Either way, you're dead. It's as simple as that. And it don't look like you're gonna get any help from outside because the fellow you left out there has already been taken care of. So, what's it gonna be?" With no wish to die, Shorty laid his gun down on the floor and stepped away from it, his hands in the air.

On the other side of the street, a little north of the bank, Hutch Purnell peered at the man holding a rifle on Jack Ramsey. He looked like the blacksmith. That, in itself, didn't look too promising for the way this bank holdup was progressing. He had heard the one single shot inside the bank. That was never a good sign, even though it was not followed by other shots. He was still trying to make up his mind what to do when the bank door opened and someone evidently told the fellow guarding Jack to bring him on inside, because that's what he did. And as soon as Jack went in the door, the man with the rifle walked over to pick up Jack's pistol. That told Hutch that there was someone waiting inside the bank to guard Jack. "I don't believe I need to stay around any longer," he mumbled. "Mama Purnell's little boy, Hutch, don't need to go to this party." Wasting no more time, he picked Reese's bay gelding for his getaway, and decided to take two of the packhorses. Thinking time was running out now, he hurriedly rummaged through the saddlebags on the other horses in search of money, tobacco, and anything else that would add to his comfort. Once he started searching, he found it hard to break off and go, but he finally told himself he was going to be caught in the same trap with his partners if he didn't get out of there. So, he took only the additional time it took to adjust the stirrups on Reese's saddle to accommodate his shorter legs. Then he climbed aboard his upgrade in horses, and rode out of the barn, leading two packhorses toward the road to Waco. Since the stable was located at the extreme north end of town, no one paid any particular attention to his departure.

Back at the bank, Ben and Mack had only two pairs of handcuffs, so they cuffed Reese's hands behind his back with one pair and cuffed Shorty and Ramsey together with the other. "There's one more of 'em somewhere," Ben said. "Wherever the horses are, I suppose. Most likely at the stable, but I'll take a look out the back door to make sure he ain't holdin' 'em back of the bank somewhere." Leaving Mack to guard his prisoners, he started toward the back when he heard the question.

"Is it safe for us to come out now?" It came from behind the tellers' cages.

"You can come out now," Mack answered at once. Like Ben, he had forgotten the two tellers were on the floor. "We've got the situation under control now." He looked at Ben and grinned.

Ben continued on to the back door, opened it and looked all around. There was no sign of the other man or the horses, so he went back inside to tell Mack. "It looks like to me that the only place the other fellow with the horses has to be is the stable. And I'm thinkin' the stable is a can't miss distance from the bank's front door with a rifle."

"I'm thinkin' the same thing," Mack said. "Might not be a good idea to march our prisoners out the front door. We'd best take 'em out the back."

"We've still got the problem of that last man," Ben said. "It might be best if you and Jim wait here a little longer and guard your prisoners while I go out the back door and circle around behind the stable. Maybe I can get the jump on him."

"Maybe I ought to do that, and you stay here and guard the prisoners," Mack replied. "You've already done more than I could expect from any citizen."

"Hell, Mack, this ain't my first rodeo. I'll get in behind the stable and see if I can flush him out. It'll take me a few minutes to get around there." He didn't wait for any more discussion and headed to the back door again, also concerned for Henry Barnes. Where, he wondered, was Henry, if the remaining outlaw was in the stable?

As he had told Mack, it took him a few minutes just to get around to the back door of the barn. He found it closed but not locked, so he eased it open slowly until he could see inside. There was no sign of anyone, but he could see a bunch of horses standing in the front part of the barn that were obviously the bank robbers' horses. With his rifle cocked and ready, he moved cautiously toward them, still with no sign of the missing outlaw. He decided the man had fled. His concern returned to Henry, so he went into the stable and called out, "Henry!"

"I'm back here," Henry replied from the stall he had been left in. Ben smiled, relieved to hear his almost casual response. "He took off," Henry added.

Ben went back into the stable and found the stall Henry was hogtied in. "Are you all right?"

"Well, I'd say I'm a bit inconvenienced, but I ain't suffered no damage, I reckon. They was figurin' on robbin' the bank, weren't they?"

"That's a fact," Ben replied.

"That one that was here was that little feller that reminds me of Tuck Tucker. I reckon he was supposed to come runnin' with the horses. Everything musta turned sour, though, 'cause he took off and left the horses."

"That's right," Ben said as he worked away to untie him. "Mack had a notion they were thinkin' about robbin' the bank this morning, so we had a reception committee waitin' for 'em. They didn't even get to see any money."

"I heard a gunshot," Henry said. "Hope none of our folks got hurt."

"Nope, it was one of them. He's dead and the other three are goin' to jail, so that leaves one on the loose. And I'd guess he's headin' for the hills just as fast as he can go." He pulled the last loop off Henry's wrists. "There you go. You don't look much the worse for wear. I reckon I'd best let Mack know that fellow's gone, so he can take his prisoners to jail and get Merle Baker to come pick up the body. I expect Lawton Grier would like to open the bank."

Ben started back to the bank and Henry went with him, primarily to take a look at the dead man, Ben figured. "I'll have to get back and get all those horses out of the barn," Henry declared. "I didn't get paid for takin' care of those horses, but I reckon I can't complain. The horses will more than make up for what they owed me."

When they walked into the bank, they found that Lawton Grier had sent Peter Best to tell Merle Baker to come pick up the body. Lawton was anxious to clean up after the body and open the bank for business as soon as possible, even though there were no customers waiting outside. So Mack was ready to march his three prisoners to the jail, waiting only for Ben to help him. "I told Horace to get the cells ready before I left the jail this morning." He was referring to Horace Chadwick, an older widower he had recently hired to take care of the housekeeping chores at the jail.

The three prisoners were marched down the middle of the street, past Howard's General Merchandise, to the sheriff's office and jail just beyond it. They were guarded by the sheriff, the owner of a saloon, and the blacksmith. A fine example of the town's citizens backing the law enforcement of the town, Mayor Cecil Howard would proclaim at the next town council meeting. Ben and Jim stayed to help Mack until the three would-be bank robbers were safely locked in a cell.

"How the hell did they know?" Reese Salter blurted after the sheriff and his two volunteers left the cell room and went into the office. "What gave it away?" He glared at Shorty Cobb. "Did you go shootin' off your mouth to that whore at the Golden Rail, maybe tellin' her you was fixin' to be a rich man right away?"

"You know better'n that," Shorty shot back. "You got no call to ask me something like that. Maybe you've got me mixed up with Hutch Purnell."

"And that makes me wanna ask another question," Jack Ramsey interrupted. "Where is our good partner, Hutch? When things got hot, he turned and ran, like the yellow dog he is."

"There ain't anything we done to tip off that simple-minded sheriff and give him the notion we was gonna hit that bank," Reese declared.

"I don't think that sheriff is that smart," Ramsey said. "I think the one who came up with it was that damn saloon owner, that Ben Savage. His bartender—what's his name?—Tiny? He said Savage was a Texas Ranger before he took over that saloon. He mighta just had a feelin' and got the sheriff turned onto it."

"That don't make no sense," Shorty said. "You sayin' Savage is some kinda mind reader or fortune teller?"

"I ain't sayin' that a-tall," Ramsey claimed. "I'm just sayin' that if a man has spent a big part of his life as a lawman, trackin' down bank robbers and killers, he might get to a point where he gets special feelings about people."

"If we see him again, I think I'll ask him if he's got any special feeling about whether Hutch is gonna try to break us outta jail," Shorty declared.

"I reckon you can forget about that," Reese said. "I expect Hutch is layin' down tracks as fast as he can."

"Whaddaya reckon they're gonna do with us?" Ramsey asked. "Little ol' town like this, they ain't got no judge or courthouse. They might just decide to give us a trial and hang us."

"I don't think so," Reese said. "Attempted bank robbery ain't a hangin' offense."

"Attempted murder is," Ramsey declared.

"Attempted murder?" Reese came back. "Oh, you mean Porter. Well, he's the only one who attempted murder and he got the death penalty for it right on the spot. No, I think we'll spend some time in this sorry jail, waitin' for a circuit judge to come to town. Then they'll give us a trial and we'll wait some more for a couple of deputy marshals to come get us and take us to prison. If we're lucky, we might get a chance to break outta this tin can they call a jail. We just gotta be ready in case somebody slips up."

While the three prisoners were bemoaning their fate, the three men responsible for their arrest were expressing thanks for the success of their ambush. "I reckon it woulda been better if we could have pulled it off without firing a shot," Ben remarked.

"I think that one shot was what kept us out of a shoot-out

in the bank and no tellin' how many woulda got shot," Mack said. "Matter of fact, I was afraid for a while that I was gonna help start it when me and that one they called Shorty was squared off ready to go at it." He shook his head and laughed. "He thought better of it after you explained what was gonna happen if he pulled that trigger." Then Mack got serious for a few moments. "I wanna thank both of you for what you did today. It was a little too much for me to handle all by myself. And I expect Lawton Grier is damn grateful for your help." He nodded solemnly to each one of them and announced, "And now, I'd best go down to the hotel and let Lacy know I've got three prisoners to feed."

Ben glanced at the clock behind Mack's desk and declared, "We've taken up most of the mornin', haven't we? It ain't gonna be long before it's time to eat dinner. I reckon I'd better go see if Rachel has sold the Coyote while I've been hidin' in the bank."

"I'll invite both of you to eat dinner in the hotel dining room with me today," Mack said. "I surely owe you that."

"'Preciate the invitation, Mack," Ben replied. "But today especially, I'm gonna have to eat at the saloon at noon, something I promised Rachel. Maybe I'll catch you in the dining room tonight for supper." He had not forgotten that the stranger who had approached Rachel and him the night before was planning to come back today at noon. He was curious to see what Rachel had found out after she contacted Caroline Carter.

"I'm gonna take you up on the invite to dinner," Jim said. "I don't feel much like fixin' up something for myself right now. And it ain't too often that the sheriff springs for a meal."

"Good," Mack responded. "I'll meet you there at noon."

They went their separate ways then, at peace with the knowledge that the robbery threat was over, and the robbers were locked up.

"Ben, wait up!" Ben heard the familiar voice behind him after he thought he had successfully walked past the Harness Shop without attracting Tuck Tucker's attention.

Knowing there was no escaping the fiery little gnome, he stopped and turned to face him. "Tuck," he acknowledged, "what's goin' on?"

"That's what I was fixin' to ask you," Tuck said. "I heard a shot a while ago, but nobody knew what it was about. I was on my way back to the Lost Coyote when I saw you and Jim and the sheriff marchin' three of them five drifters down to the jail. So I went back to the shop to get my rifle, in case you needed help roundin' up the other two. What did they do?"

"They tried to rob the bank," Ben told him. "But they didn't pull it off."

"I told you!" Tuck exclaimed. "Remember I told you when that bunch first hit town that I didn't like the look of 'em."

"I reckon you shoulda told the sheriff, instead of me," Ben said.

"You shoulda told me what was going on," Tuck said. "You know you can always count on me. I've got my rifle, so I'm ready to go after the other two with you."

"I know you are, Tuck, but there ain't no other two. One of 'em was on the receiving end of that shot you heard. The other one skipped out on 'em." He studied the precocious little man, looking much like an angry elf, and he didn't want him to think he wasn't appreciated. "You need to tell Mack that you were ready to help. I know he'd appreciate it."

"Like I said," Tuck went on, "I saw Jim Bowden with you and Mack. How did he happen to be with you?"

"He just happened to be handy," Ben said. "You know, his forge is right next to the bank, so he can see everything goin' on at the bank." He preferred not to tell Tuck that they specifically asked Jim to participate in the ambush of the bank robbers.

"Whatchu gonna do now?" Tuck asked.

"I'm just goin' back to the Coyote," Ben told him. "It's gettin' on toward dinnertime and I'm past ready to eat."

"It is pretty close to dinnertime. I expect I'd best see about rustlin' up something to eat, too. I'll be down to the Lost Coyote in a little bit." He turned back toward his shop.

"All right," Ben said. "I'll warn everybody." He was not going to escape another inquiry, however, for when he turned back around, he found Paul Hogan approaching him, notebook and pencil in hand.

"Ben," he asked, "is what I just heard the truth? Did someone just rob the bank?"

"Someone tried to rob the bank this morning, but Sheriff Bragg was sharp enough to prevent them from succeeding. He's the man you need to talk to. He's got the would-be robbers in jail right now. Or go talk to Lawton Grier. He was right there when they came in with guns drawn. I bet he could tell you how it really was inside that bank."

"That's a good idea," Paul said. "I'll go see Lawton first, then maybe Sheriff Bragg will give me an interview. Thanks, Ben." He hurried away.

"I look forward to reading about it in the paper," Ben

called after him. He shook his head slowly, thinking Paul the prime example of a useless cause. Less than six months ago, Paul set up his printing press, his ambition to give Buzzard's Bluff a newspaper. He couldn't imagine what he would write about. And as far as news that's happening now, it's usually spread all over town by Tuck Tucker. Paul was a very likable person. Ben hoped he was wrong about his chances of a successful newspaper, even one that came out only once a month.

CHAPTER 6

"You dirty dog," Rachel charged when Ben walked into the Lost Coyote. "You dirty dog," she repeated as she came to meet him at the bar. "You knew about that bank holdup last night, and that you and Mack were going to be waiting for those five in the bank this morning."

"Oh, that's right," Ben replied. "I forgot to tell you about that. I meant to tell you and I clearly forgot it. I was so interested in that meetin' you were gonna try to have at the church this morning that I forgot about mine."

"It's a good thing God doesn't snip off a little piece of your tongue every time you tell a lie," Rachel said. "You soon wouldn't have enough left to lick the gravy off a biscuit."

She was anxious to know exactly what happened, so he told her what they had planned and how it actually went down pretty much to plan. "Tiny said you only took three of them to jail. Were the other two killed?"

"One of 'em," he replied. "The other one got away. It was that little one that looks like Tuck. He was holdin' the horses over in Henry Barnes' stable, but when he saw the robbery attempt goin' to pieces, he hightailed it outta town."

"Is Mack going to try to track him down, or are you going, instead?" Rachel asked.

"Now, why do you think I'd go after him?"

"'Cause that's what you do," she insisted.

"I've got no reason to chase after him. I'm not the sheriff. Even if I was, I wouldn't go after him. Mack ain't gonna go after him. He's just glad he's gone. What's Annie cookin' for dinner?"

"Pork chops. You and him aren't going to get up a posse and try to catch him?"

"I told you, Mack's satisfied that he's gone from Buzzard's Bluff. Where'd she get pork chops?"

"Jake Massey's killing hogs, so Johnny brought us some of them. Is Mack going to hold the prisoners here, or try to get the U. S. Marshal to come get them?"

"So I reckon the hotel will be servin' pork chops tonight for supper," Ben speculated. "I imagine Mack'll hold 'em for the circuit judge. Did you talk with Caroline Carter?"

"I'm sure they will," Rachel said. "If we got pork chops, you know Lacy got some, too. Yes, I talked to Caroline."

Trapped in one of their frequent haphazard conversations, neither Ben nor Rachel noticed Annie Grey standing, waiting a few feet behind them to tell Ben she was cooking pork chops for dinner, one of his favorite meals. A silent witness to the disorganized discussion, she finally turned, exasperated, and went back to the kitchen. Noticing her rather noisy departure, Ben asked Rachel, "Was Annie wantin' to tell you something?"

"I don't know," Rachel replied. "I'm sure if it's important, she'll tell me later. Right now, I'll tell you about my visit to the church today." Ben was aware of the unusual relationship between Rachel and Caroline Carter, seeing as how Rachel was half-owner of a saloon. It was even more unlikely than that one between the preacher's wife, Marva, and Rachel, especially since Rachel had never been a regular worshiper at the Reverend Ronald Gillespie's services. But the Reverend and Mrs. Gillespie trusted Jim Vickers, the original owner of the Lost Coyote and through Vickers, Rachel Baskin. Rachel was instrumental in helping Caroline take on a new identity in the little town of Buzzard's Bluff. Rachel knew Caroline had a reason to move to a place where no one knew her, but she never asked why, thinking that was none of her business. "I hadn't been to the church in I don't know how long," Rachel said. "I was a little worried about a sinner like me walking in that door again, but it didn't collapse. The preacher was inside, working on his sermon for Sunday. He gave me a gracious welcome. I think he thought I was coming to seek the light. When I told him it was just Caroline I was seeking, he said she and her sister were in the house, or the parsonage as he called it." She paused to take a sip from her coffee cup before continuing.

"Anyway, he walked over to the house with me, and left me with Caroline and Marva in the kitchen. I didn't want to waste their time, so I cut right to it. I told her, 'Caroline, there's a man who came into the Lost Coyote last night and he's trying to find you.' I swear, Ben, when I said that, she drew back like I was a rattlesnake. I told her he said to tell her his name, and if she was willing to see him, he'd go wherever she said. I told her he said he had saved up some money for her, too. When she asked me his name, I told her, John Cochran, and her knees almost failed her. I think if Marva hadn't grabbed her, she would have collapsed right there in the kitchen."

"What did she say?" Ben asked, wishing Rachel would get to the point.

"She didn't say nothing for a while, till her sister told her to do what she felt in her heart was right." Rachel paused to judge if Ben had been moved by that. It didn't appear that he had, so she continued. "John Cochran? She asked me again to make sure she'd heard right, I guess. Then she said, yes, she'd meet him, so I said where and when? Well, she said she'd rather not have him come to the church or the parsonage, but there wasn't any place in town she could think of that wouldn't get folks to talking. So I suggested she could meet him here in my room near the back door. Nobody would ever know she was in the back of the saloon."

Ben shook his head. "I don't know if that's a good idea or not," he said. "What did she say about it?"

Rachel shrugged. "Well, she and Tommy are sitting back there in my room right now."

"Well, I'll be . . ." Ben started, then asked, "What time?"

"We told John Cochran to come back here at noon," she said. "So I guess it'll be at noon." She glanced at the clock on the wall behind the bar. "And that'll be in about twenty minutes. He damn-sure better show up, after I drove her over here in my buggy. Nobody but Annie knows she's back there. Annie fixed a plate for Tommy. Caroline said she didn't want anything to eat."

"Well, I do," Ben said, "and I think I'll go to the kitchen and get myself one before those pork chops start runnin' out."

"Where are you gonna be when he shows up?" Rachel asked, at once worried.

"I'll be sittin' right out here at a table, like I always do," he answered. "Why don't you get a plate and join me? We might as well eat while we're waiting for Mr. Cochran." Rachel followed him into the kitchen.

"You ready to eat?" Annie asked when he came in the door.

"I reckon," he teased. "Might as well eat some more beef stew."

"How about some fresh pork chops just butchered this mornin'?" Annie asked in response.

"Ah, you're playin' with me now, you ain't got no pork chops."

She speared one on a fork and held it up for him to see. "You knew it," she said, "I heard Rachel tellin' you I had pork chops."

"That's right, she did," Ben said. "Well, fix me up a plate." He poured himself a cup of coffee, waited for her to fill a plate for him, then with a knife and fork jammed in his back pocket, he walked it into the saloon. Rachel soon joined him at their regular table.

According to the clock on the wall behind the bar, it was a couple of minutes after twelve o'clock when the stranger calling himself John Cochran walked into the Lost Coyote. He paused only a minute until he spotted Ben and Rachel sitting at the table in the back where he had talked to them the night before. He went straight to the table, giving Tiny a polite nod as he passed by the bar. "Miss Baskin, Mr. Savage," he acknowledged. "I hope I'm not disturbin' your dinner."

"No, not at all," Rachel responded, "you're right on time. Maybe you'd like to eat with us."

"No, thank you, ma'am, maybe I'll eat later. Were you able to find Caroline Carter?"

Rachel nodded and smiled.

"Did she say she would meet me somewhere?"

"Yes, she did," Rachel said. Before he could ask where and when, Rachel said, "Come with me and I'll take you to her right now." His somber face suddenly seemed to take on new life, but in keeping with his polite manner, he expressed his reluctance to interrupt her dinner. "I've finished, anyway. Come on and I'll take you to Caroline." She got up from the table and led him through the rear door of the barroom.

She stopped for a moment before reaching the door to her bedroom. "Before you jump to the wrong conclusion, I need to tell you the bedrooms of the girls that entertain our customers are all upstairs. This door is my private bedroom. That last door is my partner's private bedroom, and the one we just passed belongs to Tiny Davis, our bartender. Understand?"

"Oh, yes, ma'am," he quickly replied. "I wouldn't have ever thought different. And I know for sure Caroline wouldn't be in any of your rooms upstairs."

"Just wanted to be sure," Rachel said. Then she tapped lightly on the door before opening it wide and standing out of the way for him to enter. Caroline was on her feet, holding onto a tall armchair she had been sitting in as if she needed the chair for support. When both John and Caroline rushed to embrace, Rachel quietly backed out of the room, closing the door behind her.

"Well, they ain't brother and sister," Rachel announced when she sat back down at the table with Ben. "I hope they don't make a mess of my room." Then she remembered. "They've got a five-year-old in there with 'em, surely they wouldn't . . ."

"Probably not," Ben said, when she didn't finish.

She just stared at him for a few moments before she found herself wondering about his seeming lack of interest in the people in her bedroom. "You've hardly said two words about those two. Aren't you curious at all about their story?"

He fixed a serious look upon her for several seconds before he answered her question. "Curious? I expect I have a natural curiosity about things like that. But I've also been a lawman for a lotta years, and I reckon I can't help havin' bad thoughts along with the good thoughts. For starters, why the big mystery about Caroline Carter in the first place? And why does this John Cochran, if that's his real name, have to arrange a meetin' with her like this? When she first came to Buzzard's Bluff, I thought she might be runnin' from an abusive husband. But maybe this fellow showin' up here is somebody she was double-dealin' with while she was married to somebody else. Or maybe John Cochran is wanted by the law somewhere under some other name. He's got some money to give her, he said, and I can't help but wonder where he got the money. So, I reckon I just don't wanna jump in too deep till I know what's in the water. Are you gonna eat the rest of that pork chop?"

"No," she answered and pushed her plate over toward him. "I didn't know you were such a romantic cuss," she commented sarcastically. "Now you've got me wondering all sorts of things. I know for sure, though, those two were mighty excited to see each other. I expect there's a lot we'll never know about their story."

"And the less, the better," Ben said. "Maybe after they've had their visit, he'll take off again and she can go back to live with her sister."

* * *

No matter how Ben speculated on the circumstances that brought the two young people to the Lost Coyote, he was not even close. Although he was not wanted by the law, Lucas Blaine was sought out by every fast-draw gunman in search of a reputation. In the beginning, when he first realized he possessed the speed and the reflexes to draw a pistol, cock it, and fire it while most men were still thinking about drawing it, things were different. He was too immature to realize where the road he happened upon would inevitably lead when he accused a gambler of cheating. The gambler issued a challenge to apologize for his accusation or stand to face him with six-guns. The incident was almost a blur in his memory, now more than seven years later. If he could, he would go back, apologize to the gambler and walk out of that saloon. But he didn't, and his foolish pride found him standing over the body of the gambler, whose gun never cleared his holster. Still, there might have been the opportunity to take off his gun and never put himself in that position again. Instead, he had listened to the comments by the spectators about his lightning-like speed and deadly aim. And the fact that he had killed a man seemed unimportant when the victim was a nobody, his death a loss to no one. In fact, his skill with a six-gun caught the attention of the sheriff and the San Antonio town council, and he was hired as a deputy sheriff.

It was after a year as a deputy sheriff, that he wooed and wed Miss Caroline Carter, the daughter of a small cattle rancher north of San Antonio. Caroline's father persuaded Lucas to give up his job as deputy and move out to the ranch to help raise cattle. Unfortunately, the reputation of Lucas Blaine, the fast-drawing deputy, was already in the early stages of growth. Occasionally, drifters rode through

San Antonio seeking out the deputy. But when one finally showed up at John Cochran Carter's ranch with the intention of gaining the title as the man who killed Lucas Blaine, that was too much. The nameless challenger forced Lucas to defend himself, causing John Carter to ask his son-in-law to dispose of the body and then leave his ranch. He could not defy his father-in-law's request. So Lucas left a tearful young wife, her belly swollen with his son. He had returned to the ranch once for a short visit when Tommy was two years old. It had not gone well, for John Carter was not comfortable with him around for even a short visit. It was common knowledge that Lucas no longer lived at the ranch, but still they were bothered when folks came uninvited to see the wife of Lucas Blaine. He learned on this visit that Caroline was thinking about leaving the ranch to keep Tommy from growing up with a reputation as well. She would go somewhere else, change her name back to Carter, she had told Lucas, but at the time, she didn't know where to go. Now, three years later, he had finally found her. He couldn't help thinking it a fitting place to find her, the Lost Coyote.

Holding her in his arms now, he felt that he never wanted to let her go. It had taken so long to find her. But he finally released her to take a step back to fill his eyes with her image. Then he looked at the timid five-year-old boy staring at him from the other side of the room. "Come here, Tommy, and let me get a look at you."

When the boy hesitated, Caroline said, "Come on, Tommy. Come say hello. Don't be shy."

The boy reluctantly walked up to his mother and the strange man, confused to see them still in an embrace. "Come on, son," Lucas coaxed. "I'm the last person in the whole world you need to be afraid of." He reached out and pulled the shy youngster into the embrace with him and his mother. Still the boy seemed reluctant.

"I know what's wrong with him," Caroline said. "He's not comfortable seeing a strange man kissing his mother. Is that what it is, Tommy?" He didn't answer her, but his expression told them she had guessed right. "It's all right, honey, this is your daddy. It's all right if he kisses me. He's been away for a long time, and I want him to know we missed him." They released him from their embrace, and he went back over to the lamp table where Annie had placed his dinner. Lucas and Caroline sat down on the side of the bed and began talking. He asked if she had really been forced to leave her father's house and say goodbye to her sisters and brothers. "I had to, Lucas. I couldn't even go into town without people pointing at me and asking how many men my husband killed this week. I didn't want Tommy to grow up with your name." When she saw the flicker of hurt in his eyes, she quickly said, "I'm sorry, dear. You know what I mean."

They talked on for a couple of hours until Rachel tapped on the door again. Tommy ran to the door and opened it. "I just wanted to see if there's anything you need," she said. "I know that neither one of the grownups had any dinner. Can I get you something from the kitchen? You want some coffee or something?"

Caroline shook her head, then looked at Lucas. "No, ma'am," he said. "I'm fine."

"How about Tommy?" Rachel said, giving the boy a questioning look.

"No, thank you, ma'am," Tommy replied.

"I know you told me you wanted to get back by supper-time," Rachel said to Caroline. "Let me know a little before time, so Ben can get my buggy back from the stable."

"I would be happy to take you home," Lucas volunteered.

Rachel immediately looked at Caroline, who just as quickly said, "I don't think that would be a good idea. It might greatly upset the people we're staying with. Besides, there would be three of us on your horse."

"I could have put Tommy on the packhorse," Lucas said. "But I understand how you feel."

"Just let me know when to get my buggy," Rachel said and backed out of the room. She could have told Lucas that Caroline was staying at the preacher's house, and that was not really a very long walk from there. She drove Caroline and Tommy in her buggy for the sole purpose of quickly taking her to the saloon with little chance of anyone seeing them. When she went back in the barroom and repeated the conversation to Ben, he responded by pointing out that Lucas could simply trail the buggy to find out where his wife was staying. "Oh, yes, I guess he could, couldn't he?" She shrugged. "She hasn't even told him that it's her sister she's staying with."

"I reckon it ain't really none of our business what the two of them do about their problem," Ben suggested. "I thought about askin' Mack to look to see if he had any wanted paper on John Cochran, but I decided not to because I was afraid he'd find something. Tiny said some guy told him he thought Cochran was some gunslinger named Lucas Blaine. Tiny said this fellow was so sure Cochran was really Blaine, that he didn't wanna believe him when he said he wasn't. Mack might have some paper on Lucas Blaine, but he's got enough to worry about with those three he's got in jail now. Cochran don't look like he's out to start any trouble, so maybe after today he'll be gone, and no harm done in Buzzard's Bluff."

Back in Rachel's bedroom, the same topic was under

discussion between Lucas and Caroline. And with time running out, Lucas made his plea. "Caroline, I'm weary of this life I've foolishly brought upon us. I'm tired of being hunted like a criminal when I haven't committed any crimes. I want us to be together again, to raise our son together like normal families. I miss you too much to go on this way." He tried to explain to her how his reputation with a six-gun had been his only source of income for the past several years, sometimes even in law enforcement. But most of his money had been earned as a private bodyguard for several different politicians in Austin. "I'm telling you this because I want you to know I came by it honestly. And I've saved every penny I could to ask you to take another chance on me. I've got enough money to buy us a small piece of land. Maybe you and me and Tommy can make a livin' on it."

"I don't understand how you can get away from your reputation," Caroline said. "I can't bear the thought of finding you shot dead someday."

"We'll change our names and go someplace where nobody knows us," he insisted. "We'll head for Oregon maybe, somewhere way to hell away from Texas."

"Oh, Lucas, I don't know," she fretted. It was an overwhelming proposal.

"You still love me, don't you?" Lucas asked.

"Yes, you know I do, I'll always love you. It's just so much to decide."

"Will you think about it? Please say you'll consider it. You don't have to give me a final answer today. I'm going to stay here in the hotel for a few days. Will you meet me here again tomorrow?"

"I don't want to trouble Rachel to come and get me and bring me here again." She hesitated, then made her decision. "I'll meet you at the church tomorrow."

"The church?" he asked, surprised. "The one I passed by on the south end of town?"

"Yes, that's the only church in Buzzard's Bluff," she said. "Tommy and I are living with my sister and her husband. He's the preacher."

"Marva?" She nodded. "Marva married a preacher?" He was quite surprised, remembering Caroline's sister as a gal with a wild spirit, and not likely to marry a preacher.

"She knows where I am, but we haven't told Ronald. Maybe she has told him by now, but at any rate, it doesn't make any difference because I'm going to tell him at supper tonight. If you find Tommy and me sitting on the front steps of the church tomorrow with our suitcases packed, you'll know how he took it." Then, making a decision, she said, "What I'm saying is that I'll go with you, to Oregon or wherever. I'm your wife. I belong by your side. We've already wasted too much of our lives."

Scarcely able to believe his ears, he picked her up and spun around and around with her in his arms. "For the second time in my life, you've made me the happiest man in the world! I don't know if I'll be able to stand it until I see you again tomorrow."

CHAPTER 7

Hutto's Station was a rambling two-story building built in a sharp loop of the winding Brazos River. What the soldiers would call a hog-ranch, Hutto's was a favorite hangout for outlaws and drifters of the lowest life forms. Fifteen miles below Waco, it was the place where Reese Salter and his four men were supposed to meet his brother, Brock, and two other men. On this particular night, only one solitary rider approached the noisy station, riding a weary bay gelding. He came off the horse and tied it and two packhorses to the rail with several other horses. Inside, he paused to look the crowd over. Not seeing the person he looked for, he went to the bar. "Hutch Pernell," the bartender sang out. "Brock said Reese and you boys was supposed to show up any day now. You want a drink?"

"Yeah, I need one," Hutch replied. As soon as the bartender poured it, Hutch tossed it back and slammed the glass down for another one.

"Where are the rest of the boys," Corky asked. "They outside?"

"No, there ain't nobody but me," he said and tossed the second one back. "Where's Brock? Ain't he here?"

"He's here," Corky said, "settin' in the back at that corner table. You just can't see him on account of Joyce Ann settin' on his knee."

Hutch stretched his neck up, trying to see over the people standing around in the middle of the room. "Well, I reckon I'll go give him some news he ain't gonna like a helluva lot." He tossed a couple of coins on the bar and made his way through the crowd.

"Hutch!" Brock Salter exclaimed when he saw the little rooster approaching. "About time you boys showed up. Where's Reese and the others?"

"That's just it, Brock, there ain't nobody but me."

"Whaddaya mean, there ain't nobody but you. Where's Reese?"

"Reese and the other boys are in jail in some little town called Buzzard's Bluff."

"In jail?" Brock roared and shoved Joyce Ann off his knee, causing her to land on the floor. Hutch stepped out of her way as she scrambled angrily to her feet and cursed Brock. Oblivious to her insult, he demanded, "What are they in jail for?" Before Hutch could answer, he roared, "Where the hell is Buzzard's Bluff?"

"About fifty miles south of here," Hutch said. "We spent the night there last night, stayed in the hotel."

"I don't give a damn where you stayed last night," Brock raged. "What did they do to get throwed in jail?"

"Well, it was Reese who decided," Hutch replied. "There was this little bank there that looked like it was just beggin' to get robbed. So Reese and Jack Ramsey went inside yesterday to look it over, and they said it was nothin' to it but walk in, take the money, and walk out. So we hit it this mornin' when they opened up." He shrugged helplessly.

"Well, somehow they knew we was gonna hit it, and they was waiting for us, the sheriff and some other men. And they arrested all of 'em."

"All of 'em but you," Brock reminded him. "How come they didn't arrest you?"

"Reese told me to stay outside and hold the horses," Hutch replied. "I had to hold all five of our horses plus the packhorses. And when the shootin' got started, I couldn't get into the bank to help the other fellers because every man in town musta been there with his gun. They scattered the horses, and I knew the only chance I had to come tell you what happened was to grab the first horse I could. So that's what I did and rode hell-bent for leather outta there. I picked up two of the packhorses on the way outta town, but that's all I had a shot at."

"Damn!" Brock swore. "What a sorry mess that was." He was struck with a sudden feeling of helplessness because he didn't know what to do. Reese was the undisputed leader of the gang, but Brock, because he was his brother, was next in rank behind him.

"I wish I coulda done more," Hutch lamented, "but I couldn't take on the whole town by myself."

"I reckon you done what you could," Brock told him, somewhat recovered from his panic of moments before. "It's mighty unlucky, though. How did they know to set a trap? Who told 'em that the bank was gonna be robbed this mornin'?"

"You're right about that," Hutch said. "Unlucky all right, it was downright spooky, if you ask me. There ain't nobody who coulda told 'em we was gonna rob that bank."

"Well, that sure as shootin' changes my plans," Brock said. "I've got a nice job I've been lookin' at, but I need

Reese and the rest of the boys to do it. Tell me about this little town, Buzzard's Bluff. You said they have a sheriff and a jailhouse. Are they big enough to have a courthouse?"

"I don't think so," Hutch replied. "Leastways, I didn't see any buildin' that looked like it might be one."

Brock gave it a few minutes thought before making a decision. "I doubt they've got a courthouse, or even a judge in town. Robbin' the bank ain't a minor offense, so they ain't likely to hold 'em in jail for a day or two and then let 'em go. They'll most likely hold 'em for the day a circuit judge gets to town and try 'em then. Depends on what day that judge is supposed to hit town, but unless it's today or tomorrow, we've got time to ride down there and see how hard it would be to break them outta that jail. We need those men, and I sure as hell ain't gonna let my brother set in that jail. I'll bet he's fit to be tied."

"Who else is here?" Hutch asked, thinking that if he had to ride back to Buzzard's Bluff, he hoped it would be with a gang of men.

"Just Bo Turner and Tree Forney, but that's a lot in a gunfight or a fistfight," Brock said.

Hutch had to agree with that assessment. He didn't know what Tree's name really was, but he was branded with the nickname because he stood well over six feet tall with a hard muscular body and he liked to fight. Bo was the fastest man with a gun Hutch had ever seen. That thought brought another to Hutch's mind and he commented on it. "I'll tell you something that oughta interest Bo, maybe even make him think he don't wanna go to Buzzard's Bluff."

"Yeah? What's that?" Brock asked, although not really interested.

"Lucas Blaine is in Buzzard's Bluff. Leastways that's

what Jack Ramsey said. He saw him in the saloon yesterday. He said he saw Blaine gun down a feller named Wendel Lewis in the Red Dog Saloon in San Antonio."

"What would Lucas Blaine be doin' in a little town like that?" Brock wondered aloud. "Most likely it was somebody who just looked like Lucas Blaine." He cocked his head at an angle and asked, "Did you talk to the feller?"

"Me? No, I didn't have no reason to talk to him. Jack did, though. He walked up to the bar where Blaine was talkin' to the bartender and said howdy. Blaine told him he was usin' some other name."

"Probably to keep people like Jack Ramsey from botherin' him," Brock remarked.

"Right, that's what I figured. That's the reason I didn't talk to him," Hutch commented. "Where are Bo and Tree?" he asked then.

"Upstairs workin' off some of that supper we just ate," Brock answered. "They had a contest to see who could pick the ugliest woman to go upstairs with. Danged if I don't believe it ended in a tie. I don't expect they'll be up there very long." He had no sooner said it when Tree Forney appeared at the top of the stairs. He paused there for a moment to look over the crowded floor below. Then spotting Hutch talking to Brock, he came on down the steps.

"I swear, Hutch Pernell," Tree said. "When did they start lettin' little runts like you in here?"

"When Hutto decided he was gittin' too many customers tall as trees that was dumb as stumps," Hutch fired back. "Said it was a bad influence on the high-class women workin' here. Which one did you pick?"

"Maggie Green," Tree replied. "She's ugly, but she

knows it, and she don't care. You gotta admire that in a woman."

"She ain't particular either," Hutch said. "You left that out."

"Where's Reese and the other boys," Tree asked then.

"They ain't comin'," Brock answered him. "Tell him, Hutch." Hutch started telling his story again, only to be interrupted by Bo Turner's appearance at the top of the stairs. Like Tree, he came right down to ask about the other men, so Hutch started once again.

When Hutch finished, Brock took over. "So we're takin' a little ride in the mornin' to Buzzard's Bluff," he told them. "We've gotta leave here early 'cause Hutch says it's fifty miles to that town, and that's a full day's ride. We've got two rooms here. You can sleep in the room with me, Hutch. Just throw your bedroll on the floor."

"I ain't got my bedroll with me," Hutch said. "I've got Reese's. Like I told you, I didn't have a chance to catch my horse. I had to take the first one I could grab. It turned out to be Reese's bay. I've got to go take care of him now before I do anything else. Then I've gotta find somethin' to eat. I ain't had nothin' all day but a few strips of jerky I found on the packhorses I caught."

"I swear, Brock," Tree complained, "we ain't got no food to eat on if we're gonna be ridin' a full day tomorrow." He turned toward Hutch then. "Is there any place to get something to eat between here and that town?"

"I didn't see anywhere to buy anything until I was almost here," Hutch replied. "I'da stopped there, but it didn't look like much of a place, and I decided I might as well come on here."

"That's that shabby-lookin' trading post about five

miles from here," Brock said. "Run by a little old man and his wife. We oughta be able to pick up enough there to keep us from starvin' before we get to Buzzard's Bluff." Then to Hutch, he said, "Go on down to the barn and take care of them horses. There's some grain down there, you can feed 'em. Help yourself, we're payin' Hutto enough to take care of it."

Hutch walked back outside, stopping at the bar long enough to tell Corky he needed something to eat. Corky told him that Mozelle, the cook, was still in the kitchen, so she would fix him up with some biscuits and ham. "They'll be ready by the time you get back from the barn," Corky said.

Encouraged by the prospect of relieving the emptiness in his stomach, Hutch took his three horses down to the barn. He was not thrilled by the thought of returning to Buzzard's Bluff so soon after leaving it in the manner he had. In fact, he didn't care for the thought of going back to that town at all. That morning when he was pushing Reese's bay gelding for more speed, it was his sincere intention never to set foot in that town again. He realized that he had the option to get back on the bay and leave Brock to rescue his brother. But in spite of his brash and boastful talk, Hutch needed a boss to tell him what to do and he got that from Brock, just as he had with Reese. So he took care of his horses and took Reese's saddlebags and bedroll back to the saloon where he found a plate of biscuits and ham waiting for him.

Early the next morning, Brock rousted his three men out of their beds and into the saddle. Although he was anxious to get to Buzzard's Bluff as quickly as possible, he had no desire to ride a long day with nothing but jerky to chew on. So after a ride of only about five miles, they stopped at the trading post on the bank of a creek. The store was owned by Cletus Priest, and he and his wife, Jenny, operated it. The four men arrived at the store at the precise moment Jenny pulled a pan of hot biscuits from her oven. The aroma of those golden-brown beauties was the first impression the riders got of the store. "How much you want for that tray of catheads?" Tree asked, referring to the biscuits. By the time he got a final answer, Jenny had sold them four complete breakfasts with eggs, bacon, and grits to go with their biscuits. So they began their trip a little behind the schedule Brock had planned. But it was taken with spirits high, in spite of the fact that their mission was intended, as Brock believed, to break four men out of jail, one of them the leader of their gang.

After only one stop to rest the horses, they reached a popular camping ground on Wolf Creek, just north of the town of Buzzard's Bluff. "I think it's best to just make camp here tonight," Brock said. "Our horses are dead tired and it's pretty late to get any supper anywhere. We can go in the morning and look the town over. I plan on going to the jail to see Reese and the others. I'll look the place over, and we'll decide if there's a good chance to break 'em outta there. We might hang around long enough to find out what they're gonna do with 'em. We might decide it's better to wait and see if they're gonna be transferred to some other place to be tried. Then we'd only be fightin' a couple of deputy marshals. What I'm sayin' is we need to look things over good and see what they're planning to do with their prisoners." He looked at Hutch then, who looked like he felt a pain somewhere. "What?" Brock asked. "What's eatin' you?"

"All you're thinking about doin', all that looking the town over, I can't do that. I can't go into town. I'm wanted for attempted bank robbery, same as Reese and them in the jailhouse."

Brock had totally forgotten that fact. It caused him to pause a moment before responding. He didn't want to admit that he had overlooked a blatant fact. So he said, "Of course you can't go into town. You're gonna be in charge of our camp outside of town. Me and Tree and Bo will need to go into town, leave our horses in the stable, so we can see if Reese and everybody else's horses are there."

"Reese's horse ain't in the stable," Hutch reminded him. "I've got Reese's horse."

"That's what I was fixin' to say. We've already got one of the missin' horses. Now we need to find the other horses, so when we break 'em out, they'll have their horses to ride."

When it was obvious that Brock's attempt to organize the mission to free his brother continued to give no clear plan of action, Bo and Tree looked at each other in disbelief. It became clear to them why Reese was the Salter who was the leader of the gang, and not his brother. It was Bo who interrupted his aimless wandering.

"Let me set it straight for you, Hutch," Bo said. "You can't go into town 'cause the first person to spot you would yell out and everybody would start shootin' at us, figurin' you brought us back to raid the jail. So you camp out here till we come get you to fight or fly. Now, the three of us are gonna ride into town, just like travelers passin' through 'cause we've got to be in town to find out what's what. As soon as we find that out, we'll decide our best chances. Then we'll tell you what to do. Till then, take care of the packhorses and sit here and have yourself a little vacation till it's time to go to work." He looked over at Brock and asked, "Ain't that about what you was tellin' him, Brock?"

"Couldn'ta said it better, myself," Brock said.

"I mighta just as well stayed at Hutto's," Hutch mumbled.

"We're gonna need you when we break Reese and them outta that jail," Brock told him. "And he'll be glad you took care of his horse, too." Standing out of Brock's line of vision, Tree looked at Bo and slowly shook his head. Bo nodded in return.

"Don't you think we should go ahead and ride into town tonight, Brock?" Bo asked. "Just to take a quick look."

"I suppose it could be worthwhile," Brock answered. "We might see something tonight we won't see in the morning."

"Well, let's get Hutch's camp set up so he can settle in for the night," Bo suggested. "We can string a line between the trees down on that creekbank and tie the horses there where they can reach the water. You can build you a fire and boil some coffee and eat some of that side meat we bought this morning. We'll ride on into town to get a good look at the jail and see where everything else is. Maybe we might stop by a saloon and buy a bottle of likker, so you can have a drink. We might hear something useful, too. You ain't scared to stay out here by yourself while we scout that town, are you?"

"Hell, no!" Hutch spat. "I ain't scared of nothin'. You know that."

"Right," Bo responded. "What was I thinkin'? Come on, Tree, let's take care of these horses, so they don't wander off while Hutch is eatin' his supper." Tree followed him and they unloaded the packhorses and rigged up the rope line to tie them to. When they were out of hearing distance from their two companions, Bo said, "I'd just as soon we'd left both of them two at Hutto's. Brock ain't much good without Reese to tell him what to do."

"I thought it was a good idea when Reese went back

down to San Antonio to get Paul Porter and Jack Ramsey," Tree said. "They're both good men, and I reckon Shorty Cobb is, too. We only rode one job with Shorty, but he did his part. What I don't understand is why the hell did Reese bring Hutch Purnell up here? He's like a tea kettle, makin' a helluva lotta noise when it ain't doin' nothing but boilin' a little bit of water."

After they helped Hutch get his camp set up, Brock, Bo, and Tree rode their weary horses the mile or so into Buzzard's Bluff. They figured the horses could rest all night when they returned to the camp. They didn't admit it to Hutch, but the main reason they didn't wait until the next morning, was because they hoped they might find something to eat for supper. Failing that, maybe there was a saloon there that had some crackers or something to eat with a shot of whiskey. "If they ain't," Tree remarked, "we'd best watch how much we drink. Else we'll have to find that camp while we're drunk as skunks."

They followed the road into the north end of town, passing Henry Barnes' stable on their right and slow walking their horses up the deserted street. The town was pretty much buttoned up for the night with only a couple of places with lights on inside. They figured those two places had to be saloons. The first one they came to was the Lost Coyote, so they pulled up to the hitching rail and dismounted. Inside, they found a small gathering of customers, most of them standing at the bar, a two-handed poker game at one of the tables, and a man and a woman sitting at a table near the back, drinking coffee. "I swear, Tree, that bartender is as tall as you are, but he's a little bit wider," Bo commented. He led the way to the bar.

"Evenin'," Tiny greeted the three strangers. "What can I pour ya?"

"What's in the bottle?" Brock asked, pointing to the bottle Tiny was pouring shots from.

"This is corn whiskey," Tiny answered, "but if you want something else, I've got rye."

"Corn'll do for me," Tree said. "I don't suppose you serve any supper this late, do ya?"

"No, sir," Tiny replied. "I'm sorry, but we don't serve supper at all. We just serve breakfast and dinner."

"Is there any place in this town where we could get some supper this late?" Tree asked. "We've been ridin' all day, and our supplies are kinda puny."

"No, sir," Tiny said. "The only place to get a good supper is the hotel dinin' room and they closed over an hour ago." He paused to watch Tree's obvious disappointment, then he said, "But we don't like to see anybody starve to death. Annie Grey, our cook, leaves here after dinner every day. But she always bakes up a pan of biscuits before she goes home, just in case three fellows like you come in too late to eat. Would a couple of biscuits help you out any? Maybe some molasses to go with 'em?"

"Three or four would help me even more," Tree replied. He turned to grin at Bo and Brock, silent witnesses to Tree's search for food.

"I'll see how many we've got," Tiny said. Then he raised his voice and called out, "Rachel!" When she looked up, he signaled for her to come. The three strangers, turned to watch Rachel come to the bar. When she walked behind the bar and stepped up beside Tiny, he said, "This is Rachel Baskin. She's one of the owners. Rachel, these three gentlemen just rode into town and they're in danger of starvin'.

How many biscuits are left in the oven? Do you know if there are enough to fill up three fellows this size?"

Rachel laughed at Tiny's simple humor. "I think there might be. How many do they want?"

"Well, the tall one, here, wants three or four," Tiny said. "The other two ain't spoke up yet."

Brock quickly answered. "If they're good-sized biscuits, two oughta do for me. Your bartender mentioned some molasses or something to go with 'em."

"I can eat three," Bo said.

"Nine biscuits," Rachel said to confirm. "I'll go see how many are left." She started to leave, then hesitated. "I see you're drinking whiskey. Would you like to have a cup of coffee with your biscuits?"

"Lady, if you could serve some coffee with that, you would surely be preparing a feast," Tree said. Then as an afterthought, he asked, "How much is all this special service gonna cost?"

"Not as much as you think," she said. "Why don't you sit down at one of the tables and I'll see what I can scare up for you." She went to the kitchen then. When she walked past Ben sitting at the table, she asked, "Do you want any more coffee? 'Cause I think I'm going to make a new pot."

"I swear, I've had a gracious plenty, but as long as you're gonna make it, I reckon I can soak up another cup," he said.

"I'll make a full pot then," she called back as she disappeared into the kitchen.

After several minutes, she came back carrying three plates in one hand with biscuits stacked up on the top one. In her other hand, she carried another plate with a jar of molasses and a jar of honey on it, as well as a knife and a couple of spoons. She walked them over to the table the three strangers had chosen and set them in the middle of it.

"I put on a fresh pot of coffee that ought to be ready pretty quick. There were ten biscuits left. You fellows can fight over 'em. I'll get your coffee as soon as it's ready."

"Like I said," Tree commented, "you have come up with a regular feast for three poor starvin' souls."

"Yes, ma'am," Brock saw fit to add, "this will do just fine." Only Bo remained mute, since there were no polite phrases in his vocabulary.

"I'll go check on the coffee," she said and left them to divide up the biscuits. When she walked past Ben again, he gave her a big grin, which she returned, knowing she was going to be teased when she came back to sit with him. When she came out again with three cups of coffee, he got up and went into the kitchen to pour another cup for himself. He took her cup with him, as well.

"Well, thank you very much, sir," she said when she met him coming out of the kitchen with their coffee. He handed her cup to her and they returned to the table.

"Those fellows been in here before?" Ben asked. "I don't recall seein' 'em in here, but you're treatin' 'em so nice I figured you must know 'em for sure."

"I've never seen 'em before," she said, "but I felt kinda sorry for them. The tall one that did most of the talking said they'd ridden all day and they were out of supplies. And they were hungry. Don't look at me like that," she said when he looked at her and grinned that teasing grin. "Besides, it doesn't hurt to try to encourage strangers to come back to see us when they ride through town."

"You're absolutely right," he conceded. "And after they've had their coffee and biscuits, and go to drinkin' and raisin' hell, it'll be your job to run 'em outta here, right?"

She gave him a coy smile and said, "Whaddaya think I got you in here for?"

CHAPTER 8

Ben wasn't the only one to notice the welcome mat Rachel had laid out for the three strangers. Tuck Tucker made several remarks to Ham Greeley about the special treatment the three strangers had received from Rachel. And then Ham finally said that was enough poker for him, he threw his cards in and said he was going home. "I got to get up early in the morning and go to work."

"You don't get tired so early when you're winnin', I noticed," Tuck said. "What have you gotta do tomorrow?"

"Freeman Brown wants me to build him an addition onto his kitchen storeroom. I told him I'd start it in the mornin'."

"I reckon I've had enough, too," Tuck decided. "Maybe I'll have one more drink of likker with Tiny and Henry before I roll me up for the night." He followed Ham toward the bar but paused at the table where the three strangers were sitting. "Where you fellers from?" Tuck asked.

"Well, I'll be . . ." Tree started. "Damned if Hutch ain't got a brother."

Seated with his back to him, Bo turned to gaze at the flame-haired little man straining to stand as tall as his elf-like body would allow. "Ha!" Bo responded.

Brock was quick to make amends for his two companions' rudeness. "We're from down San Antonio way, neighbor, on our way back home. First time we've ever been in your little town. We appreciate the lady findin' us some coffee and biscuits."

Tuck continued on to the bar, raising his voice to make sure Rachel could hear him. "Yep, she's good at that, all right. It'd be nice if she took care of us regular customers who spend our money in here every day as good as she's takin' care of you."

"That little chinch bug," Rachel muttered under her breath. "He never knows when to keep his mouth shut." She looked at Ben and suggested, "Maybe I should go see if those men need anything else. I was tryin' to make them feel welcome here, so they wouldn't go to the Golden Rail next time."

"Just let it lay," Ben told her. "Look at those three men, two of 'em especially. Do they look like the kind of men who would let Tuck bother them. I'm more worried about Tuck if he says anything more to them."

"It would serve him right," Rachel said.

"Now you know you don't mean that," Ben japed. "We need Tuck to run the town for us, and I figure those fellows see Tuck about the same way we see him."

Ben was right on the money with his assessment of the three at the table. "That little feller reminds me, we told Hutch we'd bring back a bottle of likker, so he could have a drink," Brock said. "Let's have one more, then see what they wanna charge us for the little supper she set up for us. I'd like to ride down the street and back, just to see where everything is."

"You know, we could go take a look at that hotel, and maybe just stay here tonight," Bo suggested.

"No, we can't do that," Brock said at once. "We left Hutch alone with all our packhorses. I ain't too sure he would stay there if we were gone all night. I expect it's too late to put our horses in the stable, anyway. It was closed when we rode in." He was unaware that the man standing at the bar, talking to Tiny, was the owner of the stable, and he most likely would have been glad to take care of their horses.

Bo shrugged. "I reckon you're the boss while Reese ain't here," he said. But he was thinking, if they were un-successful in their attempt to spring Reese, Brock's days as boss were over. The three of them got up from the table, and Brock went back to ask Rachel how much they owed.

It was then that Mack Bragg walked into the saloon, just as Tuck was walking out. "Sheriff Bragg!" Tuck exclaimed. "I figured you oughta be makin' your rounds about now." At the sound of, "Sheriff," both Bo and Tree dropped their hands to rest on the handles of their guns. "I've been keepin' an eye out," Tuck went on. "Everything's peaceful in here. We got three strangers that just showed up a little while ago. Nothin' to worry about." Tree and Bo automatically sepa-rated to spread out a little. Brock froze, standing before the table where Ben and Rachel were sitting.

"Well, that's good, Tuck," Mack Bragg told him. "It's good to know you're watchin' out for us. I reckon I can take over now."

"Can we help you with something?" Ben asked Brock Salter, when he appeared to have suddenly forgotten where he was.

"What?" Brock came to. "Oh, for a minute there, I forgot what I was gonna do. I don't know what made me do that. I was just gonna ask the lady what our total bill is for the whiskey, the coffee, and the biscuits."

"I'll take care of it, Rachel," Ben said and got to his feet. "Come on, Mister . . ." He waited for the name.

"Brock," he replied, "Mr. Brock."

"All right, Mr. Brock, come on. We'll go to the bar and check with Tiny to see how many drinks you bought, and you can tell me if that's the number you figured. Then it'll be two-bits for each one plus a nickel each for the coffee, and there's no charge for the biscuits. Does that sound fair?" He took a quick glance at Rachel, and she winked.

"That's certainly fair enough," Brock said, "and you can add a bottle of that whiskey to the bill, and we'll take it back to camp with us."

Meanwhile, Mack was attempting to get some information from Bo and Tree. "You say you rode in tonight from Waco?" Mack asked. "So you're just passin' through town?"

"Yes and no," Tree answered, stalling until Brock came back to the bar with Ben. "You'll do better talkin' to him," indicating Brock. "He's in charge."

Mack turned to face Brock. "Evenin'," he said. "I was just askin' your friends if you're just passin' through town, or if you're gonna be with us for a while. There's a night clerk still there at the hotel, if you're goin' there. He might be asleep in his chair, but you can wake him up with a little bell he keeps on the desk."

"'Preciate it," Brock said, "but we made camp a mile or so back on a creek, and we're fixin' to go there right now. We might check on that hotel tomorrow, though, if we decide to stay a day or two."

"This is Mr. Brock, Sheriff," Ben spoke up then. "Mr. Brock, this is Sheriff Bragg."

Mack gave Ben a look of surprise. It was not customary for Ben to introduce every drifter that wandered into his saloon. But he figured Ben would explain the change of habit later on. So he said, "Glad to know you, Mr. Brock."

An awkward moment followed while Brock tried to decide what Reese would do in a like situation. Aware of the sudden void of uncertainty, Brock suddenly blurted, "As a matter of fact, we were plannin' to come see you tomorrow."

"Is that so?" Mack replied. "What about?"

Hesitant and unsure just moments before, Brock suddenly relaxed his concern when a reasonable explanation occurred to him after remembering something Hutch had told him. He even winked at Bo to assure him. Then he told the sheriff his story. "To be honest with you, Sheriff, I wasn't going to come down here when I first heard about the men you're holding in your jail. At first, when I was told they attempted to rob the bank, I couldn't believe it. Those five men were paid to meet me in Waco to start moving a big herd of cattle to a new range in West Texas. I just can't imagine any of those men could have any intention of robbing a bank. So I decided it my responsibility to come to see if all this was true, and if you really do have the five men in your jail." He silently applauded himself for pretending to be unaware of Hutch's escape.

His story definitely surprised Mack and Ben, and everyone else within earshot. Mack hesitated, looked at Ben, then addressed Brock. "In the first place, I ain't holdin' five men in jail. I ain't holdin' but three. One of the five never came to the bank. He was holdin' their horses in the stable, and he took off when he saw the bank robbery was goin' bad. And one of 'em tried to shoot when he was told to drop his weapon. He's dead."

Now it was the three strangers' turn to be surprised. Only three prisoners in the jail, who was the unlucky one who got shot? Brock was alarmed that the victim might have been his brother, Reese. The sheriff's remarks about the outlaw who ran away caused all three standing there to remember Hutch's version of the incident, and the fact that he didn't know that one of them had been killed. It was a very sobering meeting with the sheriff of Buzzard's Bluff.

When each one of the three men appeared to be at a loss for words, Mack said, "If you still wanna see 'em, come by the jail tomorrow after breakfast, anytime up to noon, and you can talk to 'em." He turned back to face Ben then while the strangers filed out of the saloon. "Other than those three, anything unusual happening in the Lost Coyote tonight?"

"Wasn't that unusual enough for you?" Ben asked with a light chuckle. "Did those three look like cowhands to you?"

"Hell, I don't know," Mack answered. "Cowhands come in all shapes, sizes, and clothes. You suppose ol' Reese was tellin' the truth when they said they was on their way to Waco to move a big herd of cattle for some joker?"

"Damned if I know," Ben answered. "But if I was you, I'd keep a close eye on those three if they do show up at the jail tomorrow."

Two interested bystanders listening in on the conversation, Tiny and Henry remained silent until the three strangers had left. Then Henry said, "That one feller was a little bit taller than you, Tiny."

"Yeah, he was," Tiny replied, "but he didn't have no meat on him. Did you notice something about that one doin' all the talkin'? Didn't he remind you of that feller named Reese?"

"Yeah, he did look like him a little bit, come to think of

it," Henry said. His remark caught the attention of both Mack and Ben.

"You reckon Brock and Reese are related?" Mack asked. "Maybe even brothers?"

"I don't know," Ben replied, "but I wouldn't rule it out. This whole thing with Reese and his men has been crazy as hell. Now these three, you better be mighty cautious with these three, if they show up tomorrow at the jail."

Interested as well, Ruby and Clarice both came to the end of the bar to stand beside Rachel as she listened to the discussion between Ben and the sheriff. Rachel was especially concerned when she heard Ben warn Mack to be extra careful when he took his usual late-night check of the town. Finally, she had to comment. "Isn't it nice that I made them feel so welcome? Maybe they'll come back here after they break their friends out of the jail, and we can celebrate with them."

Overhearing her comment, Ben looked at her and smiled when it struck a thought of his own. Back to Mack then, he said, "We had a little reception for Reese and his men at the bank. Maybe we oughta have another one at the jail, just in case."

"Whaddaya talkin' about?" Mack asked. "You thinkin' about you and Jim settin' in my cell room this time as guards?"

"Well, I don't know about Jim, but it looks like you're gonna have to watch three men, so it would be a lot easier if there was at least two of us to watch 'em. I'm still an official part-time ranger, so I ought to lend a hand."

"You know I appreciate the offer, Ben, but this ain't the first time somebody's come to the jail to visit a prisoner. It'll be like any other visitors. I don't let 'em wear their guns into the cell room, and I stand guard while they're talkin' to the prisoner."

"Ordinarily, I'd say you're right," Ben replied. "But I've got a feelin' about those three. I think you're runnin' a risk of them jumpin' you in the office before you even get around to havin' 'em take off their guns." Mack hesitated, even though he was thinking seriously about what Ben was telling him. He obviously was reluctant to ever give any impression that he could not handle his job without help. "You know, Mack," Ben continued, "it's like that feelin' you had about Reese and the other four. You need a deputy, but since you ain't got one, I'll lend a hand. You're the sheriff. I'll just be your deputy." He waited for Mack's response, and when it didn't come right away, he said, "I figure it's either me or Tuck Tucker. He's waitin' for your decision."

That brought an immediate reply. "You win," Mack said. "You can wait in the office with me, and for Pete's sake, don't say anything about it to Tuck." He started to leave but paused when Rachel asked a question.

"This Brock fellow said they heard you had those men in jail for trying to rob the bank. I wonder who told him. Did he say?"

Mack exchanged a quick look of surprise with Ben. "We better be ready for four of 'em tomorrow," he said.

"You still think it's a good idea to go to the jail to see those boys tomorrow?" Tree asked Brock when they were back at the hitching rail. "Ain't you afraid Reese or one of the other ones will say something to give it away as soon as we walk in?"

"What if they do?" Brock answered. "That ain't nothin' to

worry about. That's the reason I told the sheriff they was hired to come help us move some cattle. He thinks there weren't nobody more surprised than us when we heard about that bank business." He paused to watch their reaction, then added, "There's a reason I'm the boss when Reese ain't here."

"I reckon we'll see tomorrow," Tree commented to Bo.

"We'll get on back to camp now," Brock said, "but first, I wanna ride on down the street a ways and take a look at that jail. Wonder how tough a nut it is if we end up havin' to crack it from the outside?"

"It don't matter whether we take 'em from the inside or the outside," Bo reminded them both. "We've got to get their horses first. We can't hardly break 'em outta that jail, then take a casual stroll back to the stable."

"That's absolutely right," Brock said. "That goes without sayin'." He had not, however, thought about that.

"That's right," Tree commented. "And that might take a little doin' to get their horses saddled and ready to ride, then keep 'em in the stable till we break Reese and them outta jail. We better think this thing over real good or we're liable to find ourselves in the middle of a shootin' gallery when we're trying to get outta town."

"Are you forgettin' about our horses?" Brock asked Bo. "We ain't gonna be on foot. We'll have three horses, and we're pickin' up three prisoners. We can just ride double back to the stable."

"Damn, I forgot all about that. We ain't gonna walk to the jail. But whichever way we do this thing, we'd best kill that damn sheriff," Bo offered. "If he goes down, that's gonna take the pucker right outta the rest of the town. Without anybody to lead 'em, they won't know what to do, get up a posse, or what. And I guarantee you, they're gonna think twice before gittin' up a posse to come after seven armed gunmen. So, I say shoot him down tomorrow when we go in his office. Walk out with them three he's got locked up, and ride up the street to the stable, shootin' at everybody who sticks his nose out. We'll pick up their horses and ride to hell away from here."

"That sounds good to me," Brock said, "pretty much what I was gonna suggest." He looked down the street at the jail. "It ain't that far from the jail to the stable."

"What about Hutch?" Tree asked, directing the question at Bo. "You reckon there's a lot of folks in this town who would recognize him as one of the gang that tried to rob the bank?"

"I don't know," Bo replied. "From what that sheriff said, it sounded like Hutch spent the whole time in the stable with the horses. I reckon the feller that owns the stable will recognize him. But it wouldn't make no difference if he did 'cause he'll either be dead or tied up. So Hutch could go back in the stable and get the horses saddled and ready to go. At least he'd be useful for something."

"All right, then, I reckon we know what we're gonna do," Tree said. "So we might as well go on back to our camp and take Hutch a drink of whiskey." He climbed up into his saddle and backed his horse away from the hitching rail.

"I wanna take a look at that jail before we go," Brock said.

"Ain't no need to look at that jail tonight," Bo said. "We'll see it tomorrow when we come back."

"Right," Brock replied at once, "we don't need to see that jail tonight." He got on his horse and followed the two of them out the north end of town.

After the short ride back to Wolf Creek, the three outlaws saw no sign of Hutch when they followed the creek back to their camp. The campfire was going strong, and the horses were all still tied near the water. "Hutch!" Brock called out, and after a few seconds, Hutch answered.

"I'm right here," he said and got up from the creekbank where he had been hiding.

"What the hell are you hidin' for?" Tree asked him.

"It's dark," Hutch replied. "It's hard to see who's comin' along that creek. It coulda been anybody maybe caught sight of that fire."

"And what was you gonna do if it hadn'ta been us, let 'em take the horses and everything else? We left you to guard our stuff, not hide in the bushes," Bo complained.

"You know, it's kinda funny," Hutch said, "you belly-achin' about me not standin' out by the fire, makin' a nice clear target outta myself. And the fact of the matter is I just happened to have this Winchester lined up with the front sight right on your belly button. I'da pulled the trigger if Brock hadn't hollered when he did."

"Why, you runty little rat," Bo came back at him. "How'd you like to try it when I'm lookin' at you? We can find out right quick if you're anything but mouth."

"Cool down, you two!" Brock barked. "We've got a job to do in the mornin', and we need everybody to do it. Here, Hutch!" He tossed the bottle of whiskey to him.

Hutch caught the bottle and proceeded to work the cork loose, glad to have the distraction. He wanted no part in a faceoff against Bo Turner. He tilted the bottle back and took a long pull of the corn whiskey. "Damn," he swore, "that's terrible stuff. Wish I had a gallon of it." He took another pull, then passed the bottle to Tree. It went around again before they took mercy on their weary horses. After they took care of the horses, they returned to the fire to tell Hutch what they had learned in town. He, like they had been, was surprised to find out that one of the men he had been riding with had been killed in the bank holdup attempt. "Who was it?" Hutch asked. "I heard a shot, but there wasn't but one."

"I thought you said there was bullets flyin' all around you," Bo reminded him, "'cause everybody in town was shootin' at you."

Hutch had to think quickly. "Well, there was," he said, "but I didn't hear but one shot inside the bank."

"We don't know who it was that got shot," Brock said. "We'll find out in the mornin', 'cause they didn't tell us no names. I don't think they knew anybody's name but maybe Reese's, and they didn't call his while they was talkin' to us."

Bo wasn't ready to let Hutch off the hook quite yet, so he continued reminding him of his accounting of his escape from Buzzard's Bluff the day before. "So, while you was out there in the street, tryin' to chase the horses, and every man in town shootin' at you, you just heard one shot inside the bank?"

"I reckon that's the way I remember it," Hutch answered him. "I was pretty damn busy right about that time."

"Right," Bo kept after him. "You was busy trying to catch a horse, and you just grabbed the first one you could. It just happened to be Reese's bay geldin' and two pack-horses came along for the ride." He waited then for Hutch's reaction.

After a long pause, Hutch finally said, "Yep, that sounds about the way I remember it. It was a pretty hot spot to be in. You fellers are lucky you weren't there."

CHAPTER 9

"Are you sure you're making the right decision for you and your wife?" Reverend Ronald Gillespie asked the solemn young man sitting in his study. Marva had asked Lucas to talk with her husband after supper regarding the wisdom of his and Caroline's plans to renew their wedding vows and attempt to start a new life together. "I don't doubt your sincerity in what you propose to do. But I wonder if you have given serious thought to the possible problems you may cause your wife and son. Lucas, you are a hunted man!" He paused to let that sink in. "What will happen to Caroline and Tommy when you are ultimately found by the next sick soul who wants to take away your sinful title?"

"Caroline and I have talked about that," Lucas said. "And while it is possible, it does not necessarily have to happen, if we leave Texas, change our names, and start over in a new place. We both agree that our marriage is strong enough and our love important enough to warrant our tryin' to make it work. For quite some time now, I have been avoiding any situations that would attract gunmen of any sort. I made serious mistakes in my life, for which I am truly sorry. I want to make that up to Caroline. I owe her and Tommy that."

Gillespie nodded as he studied the young man. "I believe you, Lucas. I know Marva is hoping I'll somehow talk you into leaving Caroline and Tommy here with us. But I think the two of you have come to a decision that no one will change. So all I can do for you is to wish you luck in your new life and pray that God holds you and your family in His bosom." He was genuinely sincere in his wishes for them, but he was also looking forward to having the spare room empty again and not having the extra mouths to feed. This was especially true when it came to Tommy, a five-year-old who could eat like a man. "So, when do you plan to set out for that new country you're seeking?"

"I've got money saved to buy a wagon and a team of horses to pull it," Lucas said. "I expect that might take me a few days, depending on whether I can find a good wagon here for sale. As soon as I get all the supplies I think we'll need, then we'll head out right away."

"You might check with Henry Barnes," Gillespie suggested. "He owns the stable and he's a fair man to trade with. He'll treat you right."

"I'll go talk to him in the mornin'," Lucas said. "I 'preciate it, Reverend." He returned to the parsonage where Caroline was waiting to see if her brother-in-law had succeeded in changing their plans to leave. She was well aware of Marva's feelings against their reunion, convinced as she was that Lucas, like all gunmen, would never change his ways. She gave Lucas a great big smile when he walked into the kitchen, and he nodded with a grin for her. She hurried to greet him with a hug.

"Behave yourselves you two," Marva joked. "Remember, you're at the church."

"This ain't the church, it's the parsonage," Caroline replied. "Are we still heading out as soon as you find a wagon?" she asked Lucas.

"Yep," Lucas answered. "I'm thinkin' Montana right now."

"Damn," Marva swore.

"Don't forget you're at the church," Caroline scolded.

"Well, it's gettin' pretty late," Lucas said. "I've gotta go lookin' for a wagon in the mornin', so I reckon I'd better turn in."

"I'll go tuck you in," Caroline said. "Tommy went to bed right after supper."

"I might lock you out, so you can get used to sleeping out under a wagon," Marva teased when Caroline walked out the back door with Lucas.

Sheriff Mack Bragg unlocked his office door and walked inside after his last look around the town to make sure every door was locked and there were no more people on the street. Horace Chadwick was sitting in his chair with the padded cushion in front of Mack's desk. "Everything all right with our guests?" Mack asked as he locked the office door again.

"Pretty much," Horace answered. "Ain't really heard nothin' outta 'em. Just talkin' back and forth about one thing and another."

"They might as well settle in," Mack said and walked over to a big calendar on the wall. "The judge ain't sched- uled to be here till the fifteenth, and that's a ways off yet."

He walked over and opened the door to the cell room, then stood inside the door to take a look at the prisoners.

"Hey, Sheriff," Shorty Cobb called out when he saw him, "how 'bout lettin' me outta here for about ten minutes, so I can get me a drink of likker."

"I wouldn't trust him, Sheriff," Jack Ramsey piped up. "Better let me go with him to make sure he comes back."

"I'm glad to see you're all enjoyin' your stay here," Mack replied. "You're gonna have some visitors tomorrow, if they show up like they said they would."

That caught their attention right away. Reese Salter sat up on his cot. "Visitors?" he asked. "What visitors?"

"Three interested gentlemen from up Waco way somewhere," Mack answered. "I'd tell you who they are, but like you boys, they had a hard time remembering their names. One of their names slipped out, though. Said he was Mr. Brock." This time, Mack detected a definite spark ignite in all three when they heard the name. "Anyway, they said they heard about you trying to rob the bank, and they had to come see if that was true. They acted like they couldn't believe you fine gentlemen would attempt such a thing." He studied their faces for a few seconds and decided they showed definite signs of excitement, like maybe a jail break might be scheduled for tomorrow. "Well, goodnight, I'll see you in the mornin'."

"Hutch," Reese said when Mack closed the cell-room door. "I was hopin' he'd go to Hutto's, but I weren't countin' on it. Boys, it looks like Brock will be here tomorrow. I don't know who he'll have with him, but he won't be alone."

"Ain't he takin' a helluva chance walkin' in that sheriff's office?" Shorty asked. "He might arrest him and throw him in here with us."

"What for?" Reese responded. "Arrest him for what? He

ain't done nothin' in Buzzard's Bluff. And I ain't never heard there was a law against wantin' to visit a prisoner in jail."

The morning began as every peaceful morning started at the Lost Coyote. Ben was sitting at the kitchen table drinking coffee when Annie came in the back door. "Mornin'," he greeted her when she walked into the kitchen.

"Good mornin', Ben," she returned cheerfully. "One of these mornings, I'd like to come to work and catch you still sleeping. Lord knows you don't ever get enough sleep."

"I reckon I just never got in the habit of waiting for daylight before I got up," he said.

"I know how late you and Rachel stay up at night before you close the Coyote. At least Rachel doesn't get up till seven, but that still ain't enough for a lady her age." She poured herself a cup of coffee. "But I do enjoy my first cup of coffee every morning, and my stove fired up and goin', so thank you very much."

"It's my pleasure," he said.

"What would you like for breakfast this morning? You want your usual? I was thinkin' about mixin' up some flapjacks this morning. I can go ahead and get started if you'd like flapjacks."

"Go ahead and drink your coffee," he said. "I'm not in any hurry. I'll just wait till Johnny comes in, and you can start on 'em then." He knew that wouldn't be long. Annie's husband always came into the kitchen for breakfast around six-thirty, a half hour before Rachel showed up. "I've got some business to take care of with Sheriff Bragg this mornin', and he'll see about gettin' his prisoners fed first."

When he said that, Annie's brow immediately furrowed in a frown.

"Ben, you be careful today," she said.

"I always am," he assured her, but he couldn't help thinking, *she's having another one of her feelings*. He hoped she wouldn't say anything to Rachel. Rachel believed Annie really did have some connection to things the rest of them couldn't see or hear. He didn't believe it himself, but he had to admit that it was hard to explain how often the coincidences occurred. What made it a bit annoying was the fact that Annie never claimed any such powers and she never gave warnings or made predictions. Her message was conveyed only by a worried look in her eyes, or a deep frown, like the one she made that morning. *Hell, I expect trouble anyway,* he thought.

Annie's husband Johnny failed to come in at his usual time, and Ben commented on it. "Oh, for goodness sakes! I don't know where my mind went. Johnny went deer huntin' this morning. He won't be coming in at all."

"He did?" Ben replied. "Well, I'll try to eat his share of that first batch of pancakes in his honor." There was plenty of bacon to go with them, so Ben took his time to enjoy them. By the time Tiny came in, he was ready to go to the jail, and he bumped into Rachel as he was walking out the door. "Good mornin', partner," he greeted her. "You're lucky I can't hold any more of Annie's flapjacks, or I'd have cleaned 'em out." He called back over his shoulder, "Champion flapjacks, Annie!"

"You be careful," Annie repeated, her frown of concern in place again.

Rachel saw it and turned to question Ben, but he didn't wait for it. He just said, "Enjoy your breakfast," and kept walking.

* * *

When he walked down the street to the sheriff's office and jail, he was glad to see only a few souls out and about. Less chance of somebody getting hit by a stray bullet, he thought. If there was going to be any shooting, it would likely be inside the jail, but there was always the danger that it might spill out into the street. And that was the last thing he and Mack wanted. He climbed the three steps up to the front door of Mack's office and found it unlocked, so he walked in to find Mack and Horace drinking coffee. "Want a cup?" Mack asked.

"Had one too many already," Ben replied.

"You know we've got to worry about four of these jaspers instead of the three that hit town last night," Mack said right away. "That one that got away from the bank holdup ran straight to these three. Who else coulda told 'em about the bank job? I shoulda thought about that first thing. I don't know why I didn't."

"Yeah, I know," Ben confessed and stepped aside when Horace went by him to go outside on the little platform that served as a porch. "It took Rachel last night to point that out. I figure they might think it too big a chance somebody would spot him as one of the bank robbers." He glanced over at the gun rack behind Mack's desk, the padlock hanging open on the hasp. "You gonna lock that gun rack?"

"No, I'm gonna leave it open," Mack said. He reached behind him and opened one of the two doors. "It's empty. I took all the guns out of it and put 'em under the bed in my room." He nodded toward the door to his personal quarters. "And I'm lockin' the door. When they show up here, I wanna put all their weapons in that rack. And while you and

I are in the cell room with them, I want Horace to lock that gun rack. You got any other suggestions?"

"Reckon not," Ben replied. "Just watch 'em real close, I guess."

Mack shrugged. "You reckon those men are really comin' here with the intention of breaking those prisoners out? In broad daylight? I have a hard time believin' it."

"Yeah, me, too. I reckon we're gonna find out."

Horace stepped back inside. "I see three riders way up at the end of the street," he said. "They're comin' this way."

"I can sell you any of those horses in the corral out behind the stable, Mr. Cochran," Henry Barnes said. "You look 'em over real good, and I'll take sixty dollars apiece for your pick. Take your time. I'm going in the barn and throw some of that stuff out of that wagon, so you can get a better look at it. I think you'll see it's in better shape than it looks with all that dust all over it." Henry went back inside the barn. *Nice young fellow*, he thought. *I'll make him a good deal on that wagon.* "What's that?" He sang out when he heard someone calling his name from the front barn door. "I'm back here in the barn." He walked in from between the stalls so he could be easily found, and he waited. "You!" he blurted when he saw Hutch Purnell coming toward him, his pistol drawn and pointing at him. "Are you crazy? What are you tryin' to do?"

"I'll show you how crazy I am, if you don't do what I tell you to do," Hutch told him. "You and me are gonna get them horses I left here saddled and ready to ride. Then if you don't give me no trouble, I'll let you live, just like I did last time. But don't make no mistake, old man, one move you make that don't look right to me and I'll put a hole in the back of your head. Now let's get them horses in here and get 'em saddled." It was at that point that Lucas walked into the barn, unaware of what was happening inside. "Who the hell are you?" Hutch demanded and spun around to level his gun at Lucas. Lucas reacted without thinking. In one lightning-like motion, he drew his six-gun and pumped a round into Hutch's chest. Hutch took two steps backward, then stood there stunned. He made a move to cock his pistol but crumpled to the floor before he could draw the hammer back.

Henry was as stunned as Hutch had been, for he could not believe the speed of the young man's reactions. Perhaps as shocked as either Henry or Hutch, Lucas was not certain if the man would have shot him or not. But he turned with the gun in a threatening position. There was no time to find out the man's intentions, and he was definitely threatening Henry. "Are you all right?" he asked Henry.

"I am now," Henry replied. "For a while back there, I warn't so sure."

Lucas walked over and looked down at Hutch's body. Then he looked up at Henry and asked, "Who was he?"

"He was one of the gang of robbers who tried to rob the bank here three days ago. He's the only one that got away. He hid here in my stable, holding the horses for the rest of them until it started lookin' bad for 'em, then he ran. Left me tied up in one of the stalls. The question is, who are you?" After what he had just witnessed, he wasn't sure.

"I told you," Lucas said. "I'm John Cochran. I picked out two horses I think I wanna buy, but I reckon I'd better go down to the sheriff's office and tell him what happened. When I walked in, he was holdin' a gun on you. I didn't know what was goin' on. I better go get the sheriff," he repeated.

"I expect you'd better," Henry told him. "But don't you worry, I'm your witness and I'll tell him you didn't have any choice in the matter. Chances are, you mighta just saved my life, and for that I'm grateful."

"I wanted to take another look at that wagon," Lucas unintentionally spoke his thoughts aloud. He had been so determined not to attract any attention while he was in town, and this was the worst thing that could have possibly happened.

"Well, it ain't goin' nowhere," Henry assured him. "I think I'd best go down to the sheriff's office with you. He'll be mighty interested to know that runty fellow came back here to try to get their horses. It's a wonder Mack ain't already headed up here. He musta heard the shot."

Mack did hear the shot, at about the same time Brock Salter and his two men pulled up in front of the sheriff's office. Like Brock, Mack and Ben, inside the office, he paused to listen for more shots, but there were none. It had come from the vicinity of the stable that Brock, Bo, and Tree had just passed. It was not that unusual to hear a gunshot in town. There were many reasons one might be fired, including accidents. One thing for sure, it wasn't fired by any of the three men approaching his office, so that encouraged him to dismiss it. And since the shot didn't come from either of the two saloons in town, there was a tendency to assume it was harmless, especially since there were no more to follow. Mack stepped outside on the steps. "Well, I see you kept your word about comin' to visit your men," he said. "I know they'll be glad to see you. They've had their breakfast and seem to be lookin' forward to the visit, although they might be a little shy about why they decided to rob the bank."

"'Preciate your cooperation on this, Sheriff," Brock said. "I want to hear it from them how they came to do such a thing as robbin' a bank." He motioned with his head toward Bo and Tree behind him. "I think it'll be a good lesson for these men to see where you end up if you decide to break the law."

"We're glad to help out," Mack replied. "Come right on in. Horace is standin' by the door holdin' a big box. So, if each one of you will take your guns off and put 'em in the box, we'll keep 'em for you till you're ready to leave."

There was a noticeable twitch in the expression of each one of them when he said that. Brock was already halfway through the door and looking at the large box Horace was holding. He stopped abruptly to protest. "Take off our guns? Why should we do that? We're not the criminals. We're law-abidin' visitors come to see the criminals."

"I'm sure you are," Mack said. "It ain't nothin' against any of you three fellows. It's the same rule for everybody. It's mainly for your safety, to keep one of those hombres from snatchin' your gun outta the holster if you get too close to the bars. Besides, what do you need your guns inside my jail for. Who are you gonna shoot?"

"Well, now, that's beside the question," Brock insisted.

"No, sir," Mack replied, "it's just a rule, and everybody has to follow the rule."

Brock didn't know what to do. He was the only one who was at the door. Tree and Bo were on the steps behind him. Their simple plan of overpowering the sheriff at gunpoint, locking him in a cell and walking out with the three prisoners, was dead without their guns. He turned to look at Bo, and Bo nodded his head and muttered, "Do like he said." And he started unbuckling his gun belt. So Brock unbuckled his gun belt, too, confident now that the three of them could physically overpower the sheriff. He dropped it in the box Horace was holding, and Horace stepped aside to give him room to go into the office. The procedure was repeated for Tree and Bo, resulting in three surprised outlaws facing the formidable figure of Ben Savage with six-gun drawn.

"What is he doin' here?" Brock demanded.

"He's just helpin' out in his capacity as a Texas Ranger," Mack said. "Now, to make sure nothin' happens to your guns, Horace is gonna put 'em in that gun rack behind him and Ben will hold the key. And we'll go into the cell room so you can see your friends."

"Hold it, Mack," Ben interrupted. "There's somebody at the door."

As a precaution, Mack drew his pistol and said, "Okay, Horace, open the door."

Henry Barnes walked into the office with Lucas Blaine right behind him, only to find they were part of a crowd for the small room. "Damn," he swore. "I'm sorry, Mack, we can come back later. But I reckon you'd wanna know that little runty feller that was with your bank robbers, but got away, is in my barn. He came back to get the horses them fellers you got locked up was ridin'. But ain't no hurry. He ain't goin' nowhere. John, here, shot him when he turned on him with a gun."

"I swear," Ben commented, "now that surely is one helluva coincidence, ain't it, Mack?" He looked at Brock then and asked, "Did you know he was gonna be in town the same time you were?" Brock didn't answer. His brain was still scrambled from finding that Hutch had been killed when he tried to steal the getaway horses. He was sure that effectively ended his plans to break the three prisoners out of jail. They were counting on having their horses.

"How come they don't have to take their guns off in here?" Bo demanded, the thought just occurring.

"'Cause they ain't in here to visit prisoners," Ben answered him when Mack hesitated. "If you boys just had some business with the sheriff, you wouldn't have to take your guns off. So, have you changed your minds about visitin' the prisoners?"

"No, of course not," Brock replied, afraid it would cause the sheriff to become too suspicious of their reason for the visit. "That's the only reason we rode into town. I wanna see 'em." He was still not sure his brother was not the one man killed in the robbery attempt.

"All right," Mack said. "Let's go see the bank robbers." He pointed to the cell room door and the three visitors started toward it.

Henry caught Mack's elbow and said, "I'll talk to you later about the shooting. Just want to be sure you know it was pure self-defense. John had to shoot."

"Fair enough," Mack replied. "I'll talk to you later. John, why don't you stick around. It wouldn't hurt to have an extra gun with us till they're gone. All right?"

Lucas nodded and answered, "All right, Sheriff."

They all went inside the cell room, leaving only Horace to watch the office. Reese, Shorty, and Jack were all standing at the bars of the cell when their three visitors filed in. Along with them, to Reese's regret, he saw Mack, Ben, and Lucas, all of them armed.

"You fellows don't pay us no mind," Mack instructed

them. "We'll spread out and give you room to visit. I'll be happy to answer any questions you might have about their trial, or anything pertaining to their court date." He knew, just as he was sure Ben knew, that Hutch Purnell's surprise arrival at the stable was no way a coincidence with Brock's arrival in town.

During the total time of the sheriff's instructions, the three visitors stood staring at the three prisoners without a spoken word between them. When Mack finished, Reese was the first to speak, and his voice was barely above a whisper. "Brock, what the hell? You ain't even wearin' no gun."

"They wouldn't let us in till we shucked our guns," Brock said. "I wasn't even sure you was still alive till just now. We didn't know one of you got shot till the sheriff told us last night, and he didn't know which one it was."

"Yeah, Paul Porter was with us. He tried to shoot that damn saloon owner, but he wasn't fast enough."

"Why was he gonna shoot the saloon owner?" Brock asked.

"He was one of them waitin' in the bank for us," Reese exclaimed, almost loud enough to be heard by their guards. "When the sheriff told us you were comin' to visit us, I figured you was gonna break us outta here."

"We was, and we had a plan, but it got all messed up. We didn't know the sheriff was gonna have help, so when we had to give up our guns, we still weren't worried about jumpin' him. When we got inside, there was that damn saloon ranger again, and then another feller showed up to tell the sheriff he shot Hutch Pernell when he went to get your horses. So that's why we're standin' here talkin' through the bars. We can't fight three of us against six of them. And even if we beat 'em, we wouldn't have your horses."

Reese shook his head, exasperated. "I was countin' on

you . . ." He started, then thought, "What are you talkin' about, three of you against six of them?"

"I'm talking about the three of us against them three and their three guns," Brock said. "But that don't mean we ain't gonna figure out another way. I've got Bo Turner and Tree Forney with me, and they're both good men. We've just got to come up with a new plan."

Reese nodded to each of them, now that they had moved in close to him to hear the whispered conversation. Silent until that moment, Jack Ramsey interrupted. "Whatever plan you come up with better be a good one. Those two the sheriff's got helpin' him ain't hardly no culls. The big one, that owns the saloon, is an ex-Texas Ranger, and the other one is Lucas Blaine."

That captured Bo Turner's attention. "Lucas Blaine?" he exclaimed. "How do you know that?"

"'Cause I was in the Red Dog Saloon down in San Antonio the night he shot Wendel Lewis," Ramsey replied. "Lewis never cleared his holster." Standing next to the door to the office, Lucas Blaine, alias, John Cochran could almost feel six pairs of eyes suddenly focus on him. It was a sense he knew well, and one he had hoped he would never feel again.

CHAPTER 10

The visit at the jail didn't last very long, due to the helpless position Brock Salter and his two men found themselves in. It appeared to them that the sheriff and Ben Savage were hoping they might make an attempt to free their fellow outlaws. *Save the town the expense of arresting them and having a trial for them,* Brock thought. He made it a point to study the cell room and the cells, themselves, looking for any possible point for entry. There were two small windows in the back wall of the cell room, but none in the individual cells. So there was no way to sneak a gun into the cell, other than passing it straight through the bars. And that was difficult to accomplish when they had to check their weapons in the office before they were allowed to enter the cell room. "We'll come up with something to get you outta here," Brock promised. "I ain't leavin' this town without you. One thing for sure is we're gonna have to catch that sheriff when he's alone, or maybe when he goes home at night."

"He don't go home at night," Reese said. "He stays in a room right here at the jail."

"Maybe we can catch him asleep. What about that other feller? The one he called Horace, is he a deputy?"

"No," Reese replied. "He ain't nothin'. He cleans up the cells, empties the slop buckets, and fills the water buckets. You ain't gotta worry about him."

Tree finally asked the question. "Well, what the hell are they gonna do with you? Ain't they told you nothin'?"

"I know what they're gonna do," Reese told him. "They're gonna hold us right here till the fifteenth of the month when the judge is supposed to be in town. Then they're gonna try us for attempted bank robbery."

"The fifteenth?" Tree responded. "What's today's date?" When none of the six knew, Tree called out to Mack, "Hey, Sheriff, what's today's date?"

"It's the fifth," Mack said.

"Damn," Reese swore, "that's ten days. And then ain't no tellin' how long after the trial it'll be before they transport us somewhere. I can't stay in here that long. You do something, Brock, get me outta here." Whispering lower now to make sure their guards couldn't hear him, he said, "You've got one more chance. When you leave, act like it's over and done. When they give your guns back, don't wait, shoot 'em down right there in the office. The rest of the town won't know what happened, and there ain't gonna be nobody to stop us from gittin' our horses outta the stable."

"They won't be expectin' us to do that when we look like we're fixin' to leave," Brock said, more in the way of a confirmation for what his brother said.

"That's right," Reese said. "They won't know what hit 'em. You just get me out of this cell, and I'll handle the rest of it." He looked at Bo and Tree then. "You understand? As soon as you get your guns back, cut all three of 'em down." They nodded their understanding.

"All right, visitors," Mack called out. "Visitin' hours are over. Horace is waitin' in the office with your guns. You can pick 'em up as you go out." He gave no indication that he might have overheard some of their whispering. Ben and Lucas walked back into the office to join Mack as he watched the three men take their guns out of the box Horace held.

There was a silent pause while they strapped their gun belts on, and for a moment, the three visitors stood looking eye to eye with their three guards. The room seemed heavy with a sense of anticipation from both sides. Then Bo very deliberately reached over with two fingers of his left hand and carefully drew his Colt from his holster. He waited a moment, and when there was no reaction from the sheriff or Ben, he aimed the weapon toward the window, opened the loading gate, and spun the cylinder around. He looked at Mack then and smiled wickedly. "Can I have my cartridges back now?"

"They should be in your saddlebags," Mack said. "Right, Horace?"

"Yes, sir," Horace answered. "They're in their saddlebags."

"I expect you'll be headin' back to Waco now, or wherever you came down here from," Mack said. "You talked to those men you thought you hired to work some cattle for you. And they never denied they were trying to rob the bank. So I reckon that should satisfy you that they're where they oughta be."

"It sounds like you're tellin' us to get outta town," Brock said. "We haven't committed any crimes in your town, have we?"

"Not that I know of," Mack answered. "I just figured you were a busy man, and there wouldn't be anything to keep you here in our little town."

Brock paused to consider what he was about to say. He

was not sure it was wise, but now that the sheriff had foiled his planned attack, he needed time to decide how to get Reese and the others out of jail. When nothing better came to mind, he decided to go with the truth. "I expect I coulda told you sooner," he started. "But this business is more on a personal level than I let on. You see, Reese is my brother."

"I thought there was a resemblance," Mack said. He and Ben had decided earlier that it was a possibility.

"So, you can understand why I think I should stay around long enough to go to his trial. And I'd surely want to visit him in the days he's waitin' for that trial." He paused a moment to take on a mournful expression. "I run a legitimate business involving cattle, so you can see why Reese's crossin' over the line has put a strain on me."

"Well, we sure don't wanna put you under no strain," Mack said. "You're welcome to visit your brother if you want to, but we'll have to go back to regular visitin' rules. That means only one visitor at a time, and no firearms in the cell room. Of course, if I'm doing something in town, the sheriff's office will be locked up."

"I understand, Sheriff, and thank you for your cooperation," Brock said. He went out the door, then Bo and Tree followed. They got on their horses and rode down the street toward the hotel, each man leading a packhorse.

Behind them, Mack looked at Ben and grinned when they heard, "What the hell?" It came from inside the building, from the cell room.

"There's somebody else that ain't havin' a good day," Ben commented. "That one fellow," he said, referring to Bo, "was smarter than he looks."

"That was a pretty good idea you had, Ben," Mack said. "I thought for a second there that they were actually gonna try it, but he caught on."

"I expect if one of us had reacted in some way when he reached over for his gun, that mighta caused the other two to go for their guns," Ben said. They had prepared for a sudden attempt by the three outlaws to gun them down as soon as they got their guns back. And when they did draw, and found their guns empty, Mack and Ben could simply arrest them and throw them in jail with their friends. That would have taken care of that problem painlessly, and they would have been tried with Reese and his two men. But since they made no attempt to either shoot or overpower anybody in a jail break, Mack had no charge to arrest them on.

"I would have loved to see the expressions on their faces, if they hadda tried it, though," Mack remarked. He turned to look at Lucas then. "I wanna thank you for lendin' a hand on this, John. It's mighty unusual for a stranger just passin' through town to step in and help the law out. I 'preciate it." He turned to face Ben then. "I reckon I'd best go up to the stable and see if Henry got hold of Merle Baker to pick up that body."

"I'll go with you," Lucas said. "I'm thinkin' about buyin' a wagon from Henry, and I wanted to look it over after he cleaned it up. You might need to ask me about shootin' that fellow, anyway."

"Nothin' I need to ask you," Mack said. "Henry told me what happened. You know, you'd make a helluva good deputy. I think Mayor Howard and the town council are starting to talk about the need to get me a deputy. You interested in a job as deputy?"

"I'm afraid not, Sheriff," Lucas replied. "I've already promised my wife that we're going to Montana or Oregon country to raise our son. That's the reason I'm lookin' at the wagon. I've already picked out a team of horses to pull it."

"Well, thanks again for helpin'," Mack said.

"I expect I'd better get back to the Coyote," Ben declared. "If I stay away too long, Rachel might decide to put new locks on the doors." He hadn't said anything, although he found it more than interesting to hear Mack talking to Lucas Blaine about the possibility of becoming a deputy sheriff in Buzzard's Bluff. He wondered if he should have told Mack that the most famous gunslinger in Texas had come to town. Ordinarily, he would have, but he felt he should honor Lucas and Caroline's secret, especially since Rachel, and then he, had been entrusted with it.

"That coulda been really bad back there," Tree declared. "I was just fixin' to draw my gun when Bo suddenly checked the cylinder on his .45. I thought at first you'd lost your mind, the way you was so dainty when you started to pick it up. How did you know your gun was empty?"

"They was all three lookin' like they didn't have nothin' to worry about," Bo replied. "Just struck me as kinda odd, since I was fixin' to lay 'em like cordwood on the floor. So I thought I'd better test my six-gun. And when I picked it up in the holster, it felt light to me, and they didn't spook a-tall when I took it outta my holster." He looked over at Brock. "What I wanna know now is what are we gonna do?"

"We're gonna take us a little vacation while we decide the best way to get Reese and them others outta that damn jail. I know he's hot as a Mexican pepper after we left that jail and he didn't hear no gunshots. But we're gonna stay here till we come up with a plan to get them outta jail."

"We gonna find a spot to make camp?" Tree asked.

"Hell, no," Brock replied. "We're gonna stay in the hotel like the bigshots we are."

"As long as you're payin' for it," Bo said. "Suits me just fine."

Tree was all for it as well, so they pulled up at the River House Hotel, tied their horses out front and went inside where they found the desk clerk, Rob Parker, talking to the owner, Freeman Brown. Freeman nodded politely to them, then stepped aside to permit Rob to deal with them. "Can I help you, sir?" Rob addressed Brock, since he stepped up to the desk while his two rather rough-looking companions just stood back and gawked at the furnishings of the lobby.

"I can wait till you're finished with this gentleman," Brock said, nodding toward Freeman Brown.

"Oh, no, sir," Rob replied, "this is Mr. Brown, the owner. We were just talking about something unimportant. How can I help you?"

"Mr. Brown," Brock acknowledged politely. "We were just admiring your hotel lobby. I didn't expect to find a hotel of this high quality in a town so small." Tree looked at Bo and rolled his eyes. Bo grinned and nodded in return. They were well familiar with one of Brock's favorite roles.

"Why, thank you very much, sir," Freeman responded. "We take great pride in trying to make the River House something the town can be proud of. How can we be of service to you?"

"We're going to be in town for a few days to look over the area for development. You've no doubt heard of Salter Enterprises, Incorporated."

"Well, yes, sir, I think I have," Freeman said. In fact, he never had, but he didn't want to admit it.

"Well, I'm Brock Salter, the president of that corporation. And these two roustabouts are my guides. Without their knowledge of the country, I would never have stumbled upon Buzzard's Bluff. I would like a room for myself and another one for the two roustabouts."

"We will be happy to accommodate you, Mr. Salter. Rob, why don't you put Mr. Salter in one of the rooms up front, over the street? And the other two gentlemen could share a room right across the hall." He turned back toward Brock. "Does that seem about right, Mr. Salter?"

"That sounds about right," Brock confirmed. "We'll register and take our saddlebags up to the rooms, then we'll take the horses to the stable."

"Whaddaya think, John?" Henry Barnes asked when Lucas crawled out from under the wagon after inspecting the axles. "It's in pretty good shape, ain't it?"

"Yep," Lucas replied. "I can't find anything wrong with it, and you're askin' a fair price for it. So, I reckon I'll buy it."

"Fine," Henry responded. "How about a harness? I can fix you up with that, unless you wanna buy all new stuff from Tuck Tucker."

"I'm sure what you've got will suit my needs," Lucas said.

Henry started toward the tack room but stopped when Brock Salter and his two men pulled up in front of the stable. "Here comes some more trouble," Henry muttered under his breath. "That's them three that was visitin' the jailbirds this mornin'. Lemme see what they want, John. Maybe I can get rid of 'em real quick." He didn't want anything to get in the way of his selling the wagon.

"Take your time," Lucas replied. "I'm not in a hurry."

Henry chuckled and said, "You need to rest a little bit, anyway. You've had a pretty busy mornin', so far." He walked to the door then to meet Brock. "What can I do for you fellers?" he asked.

"We're stayin' at the hotel for a few days, so we need to leave our horses with you," Brock answered.

"Yes, sir," Henry replied. "I'll take care of 'em for ya. All of 'em under one bill?"

"That's right," Brock answered.

"And that'll be Mr. Brock, right?"

"No, it's actually Salter," he said. "Brock's my first name." He thought, since he had given that name to the sheriff and the hotel, he might as well continue to do so. Hopefully, that would avoid more confusion, even for the short time they would be here.

"Oh, all right," Henry replied. "Mr. Salter then. Looks like you've got six horses to stable and board."

"Man's as sharp as a carpet tack," Bo slurred sarcastically, and started to make another comment when he saw Lucas standing by the wagon back in the barn. "There's the feller that was helpin' the sheriff guard us this morning."

"Damned if it ain't," Tree said. "And he's the one that shot Hutch right here in the stable before that."

"Watch what you say," Brock warned him, outside of Henry's hearing distance. "We ain't supposed to know Hutch was here. He weren't with us. Don't forget that." He left them there with the horses while he arranged for the care of them with Henry.

"Jack Ramsey swears that feller is Lucas Blaine, fastest gun hand in Texas," Bo added. "I wonder if he is. He don't look like the rattlesnake he's supposed to be, does he?"

"Them's the ones that fool you," Tree said. "They try to getcha to thinkin' they ain't dangerous, then they strike while you're still decidin'."

"I'll bet you I could take that feller," Bo said. "I don't care who he is."

"That's the kind of thinkin' that can get you killed," Tree replied.

"Shoot," Bo countered. "You've seen me pull and shoot. You tellin' me I ain't faster'n anybody you've ever seen draw a six-gun?"

"I reckon you are faster than anybody I've ever seen. What I'm sayin' is I ain't never seen that feller draw and shoot."

"How much are you willing to bet that I ain't faster'n that feller?" Bo insisted, growing more confident by the minute as they watched Lucas poke around the wagon in the barn.

"I don't know," Tree said. "If I bet against you, and you lose, who's gonna pay me the money?"

Ignoring Tree's sarcasm, Bo said, "I'm gonna ask him." He didn't wait then and walked into the barn where the wagon was parked. Lucas turned when he heard him coming up behind him. "Are you some kind of deputy or somethin'?" Bo asked. "Or was you just helpin' out at the jail this morning?"

"I was just helpin' out," Lucas answered. "I'm not a deputy."

"They said you shot a feller in here this morning. How'd that happen?"

"It's not something I'm proud of," Lucas said. "But I really didn't have any choice. He was fixin' to shoot me."

"I heard your name is Lucas Blaine. Is that a fact?"

"My name is John Cochran," Lucas said.

"I don't know about that. I ain't ready to believe your real name is John Cochran," Bo insisted.

"Why don't you ask Henry who I am," Lucas tried.

"Henry can tell you what my name is." Bo didn't respond to the suggestion, remaining instead to stand grinning at him as if he had caught him dealing from the bottom of the deck. When it appeared that Bo was not going to take his word as fact, Lucas asked him a question. "Why do you want me to say I'm Lucas Blaine? Has Lucas Blaine ever done any harm to you or your family?"

"If he had done anything to my family, he'd already be dead," Bo came back quickly.

"It sounds to me like Lucas Blaine ain't ever caused you any problem, so why don't you just let him be?"

"I said he ain't never done my family no harm," Bo answered. "But I didn't say he ain't never caused me a problem."

"What problem has he ever caused you?" Lucas asked, already aware of where this conversation was leading. His hope now was that Henry and Brock would return to interrupt it.

"He's walkin' around makin' people think he's the fastest gun in the state of Texas, and he don't ever go against nobody who's halfway fast. And that's a problem with me, because he ain't man enough to stand up against me."

"And you wanna be the fastest gun in Texas," Lucas said, his voice reflecting the feeling of extreme weariness for the cocky braying of yet another boastful jackass.

"I am the fastest gun in Texas," Bo declared.

"Well, congratulations," Lucas said. "But I'm not Lucas Blaine. What would he be doin' in a little town like Buzzard's Bluff, anyway? I'm John Cochran. Sorry to disappoint you, but it was an interesting talk we had."

"You're a damn liar," Bo responded.

Lucas shook his head as if exhausted. "Now, why'd you

have to call me that? Why would you think I'm lyin'? You've never seen me before this morning."

"Jack Ramsey saw you shoot a man named Wendel Lewis, in the Red Dog Saloon, in San Antonio. And Jack Ramsey is a man I trust, and he was one of the three men you saw in that jail cell this mornin'."

Lucas knew which prisoner he referred to. He was the man who approached him at the bar in the Golden Rail and asked if he was Lucas Blaine. He had already shot one man this morning. He felt that he could not risk another killing without ruining his and Caroline's plans for a fresh start in life. But he had no option, other than to keep denying his real name and claiming cowardice. "I'm not going to fight you," he said. "I've got no quarrel with you. I don't even know your name."

"My name is Bo Turner. I'm the man who killed Lucas Blaine, and that's a fact. I'm givin' you the chance to face me like a man. But if you don't, I'll shoot you down like the yellow dog you are." He stepped back toward the middle of the barn to give Lucas room to step away from the wagon. Aware only then of the challenge that had been offered by Bo, Brock and Tree stopped unpacking the packhorses, and stood shocked by what was about to happen. Brock, more stunned than Tree, started to say something to call Bo off. But Bo stopped him. "Stay outta this, Brock. If he don't stand up to me, I'm gonna kill him anyway."

With no longer any hope to prevent it, Lucas did what he had to do. "All right, Bo Turner, I'll stand up to you, if you won't give me any other choice. But if you kill me, it'll be John Cochran you killed, not Lucas Blaine." He opened his jacket and tucked the tail of it in his belt at his back. "Are you sure you want to do this?" Bo smiled and nodded. "Whenever you're ready," Lucas said.

Bo Turner suffered two wounds. The fatal one was Lucas Blaine's shot that struck him in the center of his chest. The second one was a shot through the toe of his right boot when he pulled the trigger as his gun was only halfway out of his holster. Stunned by the swiftness of Bo Turner's execution, the three witnesses could not manage to speak for many seconds after the sound of the shots. Brock Salter, still stunned by Bo's disregard for the importance of ignoring his desire for personal fame, at least until after they managed Reese's escape, could not yet form a sentence. The first to comment was from Tree Forney, who said, "Reckon that means I've got a private room at the hotel."

CHAPTER 11

There was a definite look of sadness in Lucas Blaine's eyes as he turned to watch Brock and Tree's reaction to the shooting, alert for any sign of retaliation on the part of either man. When he was satisfied there was none, he ejected the spent cartridge and inserted a new one, then returned the Colt to his holster. Unlike his early years, there was no feeling of triumph like that of a winner, because he knew he had won nothing. To the contrary, like Bo, he was a loser. The only difference was he had to continue to run, trying to hide his identity from the next rising gunman, seeking the pitiful fame of a fast gun.

"Damn!" Henry Barnes was finally able to speak. He came over with Brock and Tree to see if Bo was dead. There was little doubt.

"I swear," Tree blurted as he stared down at the body. He looked up then at Lucas and said, "If you ain't Lucas Blaine, you oughta go lookin' for him, 'cause I ain't believin' there's anybody faster than what I just saw."

"My name's not Lucas Blaine," he claimed once again, now reluctant to even say the name John Cochran for fear of it being repeated as a fast gun. "I didn't want to kill this man. He must have been crazy."

Henry made an attempt to console Lucas. "You got nothin' to feel guilty about, John. You done what you had to do to stay alive. Just be thankful you can handle a gun like you did." He turned to look at Brock then. "What made that feller do that? Had he ever done something like that before?"

Brock was at a loss for an answer, still astonished by Bo's determined effort to challenge the man. Now, he had to try to explain this to the sheriff. His only option was to play dumb.

"No, certainly not," he said in answer to Henry's question. "I don't know what came over him. I've never seen him act like this before." He turned toward Tree. "Have you, Tree?"

Tree went along with it. "No, never seen him wanna have a shootout with anybody before. But he has been actin' kinda crazy lately."

"What's the trouble here?" They all turned when they heard Mack Bragg standing in the open barn doorway, his pistol in his hand. "Henry, who's doin' the shootin'?"

"Well, it was John, here," Henry said. "He shot this feller." He pointed to Bo's body lying on the barn floor. "That was the first shot." He pointed to the body again. "He fired the second shot. Shot himself in the toe."

"That's one of your men," Mack said to Brock.

"Yes, he was one of my men," Brock replied. "I guess if I'd known he was capable of goin' off half-cocked on somebody like that, I'da never hired him. I hired him because he said he could work cattle."

Mack nodded slowly, even though he put little stock in a truthful answer from Brock. From what he had observed of John Cochran, he doubted if he had been the instigator of any gun fighting. He wanted his assumption confirmed, however, so he went back to Henry again. "Henry, you said Cochran fired the first shot. Is that right?"

"Well, yeah, Mack." Henry hesitated. "That feller, layin' there, went for his gun first, but John beat him to the draw, so he shot first. John did everything he could to talk him outta goin' at it with guns, but he told John he was gonna kill him whether he faced him or not. He thought he was some gunfighter named Lucas Blaine, and he wanted to be the fastest gun in Texas. John kept tellin' him he weren't that man, but he wouldn't have none of it."

"Is that pretty much the way it happened?" Mack asked Brock then.

"I'm afraid so," Brock answered. "We never knew Bo had such wild thoughts in his head. There wasn't anybody shocked more than Tree, here, and myself."

"You agree with that?" Mack asked Tree.

"That's the way it happened," Tree replied. "Bo called him out, but the other feller was faster when they went for their guns."

"Well, I reckon that pretty much sums it up," Mack declared. "That makes two gunfights for you today, John, and it ain't even dinnertime yet. But I can't see as how you're the cause of either one of 'em. I just hope this one is the last one."

"Yes, sir, I surely do, too," Lucas was quick to respond. "I'm buyin' this wagon and a team of horses from Henry, and I'm plannin' to leave town within a day or two."

"I hope you find your next stop a little more peaceful," Mack said. He decided he needed to have a talk with Ben Savage about John Cochran. He had a feeling Ben knew more about Cochran than he talked about. He turned his attention to Brock then. "Mr. Salter, if you and your man, there, wanna check the dead man for anything you want, go ahead and do it, and I'll have the undertaker take care of the body."

Tree unbuckled Bo's gun belt and rolled his body over so he could pull it out from under him. Then he took the pistol out of his hand and put it back in the holster. He searched his pockets and came up with a pocketknife, some chewing tobacco, and a small amount of money. "I'll take a look in his saddlebags when we go back to the hotel," he said. "He oughta have more money than this." He got up from the floor, looked back down at Bo and muttered, "Rest in peace, you damn fool."

Mack sat in his office while Horace went up to the hotel dining room to pick up the noon meal for his prisoners. Then he stood by with his weapon drawn while Horace put the plates inside their cell. Then the cell was locked, and Horace handed them coffee through the bars. Once they were settled down to eat, Mack locked the door between the office and the cell room and told Horace to stay out of the cell room. He was feeling a little uneasy about Brock Salter's decision to remain in Buzzard's Bluff for a few days. He could think of no reason, other than to attempt a jailbreak. At least one more of them had been eliminated, thanks to John Cochran. That was one other thing that troubled him, though, so he told Horace he'd be back in about twenty or thirty minutes. "Where you goin'," Horace asked. "You ain't et no dinner yet."

"To the Lost Coyote to get something to eat," Mack told him.

* * *

"Howdy, Sheriff," Tiny greeted him when he walked into the saloon.

"Tiny," Mack acknowledged in return and walked past the bar, on his way to a table in the back where he saw Ben eating dinner with Rachel.

"If you ain't had your dinner yet, you've come at the right time," Ben said. "Annie's husband killed a deer this mornin', and we're sittin' here enjoyin' some fresh venison."

"I wouldn't pass that up, even if I had eaten," Mack responded.

"Sit down, Mack," Rachel invited, "and I'll go tell Annie to fix a plate for you." She got up and went to the kitchen while he pulled a chair back.

While she was gone, Mack said, "I wanted to talk to you about John Cochran and those killings this morning. I know you heard all about the second one. I don't know how much you know about him, and I don't know how much we oughta say in front of Rachel."

"Everything I know about John Cochran, Rachel knows," Ben told him. "So, it doesn't matter what we say in front of her. I thought, after this mornin', that it was time to let you in on it."

Rachel came back to the table at that moment with a plate for Mack and a cup of coffee. "How 'bout you, Ben? You need some more coffee?" He refused it, so she asked then, "Do you need me to leave you two alone to talk business? I've finished eating, and I can finish my coffee at the bar with Tiny. He needs somebody to talk to."

"No, you're welcome to stay right here," Ben said. "Mack wants to talk about John Cochran, so you can help me out." He waited for her to sit down again. Then he couldn't resist saying, "Mack tried to hire him to work for him as a deputy this mornin'."

"If you can believe what Henry Barnes said about him, he's as fast as greased lightning with that six-gun he carries," Mack said. "Henry said that last one he killed called him out because he said he was Lucas Blaine. I've heard of Lucas Blaine, but I ain't ever seen him. But if he is Blaine, he can't be anything but bad news for Buzzard's Bluff. There'll be one damn fool after another, showin' up to try their luck against him."

"Well, he is Lucas Blaine," Ben said, "and maybe I shoulda told you sooner. But he came to Buzzard's Bluff for only one reason, to see his wife and son." When Mack recoiled in surprise, Ben said, "Caroline Carter and her boy."

"I thought she was a widow," Mack replied.

"That's what she told people," Ben said. "All they want to do now is go somewhere far away from Texas where nobody knows him and see if they can put his past behind him." With Rachel's help, they told Mack how they happened to arrange a meeting between Lucas and Caroline, and how they had felt obligated to keep their secret.

"Well, I reckon I can understand that," Mack said. "He told me they're plannin' to leave here in a day or two."

"As soon as he can get his wagon ready and supplied with whatever they need to live on, is all I know. Rachel says Caroline's sister was trying to talk her outta goin' off with Blaine, on account of the men he's supposed to have killed. You know, with Marva bein' married to the preacher and all. But Caroline says she wants to be with her husband." Ben paused when Rachel wanted to add something.

"Lucas has saved up quite a bit of money," she said, "enough to buy some land to farm he says. And he swears every penny was lawfully earned."

"Don't worry," Mack said. "I ain't got no paper on Lucas Blaine. I got nothin' to arrest him for." He chuckled then and added, "I might wanna hire him, though, until I get the Salter brothers off my hands." That became the next topic of discussion with Ben. "You know darn well that visit to the jail this morning was intended to be a jailbreak. And I ain't got no idea what they're gonna try next. You know Brock Salter ain't stayin' in town so he can go to his brother's trial."

"I don't expect he is," Ben agreed, "so I reckon there ain't no need for me to tell you to watch your back any time you're out of the jail."

"You're right about that," Mack said. "Right now, I don't like to leave the jail for very long, even with Horace there and the door locked. So, I expect I'd better get back now. Thank you for that venison dinner. I ain't ate deer meat for a while." He got up from the table and started to leave but paused long enough to tell Ben he appreciated his help at the jail that morning. Then he walked on out the door.

"Ben, how much longer are you going to help Mack police the town?" Rachel fixed an accusing eye upon him. "You know, the previous owner didn't take part in the business of the sheriff's office."

"I don't know, Rachel, as long as I can help, I reckon. Jim Vickers was a little older than I am when he retired to this saloon. Otherwise, from what I remember about Jim, I expect he woulda helped as best he could." He got up from the table and started to pick up his cup and dinner plate to take back to the kitchen, but Rachel told him she would take care of them. "Well, then," he declared, "while everything's peaceful at the moment, I think I'll throw my saddle on Cousin and take a little ride."

"Where are you going?" Rachel asked.

"Just up the river a little way," he said. "I need to give

Cousin a bit of exercise. He ain't been gettin' much these last few days. I don't want him to get as fat and useless as I am, sittin' around this saloon."

Lucas Blaine guided the buckskin gelding around behind the church where he had made his camp by a small stream. It wasn't much more than a trickle of water, but it was constant and provided enough for the buckskin and his packhorse. He had decided to leave his two horses he had just bought from Henry at the stable, along with the wagon, until he was ready to pack up everything in preparation for his and Caroline's journey. After he pulled the buckskin's saddle off, he threw it under the canvas half-tent he had constructed and left the horse to graze with the sorrel pack-horse. Then he started for the parsonage to tell Caroline that they now owned a wagon, so she had better be getting ready to go.

Tommy was sitting on the kitchen steps when Lucas approached. Before Lucas had time to greet him, the boy jumped up and ran inside the house. It was going to be a while before Tommy would be at ease in his presence, Lucas thought. He walked into the kitchen to find Marva standing by the stove. "We saved some dinner for you in the dining room," she said.

"Why, thank you very much, Marva. I 'preciate that, but you didn't have to go to the trouble."

"Weren't no trouble," Marva answered simply and turned to lead the way.

He followed her into the dining room and was surprised to find the preacher and Caroline sitting at one end of the table, opposite a plate of food at the other end. Marva sat down beside Caroline, whose painful expression immediately alarmed him. "What's wrong?" Lucas asked, aware now of the solemn faces of Ronald and Marva on either side of her.

It was the preacher who answered his question. "I was in Howard's Merchandise a little while ago," he started. "Tuck Tucker was in the store, and he was telling Cecil and several others about the gunshots that had been heard in town this morning. He said that you had shot and killed two men in the stable at two separate times. He used the name John Cochran, but he said the second man you shot came to call you out because he knew you were really Lucas Blaine. Was Tuck accurate in his report?"

It was as if he had been slammed in the chest. The almost childish look of disappointment on Caroline's face, framed by the accusing expressions of Ronald and Marva's was like that of a judge and jury. He hesitated to answer, searching for some explanation that might make the fact seem not nearly so bad. But there was none, so reluctantly, he answered truthfully. "Yes, that is what happened. But the first incident was purely bad luck because I happened to be in the stable when a man threatened Henry Barnes and myself. It wouldn't have mattered if it had been someone other than me. He was going to shoot, anyway."

"And the second man?" Ronald asked when Lucas didn't continue.

"What can I say?" Lucas replied. "He got a notion somehow that it was me. I tried to talk him out of a gunfight. You can ask Henry Barnes. He'll tell you I did everything I could to avoid facing that man, but he threatened to kill me if I didn't." He looked directly at Caroline. "It'll be different when we're somewhere else with different names. We'll be Mr. and Mrs. Smith, or whatever you like; Carter, if you'd rather. Don't let this little piece of bad luck discourage you. We'll have you and me and Tommy. That's all that really matters, ain't it?"

"Oh, Lucas," she responded as tears gathered in her eyes, "they are always going to find you, until someone kills you. Like Ronald said, if they can find you in Buzzard's Bluff, they can find you anywhere. I realize now that I can't subject Tommy to a life where we'll always have to wonder if some gunman has tracked you down."

"What are you saying?" Lucas exclaimed. "You're not tellin' me you've changed your mind? You said your place was with your husband! You said you would always love me! I told you I would do anything to make you happy! How can you just completely change your mind?" He shifted his attention to Ronald. "Was it you, preacher? Did you preach her a sermon about how evil I am?"

"Don't blame Ronald for this, Lucas," Caroline quickly pleaded, even though the preacher had engaged in a long soul-searching talk with her after he heard about the shootings. "It's my decision not to go with you. Blame it on this morning's sinful happenings that made me realize it was not the right thing for Tommy or me. I said I love you, and I always will, but I have to be realistic about the future. I will pray for you and always wish you well. My only solace is in hoping it will be better for you not to be saddled with a wife and child."

"Maybe after you think about this again, you might change your mind," Lucas said. "I think we have a good chance to start a new life in Montana or Oregon. People are going out there to start a new life, just like us, for any number of reasons. I know this is all my fault. I should have tried to change my life years ago. But it's still not too late for us."

"I'm so sorry, Lucas, but it's too late for Tommy and me. At least we have a home here in Buzzard's Bluff, and I'll always hold you in my heart."

When it appeared that Lucas was going to accept that as Caroline's final decision, Ronald attempted to heal the wound just delivered to Lucas' soul. "I hope you will see where Caroline's decision comes from, and you will feel no resentment toward Marva and myself. We certainly feel none toward you, and we want what's best for both of you. Her decision was hard for her to make, but I'm sure you'll come to see it was the right one. Marva prepared some dinner for you, so we invite you to sit down and eat."

"Thanks just the same," Lucas said, "but suddenly I just lost my appetite. I've got some jerky back at my camp. That'll do for tonight." He turned to leave but stopped when Ronald said one more thing.

"I would ask you one favor," he said. "I would greatly appreciate it if you would move your camp from behind the church. I'm sure you can understand my position as a man of God, that I cannot condone the presence of a professional gunfighter camping behind the church."

Lucas gazed at him for a long moment, but he didn't answer him. He looked away then for one last look at his wife, standing beside her sister now, her arms wrapped around five-year-old Tommy. "Goodbye, Caroline," he whispered and turned to leave.

CHAPTER 12

"Well, it don't look like you worked him too hard," Henry Barnes called out when Ben pulled Cousin back from a fast lope to a sliding stop in front of the stable.

Ben stepped down from the saddle and gave the big dun gelding an approving pat on the neck. "I think he was needin' a good run," he said. "I was needin' one, myself. It ain't good for neither one of us to sit around too long."

Henry walked beside him as he led the horse back to the corral and opened the gate for him. "John Cochran, or Lucas Blaine, whoever the hell he is, was in here a little while ago. He's changed his mind about that wagon and them two horses he bought from me."

"Changed his mind?" Ben was truly surprised. "I thought he was chompin' at the bit to get that wagon loaded up and on the road outta Buzzard's Bluff."

"It sure surprised me, too," Henry said.

"What changed his mind? Was it the money? Maybe he found one he could buy a little bit cheaper. From what he told me, he had money enough to buy some land, too."

"No, it weren't the money," Henry replied. "That's the crazy part. I figured he wanted his money back, but he said, no, he didn't want it back. He said he made a deal with me, and he had bought the horses and the wagon, and it wouldn't be right to ask me to give the money back."

"Well, I'll be . . ." Ben reacted. "If that ain't something. So you came out on the winnin' side of that deal. Kept the money and the horses and wagon, too."

"Well, I did no such a thing," Henry said. "He seemed right down in the mouth about it, like it was something he didn't really wanna do. I gave him his money back and told him it wouldn't set right with me to keep it. He made me take fifty dollars for the trouble he said I went to. I told him it weren't really no trouble, that I oughta had already fixed that wagon up. But he insisted, so I took it. Probably shouldn't have, you reckon?"

"You were right to take it," Ben said. "Sounds like he felt pretty bad about backin' out of the deal he made with you, and that fifty dollars bought him a little peace of mind." It was enough to make Ben wonder what changed Lucas' mind. "Maybe he's decided to stay here, but if he's gonna buy some land to farm, he's still gonna need a wagon." He shrugged indifferently and released Cousin to go to the water trough on the far side of the corral. "I guess I'd best get back to the Coyote and see if we sold any likker while I was out ridin' Cousin."

When he walked back into the Lost Coyote, one of the first people he saw was Lucas Blaine. He was seated at a table, eating some beef stew Annie had cooked for dinner. Ben noticed an empty shot glass on the table beside his coffee cup. "Howdy," Ben greeted him. Lucas returned the greeting. "Mind if I sit down?"

"Not at all, Ben. Have a seat. You want some coffee?"

"No thanks," Ben replied. "I ate dinner just a little while ago and drank too much then as usual. That looks like stew you're eatin'. Too bad you didn't get here earlier, you could have had some fresh venison. I reckon it went pretty fast."

"I can't complain about the stew," Lucas said. "Annie's a pretty good cook."

"Ain't none of my business, but I just came from the stable, and Henry told me you decided you didn't want the wagon or the team of horses. You decide you were gonna do something different than headin' out to Oregon?"

"No, I didn't," Lucas answered, then paused a moment before continuing. "Caroline changed her mind."

"I'm sorry, Lucas," Ben said immediately. "I didn't mean to stick my nose where it didn't belong. That really ain't any of my business."

"No need to apologize," Lucas replied. "I appreciate what you and Rachel have done to help me find Caroline again, but it just didn't work out like we planned at first. That business I was in at the stable was what changed her mind." He paused, then said, "That and all the advice she was gettin' from the preacher and his wife. I guess I can't blame her for not wantin' to take the risk. It's all my doin'. I just wish I had had a little more sense when I was younger."

Ben felt extremely sorry for the man, still young in his opinion, thinking his dream is finally going to be realized, then having it snatched away from him. "What are you plannin' to do now?"

"What I was doin' before I found her, I reckon, just drift. I ain't decided where to yet."

"Why don't you stay here in town a while, maybe things will change again." He was thinking about what Mack had said about hiring a deputy. Lucas might be willing to help again, if Brock and Reese Salter tried their jailbreak.

"To tell you the truth, I wasn't plannin' on leavin' town for a day or two. I had to move my camp from behind the church at the preacher's request. And I was gonna set it up on Wolf Creek, but now I'm thinkin' about checkin' in the hotel and let Henry Barnes take care of my horses while I'm in town. I can afford it, cause I ain't got no reason to save every penny anymore."

"That sounds like a good idea," Ben said. *If it wasn't so damn sad,* he thought. "Rob Parker will fix you up with a good room. He's the desk clerk. Mack Bragg and I always take supper at the hotel dinin' room. You could join us, if you want to. Maybe we'll see ol' Brock Salter and that one he calls Tree, if they don't go to the Golden Rail."

Lucas couldn't help smiling at Ben's attempts to cheer him up. "Maybe I'll do that," he gave in just as Rachel came from the office. Seeing them at the table, she started toward the two men.

"Hello, Lucas, I didn't know you were eating with us. Is everything all right with your dinner?"

"Yes, ma'am," Lucas replied. "Everything's fine. I'm just about finished." He didn't feel like going through the whole story with Rachel, so he decided to take his leave and let Ben repeat the story to her. He got up from the table and started for the door. "Maybe I'll see you at supper tonight, Ben."

"Right," Ben called after him, then turned to face his partner, who was standing with hands on hips, a look of bewilderment on her face.

"Well, I seemed to have scared him off right away," she said. "I didn't even know he was here." She thought about that for a moment, then asked, "What was he doing here? Why wasn't he eating with Caroline?"

"She changed her mind," Ben replied. "I expect he took off just now because he didn't wanna go through the whole story again."

"She changed her mind?" Rachel responded in disbelief. "You're teasing me, aren't you?"

"I'm afraid not," Ben answered. Then he related the whole story as Lucas had told him. As he expected, she was very disappointed in Caroline Carter and referred to Ronald Gillespie as a pompous ass.

"That poor man," she said. "What are we going to do about it?"

"Whaddaya mean, what are we gonna do about it? Not a damn thing. It ain't none of our business. That's between a man and his wife."

"What did he mean, maybe he'd see you at supper tonight?"

"He's gonna stay in the hotel for a few days, so I told him Mack and I would be eatin' supper at the dinin' room tonight."

"I'm surprised Mack is going to the dining room to eat, now that he's got those three prisoners in the jail," she commented. "Doesn't he usually send Horace up there to bring his supper back when he's got dangerous men locked up?"

"He does that when there's a great danger of a gang or somebody who might come after them. But in this case, he knows it's Brock and Tree he has to worry about, and we'll most likely be eatin' supper with them. That is, if they eat in the dining room. Anyway, he'll leave Horace in the office with the door locked and orders to let nobody in.

I hope Brock does eat in the dinin' room. It'd be a good thing for Brock to see Lucas with us. Give him something more to think about."

She thought about that for only a moment more before returning her thoughts to Lucas and Caroline. "I wonder if I should go down there and talk to Caroline."

"And tell her what? That you've decided to be her life guide? The Reverend Gillespie might work his congregation up to come burn you at the stake for tryin' to lead Caroline down the wrong path." He could see it was eating away at her. "I don't think it would help his cause for the female saloon owner to come to try to talk Caroline into hookin' up with a fast-gun who just shot down two men before dinner."

"All right, I get it," she retreated. "It just doesn't seem right."

"Like he said, he's gonna be hangin' around a few days. You never can tell what might happen. She changed her mind pretty damn quick. She might change it back just as quick. You need to get your mind back on the important business. Look who just walked in. I believe that's Mr. Tuck Tucker and he's lookin' for his poker partner. And when the two of them get to playin' cards, they might end up spending a dollar and a half in here tonight." She gave him a look of disgust for his attempt at humor.

"What the hell does Reese expect us to do?" Tree Forney demanded. "There weren't a whole lot we could do when there was three of us. And now that Bo got hisself killed, what can just me and you do?" He paused to wave Charlene away when she approached the table. "Not now, honey, maybe a little bit later on." They had spent a good part of the afternoon in the Golden Rail Saloon, most of the time discussing the execution of Bo Turner.

"We gotta come up with something," Brock said. "Reese is countin' on us to break him outta that jail, and I don't see much possibility in us shootin' our way in there. Even if the sheriff ain't there, that fellow with the shotgun—what's his name?"

"Horace," Tree supplied.

"Right, Horace—Reese said he wasn't nothin', and we didn't need to worry about him. But that shotgun don't know he's nothin', and in the small space inside that jail, you can't miss with a shotgun."

"You got that right," Tree said. "The only chance we've got is to figure out a way to pass a gun in to Reese, so he can surprise 'em and get him and the other boys outta there."

"I agree," Brock said. "That's the way to get 'em out. Now, how we gonna pass him a gun?"

"If I knew that, I'da already done it," Tree answered. He threw up his hands in frustration. "It's time that dinin' room opened for supper. Let's go eat." He got up from the table, not waiting to see if Brock was in agreement.

Charlene drifted over in front of him. "You said you wanted to go upstairs with me," she said. "I've been savin' myself for you. Where are you goin'?"

"I drank too much likker," he told her. "I've gotta get me somethin' to eat first. When you see me come back, I'll be lookin' for ya. So don't get yourself tied up with nobody."

"I won't, Tree. Hurry back. I'll wait for you." *Like hell I will,* she thought.

"That's a good girl," he said. *Like hell she will,* he thought. Brock got up and followed him out the door.

A short walk down the street took them to the River House Hotel. They went past the hotel entrance to the outside entrance to the dining room where Lacy James met them at the door. "Good evening, gentlemen, come in and sit anywhere you like." They started to do that, only to be reminded. "I have to ask that you leave your guns on the table," she said.

"Oh, that's right," Brock replied, "guns on the table. It's so easy to forget that, ain't it, Tree?"

"Yeah, it is, especially when there's three rough-lookin' fellers settin' at that back table with their six-guns on," Tree said and nodded toward the table where Ben, Mack, and Lucas were seated.

"To be fair," Lacy said, "only two of them are wearing their guns, and that's because they are lawmen. The other fellow, Mr. Cochran, put his gun on the table." It was only a half-lie she was telling. Although Ben only acted in the official capacity of a Texas Ranger once in a great while, Lacy did not require him to remove his weapon. And on occasion, it had been lucky for the dining room that he was armed.

"I reckon we oughta count ourselves lucky we've got so much protection while we're eatin' supper," Brock declared, with just a hint of sarcasm in his tone. They both took off their gun belts, rolled them up, and placed them on the table next to Lucas' gun belt. Then they went to a table by a window on the side wall. "Sheriff," Brock said in greeting as he and Tree pulled a chair back and sat down.

"Mr. Salter," Mack returned the greeting. He thought that he could almost feel the tension in the room between the two tables. "I'm tempted to arrest the two of 'em right now, instead of waitin' for 'em to make their move," he said after he lowered his voice.

"Arrest 'em for what?" Ben chuckled. "Eatin' with bad intentions?"

"There oughta be a law against that," Mack replied, a hint of the frustration he was feeling in his voice. "The whole damn county knows they're just hangin' around waitin' to make their move."

"The fact they ain't made it tells me they ain't made up their minds what they're gonna try yet," Ben said.

Lucas sat quietly, listening to the conversation between the sheriff and the ex-ranger. It seemed like a juvenile game being played between outlaw and lawman. He thought back on the short period in his life when he was a deputy sheriff in San Antonio. It was only for a little over a year, and that was when he had married Caroline Carter. Both she and her father wanted him to give up the deputy job, so he did. He wondered if he and Caroline would still be happily married if he had resisted their urging and remained in the law business. "How's that?" he asked when he just realized that Mack had asked him a question.

"You looked like you was a mile away from here," Mack commented. "I said Ben told me you was plannin' on hangin' around for a few days."

"Yes, sir, I thought I might, since I'm not in any particular hurry to go any place." He displayed a weak smile. "Is this the place where you ask me to leave town before the sun sets on Buzzard's Bluff?"

"Hell, no!" Mack responded. "I was thinkin' more about askin' if you'd like to help us out again, like you did the first time." He glanced at Ben and grinned, then added, "And the second and the third time in the stable."

Lucas glanced from Mack to Ben, his expression emotionless. Then back to Mack, he said, "I'll help you, if that's what you really want. But after that little red-headed fellow spread the word that my name is really Lucas Blaine, I'd be surprised if your mayor and town council don't want me to leave immediately."

Mack grunted, then chuckled as he looked from Ben to Lucas. "I'm more concerned they might consider makin' you the sheriff and offering me a job as a deputy."

"What about the concern about my name drawin' gunmen from all over to come to Buzzard's Bluff to test their skill with a handgun?" Lucas asked.

"We ain't gonna use your name," Mack said. "We'll keep callin' you John Cochran."

"I expect I'll be movin' on soon," Lucas said without hesitation. "I've got too much I have to forget here. And it wouldn't be good for my wife and my son to have my shadow hangin' over them. But I'll stay until you get your prisoners to trial."

"I reckon I understand that," Mack said. "I 'preciate your help."

Ben made no comment on the subject, but he had told Mack he didn't think it would be a good idea to persuade Lucas to stay on permanently in the sheriff's office. He was convinced that Lucas would draw fast-gun drifters from all over Texas, and that would surely harm the growth of the town. He was glad to see that Lucas realized it would not be best for him as well. Lucas still had a chance to regain a normal life in a new setting under a different name. He was distracted from his thoughts then when Lacy came to the

table carrying the coffeepot. "Anybody need a warmup?"
she asked, even as she was already filling their cups. "How
was the supper? Did you like the steaks?" They said they
did, and she said it was a different cut of beef than Myrtle
usually had to fry.

"Well, tell her it was tender and tasty," Ben said, aware
that they were getting all that attention because Lacy just
wanted to get a closer look at Lucas. Thanks now to Tuck
Tucker, Lucas had acquired a considerable amount of fame.

"This was your first meal with us, Mr. Cochran. I hope
you found the food satisfactory." After he came in and told
her he was a guest in the hotel, she had sent Cindy running
to the front desk to ask Rob Parker if he had signed in as
Cochran or Blaine.

"I did, ma'am," he answered. "I found it more than satisfactory, and I expect you'll see me in here again."

"Just like one big family," Tree growled when he saw
Lacy taking coffee to the sheriff's table. "I hope they didn't
put no poison in our grub."

"If they did, it didn't hurt the taste none," Brock commented. "It don't make me too happy to see that fast-gun
professional sittin' with 'em. I was hopin' he'd leave town
after he put Hutch and Bo under the ground." He was about
to complain when Lacy failed to bring them more coffee,
but Cindy came out of the kitchen with a smaller pot and
headed straight to their table.

"You fellows need some more coffee?" she asked politely.

"I sure do, honey," Tree replied and held his cup up
toward her. She filled it, then looked at Brock, but he put
his hand over his cup.

"You're gonna need to spread your fingers just a little

bit, if I'm gonna get any in the cup," she japed. Brock was in no mood to appreciate her humor. He just glared at her, so she looked at Tree and said, "Tell your father, I didn't mean to upset him." She turned and went to another table with the coffeepot.

"Ha!" Tree snorted. "She thinks you're my father."

"Shut up and drink your damn coffee and let's get outta here."

CHAPTER 13

Harley Clackum hauled back on his mules and pulled his converted circus wagon to a stop so he could read the roughly constructed sign just short of the church. "Well, I'll be . . ." he uttered, amazed as he read it aloud to his mules, "Buzzard's Bluff, I ain't never heard of a town called Buzzard's Bluff. For all the times I've drove from Madisonville to Waco, I never knowed there was a whole town right on the way. And I passed right by it. This might make this detour one helluva stroke of luck."

All because of a washed-out bridge crossing at a deep creek, east of Madisonville, he had been forced to drive his wagon over three miles south before he found a safe crossing. It was on a wagon road he'd never driven before. Since it was in pretty decent shape and seemed to go in the general direction he wanted to go in, he decided to stay on it, instead of trying to cut back north to strike his usual route. It didn't matter if it took him a little longer to get to Waco. Time was the one thing he had plenty of. And the payoff was a town he never knew existed, a new market to sell his wares and services. "Come on, mule!" He popped the reins and the colorful wagon jerked into motion.

He drove up the length of the main street, taking note of

the businesses and shops. When he got up to the stable at the north end, he turned around and drove the wagon back to the church again. There was a stream running behind the church that fed off the river and a wide grassy area between the church and the post office. It was an ideal spot for him to make his camp for a couple of days, or so, depending on what potential he found for his business. There was a good source of firewood in the trees that lined the river, and there was grass for his mules. So he pulled his wagon up into the middle of the open area, unhitched his mules and let them go to water. He wasn't overly concerned about the mules wandering. He knew they would stay close to the wagon. The only time he would tie them to the wagon was when he went off by himself somewhere, since they had a tendency to follow him, like the pets he had made of them. And with that in mind, he tied them to the wagon when they had finished drinking water, because he was going to walk up the street to the sheriff's office before he settled in for the night.

Harley made it a habit to check in with the sheriff any time he worked a new town. He had found it usually a good policy to prevent unnecessary visits from that department. Harley's business was perfectly legal, but sometimes his customers might be of a suspicious nature, so it was best not to have the sheriff suddenly decide to visit you. With that in mind, he had whistled the mules up and tied them to the wagon. Then he walked up the street to the jail.

When he got to the sheriff's office, he went up the three steps to the door but found it was locked. He started to turn around to leave, but he saw someone inside through the glass panes in the upper part of the door, so he knocked. There was no immediate response. "Sheriff must be a little deaf," he muttered and knocked again, this time louder. It got a rather reluctant response from the man inside, but he finally came to the door and peered out at him. "I'm looking for the sheriff," Harley said, speaking loud enough so the man would hear him through the closed door.

"Sheriff Bragg ain't here," Horace told him. "And he said not to unlock the door for nobody while he's gone. That's because we got prisoners locked up in here."

"How long is he gonna be gone?" Harley asked.

"Oh, he ain't gonna be gone long," Horace answered. "He's just up at the Lost Coyote, eatin' his dinner."

Harley thought about that for a moment. "I reckon I could just set down here on the steps and wait for him to come back."

"Sure can," Horace replied, "or you can go up to the Lost Coyote to see him, if it's something important."

"Maybe I'll do that. You don't reckon he'd mind if I spoke to him while he was eatin' his dinner?"

"Nah," Horace answered. "Things like that don't bother Sheriff Bragg a-tall. Besides, if it was somethin' like a robbery or a shootin', he'd be mad if you didn't come tell him."

"All right. Well, much obliged," Harley said. He turned away from the door and headed up the street. When he got to the Lost Coyote, he walked through the batwing doors and proceeded to the bar where he was greeted by Tiny. "How do?" Harley returned the greeting. "Lost Coyote," he said, "I like the name."

"I'll tell the owners that," Tiny said. "What'll you have?"

"I'll take a shot of whatever you're pourin'," Harley answered. "Feller at the sheriff's office told me the sheriff was here."

After all the recent violence in town, Tiny took a closer look at the unimposing little gray-haired stranger. He could see no indication of violence in the man's face, but he decided to ask, anyway. "Have you got a grievance with the sheriff?"

"Lord, no," Harley said at once. "I just wanna let him know I'm in town."

"In that case, that's him, settin' at the table with one of the owners of the saloon," Tiny said.

Harley stared in the direction Tiny pointed out for a long moment before he exclaimed, "Well, I'll be go to hell . . . Ben Savage is the sheriff of Buzzard's Bluff?"

Tiny recoiled in surprise. "Ben Savage is half-owner of this saloon. Mack Bragg is the sheriff."

"Oh, that's right. I remember that feller at the jail called him Sheriff Bragg." He turned to look at Tiny again. "And you say Ben Savage is half-owner of this saloon?"

"That's a fact," Tiny answered. "Do you know Ben?"

"I've done business with him, but that was a long time ago, and he was a Texas Ranger then." He looked back at the table again and said, "And I wouldn'ta even come to this town if the bridge hadn't washed out." He didn't wait to explain, put a coin on the bar for his drink then went to the table.

Ben looked up when the little man approached the table. A stranger, but he looked somehow familiar to him, like he had seen him somewhere before. "Howdy," he said when it appeared the man was coming directly to them. "Something I can do for you?"

"Yessir," Harley replied. "I was wonderin' if that tight trigger I fixed on that Colt Army .45 is still workin' like it oughta. That was some years back."

It took a second or two, but it struck him then. "Harley Clackum! That *was* a few years ago, wasn't it? In Austin, if I remember right. I gave that Colt to a friend of mine, and it was workin' fine when he got it." He turned to Mack, who was watching with interest. "Mack, this is Harley Clackum. He's been fixin' guns and rifles since they were invented, I reckon. Harley, this is Sheriff Mack Bragg." Back to Harley again, he asked, "What are you doin' in Buzzard's Bluff?"

"Same thing I was doin' the last time I saw you," Harley answered, "fixin' firearms of all kinds, personalizin' handguns and rifles. Whatever's wrong with your gun, I can most likely fix it. I was lookin' for the sheriff when I came in here. I didn't have no idea I was gonna run into Ben Savage. I didn't even know this town was here." He went on to explain how he happened to wind up in Buzzard's Bluff. "I don't know how many times I drove from Madisonville to Waco and never knew I was missin' a whole town on the way."

"What did you want to see the sheriff about?" Mack finally got a chance to ask.

"I just wanted to tell you I was gonna park my wagon in town for a day or two to see if I could do a little business. I mainly wanted to tell you what my business is, in case you wondered. But I reckon Ben and I have already told you. I just wanted you to know I wasn't up to anything against the law."

"I don't know," Mack joked, "bein' a friend of Ben's puts you under suspicion right there. I doubt I woulda thought about it one way or the other, if you hadn't told me."

"When you see my wagon, you'll see that it's painted up with signs, tellin' you some of the repairs I do on weapons. I did that to attract customers, but sometimes it makes a sheriff or a marshal think I wrote that all over my wagon to disguise what I'm really up to."

"You had your dinner yet?" Ben asked. Harley said that

he was planning to build a fire and cook something back at his wagon. "Mack and I are eatin' some pretty decent stew right here. Why don't you sit down and I'll spring for your dinner."

"Can't argue with a man who owns a saloon," Harley said, and pulled a chair back. Ben motioned to Clarice when she walked close to the table. When she came over, he told her to tell Annie to fix a plate for Harley. A few minutes later, Rachel came out of the kitchen with the plate of stew and looked at Ben. He pointed to Harley, and she brought the plate and set it before him. He beamed up at her. "Thank you, kindly, ma'am."

"Rachel, say hello to Harley Clackum," Ben said. "He's a friend from back in my days as a ranger." He looked at Harley then and said, "Rachel's my business partner. She runs the place."

"I'm tickled to make your acquaintance, ma'am," Harley replied eloquently. He nodded when asked if he wanted coffee, the wide snaggle-tooth smile never leaving his face. He felt as if he was dining at the king's table, so much so, that he felt self-conscious when he started to eat. It was better when Rachel walked away, and he noticed that he was in a saloon, sitting at a table, eating a plate filled with beef stew. He dived right in at that point, working on the stew as if afraid someone was going to try to take it from him.

Conversation dwindled for a long time while all three men concentrated on clearing their plates of food. When Ben paused to take a sip of coffee, he glanced at Harley, and was surprised to see him staring past him, seemingly frozen in shock, his eyes bulging, his mouth hanging open, and his fork loaded with stew, suspended in mid-air several inches from his mouth. He seemed to be staring at something past Mack's shoulder, so Ben looked in that direction and saw Lucas approaching the table. Ben looked back at Harley then to see the seemingly paralyzed man's eyes follow Lucas to the chair across from him and proceed to sit down. He wasn't sure that Harley had even heard Mack invite Lucas to join them. Concerned that the little old man might have had a stroke or something, he was relieved to see him start to thaw enough to finally deliver the fork full of stew to his mouth. Lucas looked at him much the same way a person would look at any unexplained curiosity. He was an odd-looking little man and one Lucas had never seen since he had been in Buzzard's Bluff. "Say howdy to Harley Clackum," Ben said. "He's just passin' through town." He decided it best to just leave the introduction right there.

"Harley," Lucas acknowledged and turned to thank Annie for bringing his plate to him, after Tiny had told her that he wanted to eat.

Harley nodded in response to Lucas' greeting. He cleaned his plate of the stew and drank some more coffee. Then he sat there for a short time, listening to their small talk while thinking, *I can't believe this. I must be dreaming. I can't believe I'm setting here with Ben Savage and Lucas Blaine and the sheriff.* When Mack said he'd best get back to the jail before Horace got worried, Harley remembered his wagon and his mules. So he thanked Ben for his dinner, and excused himself from the table. Realizing finally that he was not dreaming, he stopped at the bar to have a word with Tiny. "Looks like Ben remembered you, Harley," Tiny said.

"He sure did," Harley replied. "I'd 'preciate it if you'd tell him something for me. I woulda told him, myself, but right there at the table, I didn't think I'd better."

"Well, sure, Harley. Whaddaya want me to tell him?"

"Tell him that feller that sat down with us is Lucas Blaine."

Tiny almost laughed. "Do you know Lucas Blaine?"

"I know him, but he don't know me," Harley said. "I saw him kill a man in Johnson's Saloon in San Antonio. Feller called him out, said he was cheatin' at cards. Blaine said he didn't cheat, but that feller said he weren't gonna let him walk out. Mister, he walked out about two seconds after that feller went for his gun."

"Well, I'll tell Ben you told me," Tiny said. "But I know for a fact that Ben ain't thinkin' about callin' him out."

"Good, 'cause that man's faster'n greased lightnin'."

Harley walked back to his wagon and untied his mules. Then he went about setting up the rest of his camp. He grabbed his axe and walked over by the river to collect some wood for his fire later on. He wasn't sure if he was going to need much for supper, thanks to the load of Annie's stew he put away at dinner. There was still a good portion of the afternoon left, so he set up his display in front of the wagon. It featured two Winchester rifles; one with the figure of a mountain puma ready to attack carved into the stock, the other one with a wolf and a full moon. That was the one he liked best because he considered himself a lone wolf. "I ain't no Ben Savage," he told his mules. "But I can take care of myself. I'm old, but I ain't tired. Just like you two."

He set up his work bench and pulled his tools out of the wagon, then he packed his pipe with tobacco and sat down in his one chair to wait to see if he could attract any business. As was usually the case, he did attract some curious folks, since his colorful wagon was hard to miss. Most of them just stopped by to gawk and talk, but one fellow bought a Smith & Wesson pistol that he had rebuilt. And the preacher of the church brought his shotgun in for Harley to fix a problem caused by the top lever not properly releasing the bolt after the gun was fired. Harley couldn't complain. It certainly was better than traveling from Madisonville to Waco the way he did for years. Had the bridge not been washed out, he would have been camping that night on the side of a creek, minus all the good things that happened to him on this trip. He decided to stay in Buzzard's Bluff for another day when the sheriff stopped to talk to him that night and said he would bring him a couple of weapons to work on the next day. So he fixed his bedding under the wagon and went to bed with the double-barreled shotgun that always slept beside him.

Morning brought Harley another customer, this one interested in ammunition more than guns or rifles. He was accompanied by an unusually tall friend who appeared to lack the enthusiasm shown by his partner for special load cartridges. "Most of the black powder cartridges I make up are for huntin' bigger game," Harley told him. "They just pack a little more punch comin' out the barrel. But if you ain't careful with how you use it, you might blow your barrel up."

Brock explained again the kind of bullet he was interested in. Harley shook his head. "You're talking about a load that fires a bullet that has another load in the bullet that blows up on impact, right?"

"Yes, something like that," Brock said.

"Mister, I can't make nothin' like that. What kinda game are you huntin'?"

"Obviously, I'm talking about huntin' buffalo, and I'm looking for something that will knock one down with one shot," Brock insisted, even though he was beginning to realize his request was ridiculous.

"Far as I know, there ain't no bullets like you're talking about. It'd be safer to get a stick of dynamite and shove it in the south end of a buffalo runnin' north. But I don't sell dynamite. Best thing for you to do would be to buy a good buffalo rifle. I've got a Sharps 1874 rifle I completely repaired. It'll take a .45-90 cartridge, and that'll knock a buffalo down."

"I don't want to buy a rifle," Brock interrupted. "I just had an idea about something, and I wondered if you could do it. Obviously, you can't. Let's go, Tree, I've got an appointment to see Reese." He turned abruptly and started walking away. Tree shrugged at Harley, then followed.

"Sorry I couldn't help you fellers," Harley called after them. *You musta been smoking stinkweed to come up with a crazy idea like that,* he thought.

"Maybe we are gonna have to find some place to buy some dynamite," Tree declared as they walked up the street toward the jail. Then he couldn't resist saying, "Since he didn't have no magic bullets for sale."

Brock ignored his sarcastic remark and said, "I don't think there's any place in this town to find any dynamite."

"Even if you did find some, what good would it do us?" Tree responded, finding it hard to believe Brock was seriously thinking about it. "What would you do, blow the office door open? Then take another stick and blow the door open to the cells? Then blow the cell open? 'Course, they'd all be shootin' at us while we were doin' all that dynamitin'."

Unwilling to admit his idea to free his brother was moronic, Brock said, "Of course not. I'd use the dynamite to blow out the back wall of the jail, and go in that way, directly to the cells."

Tree knew Brock was trying desperately to talk his way back out of his stupid plan without admitting it was proposed without reasonable thought. But Tree wasn't willing to spare him. "Blow the back off the jail," he said. "Now you gotta blow the cell apart and Reese and Shorty and Jack are all gonna be blown to hell with it." They had reached the jail by that time, so Tree said, "Better not tell Reese about that plan. I'll wait for you at the Golden Rail, since the sheriff won't let but one in at a time."

"Mornin'," Mack greeted Brock when he walked into his office. Brock seemed surprised to have found the office door unlocked. "Your brother and his two partners have had their breakfast, and I told them you were comin' to see 'em this mornin'. I know they're lookin' forward to it." That was an understatement of huge proportions because Reese had been pacing their cell like a caged lion all morning.

Brock looked at Mack, sitting at his desk, a shotgun laying on the desk, close to his hand. Then he shifted his gaze to Horace, sitting in the opposite corner, holding a double-barreled shotgun resting on his thigh, with the barrels pointing at the ceiling. "I almost forgot," Brock said and started unbuckling his gun belt. He removed it, rolled it around his holstered pistol, and handed it to the sheriff.

"Thank you," Mack said. "I think it would be a good idea to let me hold that Derringer pocket pistol you carry, too." He didn't really know if Brock carried one or not, but he thought it best to be cautious.

Brock flushed scarlet and reached into his inside coat pocket to extract the little two-shot pistol. "I clearly forgot that toy was in the pocket of this coat. I'm not even sure it's loaded." He laid it on Mack's desk.

Mack picked it up and looked at it. "It's loaded. Better be careful when you put it back in your pocket." He laid it beside his six-gun and told Horace to unlock the cell-room door. Horace opened the door and left it open, so Mack and he could see into the cell room.

The three prisoners immediately came to stand at the bars of their cell when they saw it was Brock coming in. "What the hell's goin' on, Brock?" Reese demanded. "We're rottin' in this damn jail, waiting for you to do something! Where's Tree? Did he get called out by that gunslinger, too?"

"No, Tree's all right. That sheriff won't let but one of us in at a time to see you boys. Tree's waitin' for me in the saloon."

"I hope that ain't too hard on him," Shorty cracked, "settin' around in the saloon while we're havin' such a good time visitin' here in this blame jail."

"What have you been doin' to get us outta this place?" Reese demanded again and in no mood for Shorty's humor.

"It ain't as easy as you think," Brock insisted. "We've been trying to think of something that'll work. I was gonna sneak a pocket pistol in with me today, so you'd have something in case you got the right opportunity to use it. But the sheriff caught me with it."

"I doubt we'd do much damage with a pocket pistol," Jack Ramsey remarked. "Ain't you done nothin' else?"

Desperate, Brock told them he had thought about trying to find someplace to buy some dynamite to blow the jail

open for them to run out. He got the same response from
them that he had gotten from Tree. Finally, he confessed
what he already knew to be true. "Doggone it, Reese, I
can't think of anything else to try."

"There ain't but one way we're gonna get outta here,"
Reese told him. "You and Tree are gonna have to catch that
sheriff when he's walkin' his rounds of the town at night.
He does it every night before he turns in for the night.
Shoot him, take his keys and come back to the jail. You
don't have to worry about that fool Horace. He'll most
likely be asleep on his cot by the time you get here. He
won't be any trouble for the two of you, anyway. If he's
asleep, cut his throat. If he's awake and you don't wanna do
it, just back him up to the bars and I'll strangle him. I'd love
to do it. They want you to think that Ben Savage and Lucas
Blaine are helpin' the sheriff guard us. But they ain't
around here a-tall durin' the day, and they sure don't stay
here at night. So you and Tree take care of the sheriff and
Horace, and we'll walk outta this place tonight, go to the
stable and get our horses and shoot anybody down that
wants to get in our way."

Brock was plainly stunned by the ultimatum from his
brother, for he stood there speechless in response. So much
so, that Jack Ramsey said, "He's right, Brock. That's the
only way we're gonna get outta here. And they ain't gonna
be expectin' it. Tree's a good man, you and him ought not
have no trouble doin' it. What Reese just told you about
Ben Savage and Lucas Blaine is just like he said. When the
town starts to shut down for the night, ain't neither one of
them anywhere around here. Blaine goes to the hotel and
goes to bed. Savage stays at the Lost Coyote till the last
drunk goes home, then he goes to bed. The main thing is,

neither one of 'em knows what's goin' on here at the jail. After you're done with Bragg, don't forget to take his keys. Then you can walk right in the office and catch Horace asleep."

Reese studied his brother's face. He was not totally confident that Brock could carry out the simple executions he had called for, but he was desperate at this point. "Pa always said that you were the one he could count on," he told Brock. "I think Pa was right, I know I can count on you to get us outta here." He reached through the bars and gripped Brock's arm.

"I'll take care of it," Brock told him solemnly. "You can count on me."

"I'll see you tonight, after supper," Reese said. Brock nodded individually at Shorty and Jack, then a final one for Reese, then he walked out of the cell room.

When Horace closed the cell-room door again, Jack looked at Reese and asked, "You think he can pull all that off?"

"I think he'd rather not," Reese said at once. "Brock's more a talker than a doer. But, hell, he's only got one problem, and that's killin' Mack Bragg. But he oughta catch him by surprise, and between the two of 'em, there ain't no reason they can't take care of Bragg."

Jack thought about Reese's opinion for a few moments, then he asked, "Whaddaya think, Shorty? Are we leavin' here tonight?"

"Fifty-fifty," Shorty said. "No offense to your brother, Reese, that's just how I see it."

"Did your pa always say Brock was the one you could depend on," Jack asked.

"Nah," Reese replied, "I never heard Pa say anything like that about Brock."

On the other side of the cell-room door, a completely determined Brock Salter strapped on his gun belt, then took his Derringer off the desk and dropped it in his pocket.

"They have any complaints about the way they're being treated?" Mack asked.

"No," Brock answered. "They didn't say anything about that at all."

"Well, that's good. We don't want our prisoners to feel like they're being mistreated." Nothing more was said by either man as Brock turned and went out the door.

"He acted like he had a lot on his mind," Mack said to Horace.

"And none of it for a good purpose, I bet," Horace answered.

Chapter 14

Brock walked into the Golden Rail and stood looking around for Tree but saw no sign of him. He walked over to the bartender and asked, "Hey, Mickey, you seen Tree Forney? He was supposed to meet me here."

"Yeah, Brock, he's here. He just went upstairs with Charlene a little while ago. He ought not be too long. She said he don't never take too long, and that's why she likes to entertain him. You want a drink?"

"Yeah, I need one," Brock answered. "Make it a double." He watched intently while Mickey poured, and as soon as the glass was full, he tossed it back and emptied it with one gulp and slammed the glass down so Mickey could pour the second shot in the same glass. He hesitated for a couple of moments for the fire to die down before splashing the second shot down his throat.

"You threw that one back like it was medicine," Mickey commented.

"It was medicine," Brock said. "I needed it to clear my head out. Pour me one more and I'll sit down at a table and wait for Tree." As Mickey predicted, Tree was soon downstairs, and when he saw Brock sitting at a table, he signaled Mickey for a drink. Then he joined Brock at the table.

"How'd it go with Reese and the boys today?" Tree asked when he sat down.

"Nothing's changed," Brock answered. "They're still bellyaching about bein' tied down in that jail. I told 'em jail ain't supposed to be like a Sunday picnic." He tossed his whiskey back, slammed the empty glass down on the table and wiped his mouth with the back of his hand. "I'm tired of this standoff, and I've decided to do something about it. I'm takin' those boys outta that jail tonight."

That was certainly news of great interest to Tree. "Is that a fact?" he responded. "How you gonna do that?"

"*We* are gonna do it, my friend. We are gonna take 'em outta there. And here's how we're gonna do it." He paused to look around them to make sure no one was close enough to hear him talking. Then he repeated the procedure that Reese had preached to him in the jail a short time before.

Tree was almost stunned to suddenly discover an aggressive side to the man he had always read as a talker and not a fighter. When he asked him if he was sure he wanted to start with an outright killing of the sheriff, Brock told him it was the only choice they had. "We've talked about how we can break them outta that jail till we're blue in the face," Brock said. "I've thought from the start that the only way to get it done is to put that sheriff down, then go in there and get our men outta there. If you ain't got the stomach for it, I need to know right now, and I'll do it by myself."

Tree could not believe he was hearing this coming out of Brock Salter. This was more of what he would expect from his brother, Reese. It was frankly a bold and dangerous plan he was proposing. And Tree knew they would be gambling a helluva lot. But he said, "Hell, in for a penny, in for a pound. Count me in."

"Good man," Brock said. "I knew I could count on you. Now it's dinnertime. Let's go get somethin' to eat."

"Where you wanna go, Lost Coyote or the hotel?" Tree asked, those being the only choices for decent food.

"Let's go to the hotel," Brock said. "I feel like eatin' a big dinner today."

"Hello, Lucas, have a seat, you want some dinner?" Ben asked when Lucas walked back to his table at the Lost Coyote.

"Yes, sir," Lucas answered, "I thought I might see what Annie cooked up today." When he pulled a chair back, he leaned toward Ben a little to take a look at the plate of food Ben was working on. "That looks pretty good. What is it?"

"That's Annie's special meatloaf," Ben told him. "Nobody makes meatloaf like Annie's, but I have to warn you. Once you try it, you won't wanna eat nothin' else but that the rest of your life."

"I reckon I'll risk it," Lucas said and sat down.

"Tiny," Ben called out, "tell Annie we need another meatloaf plate out here, will ya?" Back to Lucas then, he commented, "You're gettin' to be a regular dinner customer at the Coyote."

"The dinin' room at the hotel always has good food," Lucas said, "at least the few times I've eaten there since I've been here. But to tell you the truth, I think Annie is a better cook."

"Glad you think so," Ben replied. "Here she comes now."

Annie came from the kitchen carrying a plate of food and a cup of coffee. Usually cheerful, she was all smiles when she placed the plate and cup in front of Lucas.

"Lucas, here, says he thinks your cookin' is better than Myrtle's at the hotel," Ben told her. Already smiling, her face blossomed with pleasure as she thanked Lucas for his compliment. When she went back to the kitchen, Ben joked, "Now, if you don't like that meatloaf, you're gonna have to carry it outta here in your pocket."

In a few minutes, they were joined by Rachel, who went by the kitchen first to pick up her own slice of meatloaf. Ben told her that he had made Annie blush and giggle when he told her Lucas admired her cooking. "We need to tell her that more often," Rachel said. "Heaven knows what we'd do without her."

The three of them were almost finished eating when Mack came in to join them. "I hope I'm not too late to get some dinner," he said as he pulled the remaining empty chair back.

"I don't think so," Rachel said. "Let me go see." She got up and went into the kitchen. When she came back, she told Mack there was enough left for a big serving. "She'll bring it out with some coffee for you."

In a matter of minutes, Annie appeared in the kitchen doorway, holding the meatloaf and a cup of coffee. The smile suddenly faded from her face, and she stopped after only a few steps into the barroom. "I think she wants you to come and get it, Rachel," Ben suggested.

Rachel got up and hurried over to take the plate and cup. "Annie, what's wrong?" Annie dropped her chin and would not look at her. "Annie, is something wrong?"

"No, nothin's wrong. Pot's boilin' over on the stove. Take the food please." She turned and hurried back to the kitchen as soon as Rachel took it.

"Here you are, Sheriff, a nice big slice of meatloaf," Rachel said, "and coffee to go with it."

"That's bigger than the slice she brought me," Lucas joked. "It pays to come in late."

"The sheriff is supposed to get the biggest slice of the meatloaf," Mack told him.

While they bantered back and forth over the meatloaf, Ben asked Rachel, "Is anything wrong in the kitchen? Annie's actin' kinda strange, ain't she?"

"I don't know," Rachel answered. "She was all right when she was at the table a few minutes ago. She just suddenly got all fearful looking. Maybe she just got another one of her *feelings*. Who knows why?"

Ben smiled, then said, "If that was what happened, we don't know who for. At least we all ate a hearty last dinner, for whoever's gonna have bad luck."

"Ben, don't tease about that," Rachel scolded. "You know as well as I that she's been right about something bad happening too many times for it to be a coincidence."

"We're gonna have to get her a long black robe with a hood on it, so she can be dressed for the part," he teased. And when he saw the irritation forming in Rachel's face, he apologized before he went any further. He knew Rachel really believed that Annie got signals and messages that the rest of them were unaware of. Quickly changing the subject, he asked, "Is that meatloaf still all right, Mack?"

"Yes, indeed," he replied. "You'd have to go pretty far to find any to beat it."

"Well, I reckon we're all agreed on the meatloaf situation in the state of Texas. The champion is right here in Buzzard's Bluff, in the Lost Coyote," Ben announced. Changing the subject to a more serious topic then, he asked Mack if everything was going along all right with his guests at the jail.

"They ain't really causin' no problems right now," Mack reported. "Brock Salter came to visit 'em this mornin'. He tried to sneak a little pocket pistol into the cell, but he never got it past me. All I had to do was tell him to put it on my desk, and he did it. I didn't have any idea if he had one or not. I was just guessin'. He claimed he didn't know it was in his pocket. I coulda hassled him about it, but I didn't. I didn't go in the cell room to watch 'em. Just left the door open. He didn't stay very long, and it sounded like his brother did most of the talkin'."

"Doesn't seem to be much doubt about who gives the orders in that family, does it?" Lucas commented.

"It's kinda like this saloon," Ben joked. "There ain't no doubt who calls the shots in the Lost Coyote."

"Well, I would surely hope so," Mack said, going along with the joke. "I'd hate to see what would happen to this place if you were making all the decisions."

"Well, I can see the conversation has turned to nonsense now," Rachel announced. "I'm gonna go and help Annie clean up her kitchen, so she can go home." She excused herself, picked up a stack of dirty dishes, and left the table.

After Rachel left, the conversation returned to the topic of the prisoners in the jail and particularly the presence of Brock Salter and Tree Forney. "I can't believe they're gonna hang around here until the fifteenth, so Brock can go to the trial," Lucas commented.

"I don't think they had planned to," Mack said. "But they can't figure out how they're gonna break them out without a fight with the three of us. And that's something they ain't too anxious to try. So, there ain't too much they can do. I really think they've decided to stick around and look for an opportunity to jump us when the prisoners are out of the jail, either in the court or in between the court and the jail. I don't know what else Brock is capable of doin'."

"You may be right, Mack," Ben said. "The only other possibility might be if Brock and Tree are just waitin' for help to arrive from somewhere. I reckon all we can do is just wait and watch."

"Things bein' what they are," Lucas remarked, "I'll be there to help out until after the trial."

"Do you know where you'll be goin'?" Ben asked.

"No, I don't. Just somewhere I ain't been before, I reckon."

Neither Lucas nor Mack sat around the table very long after that. Mack said he didn't like to leave Horace alone at the jail for too long a time, and Lucas wanted to talk to Jim Bowden about some new shoes for his buckskin gelding. Ben walked out to the front porch with them and stood there a while after they had disappeared. He was about to turn around and go back inside when he saw the colorful wagon, with Harley Clackum on the driver's seat, coming up the street. When Harley saw Ben standing on the porch, he pulled his mules up to a stop when he reached the saloon. Ben walked out in the street to talk to him. "Afternoon, Harley, you leavin' town already?"

"Yes, sir, I figure I'd best get on my way on up to Waco. I wanna thank you again for your hospitality last night. I still ain't got over the fact I didn't know this town was here until I tripped over it."

"It is kinda out of the way," Ben said. "But now that you know where it is, we'll expect to see you back again."

"Sure will," Harley responded. Then he leaned over toward Ben a little, like he was afraid somebody might hear him, and said, "Did that big bartender of yours tell you what I said to tell you?"

"What was that?" Ben asked, not recalling any message from Tiny.

"About the feller we was eatin' with," Harley said. "I told him to tell you that feller was Lucas Blaine."

"Oh, that," Ben replied, "yeah, Tiny told me you did. I 'preciate the warnin'." Actually, Tiny hadn't said anything about it, since Ben knew who Lucas was. Harley promptly repeated the story he had told Tiny, about the time he had witnessed a shooting Lucas was involved in. When he finished, Ben said, "That's something not many men have witnessed. You take care of yourself, Harley, and we'll see you next time you get lost and wind up in Buzzard's Bluff."

But Harley wasn't through talking. "There's somethin' you might wanna tell that sheriff, too. I had a couple of fellers come by my wagon askin' me if I could make up some magic cartridges that could fire a bullet that had another charge in it. I told 'em hell, no, and I didn't think anybody else could, neither. I asked 'em what on earth they was huntin', and they said they wanted to knock a buffalo down with a shot that would blow a hole in him. I don't know why they'd want somethin' like that 'cause there ain't no buffalo no more."

Ben couldn't imagine what he could be talking about, but he was curious. "You don't remember who those two men were, do ya?"

"Well, no, I didn't ask them their names. I tried to sell 'em a Sharps buffalo rifle, but they weren't interested." He thought for a few seconds. "One of 'em was tall as that bartender of yours, but not as big. The other one did all the talkin'. He was just a regular-lookin' feller, and you could tell he didn't know as much as he thought he did."

Brock Salter and Tree Forney came immediately to mind, but what they were asking Harley about made no sense to him. Unless, he thought, they were thinking about blowing a hole in the jail to get their friends out. "Did they ask you if you had any dynamite?"

"No, they didn't," Harley said, "'cause I told 'em I didn't sell dynamite."

"Well, take care of yourself," Ben said again, "and we'll see you next time you're in Buzzard's Bluff."

"You take care of yourself, too, and take care of that little lady you're in business with," Harley said.

"I'll do that," Ben said as he stepped back from the wagon.

"Ha! Mule!" Harley barked, slapped the reins across the mules' rumps, and the wagon lurched into motion. Ben watched it until it rolled past the stable at the north end of town. Then he turned back toward the door of the saloon in time to see Tuck Tucker approaching.

"Hey, Ben," Tuck blurted. "What was that old drummer tryin' to sell you? Some old piece of a pistol he put together?"

"No, Tuck, we were just talkin'. Harley does pretty good work. I knew him before I came to Buzzard's Bluff. He repaired a revolver for me once. Did a good job on it. I'll do business with him again, if I need a weapon fixed."

"He try to sell you holsters or belts?" Tuck asked.

"No, he just works with iron and steel. If I need leather goods, I'd come to you."

"I'll always treat you right. You know that for a fact, right?"

"I know that's true," Ben japed. "'Course I don't know how much longer you'll be in business, if you keep playin' cards with Ham Greeley."

"Shoot! That wood butcher! That'll be the day when I let Ham Greeley take me in a game of poker. Is he in the saloon now?"

"Ain't seen him today," Ben said. "He must be doin' some carpentry work somewhere."

"He might as well come on out of his hidin' place and take his daily whippin'," Tuck said.

"I expect he'll show up as usual," Ben said. He'd never seen friends as close as Tuck and Ham who bad-mouthed each other so much. They walked into the Lost Coyote to find Ham Greeley standing at the bar, talking to Tiny. "He must have come in while I was talkin' to Harley Clackum," Ben said. It appeared that it was going to be a busy Friday night at the Lost Coyote with some of the regulars showing up before suppertime. Ben checked with Rachel to see if she wanted anything from him before he walked up to the stable to spend some time with his horse. When he returned to the saloon, there was already a card game in progress in addition to the usual two-handed poker game between Ham and Tuck. Already this busy on Friday, he wondered if they might have an even busier Saturday. When it was time for the hotel dining room to open, he walked down the street to the hotel.

Chapter 15

"Evenin', Ben," Lacy James greeted him when he walked in. "The sheriff's already here. He was here when I opened the door."

"Evenin', Lacy," Ben returned. "He must be extra hungry tonight." He couldn't help thinking about the big fuss they had all made over the meatloaf at the Lost Coyote at dinner. Maybe it didn't have the staying power they thought it had, although he wasn't especially hungrier than usual.

"Is Mr. Cochran going to join you tonight?" Lacy asked, still calling Lucas by that name.

"I don't know for sure," Ben answered. "I expect he might." He walked on over to the table. "Evenin', Sheriff Bragg, may I join you, or are you expecting company from the governor's office?"

"I thought you were the governor," Mack japed back. "Cindy, bring a cup of coffee for the governor."

"For who?" The young waitress asked, looking around at the nearly empty dining room. Mack pointed to Ben. She brought him a cup of coffee. "Evenin,' Ben." Then she looked at Mack and asked, "Who did you say you wanted coffee for?"

Mack shook his head and laughed. He saw Lucas come in the door, so he said, "The next person who walks in here is who I said."

She turned around to see Lucas coming toward them. "Oh," she said. "Mr. Cochran, I thought you said. . . ." She paused then declared, "I don't know what you said. I'll get Mr. Cochran a cup." She went to the kitchen to get it, and Lacy came over to the table.

"Mack," Lacy scolded, "please don't mess around inside Cindy's head. We need her brain working like a clock tonight."

"What's special about tonight?" Ben asked.

"Nothing," Lacy answered. "It's just that there are more folks in the hotel for a Friday night, like Mr. Cochran, here." The door opened then and Brock and Tree walked in. "And those two gentlemen." She hurried to greet them, but called back over her shoulder, "And I heard the governor is gonna be here." That sparked a chuckle from the three men seated at the table. It caught Brock and Tree's attention as they unbuckled their gun belts.

"What's so funny?" Tree asked Lacy.

"Nothing, really," she answered. "They were just laughing at something the sheriff said."

"Good," Brock said. "I'm glad the sheriff's feelin' good tonight." After she left them at a table, he said, "It's a good thing for a man to feel good on his last night on earth."

The two of them had talked at length about the executions they planned to perform that night. They were convinced that they could be accomplished as easily as Reese had told Brock, and Brock had told Tree. But they were not willing to trust entirely on their victims' usual routines. So they intended to keep an eye on all three of the men sitting at the table near the kitchen door, at least as closely as possible. Take no chances was the watchword. If any of the three men varied from their routine, they would call it off and try the next night. With that in mind, they were confident that their plan would be successful. "We'll have us a nice supper," Brock said. "Then we'll go to the saloon and enjoy a few drinks and wait for the sheriff to make his last walk around town."

"And it will be his last walk around town," Tree emphasized. They both enjoyed a chuckle for that remark.

At the table near the kitchen door, Ben couldn't help noticing what appeared to be good spirits between Brock and Tree. Whereas their usual dining atmosphere had been dour at best. He also noticed that they seemed to be throwing many glances in their direction, more so than the last time they all ate in the same room.

The customers of the hotel dining room were treated to baked pork chops that night, and they proved to be a hit at both tables. The sheriff was in no hurry, since he had arranged for Horace to pick up four supper plates before the dining room opened. Mack had guarded the three prisoners while Horace put the plates in the cell, then he left Horace to eat the fourth supper while he went to the dining room. He and Ben lingered a while to drink coffee while Lucas announced that he was going to take a bath and go to bed. So he headed for the hotel wash room. Overhearing his comments, Brock and Tree took note of where the fast gun was going to be—in the hotel, a good place for him they thought. Now, with only Ben and the sheriff to worry about, their job seemed much better.

When Mack finally decided he'd best get back to the jail to make sure everything was okay, Ben left with him. When they walked past Brock and Tree's table, they exchanged grunts of acknowledgement before going out the door. "Mack," Ben said outside the dining room, "those two have something up their sleeves. They're gonna try something to get the other three out of jail."

"I agree," Mack said, "but I think they ain't figured it out yet. Like you told me what that fellow with the circus wagon said. They're tryin' to find magic bullets and dynamite, and there ain't none."

"Maybe you're right," Ben conceded. "I just don't see them waitin' to go to the trial. I think there's only one reason they're still hangin' around."

They walked back down the street, and Ben left Mack at the sheriff's office while he continued on to the Lost Coyote. When he went back inside, it was to find the saloon enjoying a fairly busy evening. He joined Tiny and Rachel at the end of the bar, and Rachel asked, "What was Lacy serving tonight?"

"Baked pork chops," Ben answered, "served with fried potatoes and pinto beans, and boy were they good."

"Mmmm," Rachel said, "that does sound good."

"I always invite you to go with me," Ben replied, "but you never do."

"I just never feel hungry at suppertime. That's why I don't eat anything until later in the evening."

"Not me," Tiny declared. "I'm hungry at suppertime, and I'm hungry again by the time you wanna eat."

"Well, you're still a growin' boy," Ben joked.

Their conversation was interrupted then by a loud voice from the opposite side of the room where three men were sitting at a table, drinking from a bottle of whiskey. Ben looked at Tiny and Tiny explained. "That's three young cowhands from the Double-D. They pitched in and bought a bottle of corn whiskey. They got in an argument over who was gonna go upstairs with Ruby first. But they settled down a little bit since then. I think Tuck told 'em they was gonna have to quiet down, or he was gonna order 'em to leave. They've been grumblin' about that for a few minutes."

"Tuck told 'em?" Ben asked. "Well, that ain't especially good. I'm sure that scared the hell outta those three cowhands. I swear, we need to get Tuck to make a leather muzzle for himself to keep from gettin' shot one of these days." He had no sooner said it when one of the cowhands stood up and drew his six-gun. There was an immediate clearing out of a circle around that table, as the alarmed patrons backed away from the drunken cowhand. "Uh-oh," Ben gasped and moved quickly to get between the drunken man and Tuck, who stood in shock from the unexpected action of the young man.

"Put the gun away," Ben told the bleary-eyed aggressor.

"Who the hell are you?" the drunk asked, his six-gun pointed at Ben now.

"I'm one of the owners of this saloon," Ben answered him calmly but sternly. "And I'm gonna have to ask you to holster that weapon. We don't allow any gunplay in here."

"I told him to quit makin' so much noise or I was gonna throw him outta here," Tuck spoke out, now that the formidable person of Ben Savage was standing between him and the danger.

"Shut up, Tuck!" Ben roared. "Ham, drag his ass away from here!" Back to the drunken cowhand then, he said, "Now there's no more trouble with him, so put the gun away. We don't want anybody to get shot."

The cowhand looked as though he was giving the situation some thought, but then he came to the wrong conclusion.

"I ain't lettin' that little rat talk to me like that. It's time he stands up to back up his mouth. If you don't get your big butt outta my way, I'll shoot you down first."

"Now, if you think about it for a minute, you'll know you don't wanna do that. You can see I'm not wearin' a gun, so if you shoot me, it'd be murder. And you'd earn yourself a hangin'. So, put the gun away, all right?" He looked around at the other two cowhands and decided they showed no signs of backing their friend up. "You think you boys have had about enough for the night?"

"Yes, sir, I expect we oughta be thinkin' about gittin' back to the ranch," one of them replied. "I don't think Red knows how much of this bottle he drank." He got up from the table and said, "Come on, Red. Me and Tom are ready to go. It's a long ride back to the Double-D." Red thought about it again, then holstered his gun. Ben stepped aside to let them pass, but suddenly, Red drew his six-gun again and aimed it at Tuck. Ben didn't hesitate. He swung his left arm up under Red's right just as Red pulled the trigger, sending a bullet into the ceiling. With his right fist, Ben issued a right cross that cracked Red's jaw and laid him out flat on the floor. While Tom and the other cowhand watched in shocked amazement, Ben reached down and took the weapon out of Red's hand. He spun the cylinder around, ejected the remaining cartridges and handed them to the cowhand he had been talking to. "I don't think you boys meant to cause any trouble, so I ain't gonna send for the sheriff to lock your friend in the jail for a night or two. I'll help you put him on his horse if you want me to, and you can take him home. You may have noticed that the Lost Coyote is kind of a family type saloon, but you fellows are welcome to come back, if you're looking for that kind of place."

"Yes, sir, thank you, sir," the cowhand said. "I think me and Tom can get him on his horse. Thank you for not throwing him in jail." Ben might have ordinarily called Mack to haul the young man into the jail, but at this particular time, he decided Mack had enough to handle without dropping a drunken would-be gunfighter in his hands. The would-be assassin was carried out of the saloon by his two friends.

Still standing at the end of the bar, Rachel looked at Clarice and remarked, "That's the reason I like having Ben Savage as a partner."

At the other end of the bar, closest to the door, two more spectators watched with particular interest. Unnoticed when the disturbance was underway, Brock Salter and Tree Forney walked into the saloon. "Looks like the boss is pretty busy tonight," Brock said when Tiny came to wait on them.

"Yep," Tiny replied. "Every so often, he's called on to handle some trouble with a customer. He's pretty good at it. He says he tries to be diplomatic. This time, he had to be diplomatic with a right cross, but it did the job. Whatcha gonna have?"

"Give us a bottle of rye whiskey," Brock said. "And we'll sit down and have a few drinks before we call it a night." Tiny got them a bottle and a couple of glasses, and they took them over to a table near the center of the room. As Brock had told Tiny, they appeared to be at their leisure, pouring only occasionally from the bottle of rye. Brock was very strict about the amount of whiskey imbibed. There was too much at stake tonight to overindulge in alcohol. As they sat there, quietly minding their own business, they were gratified to see that Ben Savage showed no signs of leaving the saloon for any reason. They were also satisfied to see no signs of Lucas Blaine showing up for a late drink. So they felt safe in taking him at his word when he left the dining room, saying he was going to get a bath and turn in early. They remained there until the sheriff came in and joined Ben and Rachel at a table in the back part of the room. The customers were beginning to thin out by then, and they could assume that it wouldn't be long before the whole town would be winding down. "We'd best get to our ambush place now, I reckon," Brock said. "We gotta be sure we get there before he does."

"What if he's already took his walk around, and he's just back here to take a drink before he goes to the jail for the night?" Tree wondered.

"The reason he takes that last look around is because he wants to make sure everything's locked down for the night," Brock said. "Right now, there's still too much goin' on to do it. We've got time yet."

In the back of the room, Ben remarked to Mack, "I was surprised you didn't sit down at the table with Brock and Tree when you came in, since they're visitin' you so often. At least Brock is."

"If Rachel hadn't been sittin' here with you, I might have, because the company woulda been better," Mack responded to Ben's sarcasm.

"Thank you for the compliment—I think," Rachel said to Mack.

"I reckon we oughta be honored that they came here to do their drinkin', instead of goin' to the Golden Rail," Ben commented.

"It's quieter here," Mack said. "They can think better." No sooner had he said it than they got up from their chairs and started for the door by way of the bar. They paused there to say goodnight to Tiny and to say they were going to turn in early. When Tuck and Ham put the cards away, Tuck stopped briefly at the table to tell Ben he appreciated his stepping in to confront the drunken cowhand, but he had been more than ready to handle the situation.

"Right, Tuck," Ben answered him. "But I was afraid you mighta been too rough on those boys."

"That's all I need to hear," Mack said as Tuck walked away. "I'm gonna go make my rounds now." He got up to leave.

"You be careful," Rachel said.

"Always a good policy," Mack said in return. He said goodnight to Tiny as he walked by the bar.

"Now, I'm hungry," Rachel announced and got up from the table. "I saved a little slice of that meatloaf Annie made today. I'm going to warm it in the oven while it's still got a little heat left in it. Can I get you something?"

"No, thanks, Rachel," Ben replied. "I'm still full from those pork chops I had at the hotel tonight."

"Are you sure?" Rachel insisted. "I can share my meatloaf with you. It was mighty good meatloaf."

Ben had to chuckle when he thought of the fuss they had all made over the meatloaf. "Yep, that was good meatloaf, but I'm really not hungry. Besides, I've seen the portions of food you've saved for yourself before. Hardly enough to keep a butterfly alive. If you split your meatloaf with me, I bet there wouldn't be enough to leave a taste in your mouth. Go get your meatloaf," he ordered.

She laughed and went to the kitchen, and he sat there fiddling with his empty coffee cup, still thinking about the fuss they had made over the meatloaf. How delighted

Annie had been, blushing and giggling in response to the compliments. And then he remembered, all of a sudden, she had one of those *looks* of hers. She stopped and wouldn't bring any more meatloaf out to the table. Rachel had to go and get it. He wasn't sure he could accept the thought that Annie had any such special thoughts. Most likely she suddenly suffered one of those female pains that all women get. He shook his head slowly and thought, *but Rachel sure believes Annie gets them.*

Now it was beginning to bother him to think about it, and he thought back to remember the scene, Annie grinning and blushing at the compliments paid her when Lucas first tried it. Then when she had the opportunity to receive more praise, she balked and refused to give the plate to Mack. Why Mack? Rachel would insist that the feeling Annie had experienced was a warning for Mack. Then he remembered that when Mack said goodnight a short while before, Rachel had told him to be careful. That was not customary for her. "I swear," he muttered to himself, "she'll have me believin' that nonsense." *I know one mystery that works,* he thought. *Doing all that thinking about that meatloaf makes you want to go to the outhouse.*

A few minutes later, Rachel came from the kitchen with her warmed-up plate of meatloaf. Looking around the room, she asked Tiny, "Where's Ben?"

"I think he went to the outhouse," Tiny answered and laughed. "He went out the back, mumblin' something about meatloaf." They both laughed then.

The spot they selected for the assassination was at the very southern end of the town, in a vacant area between the post office and the church. At night, it was the loneliest part of the town. It was mostly covered by large bushes and some trees. There were plenty of places to hide and lie in wait for the sheriff when he walked from the post office on his way to check the church. They had waited for what seemed like a long time when Tree asked, "What if he don't check this far down the street?"

"Why wouldn't he?" Brock replied.

"Because there ain't nothin' down here but the post office and the church." Tree pointed farther down and across the street. "There's the doctor's office down there. But, hell, everything else is back up that way." He pointed up the street.

"He's the sheriff," Brock said. "He's supposed to check the whole town. What kinda sheriff would he be if he didn't check the church. There might be a fire or something goin' on inside."

"If we're wrong, we're just settin' out here in these bushes while he's already back in the jail, all locked up again."

"Hush! Here he comes," Brock exclaimed and pointed toward the other side of the post office, where Mack suddenly appeared approaching the entrance.

"Why don't we just shoot him?" Tree asked. "Ain't that what we came out here for?"

"Yes, but I ain't takin' any chances. That's a long shot for a pistol. We'll wait till he leaves the post office and walks by us on his way to the church. When he's past us, we'll step out of these bushes and shoot him in the back. That way, there ain't no chance he could draw his weapon and hit one of us. And take dead aim, don't rush it. We don't want but two shots fired, and both of them right between his shoulder blades. If there's more shots than that, it's liable to roust folks out into the street."

"That sounds like a good idea to me," Tree said. "Then we'll pull him into these bushes and get his keys, and anything else he's got." So they waited and watched as Mack tried the door to the post office, and finding it locked, continued on toward the church.

When he passed by their hiding spot, they stepped out of the bushes into the street behind him, their guns drawn and pointing at him. As they both raised their pistols to take dead aim, Ben shouted, "Mack!" Running as fast as he could, a Colt .45 in each hand, he didn't wait for Mack to react. He pumped a .45 slug into Tree's chest when he turned to meet him. Brock turned at the same time, but seeing Ben charging toward him, turned back to shoot the sheriff. In the time it took him to do that, Ben put a round into his back before he could pull the trigger. "Mack, you all right?" Ben asked as he hurriedly checked both targets to make sure they were finished. Tree was dead, the shot in his chest a fatal one. Ben pulled the unfired pistol from Brock's hand. He was not dead, but he was obviously mortally wounded. Knowing he was no longer a threat, Ben turned to Mack then. "Are you all right?" he repeated because Mack looked fairly shook.

"Damn!" That was all Mack could say for a few moments. "Damn!" he repeated. Then he gradually recovered his senses. "Both of them dead?"

"One dead, the other one dyin'," Ben answered.

"Where did you come from?" Mack asked, amazed.

Ben couldn't help grinning. "The Angel Annie sent me."

"What?" Mack asked, confused.

"Oh, nothin'. I'll explain it sometime. Right now, let's

do something about these two. I think I figured out what their plan was to free Reese."

"What?" Mack asked, still a bit too shaken to realize that Ben was making a joke.

CHAPTER 16

With the problem of two bodies to take care of this late at night, Ben volunteered to go to Merle Baker's place of business to see if he was still up. Mack stayed there with the bodies in case someone came along to discover them. When Ben got to the undertaker's establishment, he found it locked and the lights out. He was not dismayed, however, because Merle always left his handcart parked outside the building for just such an occasion as this. Then he would take care of the bodies when he discovered them in the morning. There was the question of whether or not they should take Brock's body to the doctor instead of the undertaker. But that problem was solved when Brock was considerate enough to die before Ben returned with the cart. "You didn't try to encourage him to hang on, I don't reckon," Ben said when Mack informed him.

"No, I didn't," Mack answered him, "but I didn't try to get him to give up. I took a look right after you left, and he was gone, most likely in time to catch the same train to hell that his partner, Tree, was on." So they loaded the two bodies on the handcart and covered them with the canvas sheet Merle left on the cart for the purpose. Then they pushed the cart back to Merle's funeral home and left it by the back door. "I swear," Mack commented, "this sure is gonna be a piece of bad news for those boys back at the jail, ain't it?"

"I expect so," Ben agreed.

"When are you gonna tell me what you were doin' down by the post office this time of night? I left you settin' at the table with Rachel."

"I just felt like takin' a little walk before I went to bed," Ben told him. "Just wasn't sleepy, I reckon."

"Horse turds," Mack responded. "You saved my life tonight! If you hadn't showed up when you did, I'd be the one on that handcart, and they'd be in the jail right now, lettin' Reese and the other two outta there. And I expect Horace would be dead, too." He paused when he remembered what Ben had said at first. "What were you talking about when you said something about the Angel Annie?"

Ben really didn't want to confess what inspired him to come looking for Mack. He was already convinced that Rachel had a loose screw for thinking Annie had psychic connections. "I don't know, Mack, I was just out takin' a little walk. I don't even remember what I said."

"Out takin' a little walk?" Mack repeated, then added, "With an extra handgun for your protection, right?" He gave Ben a long look. "Anything you say, all right? But I want to thank you for savin' my life. I'll never forget that." There followed a long moment of awkward silence when Ben only shrugged in response. Then Mack asked, "You wanna go to the jail with me to give Reese, Shorty, and Jack the good news?"

"I reckon I'd best get back to the Coyote. Rachel's probably wonderin' where I am. I didn't tell anybody I was going for a walk."

* * *

Ben was accurate in his thinking that Rachel might be wondering where he had gone. By this time, she and Tiny were both worried about what could have happened to him and were especially concerned when they had heard the sound of gunshots somewhere down the street. Earlier, after she had returned from the kitchen with her late supper of meatloaf and wondered where he was, Tiny had assumed he had gone to the outhouse. When he had still not returned by the time Rachel was finished with her supper, they even joked about it.

"I hope that meatloaf doesn't affect me the same way it affected him," she had said.

When he still had not returned for a long time after that, they became a little more concerned, and Rachel sent Tiny to the outhouse to check on him. "He would have told us, if he was going somewhere," she thought aloud. It was a little after that when they heard the gunshots, and Tiny volunteered to go in search of him. There were no more than the two shots, so she told him to wait. Finally, she could stand to wait no longer and told Tiny to go, but he met Ben coming in the front door. "What happened to you?" Rachel yelled from the bar, where she had gone to stand in for Tiny, in case a late customer wandered in.

"I was just goin' to look for you," Tiny told him. "You had us worried. We didn't know where you were."

"I was just helpin' Mack take two bodies to the undertaker's," Ben told them, hoping to avoid going into too much detail. "I'm sorry if I had you worried. I should have told you I was gonna take a little walk, but I didn't know I was gonna be gone that long."

Tiny, being a bit more perceptive than Ben gave him credit for, commented, "He took two pistols with him when he went for a little walk." He turned and looked at Rachel.

"Once a ranger, always a ranger, right, Ben?" Rachel asked. "Who got shot?"

"Brock Salter and Tree Forney," Ben said. "They were waitin' in ambush for Mack, but we turned the table on 'em. We figured they were gonna try something to break those three outta the jail, just didn't know when. Well tonight was the night."

"You never said anything about that," Rachel said.

"I know, but I don't tell you everything, partner," he replied with a wide grin.

"I guess that calls for a drink," Rachel suggested.

"I'll second that," Ben said. "Tiny, break out a bottle of the good stuff, and we'll drink a toast to the engineer drivin' the train to hell tonight."

"That's the only stuff Rachel will drink," Tiny responded and opened the cabinet on the wall behind the bar. Rachel put three glasses on the bar for Tiny to fill. Then they saluted each other and downed the expensive Scotch whiskey.

There would be no celebration down the street at the jail where the evening had started with high anticipation of a reckoning with Sheriff Mack Bragg. Horace told Mack that all three of the prisoners had seemed on edge when he left the jail to make his rounds of the town. He said when they heard the two shots fired, the three of them reacted with strange little sounds of excitement. He said he even went to make sure the cell-room door was locked. He knew he was not supposed to unlock the cell-room door while Mack was gone, but he said he had to open it a crack to take a peek inside. He wanted to make sure their cell wasn't open. He said they were all pacing around the cell, not just Reese. "I'm dang glad to see you back," Horace said.

"Well, come with me," Mack said, "and I'll show you how to take the starch out of 'em." He took the cell-room keys from Horace and unlocked the door. When he opened it and walked into the cell room, all three prisoners were standing at the bars, with eyes wide in anticipation. He was wrong with his prediction that they would calm down. In contrast, Reese roared a series of profane exclamations, while Shorty and Jack rocked back and forth on the iron bars like apes in a cage. It was a gratifying sight to Mack Bragg. "If you boys will calm down for a minute, I've got an important announcement you'll be interested in. Reese, I'm sorry to have to tell you that your brother, Brock, has died. His companion, Tree Forney, has also passed away."

"Damn you," Reese swore.

"If you're interested in the cause of death," Mack continued, enjoying every bit of it, since he was their intended victim. "As near as we can tell, it was lead poisonin' and it was the same for both of the deceased." He watched as Reese sank his teeth into his lower lip until he drew blood. It was the maddest he'd ever seen a man since he'd been a sheriff. "We're gonna rule their deaths as accidental," he continued, "on account of them somehow thinkin' it ain't against the law to try to shoot the sheriff in the back. Seems like a waste of two outstanding men."

"You sick excuse for a sheriff!" Reese growled. "Who shot them? Was it you?"

"No, wasn't me," Mack answered. "I don't know who it was. I think it was some strangers, ridin' through town who gunned 'em down when they saw what Brock and Tree were fixin' to do. After they shot 'em, they musta figured it wasn't healthy to hang around Buzzard's Bluff." He did not want to name their killer because he couldn't see the future when it came to Reese Salter. During the trial, after the trial, on the way to prison, in the event he escaped, he didn't want him seeking revenge from Ben Savage.

In a fit of rage, Reese grabbed the end of his cot and hurled it at the bars where Mack was standing. Then he kicked at his bedding that was now on the floor. "All right," Mack said, "that's one of ya that don't want any breakfast in the mornin'. Anybody else?" Reese stood glaring at him, still in his rage. Then he turned and glared at Jack and Shorty as if waiting for them to do the same with their beds. Neither of them could see the sense in forfeiting their breakfast when it wouldn't change anything. Their lack of action deepened his rage.

"You can't do that," Reese roared back at Mack. "You got us in jail and you've got to feed us. That's the law."

"It might be the law somewhere, but it ain't the law in Buzzard's Bluff. I'm the law in Buzzard's Bluff, so when I say you don't get no breakfast, you don't get no breakfast. So does anybody else wanna challenge my authority?" No one spoke up. "All right, then. That's two for breakfast in the mornin'. I'll check later to see if anybody changed their mind. Goodnight, boys." He left the cell room and locked the door, smiling to himself when he heard the sound of Reese's cot skidding across the floor of the cell.

Back in the office, Horace was waiting for him. "I swear, Mack, they're liable to make a mess of that cell. I'm gonna have a devil of a time puttin' it right again."

"There ain't really much they can hurt in that cell," Mack told him. "If they make a mess in there, we'll just let 'em live with it, until the trial and we get 'em outta there for good."

* * *

When Annie came into work the next morning, Ben was in the kitchen as usual, the coffee was made, and there was a good fire going in her stove. He told her not to fix breakfast for him because he was going to go to the hotel to have breakfast with Mack. The frown she was wearing immediately disappeared, replaced by her usual smile. "That's good you're going to meet him." She seemed relieved, and when he said so, she shrugged and said, "I'm just glad you're not skipping your breakfast."

"I thought maybe you were worried about Mack last night when he left the Coyote," he persisted.

"Me? No, I wasn't worried about anybody. Why would I be worried about him? He's the sheriff."

"He was in trouble, though," Ben said. She never admitted that she had those *feelings,* and he wanted her to admit it this one time, if in fact she actually had them.

"But you said you were going to meet him at the hotel this morning," she said.

"I am," he replied, "but he was in trouble last night, dangerous trouble."

"But you were there," she said.

"Whoa! What makes you think I was there?" He was sure he had her now.

"You said he was in trouble," she answered.

"Oh, that's right, I did, so I had to be there." He felt that she knew what he suspected she knew now and was just still determined not to admit it. "All right, I give up. Pour me one more cup of coffee and that oughta see me to the hotel dining room."

She brought the pot over and poured his coffee, then asked, "What kind of trouble was the sheriff in last night?"

He gave her a look as if she should know what kind of trouble he was in, but he answered her frankly. "He was set up for an ambush. Brock Salter and Tree Forney were waiting for him last night when he was making his rounds."

"You shot them?"

"Uh-huh, but I hadn't planned on tellin' anybody that," he confessed. "But I think you already knew that."

"That's crazy. How would I know that?"

"You're right, that's crazy all right," he declared. "I gotta get on up to the hotel to meet Mack." He took a couple of quick slurps of hot coffee and got up from the table. He met Johnny coming in the back door. "Mornin', Johnny. Your wife's in the kitchen where she was tanglin' my mind all up."

"Is that right? She tangled mine up fifteen years ago."

He was a little bit early for breakfast, but Lacy saw him waiting outside the door, so she opened it for him. "Well, good morning, Ben. Why didn't you knock? I'd have let you in."

"I didn't wanna get in the way," he told her. "I know I'm early. I wanna catch Mack this morning." He knew Mack would be early, so he wouldn't get back to the jail too late with breakfast for his prisoners. And he had an idea he might be picking it up this morning instead of sending Horace.

"Well, come on in and sit down at your usual spot and we'll get you started on some coffee." He started to remove his gun belt, so she stopped him. "I told you it's all right to keep it on. I feel better if both you and Mack keep them on when we've got people like Brock and Tree coming in here to eat."

"I can take it off if you want me to," Ben said. "They won't be in here this mornin'."

"How do you know that?"

He motioned back toward the door. "'Cause here comes Sheriff Bragg, and he woulda sent Horace up early to get breakfast for his prisoners if he thought Brock and Tree were still in town."

She gave him an inquisitive look before going to the door. "Have they left town?"

"That's what I hear," he answered and walked back to the table while she met Mack at the door. "Mornin', Cindy," he greeted the young waitress when she met him at the table.

"Well, good mornin', Mr. Savage," Cindy responded. "Does Annie Grey know you're eating breakfast with us?"

Ben laughed and said, "She does and she gave me special permission to have all I want to eat. So bring it on."

"I see the sheriff," she said. "How 'bout Mr. Cochran? Is he going to join you for breakfast, too?"

"I wouldn't be surprised, but I don't know for sure. Mornin', Mack." He greeted the sheriff.

Lacy followed Mack back to the table. "Ben said Brock and Tree left town," she said, "and that's not bad news as far as we're concerned here."

Mack looked up at her and asked, "Did he tell you that? They're still town." He waited for her reaction, and when she looked at Ben in confusion, then back at Mack, he said, "They're over at Merle Baker's place."

"They're dead?" Lacy exclaimed.

"Well, I hope so," Mack replied. "'Cause if they ain't, I'll have to arrest Merle for assault and battery."

"Doggone you, Mack Bragg," Lacy responded. "Cindy, take the sheriff's breakfast outside to the outhouse. That's where he oughta eat today." Back to Mack then, she said, "Now, how 'bout telling me the truth."

"I'll tell you," Ben said. "Those two made an attempt on the sheriff's life last night and ended up gettin' themselves killed."

"Who killed 'em?" Lacy asked.

"It don't matter who killed 'em," Mack answered. "They're dead, and that's that. I just know that I'm grateful they came along when they did."

"I bet I know who killed them," Cindy said when she turned to see Lucas come into the dining room. By this time, thanks in great part to Tuck Tucker, everyone in Buzzard's Bluff knew that John Cochran's real name was Lucas Blaine, even though they might still address him as John Cochran.

Lucas seemed puzzled by the outright staring he received from the two women standing by the table. "Mornin'," he mumbled. "Do you want me to sit somewhere else?"

"No, no," Lacy answered him. "We want you to sit right here with Mack and Ben. I know Mack wants you to sit with them."

"All right," Lucas said, puzzled by her rather strange behavior this morning. *She asked as if she knew*, he thought. *But how could she?* "What's goin' on?" Obviously, something was by the grins from the two men and the knowing looks from the women.

"A case of somebody comin' to the wrong conclusion," Mack answered him. "Somebody shot and killed Brock Salter and Tree Forney last night." He turned to look directly at Lacy. "And ladies, it was not Lucas Blaine. Now, can we get some coffee and something to eat?"

Lacy was immediately deflated. "Are you telling the truth?"

"I assure you, I am," Mack said. "The man's tryin' to live down a reputation, not add to it." That sent Lacy back to the front and Cindy to the kitchen.

"Is that a fact?" Lucas asked. "What you said about Brock and Tree, what happened?"

"When I was makin' my rounds last night, the two of 'em were hidin' between the post office and the church. They came up from behind me, but Ben came outta nowhere and cut both of 'em down before they could get off a shot. Two shots and it was over."

"Well, I'll be damned," Lucas reacted, relieved. "I heard the two shots when I was in bed. I listened for several minutes for more, but there weren't any more, so I went back to sleep." *And when I woke up this morning, she was gone,* he thought. *She slipped out of the room sometime during the wee hours of the morning.* When he walked into the accusing gazes of Lacy and Cindy, he thought for sure they knew that Caroline had slipped into his hotel room last night. Maybe there was hope after all. She had gotten his room number from the night clerk on the pretense that she wanted to slip a thank you note under his door for a courtesy he had performed. She confessed that she had to see him again, even if it was for the last time. But since she slipped out while he was asleep, there was no final goodbye, so he was in hopes that their marriage still had a chance to survive. "What?" He suddenly realized that Ben and Mack were both staring at him.

"I thought you went back to sleep again for a minute there," Mack said. "What I was sayin' was the reason the girls were actin' the way they did was because they thought it was you that shot Brock and Tree. I didn't tell 'em it was Ben who did the shootin' 'cause I didn't think he'd want it talked about."

"I druther it wasn't," Ben interrupted.

"It's gonna come out eventually," Mack continued, "but hopefully at least not till after those three in the jail have been tried and transported to prison. That reminds me," he said and signaled to Cindy. When she came over to the table, he told her to tell Myrtle that he only wanted three breakfast plates for the jail that morning. Reese Salter was going without one. That caused Ben to ask how the prisoners had responded to the news about Brock and Tree. Mack told him about the looks of disappointment on their faces when the cell-room door was opened, and it was him who walked in. They had expected to see Brock march triumphantly through the door with the keys to their cell. "I'm gonna tell you they didn't take it too well, and Reese acted up so much it cost him his breakfast this morning."

"Well, I expect that business last night has got to lighten our load a helluva lot," Ben commented. "Without Brock and Tree hangin' around to keep us on our toes while we're waitin' to see what they're gonna try, it's just a matter of waitin' for the trial."

"That's pretty much the case," Mack agreed. "I think things can go back to normal here in town now. But I sure want you two to know how much I appreciate you lendin' a hand when I needed one. Doggone it, they almost pulled the stunt that I was afraid of last night. I reckon I ought to really thank you, Lucas. Ben and I have a lot invested in the town, but you were just passin' through and you stepped up to help. I reckon you're anxious to move along now that there ain't nothin' holdin' you back."

Lucas hesitated before answering. "It's a funny thing,"

he said. "I ain't as anxious to leave as I was. I figure I might as well hang around a while longer, at least till after the trial." He paused before continuing. "Of course, you might be wantin' me and my reputation to move on to some other town."

"Hell, no," Mack said at once. "As far as I'm concerned, you're welcome here for as long as you want." He'd decided that having Lucas around outweighed all the negatives.

"I 'preciate that, Mack. I'll try to stay out of trouble, so you won't regret sayin' that."

"I don't know what you're gonna do with yourself while you're hangin' around Buzzard's Bluff," Ben said. "But you can always come to the Lost Coyote to find a drink, a card game, or a conversation." That reminded him. "I'm gonna have to get back there and explain to Rachel why I ain't been doin' my share of the work. She's liable to come down hard on me. And I've got a feelin' she isn't finished grillin' me about the episode with Brock and Tree."

CHAPTER 17

"I don't understand, Ben, you say there was a short gun battle you and Mack were in with those two men. What were you doing down there at the church? You walked out the back door, we thought to the outhouse, and you wound up at the church? Why did you go there? There was a short gun battle? I'll say it was. We heard the shooting. There were only two shots." Rachel threw up her hands. "I wish you would just tell me the truth. What are you hiding? I know that you and Mack suspected Brock and Tree of planning a jail break. Did you just decide to murder them to keep them from breaking the others out of jail? Did you take them down to that dark end of town and kill them?"

"Damn, Rachel, you make it sound so bad," Ben replied. "I stopped an ambush. It wasn't murder. Do you really think Mack or I would do that?"

"That's what your story sounds like. It disappoints me to hear it, but that's what it sounds like."

He couldn't let her think that of him. "All right," he finally surrendered. "Here's what happened." Then he told her that Annie's apparent attack by one of her *feelings* caused him to go out in search of Mack, to make sure he was all right. By coincidence, he said he happened to find the two killers about to assassinate Mack. He described the trap they had devised, and he was fortunate enough to get to them before they had time to shoot Mack in the back. "If you don't believe it, ask Annie."

She nodded slowly. "I thought it was something more like that," she said. "You shot both of them to save Mack's life. Why didn't you just tell me that? You've got to be the world's worst liar." She shook her head. "But you're the world's best partner."

"Hell, everybody knows that," he declared.

As the days became closer to the fifteenth, the town of Buzzard's Bluff reverted back to its normally peaceful self. If you weren't aware of the three bank robbers in the town jail, you might think it was the perfect town. To the surprise of those who knew him at all, Lucas Blaine moved out of the hotel, but he didn't leave town. Instead, he built himself a small shack on the creek that ran behind the church, but it was up the creek about seventy-five yards from the church. It was not meant to be a permanent dwelling, but it was better than camping on the ground. Ben and Rachel saw Lucas quite often and were surprised by the change in his outlook for the future. Rachel was certain he had reconnected with Caroline. Ben was afraid Lucas was riding for another fall, but if he chose to take the ride, then he wished him luck. He figured Lucas was born to be a wanderer.

About fifty miles northwest of Buzzard's Bluff, another wanderer was looking forward to a drink of whiskey and a good supper. Harley Clackum guided his mules down the path to the sprawling two-story building on the bank of the

Brazos, called Hutto's Station. At the end of the path, he parked his circus wagon up under the cottonwoods while he went inside the saloon. "Whatcha say, Corky?" He called out when he went inside the door and stepped up to the bar.

"I swear," Corky came back. "Harley Clackum! What you doin' up this way? I ain't seen you since way before last winter. Whatcha drinkin'?"

"I'll take a lick of whatever that is in that bottle," Harley said. "I had some business to take care of in Waco, so I thought I'd drive down this way, since I ain't been here in a good while." He picked up the shot glass Corky just filled and tossed it back. "It's gonna take another'n," he said and pushed the empty glass back for a refill. After he tossed that one back, he smacked his lips and declared, "Sweeter than the kiss of a virgin. Is that woman, Mozelle, still cookin' for ya?"

"Yep, she's still here," Corky said, "and you've hit here at a good time if you're wantin' to eat."

"That's what I had in mind," Harley said. "Pour me one more of that stuff and order me some supper."

"Pick you out one of them tables and have a seat." He poured the whiskey. "Here's your likker, I'll go tell Mozelle to bring your supper." Corky walked to the kitchen door and called the cook. When she came to the door, Corky pointed to Harley. She went back in the kitchen to fill his plate and Corky went back to the bar. In a few minutes, Mozelle reappeared, this time, carrying a plate filled with a beef hash and two squares of cornbread. She asked Harley if he wanted coffee, then went to fetch it when he said he did.

Harley looked around him while he ate. The saloon was fairly busy for this early in the evening. There were a couple of card games in progress, and the bar was beginning to attract a line of drinkers. He crumbled up one of the cornbread squares and sprinkled it over his hash, then attacked it with a vengeance. When Mozelle set a cup of coffee down on the table, he immediately grabbed it and took a cautious sip of the boiling hot liquid. He smacked his lips and gave Mozelle an approving smile. She responded with the same bored expression she had worn when she brought his plate, turned around, and returned to the kitchen. Maggie Green walked by his table and gave him a warm smile, but she didn't stop to talk. He answered her with a smile in return, not expecting her to stop. None of the women working the saloon ever stopped to entice the odd-looking little gray-haired man who fixed firearms. *Probably afraid my heart would give out, if they ever got me in the saddle, and they'd have a dead man on their hands,* he thought. *I'd be kinda scared of that, myself, but it wouldn't be a bad way to go.*

He was not going to go without some conversation, however, for he was just eating the last of his cornbread when Ward Hutto came by his table. He was carrying his own cup of coffee and he said, "Howdy, Harley, mind if I sit down?" He didn't wait for an answer before pulling a chair back.

"Not at all," Harley replied. "It'd be a pleasure."

"Ain't seen you in a while," Hutto said. "Corky said you came in, so I thought I'd ask you something about my ten-gauge, my bird-huntin' gun."

"What's it doin'?" Harley asked.

"I went bird huntin' last week and my dog flushed a pair of quail. I had a good chance to get both of 'em. It's a single barrel, you know, and I knocked the first bird down, and swung around to shoot the other one, but when I tried to eject the empty cartridge, I couldn't get the dang spent cartridge out. That ejector thing wouldn't work. And that ain't the first time it's happened."

Harley listened with interest, then he asked, "You ever oil that gun?"

Hutto shrugged. "Yeah, whenever I think of it."

To Harley, that meant never. "I'll be glad to take a look at it. Most likely ain't much wrong with it." He started to tell Hutto if it was just needing cleaning, he wouldn't charge him, but he was interrupted by a dispute that was about to get out of hand at one of the card games. One of the players stood up, knocking his chair over when he did.

"Uh-oh," Hutto said, "Nate Castor." He got up from his chair and went over to the table. "What's the trouble, boys?"

"Ain't none I can't handle," the man standing declared. "I just ain't believin' this jasper is so dang lucky every time it's his deal, and I'm callin' him on it right now."

Hutto looked at the man Nate was accusing, a stranger to him. "What do you say about that?"

"I say he's a lousy card player, and he don't know what he's talking about. I don't cheat, and I don't appreciate him sayin' I do."

"Then maybe we oughta step outside and settle it with six-guns," Nate said.

"Maybe we ought to at that," the stranger said.

"You know my rules, Nate," Hutto said, "but I'll tell you, so you don't shoot nobody in the back. There ain't no gunplay inside this saloon. If you wanna settle it between ya, ya take it out beside the buildin'."

"Them's the rules," Nate said. "Now, let's get at it. I'm tired of lookin' at your face."

"Wait a minute!" the stranger exclaimed and looked at

Hutto. "You called him Nate. Nate what? It ain't Nate Castor is it?"

"Yeah," Hutto said, "Nate Castor."

"Hell, no!" the stranger declared. "You didn't say you were Nate Castor. I ain't pullin' on no professional gunfighter." He started to rake his money off the table. "You can work on your reputation with somebody in your class. It ain't gonna be me."

"If you walk outta here with your tail between your legs, you leave that money on the table, you yellow dog," Nate said.

The stranger hesitated, then backed away a few steps. "It's my money fair and square, but I'll leave it. It ain't worth dyin' for." He grabbed his hat off the back of the chair and headed for the door. Castor sat back down and raked the stranger's money over to his side of the table. No one suggested it should be split between all the players.

When Hutto came back to Harley's table, Harley said, "Nate Castor, huh? I think I mighta heard of him. I ain't sure. I'll tell you one I have heard of, though. If Castor wants to add to his reputation, he ought to take a little ride down to Buzzard's Bluff and try that feller out."

"What feller?" Hutto asked.

"Lucas Blaine," Harley said.

"Lucas Blaine? What in blazes would Lucas Blaine be doin' in Buzzard's Bluff? Are you sure it was him?"

"Sure, I'm sure," Harley insisted. "As sure as I'm settin' here in Hutto's Station. I reckon I oughta know it was him 'cause I was settin' in the Lost Coyote with him and Ben Savage, and the sheriff of Buzzard's Bluff."

"Well, I'll swear," Hutto started, then he yelled over to the card game. "Hey, Castor, if you're itchin' to show off your skill, why don't you try somebody your own size?"

"Yeah, Hutto, who is that?"

"Lucas Blaine," Hutto answered.

"Lucas Blaine?" Castor responded at once. "I'd like to try him out. If he ever came out of hidin', I'd be the first one to call him out."

"He ain't hidin'," Harley said to Hutto.

Hutto forwarded the message. "Feller here knows him, sez he ain't hidin'."

That was enough for Castor. He got up from the table and walked over to stand over Hutto and Harley. He gave Harley a look-over and automatically decided he was bluffing. "Big talk from a little man," Castor said. "You wouldn't know Lucas Blaine from your grandma, if they was both neckid. Where'd you see Lucas Blaine?"

"I seen him in Buzzard's Bluff," Harley said. "And he was still there when I left there. He's a friend of Sheriff Mack Bragg and Ben Savage, who owns the Lost Coyote Saloon. And that ain't the first time I saw him. I also seen him gun down a man in Johnson's Saloon in San Antonio."

That was enough to cause Castor to think about it. "San Antonio, huh? That was a while back. Last I heard of him, he was in Austin." He thought on it some more. "Where the hell is Buzzard's Bluff? I ain't never heard of it before."

Hutto looked at Harley to answer the question, and Harley suddenly realized that he was helping Nate Castor track Lucas Blaine down. He wasn't sure he wanted to be a party to that. So he didn't tell them that he was going back to Buzzard's Bluff himself. When he went depended on how much business he drummed up at Hutto's. Before he stumbled upon the little town of Buzzard's Bluff, he would have gone straight back to Madisonville. But he kinda liked what he had seen of Buzzard's Bluff, so he intended to go that way from now on. He sure as shooting didn't want to take a chance on Nate Castor wanting to go with him. So he said, "It's on the Navasota River, about sixty-five miles southeast of Waco, which puts it about fifty miles from here. It ain't really hard to find. You get on that road outta Waco, and just stay on it. A little over halfway down there's a fork off to the east and a sign that says Madisonville. Don't take it, keep goin' straight and it'll take you to Buzzard's Bluff."

"If I ride down that way and he ain't there, then I might start huntin' you," Castor threatened.

I hope he is there if you ride down there, Harley thought. *I just hope I get to see it*. To Castor, he declared, "I ain't got nothin' to do with where he goes. All I'm tellin' you is that he didn't say nothin' about leaving." One of these days, he realized, he was going to have to learn to keep his mouth shut.

Castor went back to the card game, still grumbling about the stranger who wisely chose cowardice over suicide. His display of violence was effective in eliminating any thoughts of cheating by those who remained in the game. Hutto was satisfied to have prevented a bloody shootout inside his establishment, so he returned to the matter of his shotgun. Harley suggested that he should take a look at it. He took it back to his wagon that night and found that the problem was what he had suspected. So he took the gun apart and cleaned and oiled every part. And when he put it back together, it worked just like new. He brought the gun to breakfast with him, only to find that Hutto didn't come down until later in the morning. So he hung around after he had eaten, talking to Corky until Hutto made an appearance.

"Mornin'," Harley said. "I brung you your shotgun. Thought you'd like to take a look at it."

"What?" Hutto asked, his mind still abed. "Oh, my ten-gauge. Hell, you didn't have to wait around for me. You coulda just left it with Corky."

His attitude was quite disappointing to Harley when he thought about how concerned the man was last night. "I thought you'd wanna see it. Like I figured, there was nothin' seriously wrong with it. I took it apart and made some adjustments that needed to be made, and I think you'll find it works like a new one now."

"Is that a fact?" Hutto replied and took the gun from him. "It does feel better," he said after he practiced jerking it to his shoulder and aiming a couple of times. "It even looks like a new shotgun," he said, admiring the shiny, oily firearm. "Corky, reach under the bar and fetch me a couple of shells." He took the shells from Corky and said, "Come on." And Harley followed him out to the front porch where Hutto broke the barrel open, dropped a shell in it and closed it again. Then he looked around the trees, looking for a target. Spotting a crow, he raised the gun and fired, killing the crow. Then he broke the barrel open again and extracted the spent shell. Pleased, he looked at Harley and smiled. "Just like new," he said. "Looks like you made the right adjustments." He dropped the other shell in and repeated the test, again selecting a crow as a target. This time, he missed the crow, but the shotgun performed flawlessly. "Can you make some adjustments on my shootin'?" He joked. "It's perfect," he said then. "How much do I owe you?"

"A job like that, I usually charge a dollar and a half, but I ain't plannin' to charge you anything. I figure I was doin' somethin' for a friend." He had actually made no adjustments on the shotgun. There was nothing to adjust.

"Nonsense, Harley, you ain't never gonna get rich doin'

favors for friends. I got where I am today by shuckin' my friends harder than I did the strangers. I'll pay your regular charge."

"I tell you what," Harley offered. "I ain't paid for my breakfast yet, so how 'bout we call that your payment?"

"That ain't hardly fair. Are you planning to be here another night?" Harley said that he was. "Good," Hutto continued. "We won't charge you for any of your meals all day, or breakfast in the morning."

"That's more than fair," Harley said. When they went back inside Hutto repeated the deal to Corky, so Harley was pleased with his arrangement for his food. He had thought about pushing for a room for the night as well, but considering Hutto's typical customers, he preferred to sleep in his wagon to keep an eye on his possessions. But for the rest of the day, he would entertain himself watching the saloon ladies working the customers, and if he was lucky, maybe by selling a gun or two. As it turned out, his stay was extended, thanks to Hutto's enthusiastic endorsement of his repair work. He picked up enough new customers to keep him busy for a while.

Unlike Lucas Blaine, Nate Castor had one thought in mind when he discovered he was faster than most men when it came to drawing and shooting accurately. That thought was to become known as the fastest gun in Texas. In the beginning, after he had won his first contest in a saloon in Tyler, Texas, he had spent hours practicing his quick-draw, constantly looking for more speed. It was after his second confrontation with a drunken cowhand that he became aware of a measure of some respect, although it was grudgingly given. The fact that his new-found respect was built on the deaths of two men was not troubling to his conscience. The victims were just numbers. So he began seeking situations that might provide opportunities to increase the number and expand on his reputation. He soon became addicted to the respect he received in the barrooms and dance halls. Sometimes it afforded him other rewards, like the stranger's money left on the table after he heard his name. The man had rather lose the money than test Nate Castor. And sometimes, his particular skills earned him a nice payday.

Now, this comical-looking little gray-haired man comes along and brings up a name that is more widely known than his. It was especially infuriating because he had ridden to Austin to seek him out, only to find that he had left Austin, and no one knew where he had headed. As irritating as Harley was, still it was a lucky day for Nate when he came to Hutto's. Otherwise, he would never even know of the existence of the town of Buzzard's Bluff, and that Lucas Blaine was hiding out there. Just fifty miles away, he would make two days of it, so he would arrive fairly early the second day. Though anxious to get on the road, he had to wait at Hutto's in order to collect payment for having solved a problem between two competitive businessmen.

Harley had spent most of the morning sitting beside his wagon, to see if there was any more potential for his skills. So far, there had been nothing. When it was dinnertime, he went inside to eat and that was when Corky told him that Castor had left there after breakfast and said he was going to Buzzard's Bluff. As much as Harley would like to witness a showdown that would be one to talk about for the rest of his life, he decided it not worth the risk of running into Castor along the way. He would wait till the following morning to leave, figuring it surely wouldn't happen for a day or two and he'd have a good chance of being there for it.

CHAPTER 18

Sheriff Mack Bragg received a surprise visitor on the morning of the thirteenth of the month, when a tall, rawboned individual with solid gray hair and a neatly trimmed beard strode forcefully into his office. "Sheriff Bragg?" he enquired confidently.

"Yes, sir," Mack replied. "What can I do for you?"

The man reached inside his coat pocket, pulled out an envelope, and handed it to Mack. "I'm Judge Willard P. Gardener. I'm here to hold court as previously scheduled. These are my papers to prove who I am."

Bragg took only a few moments to take a look at the papers. "Yes, sir, Judge, we didn't expect you till the fifteenth."

"Well, I'm here early. You gonna send me back to Waco? If not, we can get set up and we'll have a trial tomorrow. Is there any reason we can't do that?"

"No, sir," Mack replied, "no reason a-tall. I'll just have to get your courtroom set up in the Lost Coyote."

"Good," Gardener said. "I'll need accommodations in the hotel tonight and tomorrow night. One room for me and one room for two men accompanying me."

"You got two men with you?" Mack asked and craned

his neck in an effort to see if there was anyone in the doorway behind him.

"That's right, two U. S. Deputy Marshals. They're outside with the horses." He watched Mack impatiently as if he expected immediate action.

Mack took the hint. "Yes, sir." He got up from his desk and told Horace to lock the door when they left. "We're going to the hotel to get the judge settled." They walked outside where Mack saw the two deputy marshals standing with three saddled horses and four packhorses. One of the packhorses was carrying what looked like a wooden box that Mack guessed would hold his official tools for trial and might also serve as the bench.

"This is Deputy Marshal Clem Douglas and Deputy Marshal Ralph Bell," the judge said. "Two good men who had the bad luck to be assigned as my nursemaids on this circuit. Men, say howdy to Sheriff Mack Bragg."

Mack stepped up and shook hands with each of the deputies. "You came in by the stable, so you know where that is," he said. "Let's go down to the other end of the street to the hotel and see about gettin' you some rooms." The judge climbed back up into the saddle. He was riding what was now called an Appaloosa gelding. The two deputies walked with Mack and led all the other horses. When the judge nudged his horse and moved on up ahead of them a little, Mack commented to one of the deputies. "The last judge we had came down in a fancy buggy with a wagon carryin' all his things."

"Not ol' Wild Will Gardener," Clem Douglas said, speaking softly to take no chance on the judge hearing. "He's like ridin' with the Pony Express, hell-bent for leather. Ain't that right, Ralph?"

"That's right," Ralph said. "We were afraid we were

gonna have to shoot that Palouse he's ridin' to rest our horses. He runs a trial the same way, get the facts, make a decision, and hit the trail to the next stop."

"That's a fact," Clem said. "We're supposed to be here for his protection. But that's just because the department says all circuit judges get protection. He don't need any protection. He's wearin' an Army model Colt .45, and it ain't just for show. I feel like me and Ralph have him for protection." By then, the judge had given his horse a little kick and the Appaloosa loped on down to the hotel. When they got there, he was at the front desk, talking to Freeman Brown, the owner.

"Oh, Mack," Freeman said when they walked in, "I was just telling Judge Gardener that you told us he would be here on the fifteenth."

"Don't tell me you don't have any vacant rooms," Mack responded, somewhat alarmed.

"No, no," Freeman said. "We've got rooms and we've saved the best for the judge. It's just that we planned to put up some additional furniture and things to make them even more comfortable."

"You shouldn't worry about that for a second, sir," Judge Gardener insisted. "Last night, I slept on a bedroll on the ground. Any rooms you have will be luxurious."

"Rob," Freeman instructed Rob Parker, his desk clerk, "put the judge in two-hundred." He turned back to Gardener and said, "That's our best room, upstairs, first room on the left. What would you like for the other two gentlemen? One room or separate rooms?"

"Are there two beds in the rooms?" Gardener asked.

"Well, no, sir, but they have full size beds," Rob answered him.

"Then put them in separate rooms. Two men shouldn't sleep together in the same bed."

"My thoughts, exactly," Freeman said, and while the judge and his men signed in, Freeman went on to tout the quality of the hotel dining room. "We will try to make your stay as enjoyable as possible while you're with us," Freeman continued. "Can we help you carry your luggage up to the room?"

"No, thank you," the judge answered. "We're three able-bodied men. I think we should be able to handle it." They took the keys Rob handed them and went outside to get their saddlebags and war bags with their personal items. Mack waited downstairs at the front desk while they took their things up to their rooms.

"Have you been in those rooms this morning?" Freeman asked Rob. "I hope to hell those women cleaned them properly."

Rob shrugged. "I didn't go in 'em this morning," he said. "I didn't have any reason to. There ain't been anybody sleepin' in 'em."

"I hope they ain't in too bad a shape," Mack japed. "That ol' boy means business. He's liable to condemn this place and order you to shut it down."

"It can't be too bad, Boss," Rob said. "A little dust on the tables maybe, but there ain't no reason the room would be messed up."

"Well, if it is, we're bound to hear about it," Freeman said. He reversed his frown when he heard them coming back down the stairs. "Did you find the rooms satisfactory?"

"Yes, they'll do fine," Gardener said as he breezed by the desk. "The chamber pot in room two-hundred needs to be emptied."

"Oh, my Lord," Freeman gasped and looked at Rob.

"That's why you should have looked in that room this morning."

"Hell, Freeman, that probably means he just used it," Mack said, then rushed out the door after them.

Freeman looked at Rob and said, "Quick! Run up there and see if it feels warm!" Then he went at once to the dining room to alert Lacy to be on her toes.

Mack caught up with them as all three were now walking. "Show me my courtroom," Gardener said to Mack.

"Comin' up on your left," Mack pointed, "the Lost Coyote Saloon. It's the saloon that catches most of the local folks' business, on account they don't stand for any wild goings on. You wanna go inside?"

"No, I just wanted to see which building we were gonna be in. We'll go in after dinner today and have a drink. Then I'll tell them how I want it set up." They proceeded on to the stable where Mack introduced them to Henry Barnes. The judge gave Henry specific instructions on the care he wanted for his horse while Ralph and Clem unloaded the packhorses and put the packs in one of the stalls. When they were through there, they walked back through town until coming to the jail. "I'll let you get back to your work, Sheriff," the judge told him. "What time does the dining room open for dinner?" Mack told him. Then the judge asked, "Do you eat there?" Mack said he did, so the judge said, "Fine. We'll meet you there and we'll discuss the case we'll be working tomorrow at that time."

Mack went back inside his office to find Horace waiting by the door. "Man, he's a real pistol, ain't he?" Horace exclaimed.

"He sure is," Mack replied. "You shoulda seen him at the hotel. I thought Freeman Brown was gonna wet his

britches before we got outta there. According to the two
fellows with him, he don't know nothin' but full speed
ahead. I don't think ol' Reese and his boys are gonna have
a very long trial. You'll have to go to the dining room and
pick up dinner for our guests. The judge wants me to meet
him there to talk about the trial. So, I might not be back for
a while. Just lock up when you go. You all right with that?"
Horace said that he was, now that Brock and Tree had been
taken care of. "Good," Mack continued. "I've gotta go now
to tell Ben and Rachel that the judge is planning to go there
after dinner this afternoon to show them how he wants the
room set up for his trial."

"The judge showed up a little early, didn't he?" Ben
asked Mack when he walked into the Lost Coyote and
found Ben and Rachel standing at the end of the bar, talking to Tiny.

"Yeah, two days before he was supposed to," Mack
answered. "You see him go by?"

"No, we didn't see him," Ben answered. "But Tuck saw
you when you walked by his shop when you went to the
hotel. Then he followed you till you got back to the Coyote.
He came in and gave us the news. He said there was a
fellow ridin' an Appaloosa and there were two other men
with badges. So I figured it had to be the judge."

"Well, that's a fact, and he's a pistol," he said, using
Horace's description of the judge. He went on to describe
the judge and his controlling manner, including the comments the two deputy marshals said about him.

When Mack was finished, Ben asked a question. "By
any chance, is this judge's name Gardener?"

Mack looked surprised. "Matter of fact, it is," he answered. "You know him?"

"I know who he is. I've worked on a couple of cases that ended up in his court in Austin. He wasn't workin' the circuit then. He was just a regular judge in the rotation, but he was different from the other judges. I ain't surprised to hear what those deputy marshals said about him."

"Well, I came to tell you and Rachel that he's plannin' on comin' here after dinner to talk about how he wants the room set up for his court, which I also wanna tell you is gonna be tomorrow."

"Tomorrow," Rachel repeated. "I hope he plans on getting started pretty early, so we aren't shut down when customers usually start coming in."

"From what I saw of this fellow," Mack said, "he'll be in early and done pretty quick. I'm supposed to meet him down at the hotel dining room for dinner. You wanna go with me?" He was looking at Ben when he asked but then looked at Rachel and said, "Both of ya?" This, even though he knew she wouldn't accept. She never ate at the hotel. As he expected, she declined.

"I reckon I'll pass it up, too," Ben told him. "Sounds to me like he wants to talk about your prisoners. Besides, I'd have to explain it to Annie, and she might have one of her *feelings*. And one of us might get shot at."

"Ben! Shame on you. Don't go joking about that. What if Annie would hear you?" Rachel gave him a stern look.

He apologized and said he would never tease her personally about it. "Especially right now, just before she serves dinner," he added.

"I declare," Rachel scolded, "I hope she heard you." As if on cue, Annie came to the door of the kitchen then to tell Rachel that dinner was ready and asked if she and Ben were ready to eat it. "Yes," Rachel answered. "We'll be right in to fix a plate." Then she looked at Ben, her eyebrows arched, and eyes opened wide, and she nodded as if warning him.

"Maybe I had better go eat with you, Mack," Ben joked as the sheriff started for the door.

"Good afternoon, gentlemen," Lacy James greeted the judge and his two deputies. "Welcome to the River House Dining Room. Please pick any table you like." Having been briefed by Freeman Brown to expect the judge's party, she refrained from asking Judge Gardener to remove the six-gun he was wearing. The judge headed straight for the table in the back corner of the room, opposite the kitchen. Lacy followed the three of them, and when they were seated, she asked what they preferred to drink. They all ordered coffee. *Why did I ask?* she thought. Then she said, "The special noontime meal today is beef stew, but if you prefer, we have fresh pork chops for supper. We can fix one of those for you. Cindy will take care of you. Just let her know which you prefer."

Mack arrived before Cindy came to the table, so she brought four cups of coffee. Before she could ask, the judge said, "I'll have the stew. I'll wait and try the pork chops tonight for supper." That seemed to set the standard for the deputies, so they followed his suggestion. Mack shrugged and said she might as well make it four.

While they ate, Mack brought the judge up to date on Buzzard's Bluff's history with the Salter brothers and their gang. He told him about the original charge of attempted bank robbery against Reese and the other two the judge would be trying. Then he told him about the first attempt to break them out of jail by Reese's brother, Brock. And lastly, he told about the second break attempt that resulted in the death of Brock and Tree.

"So basically, what you're telling me is, in spite of all the attempts to break in the jail, and the killings that resulted, the only crime the three who are on trial for is attempted bank robbery. Is that correct?"

"Yes, sir," Mack answered. "I reckon that's about it."

"It cannot even be proved that the three in jail knew there were attempts to free them, or even if they wanted to escape." Gardener waited for a comment.

"No, sir," Mack replied. "I reckon you can't find 'em guilty based on assumption."

"So we're trying them on attempted bank robbery," Gardener concluded. "And we have witnesses to that charge?"

"Yes, sir, there ain't no doubt on that charge. We've got plenty of witnesses; the president of the bank, the two tellers, the blacksmith, the owner of the Lost Coyote, and myself. One of the robbers was killed inside the bank. Yes, sir, there ain't no doubt about that charge."

"Attempted bank robbery, it is. Can you have all those you just named at the trial tomorrow?"

"Yes, sir," Mack answered. "I sure can."

"Very well," the judge said. "This shouldn't take long at all. I want to call the court to order at nine o'clock." He waited for Mack to indicate his okay, then he looked at his deputies. "We should be ready to start back to Waco before noon tomorrow." Mack could see the look of disappointment in the faces of Douglas and Bell. They had obviously been looking forward to a couple of nights in the hotel, three nice meals a day in the dining room, and perhaps some time in the saloon.

They finished their dinner, and the judge signaled for Lacy to come to the table. When she came over, he announced grandly, "I am ready to make a judgement on this dinner we had here today. I rule that it was excellent, and I look forward to my supper here tonight."

"Why, thank you, sir." Lacy beamed. "I'll pass your judgement on to Myrtle, our cook. And we look forward to serving you again tonight."

From the dining room, Judge Gardener's party retired to his room to work on some papers he had brought with him. He advised his two protectors that he needed no protection, so they were free to do whatever they wanted until two o'clock, at which time he would meet them at the Lost Coyote. "You're welcome to meet us there as well," he said to Mack. "I've taken quite a bit of your time already, so it's entirely up to you."

Mack stopped in the Lost Coyote on his way back to the jail just long enough to let them know that the judge and his party planned to be there at two. Then he went to see how Reese and his two men were taking the news of their trial the next day.

Clem Douglas and Ralph Bell walked into the Lost Coyote Saloon at a quarter to two, knowing well that Judge Gardener would walk through the door at two o'clock on the second. Having spent most of the time between the end of dinner and a quarter to two at the Golden Rail Saloon, they went at once to the bar where they ordered a shot of whiskey from Tiny. Their purpose, of course, was to have the judge come in while they were having a shot at the bar, which would account for the smell of alcohol on their breath, should he get that close. Tiny, or anyone else in the saloon could tell the judge they had just walked in minutes before him and had only one drink. The judge enjoyed a few drinks, himself, but he had no tolerance for those who overindulged.

As they had anticipated, the judge walked in at the stroke of two, and seeing his deputies at the bar, strode forth to join them. "We just got here a few minutes ago," Clem said. "Thought it wouldn't hurt to have a little shooter while we waited for you."

"No, no harm at all," Gardener said. He turned his attention to Tiny then. "You're a big fellow. Can you direct me to the owner of this establishment?"

"Yes, sir," Tiny answered. "There's two owners, and they're settin' at that table near the back of the room."

"The man and the woman?"

"Yes, sir."

"Are they man and wife?"

"Ah, no, sir," Tiny said. "They're co-owners, just partners. I'll take you back to see 'em." He didn't have to, for Ben and Rachel noticed the strangers at the bar then, and Ben was sure that he recognized the tall, slim man as the judge. So they came to greet him.

"Welcome, Judge Gardener," Ben greeted him. "We're the owners. This is Rachel Baskin, and my name's Ben Savage."

"It's a pleasure to meet you, ma'am," the judge said, recognizing a quality in her above the common saloon hostess. He turned then to look at Ben, and a faint spark ignited his memory. He extended his hand and said, "Ben Savage, we've met before. Ben Savage," he repeated. "Were you ever a Texas Ranger?"

"Yes, sir, a couple of years ago. Quite a few years back, I was the arrestin' officer on a couple of your cases."

"Well, well." The judge grinned. "Of all the places to run into you, Buzzard's Bluff. How did you wind up the owner of a saloon?" Ben had to go through the story of how he ended up inheriting the Lost Coyote.

When he finished, he let Rachel continue when Gardener wanted to know how the saloon came to be called the Lost Coyote. The judge was fascinated by the happenstance that brought Ben to this small out-of-the-way town. "So you gave up the chase for the law-breakers and scallywags that pester our citizens."

"That's right, I'd have to say that, but once in a while I still try to help out, if help is needed. My boss, Captain Randolph Mitchell, never retired my badge, so he occasionally calls on me to pin it back on for one thing or another."

"I can see why you were waiting in that bank with Sheriff Bragg," the judge said.

"Lucky it doesn't happen too often, or my partner, here, would lock me outta the saloon." Ben chuckled.

"I understand," Gardener said. "Well, let's get down to business. I see the sheriff has joined us." That reminded him that he had ignored his two deputies. "Let me introduce Ralph Bell and Clem Douglas. They are deputy marshals, and they accompany me on the circuit." Looking toward Mack then, he said, "They'll be available to help you transfer your three prisoners from the jail to this courtroom." Mack acknowledged with a nod and welcomed the assistance. Rachel signaled Tiny, and he came over to determine what everyone wanted to drink. Since everyone wanted whiskey, she had Tiny bring a bottle of the judge's choice, and glasses for everyone.

Having set up his courtroom in many saloons across Texas, Gardener wasted very little time. He showed Ben and Rachel where he would set up his bench and told them how many of their small tables he wanted to make it. Then he picked a spot where he wanted the defendants seated on one side and the witnesses seated on the other. He pointed out the place for Mack to sit and designated him as the prosecutor. When Mack started to question that, the judge explained that he wouldn't have to present a case. He just might have to answer some questions. "That about does it," Gardener said. "As far as spectators, you can set up as many chairs as you think you might need. I really don't care about that. I intend to call the court to order at nine o'clock sharp. The bar must remain closed until court is adjourned. Now, does anyone have any problem with any of that?" No one did until one question came from behind them.

"What about the jury? Where are they gonna be settin'?" Everyone at the table turned to see Tuck Tucker standing just inside the door. "I'm volunteerin' to be on the jury." He was about two hours earlier than his usual appointment there with Ham Greeley.

"His nose just naturally sniffs out anything unusual going on," Rachel said and got up to take care of it. Gardener motioned for her to ignore it, so she remained standing by the table.

"I think everybody knows what we're going to do," the judge said. "So we're through except for a couple more drinks. Nine o'clock tomorrow," he reminded them.

"We'll arrange the table and chairs just like you said," Ben told him. "If I get it wrong, Rachel will straighten me out."

"Fine," Gardener said and got up to leave. "Thank you very much for your cooperation and your hospitality. Just make out a bill for the whiskey and give it to me tomorrow. You'll receive payment from Waco along with the payments for my other expenses. They'll all go to Sheriff Bragg and he'll give them to you."

"We appreciate it, Your Honor," Rachel said, "but there won't be any charge for that bottle tonight."

"Well, thank you very much, ma'am. You are most gracious. I will see you all in the morning. Sheriff, remember, prisoners here at nine o'clock."

"You want us to walk back to the hotel with you?" Clem asked when Gardener started for the door.

"Not necessary, Clem, stay here for a while if you like. You know when supper is served at the hotel. And there'll be pork chops tonight."

"Yes, sir, that's right, pork chops tonight," Clem said and winked at Ralph. *But I mean to finish that bottle on the table this afternoon,* he thought.

Tuck was still standing by the door when the judge walked out, so Gardener paused long enough to say, "This won't be a trial by jury. I will simply rule on it by the evidence I see. Had it been a jury trial, I am sure you would have been the first name called out." Tuck turned around to grin at everyone in the saloon, anxious to see if they saw the judge stopping to talk to him. No one he knew would escape hearing his version of the short meeting between him and the judge. It was a version that implied more than could have been said in the short meeting they had.

CHAPTER 19

The morning of the trial began as all other mornings did at the Lost Coyote. Coffee and a hot stove were waiting for Annie when she came in to work. But this morning, Ben didn't linger in the kitchen while Annie started preparations for breakfast. He figured he'd get a head start on the courtroom arrangement, so he went into the barroom and started moving tables and chairs around. He was careful to make enough noise to awaken Tiny, and when he came out of his room, he was quick to offer his help. By the time Annie called them in for breakfast, they had the chairs and tables arranged as Ben remembered Gardener's instructions. Before they were finished eating, Clem and Ralph came in with the things the judge would need from their packs in the stable. Among the items was the large wooden box that one of the packhorses had carried. It turned out to be the judge's *bench,* and inside it, among other things, was his robe and gavel. The deputies also brought a small professionally painted sign that read, COURT TODAY—BAR CLOSED—NO FIREARMS INSIDE. This they propped in a chair and set the chair right outside the door. When the deputies determined that everything was arranged the way the judge usually ordered it, they accepted Ben's invitation to eat breakfast at the Coyote, since they were now running short of time before they would have to go to the jail to help Mack transport the prisoners.

Down the street at the jail, Reese Salter was pacing around the cell again, trying to calm his nerves. Shorty Cobb and Jack Ramsey, although as anxious as Reese, were sitting on their cots, waiting for the sheriff to come to get them. Reese stopped his pacing and turned to them. "You two be ready," he charged. "I don't know what's gonna happen once we get outside this jail. But if there's any chance at all, I'm takin' it. So be ready."

"I'll be ready," Ramsey said, "but I ain't gonna commit suicide." Shorty didn't say anything, but he felt the same as Jack. They were both a little concerned that Reese was now so frantic about being locked up, that he might get them all killed. "They're just takin' us to trial today," Ramsey said. "No matter what that judge says, they ain't takin' us nowhere today. We'll be right back here in this cell for who knows how long before they send a jail wagon to get us. That's plenty of time for somebody to get careless, and we might get our chance to get outta here."

"You be ready today!" Reese pointed his finger at him in anger. "If we get a chance to break free, and you don't back me, I'll kill you with my bare hands when we get back here."

"You ain't got no business talkin' to me like that," Ramsey said. "I ain't ever give you no reason to threaten me. I wanna get outta here just as bad as you and Shorty do."

"What about you?" Reese demanded, looking at Shorty now.

"I'll be ready, if there's a chance we'll make it," Shorty

replied. "But I'm like Jack, I ain't gonna throw my life away when there ain't a chance we'll make it."

"Well, I'll be . . ." Reese started, then paused to look at each one of them individually. "I reckon I found out what kind of men I've been ridin' with." He was about to say more, but the cell-room door opened then and two men they had never seen before walked in. "Who the hell . . . ?" He started again, then saw the badges they wore. This was another stroke of bad luck as far as Reese was concerned. He had counted on just the sheriff and Horace to march the three of them to their trial.

Ralph and Clem said nothing but just took a look at the prisoners. In a few moments, Mack came in carrying his handcuffs. "All right, boys," Mack said, "all of ya back up to the bars and stick your hands between 'em behind your back. We're gonna take a little walk." Reese's reaction right away was to resist, so he didn't comply when Shorty and Jack backed up to the bars.

Clem cast a grim, bored look at him and said, "It's gonna be a helluva lot harder on you if I come in there to do it." With no more than a few seconds of defiance, Reese backed up to the cell wall beside Shorty. He put his hands together and pushed them through the bars.

When all three were handcuffed, they had to twist their wrists to pull the cuffs through the bars. Reese made a problem of it with his until Clem gave him a forceful assist. "So this is the one," Clem said to Mack. "There's always one that thinks he's got a lotta hard bark on him."

"He's the one, all right," Mack answered. "He's the leader of a little gang that got whittled down to just these three. But I reckon he's got good reason to be a sorehead. His brother just got himself killed tryin' to break him outta here. We still don't know who shot him."

"I know who shot Brock," Reese blurted. "I know damn well who did it. It was Ben Savage. I know it was him, and so do you."

"Now, why would you say that?" Mack responded as they herded them out of the cell. "You don't know that to be true."

"I know they weren't nowhere near this jail when you say they was killed tryin' to break us outta here. So where were they? And where were you and Ben Savage? That's what I'd like to know."

"I expect Ben Savage was at the Lost Coyote, and I was makin' my last check of the town before I came back here, hopin' that no-good brother of yours wasn't tryin' to slip up behind me, like the back-shooter he was. Now get movin'!"

Finally, Jack Ramsey said, "Come on, Reese, let's get this damn trial over with. You're just makin' it harder on yourself."

When they walked out on the street, they found Paul Hogan waiting to walk with them to the Lost Coyote. With pencil and notebook in hand he started to walk up beside Reese, prompting Clem Douglas to draw his weapon and Mack to issue a warning. "Back off, Paul! Don't walk too close to the prisoner."

"I just wondered if he wanted to give me his thoughts on being tried for bank robbery," Paul said.

"Paul's the owner of a monthly newspaper," Mack explained to Clem. "He's the owner, the reporter, and the pressman for the *Buzzard's Bluff Banner*." Back to Paul then, he said, "They'll still be here after the trial. You can come to the jail to talk to 'em. Anything he's got to say right now might not be fit to print in your newspaper, anyway."

Paul backed away, but he called out to Reese. "Do you have anything to say about that, Mr. Salter?"

Reese's answer was less than kind and laced with colorful whorehouse language. "I told you so," Mack said. Paul retreated to the courtroom to report on the actual trial as conducted by the Honorable Willard P. Gardener.

Once the prisoners were inside and seated in the chairs designated for them, Ben came out of the kitchen, where he had been drinking coffee with Rachel and Annie. He went over to the witness section and sat down with Jim Bowden, Henry Barnes, Lawton Grier, and his two tellers from the bank. At nine o'clock, Judge Gardener, dressed in his official robe, came in from the office to take his place behind the wooden box on the middle table. Ralph Bell called for all to rise, and he announced that the trial was officially open.

Judge Gardener took a long look with a critical eye at the defendants before he began. But true to his reputation, once he got started, he charged straight ahead. He called out their names, "Reese Salter, Jack Ramsey, Calvin Cobb." Both Reese and Jack looked at Shorty, never having heard his given name before. Shorty just shrugged in response, as the judge continued. "You three have been charged with the attempted robbery of the First Bank of Buzzard's Bluff. How do you plea, Mr. Salter?"

"Not guilty."

"Mr. Ramsey?"

"Not guilty."

"Mr. Cobb?"

"Not guilty."

"Very well," Gardener said. "Sheriff, call your first witness."

"Your Honor, the prosecution calls Mr. Lawton Grier to the stand." The judge questioned the bank president briefly, and Grier explained in detail how the three men, along with a fourth, who was killed when he tried to shoot Ben Savage, came into his bank with guns drawn, demanding money. The judge called one of the tellers up to testify, and he said it happened just like Grier said it did. Then Gardener asked the rest of the witnesses as a group if they agreed that it happened that way. They all did.

"Your Honor!" Reese blurted. "It was a trap! They were set up, waitin' for us."

"Is that your defense, Mr. Salter?" Gardener asked.

"Why, I don't . . ." He stumbled. "I reckon it is."

"Very well, I'm ready to rule on this case. In the case of the First Bank of Buzzard's Bluff against the defendants, Reese Salter, Jack Ramsey, and Calvin Cobb, I find the defendants guilty as charged, and I sentence them to ten years incarceration in the Huntsville Unit of the Texas State Prison System. Court dismissed." He looked at Ben then and said, "You can open your bar now."

"You call that a trial?" Reese yelled when the judge turned and walked back to the office to get out of his robe. Reese looked at Mack then and said, "What the hell did you drag us over here for?"

"I thought you'd enjoy a little walk," Mack answered. "Get you a little exercise, work up an appetite for your dinner. I reckon we'll take you back now, if you're really homesick."

After Mack and the two deputy marshals marched the prisoners back to their cell, which had been thoroughly cleaned by Horace while it was empty, Mack and the deputies came back to the Lost Coyote. They arrived to find His Honor, the Judge, having a cup of coffee with Ben and Rachel. When he saw them come in the saloon, he called them back to the table. "It went about like I expected," he told them. "So, I see no reason why we can't get started back to Waco this afternoon." Both deputies tried to hide the look of disappointment on their faces. "I think we should try to put the saloon back to the way we found it. Then you should have time to get the horses packed up and ready to go, and we'll eat dinner at the hotel after we check out. Then we'll be on our way. Do you see any problem with that?"

"No, sir," Clem answered. "We'll need to pick up some more flour and coffee for the trip back. I think everything else is okay."

"If it'll help," Ben suggested, "Tiny and I can take care of puttin' the room back the way it was."

"That would be a help," the judge said. "We'd appreciate it."

"I was wonderin', sir," Mack asked, "will you be sendin' a jail wagon to pick up my prisoners when you get back to Waco?"

"No," the judge replied. "That's not under my authority. The U. S. Marshal handles prisoner transportation. But that won't come from Waco, anyway. The jail wagon will be sent from the Huntsville Unit, since that's where they'll be serving their time."

"Well, that makes sense," Mack said. "I forgot about that. I just wish I knew how much longer I'm gonna be stuck with those three."

Rachel tended bar while Tiny helped Ben put the saloon back in its proper order in plenty of time for the modest dinner crowd that customarily ate Annie Grey's cooking. Ben was invited to join the judge and the two deputy marshals for dinner at the hotel dining room, but he decided to stay and eat at the Lost Coyote. It always pleased Annie when he opted for her cooking over that of Myrtle Johnson's. Ben was talking at the bar with Ham Greeley and Jim Bowden when Lucas Blaine came in the saloon. Seeing Ben at the bar, he walked over. "John," Ben greeted him, still not sure if Lucas was still trying to keep his real name to himself or not.

"Howdy, Ben," Lucas returned and nodded politely to Ham and Jim. "Can I talk to you a minute? If I ain't disturbin' your conversation here."

"Sure," Ben replied. "Come on back by the kitchen. It's almost time to eat dinner." He led him back to the table he and Rachel usually shared.

"Actually, I oughta talk to Rachel, too, if she's around."

"She's right there in the kitchen," Ben said. "Sit down and I'll get her." He went into the kitchen where Rachel was helping Annie get dinner ready. "Rachel, can you turn loose here for a minute? Lucas Blaine is out there, and he wants to talk to both of us. He kinda acts like it's important."

"He does? Well let's go see what's on that young man's mind. He's about due to tell us something good is happening with him and Caroline." She looked at Annie. "Do you need me to help you finish those potatoes?"

"No, scat, you're mostly in my way, anyway," Annie teased.

They went back outside the kitchen, and Rachel greeted Lucas warmly. "How have you been doing, Lucas? Ben told me you built yourself a little cabin down a-ways from the church."

"That's right, I did," Lucas said. "It's just a little temporary shack to keep me out of the rain. I never meant for it to be a permanent cabin."

"Ben said you wanted to talk to us about something. Is anything wrong?"

"No, ma'am, nothin's wrong," he said. "I just thought I'd like to tell you some good news. At least, it's good news to me. I've decided to buy that wagon and that team of horses back from Henry Barnes."

"Does that mean what I think it means?" Rachel gushed.

"Yes, ma'am, it surely does. Caroline and I have been seein' a lot more of each other the last couple of days. And I've gotten to know my son, and I think he actually likes me now. So the plans we made to leave Texas are back on again. We'll be leavin' here in a day or two."

Nothing could have pleased Rachel more. "Oh, Lucas," she said, "that's about the best news I could have heard all day. I'm so happy that you and Caroline worked it all out. Have you settled it peacefully with Marva and the preacher?"

"Yep, Marva's okay with it, and the preacher even gave us his blessing," Lucas answered. "I just wanted to come by and let you folks know about it, and to thank you for helpin' me get back with Caroline."

"Well, you certainly have my blessing, as well," Rachel said. "I just wish you two, and Tommy, of course, the best of luck in finding your new home."

Ben grinned and shook Lucas' hand. "I reckon you can have my blessin', too. I can't think of no other use for it."

"Are you going to stay and have dinner with us?" Rachel asked.

"No, I reckon not. Caroline's fixin' dinner for us back at the parsonage. So, I expect I'd best drive my new wagon back pretty quick." He grinned at the thought of it.

"I'll walk out with you," Ben said. They got up from the table and walked out the front door where Ben saw the wagon at the hitching rail. "It looks like it's ready to make the trip. Gotcha a canvas cover and everything. You make the ribs for that canvas?"

"No, Jim Bowden made those and attached them to the wagon. Everybody's been real nice about helpin' us. I wouldn'ta been surprised if Henry Barnes had charged me double for the horses and the wagon, after I backed out of the first sale, but he didn't."

"Well, you made a lot of friends here in the short time you've been with us," Ben told him. He stepped back when Lucas climbed up onto the wagon seat. "Good luck to ya," he said as Lucas pulled his wagon out into the street, his saddled buckskin tied on behind it. *Well, I reckon that's the happy ending for that story,* he thought, and turned to go back inside.

Rachel was waiting for him when he came back inside. "What's the matter with you?" He asked because of the deep frown she was wearing. "Did Annie burn the biscuits?"

She ignored his attempt at humor. "When you and Lucas left, I went in the kitchen to ask Annie if she didn't want to wish Lucas a safe trip to a new home. She made that face of hers and turned away trying to keep me from seeing it. Ben, she's got one of her feelings about Lucas. I know she has."

This was not what Ben wanted to hear. "Now, Rachel, you don't know that for sure. She mighta been havin' a cramp or something."

"She wasn't having any cramp," Rachel insisted. "She feels something bad is going to happen to Lucas or Caroline, or both of them."

"Even if what you say is true, it doesn't necessarily

mean something drastic is gonna happen to him. It just means she thinks he's gonna have some trouble. Just like when she had a feelin' about Mack. And he had some trouble, but he wasn't killed or wounded. And that's if you really believe in that kind of stuff, which I ain't sure I ever could."

"I don't know why I bothered telling you about it," she told him, and started walking toward the kitchen. Then she stopped after taking a few steps, for one more comment. "And as far as that thing with Mack, I should remind you that you got to thinking about her feeling that night, so you went looking for Mack. And if you hadn't, Mack would be dead." Then she spun on her heel and went to the kitchen.

Well, she's got me there, he thought. *But I still don't believe it.*

Rachel came back to the kitchen door again and asked, "Are you ready to eat?"

"Yessum," he replied, "I surely am. What are we havin'?"

"Ham," she said, "but I told her to fix crow for you."

He was still sitting at the table, drinking coffee, when Tuck walked in the front door and announced, "The judge and his party are leavin' now. Goin' back to Waco."

"You heard the town crier," Ben said, then got up from the table to go and give Judge Gardener a word of thanks. Out in the street, he saw the judge's party coming up the street and Mack following along behind them. When the judge reached the Lost Coyote, Ben stepped out into the street and thanked him for his service and wished them a comfortable journey back to Waco.

"It was good to see you again, Savage," the judge responded. "Thank you again for your hospitality." Both deputy marshals gave him a two-finger salute to the brims of their hats.

Mack walked up behind them and commented to Ben. "There he goes, Wild Will Gardener. The only thing wrong is he didn't take Reese Salter and his partners with him."

"Yep," Ben said. "I reckon we can get back to normal now."

CHAPTER 20

It was mid-morning of the following day when Tuck Tucker announced the departure of the next important party to leave Buzzard's Bluff. Tuck took time out from his shop to inform his friends at the Lost Coyote that the famous fast-draw gunman, Lucas Blaine was leaving town. He had Caroline Carter and her son with him, and judging by his covered wagon, it appeared he was going for good.

As he had the day before, Ben walked out to wish them well. This time Rachel came with him. Caroline was on the seat beside Lucas and five-year-old Tommy was sitting on Lucas' buckskin horse, which was tied to the wagon along with his packhorse. Caroline and Lucas were all smiles as he pulled the wagon to a stop. "Well, we're on our way," Lucas said. "A little later start than I planned, but we don't care, we're not in a hurry." Caroline thanked them for their help in getting their family back together.

"My goodness," Rachel protested. "We didn't do an awful lot for you."

"Have you figured out where you're headed?" Ben asked.

"To be honest with you, not exactly," Lucas said. "I'm thinkin' about Colorado or maybe Montana. We're just gonna go up through Waco and take that trail north up through Indian Territory, up into Kansas before we turn west. I reckon we'll just ride till we come to a spot we like and then we'll make it our home."

"My goodness," Rachel said again. "That sounds like quite an undertaking. Are you sure you're up to it?"

Caroline laughed and answered, "I'm sure I'm up to it. As long as I've got my two men with me. One thing I know for sure is it'll be a whole lot better than the past five years without both of them."

"We'd best not hold 'em up any longer," Ben said. He reached up and shook Lucas' hand when it was offered. "Take care of yourself and your family, young man."

"You can count on it," Lucas said, and he started his wagon off again.

Ben and Rachel stood and watched them ride out the north end of town on the road to Waco. "I don't know," Rachel speculated. "That's a big undertaking. I hope they're up to it."

"Lucas is a good man," Ben replied. "I think they'll make it."

Nate Castor was beginning to lose his patience. "How much farther is this damn town?" he asked his horse. "That scaly little runt put me on the wrong road," he complained, referring to Harley Clackum. "If there ain't no Buzzard's Bluff at the end of this road, I'll track him down and kill him!" He was going to have to stop and rest his horse before very much longer, and he was hungry. He had been hoping he would strike the town before he had to rest his horses. The flea-bitten gray gelding had cost him a good bit of money, but he thought he had to have it. It suited his style more than any other horse, just as his black coat and trousers fit his personality. He considered himself walking death and when he wore black, from his flat-crown, medium-width-brim black hat, to his black boots, he thought that he could feel the strength they created.

Reluctantly, he decided to rest his horses at the next stream or creek he came to, when he saw the wagon approaching him. It was a man and a woman driving a covered wagon, two horses tied on behind with a kid sitting on one of them. They were the first people he had met on the road since he left his camp this morning. When they met, he pulled the flea-bitten gray to a stop, so they stopped as well. "I ain't got no idea if the fool who told me how to get there told me right or not," he blurted. "Is there a town down this road somewhere?"

"Sure is," Lucas answered. "You're almost there, about three miles, I'd say."

"What's the name of it?" Nate asked.

"Buzzard's Bluff," Lucas said.

"Is there any place to eat there?"

"Three places," Lucas answered. "Hotel's got a dinin' room that's good, or you can get some dinner at the Lost Coyote Saloon. The Golden Rail serves a wilder crowd."

"Obliged," Nate said and wheeled his horse away to continue down the road. Three miles, he was thinking. I'll water 'em there and get myself somethin' to eat.

"Well, he was a real charmer, wasn't he?" Caroline remarked. "Maybe he's just having a bad day."

"He looked like the kind of man who specializes in givin' somebody else a bad day," Lucas said. "Take a look back of the wagon and see if our son is still there."

She laughed and said, "That's right, he did say he was hungry."

* * *

Nate was about to curse the man in the wagon for giving him the wrong distance to Buzzard's Bluff, when the road took a sharp curve and, suddenly, he was looking down the main street. "Good, that's handy," he muttered to himself when he saw the stable on his right. He guided the weary gelding toward it. "I need to rest my horses and water 'em while I go get somethin' to eat," he said to Henry Barnes when Henry walked out to meet him.

"Fix ya right up," Henry said. "You wantin' to keep 'em here overnight, or just long enough for you to get somethin' to eat?"

"I said water 'em and let 'em rest. Are you hard of hearing? You've got a corral, and yonder's a waterin' trough at the other end of it. What are you trying to take me for, grandpa?"

"I ain't tryin' to take you for nothin'," Henry told him. "I'm trying to save you money. Yonder's the river." He turned and pointed to it. "And there's plenty of grass to graze on. Won't cost you a dime. If you leave the horses here, I'll have to take care of 'em and be sure they get enough time at the trough between the other horses in there. If you want me to give 'em some grain, I'll charge you for that. So, if you're figurin' on bein' gone just long enough to eat dinner, I charge twenty-five cents for each horse. If I feed 'em grain, that's another twenty-five cents. It would just save you money to hobble your horses over there by the river and spend that money to feed yourself and have a drink of likker."

Nate just stood there gaping at Henry for a few moments, trying to make up his mind how he was going to respond. Finally, he decided. "Is everybody in this town as crazy as you?"

"It'd be about half and half, I'd say," Henry answered.

"Like I said when I came in here, I'm gonna leave my horses here while I'm in town. I ain't sure how long that'll be. But I want 'em watered and give 'em a portion of grain. I want the saddle and the packs took off and put where nobody can bother 'em. I'll pay you what I owe you when I'm ready to leave. My name's Nate Castor. You heard of it?"

"Why, no, right off hand, I can't say as I have," Henry answered a little more concerned than he was.

"I expect that you will," Nate said. "What's your name?"

"I'm Henry Barnes."

"Good. I'll know what name to put on the headstone if you screw my horses up." He took the gray's reins and whipped them across Henry's wrists, turned and walked down the street.

The place to find anybody in a strange town is the saloon and he remembered the name of one the couple in the wagon had mentioned. It was the first saloon he came to, the Lost Coyote. He chuckled at the thought, *maybe it'll be the place where I find my coyote.* He paused at the swinging batwing doors to take a look inside before he walked in. Seeing nothing that posed a problem for him, he walked on inside, directly to the bar. He took a look at Tiny and said, "Damned if you ain't a big target. Whadda they call you, Tiny?"

"That's right," Tiny said, "what can I get you?"

Nate stepped back and looked right and left as if making sure. "This is a bar, ain't it? How 'bout whiskey?"

Tiny wasn't amused. He poured the whiskey and said, "Two bits."

"Let's see if it's worth it first," Nate said and tossed the whiskey back. He reached in his pocket, pulled out a quarter and tossed it on the bar. "Say, Tiny, I'm lookin' for a fellow I'm supposed to meet here. His name's Lucas Blaine. You seen him today?"

Tiny was immediately alert. "Lucas Blaine," he repeated. "Don't recollect anybody by that name in here. Was it this saloon he was supposed to meet you at? Mighta been the Golden Rail. It's right down the street." He was sure Lucas didn't frequent the Golden Rail, so he thought it would be a lot better for this gunman to be sitting around there, instead of asking people in the Lost Coyote. And he was certain the man was a fast gun, seeking a reputation.

"Maybe I'll check there later, but some folks I was talking to said I could get some dinner here, so I'll do that while I'm here. Who do I tell to get me something to eat?"

Damn! Tiny thought, not sure what to do. "I do that," he said, not wanting to seem like he was stalling. "Have a seat at one of the tables, and I'll go tell the cook to fix you a plate." Nate turned around and looked at the tables, then walked over and sat down at one against the wall. "I'll tell the cook," Tiny said again and went to the kitchen. Ben was sitting at his usual table by the kitchen door. He looked up when he saw Tiny coming toward him. But instead of going to Ben's table, he motioned frantically with his head and went into the kitchen.

Ben got up as casually as he could affect and went in behind him. "What is it, Tiny?"

"That fellow out there at a table came in here lookin' for Lucas!" He turned quickly to Annie and said, "Fix him a plate of food, I forgot to ask him what he wants to drink with it." Back to Ben then, "He said Lucas was supposed to meet him here. You take one look at him and tell me he ain't one of those fast-draw gunmen. I told him I'd never heard of anybody named Lucas Blaine. I don't know if he believed me or not." He looked frantically back and forth at Annie and Ben. "I told him he mighta meant the Golden Rail."

"You did the right thing," Ben told him. "We'll just try to keep him here as long as we can to give Lucas as much head start as we can. As long as he doesn't know they've left town, Lucas and Caroline have a pretty good chance of getting away. You go on back to the bar. I'll go talk to this fellow." He took the plate of food Annie had fixed and went out the door after Tiny. He walked over to the table, and when Nate saw him coming toward him, he immediately dropped his hand on the handle of his pistol. "Here you go," Ben called out, "one plate of beef and potatoes."

"Who the hell are you?" Nate asked, a little concerned about the size of the man confronting him.

"I'm Ben Savage. I'm the owner. Tiny forgot to ask you what you wanted to drink. I'd guess coffee. Am I right?"

"Yeah, I'll take coffee," Nate said. "I'm looking for a friend of mine. Maybe he comes in here, Lucas Blaine."

"Who?" Ben asked.

"Lucas Blaine," Nate repeated.

Ben paused and acted like he was trying to remember. "Don't recall anybody by that name. You sure you got the name right?" When Nate started to show a little irritation, Ben quickly said, "I reckon if he's a friend of yours, you oughta know his name. I'll bring you some coffee." He turned and went back to the kitchen.

Rachel was in the kitchen when he got back. "Annie told me," she said when Ben walked in. "What are you going to do?"

"Take him a cup of coffee," Ben answered with a look of disbelief.

"No, you know what I mean. What are you going to do about him looking for Lucas?"

"Nothing I can do," Ben told her. "Whadda you think I oughta do? Go get Mack to run him outta town? Shoot him, myself? What? The only thing he's done so far is lie about being a friend of Lucas', and without Lucas here to deny it, we ain't sure if that's a lie or not. Even if he is here to challenge Lucas, if Lucas refuses to face him, and the man goes away, there ain't nothing for Mack to arrest him for. That's why the best thing we can do is keep him here, so Lucas gets way to hell away from here. Because, without any witnesses, he likely won't give Lucas any choice. He'll kill him if he doesn't fight."

"Damn," Rachel responded. "I see what you mean." She thought hard about the problem for a minute, then repeated her swear word. Then she said, "Let me take him his coffee."

"Suit yourself," Ben said. He was tempted to suggest that they send Annie out with the coffee. Then, if her face didn't get all screwed up in one of her expressions, maybe that would indicate the man wasn't as bad as he looked. But he thought better of the idea when he thought how Annie and Rachel might react to it.

Rachel picked up the cup of coffee Ben had just poured and took it to the table where Nate was already busy with his knife and fork. He looked up at her when she placed the cup on the table. "Looks like you've already gotten a good start on your dinner. How's the food?"

"Better'n I expected," was his gruff answer. Then he asked, "Who are you?"

"I'm the owner," she answered.

"The big feller over there said he was the owner."

"He is," she said. "We both are. We're partners in this

business. And we want to be sure when a new customer comes in, he gets treated right. So you just enjoy your dinner, and if you need more coffee, just hold up your cup. One of us will see it."

She turned to leave, but he asked quickly, hoping to catch her off guard, if they were playing dumb with him, "How often does Lucas Blaine come in here?"

She stopped and asked, "Who?" He repeated the name and she pretended to be searching her memory. "I'm afraid I don't know anyone by that name. Is he someone important?"

"Never mind," he said, returning to his gruff manner, convinced by then that Blaine must not have been here, or if he was, he was using another name. He decided to try the other saloon when he finished his dinner. The folks in the wagon seemed to think it attracted the wilder crowd of customers. He figured he should have looked there first, but this food was good, so he was glad he came here. Rachel returned to the kitchen.

"I don't think we've made a mistake," she told Ben and Annie. "He looks like pure evil." She stood inside the door just far enough to see his table without giving him a clear sight of her watching him. In a couple of minutes, his hand went up with his coffee cup. "He wants more coffee," she said and turned to come get the pot.

"Let me get it," Ben said. By now, it had almost become a game to see how long they could delay his departure. He picked up the coffeepot and went out the door. When he filled the cup, he asked, "Everything all right? Is that grub worth a quarter?"

Nate belched loudly. "It's all right."

"You know," Ben started. "Maybe that fellow you're lookin' for might show up lookin' for you after you leave here. Maybe you beat him here. Why don't you tell me your name, and if he comes in here, we'll know what to tell him."

Nate favored him with a patient smile, thinking, *so you can run down the street to that jailhouse and see if the sheriff's got any papers on me.* He knew he didn't have, so he said, "My name's Nate Castor."

"Nate Castor," Ben repeated, and pretended to think for a moment. "That name sounds familiar for some reason. Nate Castor," he repeated. "Have you been in here before?"

Nate couldn't help the feeling of pride he felt from the thought of his name being known in this out-of-the-way town. "Nah, I never been here before."

"Maybe it'll come to me where I heard it," Ben said. "Anyway, I'll remember Nate Castor, and if anybody comes in looking for you, I'll know who it is." He started to leave but stopped again. "What should I tell him? Are you gonna be in town a while?"

Nate answered honestly. "I ain't gonna spend but a day in this town. If I don't find him by tonight, I'm leavin' in the mornin'." *And then I'm gonna go back to Hutto's Station and find that little rat that sent me all the way down here for nothing,* he thought.

Ben went back into the kitchen to let Rachel know he was going to the sheriff's office to look through Mack's files for any paper on Nate Castor. "If there is anything, that'll solve our problem. Mack can arrest him and let him get to know Reese and his partners."

"He looks like he'd be good company for them," Rachel said.

Ben went out the back door, so Nate wouldn't know what he was doing. When he got to the jail, he explained to Mack what was going on at the Lost Coyote. "Let's take a look at your file to see if you've got anything for Nate Castor."

"Well, I know I ain't got nothin' recently on that name," Mack said as he took a large box out of his lower desk drawer. "I got everything in this box I've received in the last two years. I burned everything earlier than that. Here," he said and handed Ben half of them. They went through them page by page. "I shoulda done this earlier," he remarked when he started pulling out pages on suspects who had been caught or killed. It took some time, and it was to no avail, so Ben went back to the Coyote to report to Rachel that the search was unsuccessful.

He went back out into the barroom in time to see Nate gulping down the last swallows of his coffee, already on his feet, preparing to leave. Ben walked over to the bar to wait for him to come settle up with Tiny. When he did, Ben said, "I hope you feel like you got your money's worth, Mr. Castor. We're gonna remember your name, in case that Blaine fellow shows up lookin' for you."

"Yeah, you do that," Nate remarked. "Tell him it's a funeral party he won't wanna miss." He put the money on the bar for his dinner.

"You want a shot of whiskey to settle that dinner you just finished?" Ben asked.

"I'll get that at the Golden Rail," Nate answered, and turned to leave.

CHAPTER 21

Ben and Tiny watched him as he walked out the door and turned toward the Golden Rail. "I reckon that's about as long as we could expect to delay him. I doubt he'll get much more help at the Golden Rail than he did here. I don't think Lucas ever went in the Golden Rail."

"He told me he was there once," Tiny said, "but briefly. It was when he first got to town and he was looking for information on Caroline."

They stood there talking for a few minutes when they spotted a familiar hat and head just above the middle of the batwing doors of the saloon. "I reckon it is about time for Tuck to show up," Tiny remarked. But he didn't come in. They could see that he had turned in the direction of the Golden Rail, but he was still in front of the door.

"Oh, hell," Ben blurted, but it was too late, for Nate Castor appeared in front of the door then, and they were obviously having some conversation. It didn't last very long, however, and Tuck pushed on through the batwing doors to stand looking around the saloon to see if Ham Greeley was already there. "Tuck," Ben called out. "What did you say to that fellow?"

"Who?" Tuck responded and walked over to Ben and Tiny at the bar.

"The man you were just talkin' to outside the front door," Ben said.

"Oh, him. He wanted to know if I knew Lucas Blaine. He said he was looking for him. I told him, sure I know Lucas, but you just missed him. I told him Lucas and his lovely wife, and their little boy just drove a wagon outta town this morning on the road to Waco." He laughed and added, "Boy, if that didn't light a fire in his tail. He took off, didn't say another word." He paused then when he saw the looks of horror on the faces of Ben and Tiny. "What?"

"The one thing I didn't take care of," Ben said to Tiny, referring to Tuck.

"What's that, Ben?" Tuck responded. "What thing didn't you . . . ?"

That was as far as he got before Tiny pulled him away from Ben. "Never mind, Tuck, don't bother Ben right now. It might not be good for your health." Ben turned and went back to tell Rachel he had to go somewhere, and he didn't know how long he would be gone.

"What?" Rachel responded in panic, seeing the look on his face. "Where are you going?"

"Tiny will tell you. I haven't got time right now to talk. Don't worry." He rushed back to his room to get the things he knew he might need for what he had to do. But Rachel was not going to settle for no explanation. She followed him to his room where she found him shoving things into his saddlebags.

"You're going to do something that's liable to get you killed again, aren't you?" she demanded. "Something you should let Mack handle, I bet. Ben, tell me what's happened."

He realized that she had a right to a full explanation.

She was his partner. So he stopped and told her that their little delaying game had worked well, but Tuck blew it all up in about ten minutes worth of conversation with Nate Castor, just a little while ago. "He not only told Castor that Lucas had been here. He told him that Lucas and Caroline and Tommy were on a wagon and told him they were on the road to Waco. Now, do you see why I've got to go? I've got to try to stop Castor before he catches up to that wagon, if I can. I don't want Lucas to make that decision if Castor catches up with them."

"Don't you think the sheriff should be doing this instead of you?" Rachel asked.

"It's really not the business of the sheriff's office at this point," Ben said as he picked up his rifle after strapping on his gun belt. "I feel like it's my responsibility, since we had a big hand in gettin' those two together again. You understand that, don't you?"

"I guess I understand the way you feel about it," she relented. "You be careful, that man looks like Satan, himself. And I don't want to run this place by myself."

They walked back out into the hall and found Annie waiting for them, holding something tied up in a dish towel. "I don't know how long you're gonna be gone. You take these biscuits left over from dinner. They'll at least fill your belly."

"Thanks, Annie, I'm sure I'll be glad I've got 'em. I've got some things in my packs at the stable I might be able to add to 'em. I'd best get going now, he's already got a head start." When he got outside, he looked up and down the street. He didn't remember seeing any horses tied out front, so he was thinking Nate's horses were probably at the stable. He assumed he had a packhorse, and he was counting on him having to take the time to load the packs on the horse again, as well as having to saddle his riding horse. When he ran up to the stable, he saw no sign of Nate Castor.

Henry was back in the stalls, and when he saw Ben run in, he called out, "I'm back here, Ben. You needing Cousin? I just gave him some oats." He walked out into the alleyway between the stalls, carrying the empty bucket. When he saw Ben with his rifle and saddlebags, he asked, "You fixin' to go bear huntin'?"

"You could call it that, I reckon," Ben said. "Did a fellow just ride outta here in a big hurry?"

"Sure did," Henry said, "'bout a half hour ago, maybe more'n that. He was in a helluva big hurry, even left his packhorse here. Said he'd come back to get him. He didn't have time to load him all up. I told him I'd help him, but he said he didn't have time right then to do it. Said he didn't wanna fool with a packhorse, anyway. I asked him who he was tryin' to catch, and he said it was none of my business."

That was disappointing news to Ben. He had really hoped he was going to catch up with him while he was still in the process of loading his packhorse. Now, Castor had a sizable head start on him. And from the way Henry talked, he could assume that Castor was going to push his horse for every bit of speed it had. "What is he ridin'?" he asked Henry.

"One of them peculiar-lookin' horses," Henry said, "a flea-bitten gray."

"Did you hear that, Cousin?" Ben said to the dun gelding as he threw his saddle on him. "You ain't gonna let an old flea-bitten nag run off and leave you, are you?"

Henry heard him and felt like he had to say, "Them horses sell for a lotta money. That feller had to pay a lot for that horse, unless he stole him. Now that I think about that feller, I'd say he most likely stole him."

"We don't care how much he cost, do we, Cousin?" He

got his war bag from the packs he kept in the stable and put Annie's biscuits in it. He didn't take the time to look for anything else and hoped it wouldn't be necessary, anyway. He led the dun out of the stable, climbed aboard and started out at a fast lope. After about a quarter of a mile, he pulled Cousin back to a more forgiving lope, and he planned to alternate between the lope and walking. He figured that to be his best chance of overtaking Castor without breaking his horse down. He was counting heavily on Castor over-working his horse in his efforts to overtake the slow-moving wagon. Even if Lucas was driving a wagon, he had a sizable gap for Castor to close. There was a good chance Castor's horse might have to quit, if he held him to a fast pace for too long.

As he rode mile after mile with no sight of Nate Castor ahead of him on the road, it was hard not to become discouraged. He felt he had no choice but to continue his present pace. And he couldn't help but have thoughts that maybe Castor was not as dumb as he assumed, and he was alternating his horse's pace the same way. And they were merely maintaining the same gap between them, neither one gaining on the other. It was just something else to worry about because he knew it was inevitable that they would catch up to the wagon and Castor would get there before he would. He had one thing that could work in his favor, however, and that was the time Lucas and Caroline decided to stop for the night.

It was a better than even shot that Lucas would drive until darkness began to set in before he made his camp for the night. Then Ben could imagine a situation where Castor might catch up to them after dark, then he would catch up with Castor after that. At that point, it would depend upon Castor's pride. If he had no honor, he might simply try to murder Lucas and claim he met him face to face. If that was the case, Ben's only option would be to try to protect Lucas as best he could. That was, if he could get there in time. But he felt strongly that Castor would not try to bushwhack Lucas. Castor was unlikely to have any honor, but his ego was enough to make him think he could take Lucas in a fair contest. And this was his goal, to prove to the world, but also himself, that he was the fastest gun alive. For that reason, Ben believed that fate had taken a hand in this drama.

"Damn you sun!" Nate Castor roared as the last scarlet fingers of light played among the leaves of the trees, and the sun settled beneath the road far ahead with still no sight of the wagon. Nothing to do but keep his weary horse plodding along the road until he eventually came to their camp, and eventually he did. He almost passed it up in the heavy darkness that had now descended upon the land. When crossing a shallow stream, he almost missed the fact that there were no wagon tracks on the other side. To be sure, he had to stop and lean way down from the saddle. He wheeled the tired gray around without letting the horse drink from the stream, and he rode back a little way until he found where they had driven the wagon off the road into some pine trees. They probably parked the wagon close by the stream, he thought, but in the darkness he couldn't tell. As he sat on his horse staring at the grove of pines, he suddenly caught sight of a flicker of light and a spark rising in the trees here and there. He knew he had found their campfire.

The thought ran through his head that it would be so easy to sneak up on that camp and shoot all three of them.

Then he could simply take Blaine's gun belt and any other personal items as proof that he had bested him in a face-off. Rumor had it that Blaine carried a picture of his wife in his wallet, although he had not lived with her for years. That would do for proof, he thought. That would be the easiest way to gain his rightful place as the best. But he knew he would never be satisfied with a paper crown. It was best to have an eye witness to the contest, and that was what worried him. He was the best, and he knew he was faster than any man with a six-gun. "No, Mr. Lucas Blaine, you have a date with death when the sun comes up in the mornin'. And your wife and child will be left to verify that you were shot in a duel by Nate Castor, fair and square." This was why murder would not accomplish what he needed. With that settled, he would now find a spot for his camp.

When he came to the stream that crossed over the road, it occurred to Ben that it was the first sign of water he had come to for quite some time. He thought it a possibility that this might have been Lucas' thought, as well, prompting him to decide to camp there for the night. He crossed to the other side and dismounted. He saw at once that there were no wagon tracks on the far side of the stream, so Lucas must have decided that he wanted to camp on the near side. That fact was confirmed by the obvious tracks of the wagon turning off the road, even in the dark. But he noticed that, while there were no wagon tracks on the far side, there were tracks left by a single horse, telling Ben that Castor had decided to make his camp on the far side of the stream. It was decision time. Ben had to decide if he should ride on into Lucas' camp to alert him of the danger awaiting him. Or should he not make his presence known and lie in wait for Castor to make his move, and possibly take him out with a rifle shot when he showed signs of an outright murder. In that case, he would need to find where Castor was hiding tonight and take a position to watch that spot. And in the morning, it would be up to him to shoot Castor before Castor shot Lucas. The more he thought about it, the more he was persuaded to think he should alert Lucas tonight, so he could make sure Caroline and Tommy were in a safe place, if bullets started flying in the morning. That was best, he decided.

With the decision made, the next thing to do was to find Lucas' camp. Like Castor, he saw the sparks from the campfire, so he knew approximately where the camp was. He took Cousin's reins in hand and led him off the road where the wagon had left it. He walked through the pine trees until he saw the dark form of the wagon and the fire on the other side of it. He continued toward it until he caught sight of movement between the fire and the wagon and knew it was Lucas or Caroline moving about the fire. He continued to approach the camp until Lucas' horses became aware of Cousin's presence and inquired with a whinny. Lucas became immediately alert and told Caroline and Tommy to get back by the wagon. Then he walked out of the firelight to the edge of darkness. Close enough now to be heard without calling out too loudly, Ben had to be concerned with Lucas' reputation as a fast gun. Using a medium-sized pine for protection against any automatic reaction, he called out softly, "Lucas." In an instant, Lucas drew his gun and turned in Ben's direction. "Lucas," Ben called again. "It's me, Ben Savage, don't shoot."

"Ben?" Lucas asked, astonished, but he didn't holster his .45. "What are you doin' here?"

"I had to find you to warn you," Ben answered.

"Come out where I can see you," Lucas said.

"All right, but don't shoot me." Ben stepped out from behind the tree and walked up to the edge of the firelight.

Lucas holstered his gun. "I'm sorry, Ben, but I had to be sure it was you. Caroline and the boy . . ." He started but was too embarrassed to finish.

"I know," Ben said. "I'm glad to see you ain't takin' no chances. I'm sorry I had to come find you, but I had to tell you I ain't the only one hidin' out here in the dark."

"What are you talking about?" Lucas responded, at once alarmed.

"Do you know of a man named Nate Castor?"

"Nate Castor?" Lucas repeated. "No." He turned around when he heard Caroline call from the wagon. "It's Ben Savage, honey. He came to find us."

Caroline came to them immediately. "Ben, what is it? What's wrong?"

"I'm awful sorry to have to find you to bring you bad news, but it's important that you know you've got some trouble, and I've come to help you, if I can."

"Who's Nate Castor?" Lucas asked, already pretty sure what Ben was going to say.

Ben proceeded to tell them about the sudden appearance of Nate Castor in Buzzard's Bluff soon after they had left. He told them that Castor had said he had come to town to meet Lucas and how they had played their game with him in order to delay him as long as they could. Lucas interrupted when he asked, "What kind of horse was he ridin'?" When Ben said he rode a flea-bitten gray, Lucas said, "We met that fellow about three miles north of town. We told him how far it was to Buzzard's Bluff."

"Oh, Dear Lord," Caroline sighed, fully aware of what

was taking place. "I remember thinking I was glad that man was going in the opposite direction."

"I'm sorry, but I think he's found you," Ben said. "Our little game we played was working fine until he ran into Tuck Tucker. Tuck didn't know what was going on, and he told him everything he needed to know. It's my honest opinion that Castor is waiting to call you out when it's light enough to see, but I wouldn't expose myself to a rifle shot. Your life means nothing to him. It's your title he wants, your reputation, and the only way he can get it is to beat you in a face-off. And he figures he has Caroline and Tommy to verify that it was a fair fight. So at least he has no reason to harm either of them."

"Oh, wonderful," Caroline groaned sarcastically. "That makes me feel so much better."

"I'm sorry, Caroline," Ben apologized again. "I was hopin' I'd catch him before he caught you, but he had too much of a start on me."

"I appreciate the trouble you took to warn us, Ben," Lucas said. "I'll be ready for whatever happens, now that I know. I expect you might want to go on back now while you still have the cover of darkness."

"Go back?" Ben responded, surprised. "Why would I wanna go back? I came to help you."

"How?" Lucas asked.

"Any way I can to keep him from shootin' you, if you refuse to face him," Ben explained. "I figure you gave up that part of your life, and when you tell him that, he's gonna threaten to shoot you if you don't face him. I don't aim to let him do that."

"Like I said," Lucas replied, "you're a good friend. And I don't wanna put you in a position where you might have to kill a man that you ain't even got an argument with. And

I'd feel twice as bad if something happened to you. I know you were a Texas Ranger for a long time, but I can handle this myself."

Ben was at a complete loss when confronted by the surprising attitude Lucas had taken. He felt like he had just politely been told that he was trying to stick his nose in somebody else's business. Up to now, he had looked at Lucas as a very levelheaded young man. Maybe he was wrong. Maybe Lucas was not sincere when he claimed he wanted to escape his name and reputation. He thought for a moment before he responded. "Well, I rode a long way to catch up with you. My horse is tired, so I need to let him rest and graze a little. Is it all right with you if I hang around to see what happens, so I can tell the folks back in Buzzard's Bluff? There's some folks back there who care about you and Caroline and Tommy. I'll not get in the way of whatever you decide to do unless you ask me for help. Then if things don't go the way you expect, I'll drive your wife and son back home for you. Fair enough?"

Lucas laughed. "Fair enough," he said.

Caroline wasn't quite sure what she should make of the conversation she had overheard. Like Ben, she thought at first that Lucas was asking Ben to leave, and that didn't make sense. He walked away, but came right back, leading his horse, so he was staying. *Good,* she thought. He led the dun gelding over by the stream with their horses and took the saddle off. When he came back from the stream, he was carrying his rifle and a cloth tied up to form a little bag. It occurred to her that he had had no supper, and she had saved nothing from theirs. She promptly apologized for it and offered to fix him something.

"No, thank you very much, but I've got a little sack of biscuits Annie gave me when I left the Coyote. Although, if there's anything left in that coffeepot, I'd be obliged to have a shot of that."

"You're in luck," she said, "there's a tad left, but I expect it's strong enough by now to raise blisters on a turtle's back."

"The stronger, the better," he said. He sat down out of the firelight and untied Annie's biscuits and was surprised to find a little slice of ham in each one. It brought a little smile to his face, even in the uncertain conditions he found himself.

CHAPTER 22

The night was passed peaceful enough, considering the ominous threat awaiting in the dark forest on the other side of the stream. Lucas put his wife and son to bed inside the wagon while he slept under the wagon in his bedroll. Ben positioned his bedroll on the opposite side of the fire from the wagon, between two trees. It was questionable if the two men were able to get an hour's sleep between them. Toward the early hours of the morning, it was hardest to stay awake, even though they were both convinced by then that Castor was not going to show until daylight. When daylight finally came to the stream, both men were out of their blankets and began the chores of packing up to get on the road again. There was no sign of Nate Castor, so there was no reason to wait. Lucas hitched up the horses, Ben saddled Cousin, all the while scanning the woods around them with sleepy eyes. Still, there was no sign of Castor. He was just beginning to think he had been mistaken when the call came directly from a clump of willows on the opposite side of the stream. "Lucas Blaine," the call caused the flutter of leaves as some small birds were startled into flight. "Lucas Blaine," the voice came again hoarse and strong. "You have somethin' that belongs to me. I've come to get it. I'll wait for you to come out in that clearin' to the right of your wagon, and we'll settle it man to man."

"Castor," Ben called back to him. "Lucas isn't in that business anymore. So go on your way and let these people alone."

"Who is that?" Castor demanded.

"Ben Savage, and I speak for Lucas and his family. Be on your way."

"So, Blaine, you bring somebody to protect you. I knew you were yellow. I shoulda shot you last night while you were settin' by the fire with your sweet little wife."

"Castor," Lucas called out then. "He speaks for himself. No man speaks for me. But what he says is true. I no longer fight these contests. I have no desire to kill you. So go away and live to challenge another man. I no longer play this game."

"You are yellow to the bone," Castor came back. "You'll not leave this place alive, and then I'll call on you, Ben Savage, for stickin' your nose where it don't belong."

"All right, Castor," Lucas said. "This is your last chance to see another day. I'll go to that clearing, my gun in my holster. If you know what's good for you, you'll go the other way."

"Lucas!" Caroline cried. "What are you doing? Don't do this! Ben! Stop him!"

"Ben," Lucas demanded, "stay out of this. I know what I'm doing." He didn't wait any longer but walked out into the clearing, and the first real rays of the sun began to light the sky above the trees. Ben saw that he had left him little choice, but he picked up his rifle and went to the edge of the clearing, still undecided if he was going to shoot Castor before he had a chance to draw his weapon. He decided he couldn't risk the chance that Lucas would be killed, so he stood ready to shoot.

Lucas, already in place, stood patiently waiting the arrival of Nate Castor, his feet planted squarely shoulder width apart, his arms hanging relaxed at his sides as he watched the willows on the other side of the stream. And then, Castor appeared, wading across the shallow water. When he got to the near side, he made a show of stomping his boots to rid them of water. Then, without warning, he drew his gun and fired a shot into the ground before doubling up from the bullet that ripped into his belly. Castor's sneaky attempt happened so fast that Ben had no time to raise his rifle and fire. Yet Lucas reacted faster than the blink of an eye. It was a reaction that Ben would never forget having witnessed. Lucas walked over to Castor who was doubled up in pain, but still trying to raise his pistol to shoot, so Lucas put him out of his pain with a round to the head. Ben walked over to join him. Lucas looked at him and said, "Now I'm finished with this business."

"Do you really mean that?" Ben asked. "You're the best I've ever seen."

"Yes, I mean it," he answered. "This is no way for a man to live. I have a wife and child. I want to live like a man who has a wife and child."

Ben could see the sad look of regret in the young man's eyes, and he knew that he meant what he said. "Then why don't you let me bury you here? You have taken a new name, you are on your way to new country. Let me bury Lucas Blaine right here on this lonely stream and let John Cochran and his family drive on to their new home. I'll take whatever personal possessions you can give up. How about your six-gun? Is there anything special about that?"

They were momentarily interrupted at that point when Caroline ran screaming joyously to throw her arms around Lucas, tears streaming down her face. Lucas calmed her for a few minutes. Then when she relaxed, Lucas told her, "Ben and I are killin' me right now." He drew his Colt .45 again, and holding it by the barrel, held it up to show Ben his name engraved on the handle.

"That would be perfect," Ben said. "Can you live without it?"

"Yeah. It's a good gun, but my spare is just as good. You can take it." When Ben asked if there was anything else, Lucas said, "Yeah, my belt buckle, the same fellow engraved my name on the back of it. But you have to look close to see it."

When Caroline realized what they were doing, she suggested something. "How about that terrible old picture of me you keep in your wallet? You should be glad to lose that." She looked at Ben and said, "I wrote on the back and signed my name."

"Good," Ben said. "I think we're gettin' enough evidence to make this work. I'll spread the word. Famous gunman, Lucas Blaine, gunned down by Nate Castor. Castor wanted to be famous, so he oughta like that. I'll get a display case made up to show these personal items. It'll help me sell more whiskey in the Lost Coyote. I'll bet the Golden Rail will be jealous of that." He looked over at the body lying in the weeds. "He might have a decent gun you can swap for this one. Take a look at anything else we can find on him that you can use. He might have some money on him. I know he'd want you folks to have that. Whaddaya think, John? Are you about ready to roll again? I'll take care of Mr. Castor. Nobody knows where he drifted off to. Of course, I'll have to come up with a good story on how I happened to come upon those souvenirs."

While Lucas and Caroline gave the campsite one last check, Ben went across the stream and found Castor's horse. When he led it back to the wagon, Lucas looked at it and said, "I forgot about that crazy-lookin' horse of his."

"You wanna tie it on the back of your wagon with your other horses?" Ben asked. "You oughta be able to sell him for good money. Maybe you might wanna keep him and put him up to stud and raise the blame things. Pretty good saddle, too. Might be something in the saddlebags."

Lucas looked at Caroline for her opinion and she just shrugged. "Maybe you want him," he said to Ben.

"I'm afraid I've got enough lies to tell when I get back. I don't think I could come up with a believable one for where I got that horse," Ben said. By the time they were finished, the Cochrans had acquired quite a bit of wealth. Castor was carrying a lot of money, and Lucas suggested that Ben should share it to compensate him for the trouble he had gone to. "No, thanks," Ben replied. "You folks are gonna need all you can scrape up to start your new life. I'm already fixed up. I've got Rachel back in Buzzard's Bluff runnin' the Coyote, and she'll keep me outta the poorhouse."

"You're too kind, Ben," Caroline felt inclined to say. Then she looked into Lucas' eyes and smiled. "Start our new life," she said, repeating Ben's remarks. "I like the sound of that." While struck with the thought, she looked back at Ben and asked, "What about you and Rachel? Any chance you two might get married and be partners for life?"

Ben shrugged. "Never thought about it," he said. "I doubt she ever has, either. I think we get along too good to get married. Besides," he joked, "I don't think she can work up the nerve to propose." On that note, they said their goodbyes and wished each other good fortune. Then Ben helped Caroline up on the wagon seat and set Tommy up on his daddy's buckskin gelding. He watched them until they pulled out onto the road again, then he turned his attention to the body of the late Nate Castor, his gun and holster gone, his clothes slightly disheveled from the search of his body. "Well, Nate," he said, "if they've got any windows in Hell, maybe you can look outta one of 'em and see how happy you've made that young couple. You gave that young fellow a new name, and you got what you wanted, too. You'll be remembered as the fellow who gunned down Lucas Blaine."

Left with the problem of disposing of the body, he looked around him for a solution. He had no tools to dig a grave for Nate. Had he thought about it, he would have buried the body before Lucas and Caroline were ready to go. He could have used the shovel he saw on the side of their wagon. "Best I can do for you, is drag your ass away from the stream, so you don't contaminate it, and maybe the buzzards will take care of you before anybody stumbles on you." So he pulled Castor's body up from the ground and stood him up against Cousin. "Hold still, horse!" He scolded when Cousin started to sidestep. Then he bent down and grabbed the body around the legs and lifted it up until it fell across the saddle. When he was sure it was securely settled, he led the horse off deeper into the woods. "I woulda just tied a rope around your boots and dragged ya, but I didn't wanna leave a trail through here."

He didn't want to leave the body anywhere near the tracks left by the wagon, so he led Cousin almost a quarter of a mile until he came to what appeared to be a cabin through the trees. "Damn," he uttered, "just my luck." He started to turn around but then decided to take a closer look. He tied Cousin to a tree limb and then made his way carefully through the trees until he got close enough to see it clearly. He discovered it to be an abandoned shack, so he walked on over to get a closer look. It had evidently not been used for quite some time and was in pretty pathetic condition. "Perfect," he said. When he turned back to get his horse, he noticed the well beside the cabin, the well box around it broken down like the cabin. He walked over and looked down in the well and saw a dry bottom. *Maybe the reason the cabin's abandoned,* he thought.

He went back to get his horse and led him back beside the dry well. "Welcome to your new home, Nate," he said and pushed the body off into the well. He checked his saddle to make sure there was no blood on it, then mounted and turned Cousin at an angle he estimated might be right to strike the road again, heading back toward Buzzard's Bluff. He hadn't gone far when it occurred to him that there might still be a path from the cabin to the road. A brief scouting found it. Although it was almost overgrown, there were traces enough to show him where it had been. So he used it as a guide and he was soon back on the road to home.

He was not going to work Cousin as hard on the return trip as he had when he was chasing Castor the day before. Having traveled the road between Buzzard's Bluff and Waco before, he knew where he would stop to rest his horse on other trips. The spot he picked was where the road crossed a good-sized creek, and it was only about six miles from town. With a much-earlier start than when he was going in the opposite direction, even after resting his horse, he expected to arrive in Buzzard's Bluff fairly early in the afternoon. He was feeling pretty good about the outcome of his trip, and the only problem he had was his hunger. He was glad he had saved one of Annie's ham biscuits to eat on the way back, but he knew that was only going to be enough to tease his appetite. Ordinarily, on a trip of this length, he would have a packhorse with something to cook and coffee to go with it. He sometimes hunted for game if there were signs where he stopped. But without a coffeepot, he didn't want to bother with building a fire, and he didn't want to take the time to hunt. As soon as he thought Cousin was ready, he was going to go.

When he felt it was time, he got back into the saddle and started for home. He rode into the stable in the early afternoon. "Ben!" Henry called out, excitedly. "What happened? Did you catch him?"

"I almost caught him," Ben answered, having already decided he was not going to share the secret with everyone. "I didn't quite make it in time to stop it. I got there just in time to see Lucas and Nate Castor square off against each other. I ain't ever seen anybody faster."

"Who won?" Henry pressed, hardly able to wait.

"Well, that's the sad part," Ben replied, shaking his head. "Lucas is dead. I buried him, myself. But he put a bullet in Castor, too. Castor rode off somewhere to die. I didn't care enough then to try to go after him."

"What about Lucas' wife and son?" Henry asked. "What happened to them? Are they comin' along after you?"

"No, and that's another worrisome thing. I couldn't persuade her to come back here with me. I offered to drive her wagon back, but she said she could drive her own wagon, and she wasn't ever comin' back to Buzzard's Bluff. Said it was bad luck for her and Tommy. I asked her where she was goin' and she wouldn't tell me." He could see that Henry was winding up to ask a basketful of more questions, so he said, "Take care of my horse. I worked him hard. And I ain't had nothin' to eat, so I'm starvin'."

"I'll take care of him," Henry said. "That sure is sorry news about Lucas, though."

"It is that," Ben said and took his saddlebags, rifle, and his war bag with the articles of proof in it, and started for the Lost Coyote. He hadn't gone far when he was spotted by Tuck Tucker. *I shouldn't have to tell my story but one more time,* he thought. *Tuck will take care of informing the rest of the town.*

"Ben!" Tuck yelled and came running. "I heard what happened and I was comin' to help you, but you'd already gone. Did you catch up to that lowdown dog?"

"I'm trying to get to the Coyote before Annie cleans up the kitchen. I'll tell you all about it there." He kept walking and Tuck fell in step with him, so they walked into the saloon together. As soon as Tiny saw them, he yelled to Clarice to tell Rachel that Ben was back. In a few seconds, Rachel and Clarice were out in the barroom to meet him.

"Has Annie thrown everything out yet?" This was his first question.

"She's about to," Rachel answered. "I'll tell her you're hungry." She stuck her head back inside the kitchen door and delivered the message. "Now," she said when she came to meet him. "What happened? Did you make it in time?"

"I almost made it," he said and shook his head sadly. By this time, Ham Greeley had joined them. "But I was too late to prevent the shootout, but just in time to see it happen." He read the shock in Rachel's eyes, but he continued to repeat the story he had just told at the stable. He thought he detected a tear in Rachel's eye, but he laid out the entire sad encounter that resulted in the tragic death of Lucas Blaine and the disappearance of Nate Castor. A lot of the small gathering shook their heads sadly for the loss of a young man they had come to know in such a short time.

"But why wouldn't Caroline let you drive her wagon back here, Ben?" Rachel asked, obviously upset and worried about her. "What is she planning to do? A woman alone, with a young child. She clearly wasn't thinking right."

"I know, I told her that, myself, but she said she'd rather die than come back to the place that killed her husband," Ben said. He could see that she was not satisfied with his answers, so he said, "You're right. She shoulda come back with me, but I couldn't persuade her to do it. And I didn't think I had the right to force her to do it. I figured when she thought about it for a while, she'll most likely show up here one day." He turned to address the spectators. "Lucas Blaine may be dead, but I'm gonna make sure the folks around here remember him. I took the liberty of bringin' back a few of the personal items he wore." He reached in his war bag and pulled out Lucas' gun belt and Colt .45. He pulled the gun out and showed them the name engraved on the handle. "Same as engraved on the back of this belt buckle," he continued. "And this," he said, holding up the picture, "a picture of Caroline he always carried. And she wrote on the back and signed it. I'm gonna get a frame made for 'em so everybody comin' in here can see it." Rachel had heard enough. She turned about and returned to the kitchen.

Ben stayed a while longer at the bar, answering questions, most of which pertained to the speed of the two combatants. He assured them all that it was the fastest display of gunfighting he had ever seen. He left them to talk about it then and went into the kitchen to see if Annie had saved him anything. When he went in, he found Rachel sitting at the kitchen table, drinking a cup of coffee. Annie turned away from her and took a plate out of the oven, she had been warming for him. He had evidently interrupted their conversation. "Pardon me," he said. "Want me to take this out in the saloon?"

"I guess you can eat it anywhere you want to," Rachel said. "You're the half-owner."

"In that case, I'll eat it in here, so I can visit with you lovely ladies. I hope to hell there's some coffee left in that pot. I need it more than food."

His remarks were met with an emotionless face from Annie and a deep frown from Rachel. Finally, she could hold it no longer. "Ben, that was wrong what you did out there. You should not have left that woman out there alone," she said. "And with a five-year-old boy? What were you thinking? And then make a carnival gunman figure out of Lucas. He deserves better treatment than that."

He waited until Annie placed his coffee on the table, in case she decided to throw it at him, before he replied to Rachel's remarks. "Ah," he sighed with pleasure, after a couple of sips, "that's what I really needed. I swear, I can't go very long without a cup of coffee. Now, in the first place, I think it's fitting that we remember the late Lucas Blaine. That's why I brought those things of his back with me. In the second place, I didn't try to get Caroline to come back here with me to Buzzard's Bluff because she clearly preferred to go on to Montana or California, or wherever they wind up, with her husband and her son. End of story."

Rachel didn't reply at once. Clearly confused by his remarks. After a few moments, she said, "Wait, you're saying that . . . What are you saying?"

"I'm sayin' that Lucas Blaine ain't dead, and nobody

knows that but you and Annie and me." He paused. "Well, if you don't count him and Caroline and Tommy. But nobody else. And, anyway, if you still object, it's too late 'cause Tuck Tucker was out there, so it'll be all over town. If we can get Paul Hogan to print a story about it, maybe some more of the other Nate Castors out there will have someone read it to them, and they won't bother comin' to Buzzard's Bluff lookin' for Lucas Blaine."

"I swear, Ben Savage, that's brilliant!" Rachel exclaimed. "I should have known better than to think you had no more class than that."

"Now, wait a minute," he said. "Let's not get crazy about this. Just once in a while I think of a good idea, though."

"Brilliant," Rachel repeated. "Isn't he, Annie?"

"Sometimes, I think, maybe," Annie said guardedly, causing Ben to laugh.

"Since you know the truth about the story, would you like to know the truth about the actual meeting between Lucas and Castor?" Rachel said she would, so he told them. "I thought I was going to try to cut Castor down before he had a chance to draw his weapon. But I didn't quite get there on time. Ya see, I thought Lucas was going to refuse to draw on him, and Castor would just shoot him down anyway. I shoulda known Lucas has better sense than that. When I got there, I tried to talk Lucas out of facing Castor, but he told me he would handle it himself. I'd already made up my mind that I would shoot Castor before I let him shoot Lucas. He told Castor he didn't want to face him. Castor said he was gonna shoot him, anyway. So Lucas told him he would face him, and that's when I got ready to take Castor out with my rifle. I never got the chance. Castor had to walk across this tiny little stream, and when he came out of it, he acted like he was stomping his feet to knock off some water. Then he drew before he even stood up to face Lucas. Lucas cut him down so fast, it wasn't even close. In my mind, he's the fastest one out there. He didn't need me stickin' my nose in his business."

"Lucas just didn't know he had a publicity agent," Rachel said, now that she could joke about it. "Maybe we should make that little memorial you threatened to hang up somewhere in *our* saloon." She emphasized the word, *our*. They all laughed at that.

Ben had one more thing he was concerned about relating to the *death* of Lucas Blaine. So he asked Rachel her opinion, and just as he had when telling the true story about the shootout, he asked it in Annie's presence. They both felt that Annie was like a priestess or something. They were sure she never repeated anything of a confidential nature, not even to her husband, Johnny. "Do you think I should tell Mack the true story?" A matter of principle they felt, so they decided to think about it later.

CHAPTER 23

Mack didn't come by the Lost Coyote that afternoon, so Ben figured he'd see him that evening at the hotel dining room. And when he went to supper, he found that the sheriff was already there, sitting at his usual table. Lacy greeted him cordially when he walked in and commented on the sad news about Lucas Blaine, Tuck Tucker having made sure everyone had the news. "Yep," Ben responded, "sometimes things just don't work out the way they should." He nodded to Cindy as he walked back to Mack's table. "Can anybody sit at this table?" he asked Mack when he looked up.

"Sure can," Mack replied, "long as he ain't a Texas Ranger." Ben sat down and thanked Cindy for the coffee she placed on the table for him. "I heard the news about your trip up the Waco road to catch up with Nate Castor. I was sorry to hear it turned out the way it did. I liked that young man. He had no business bein' caught up in that fast-gun game. He got into it when he was too damn young to know what he was bargainin' for. I wish we coulda done something to help him. And it really galls my butt to have him gunned down by some worthless drifter like Nate Castor." He took a couple of gulps of coffee. "I kinda figured you'd stop by the jail this afternoon to tell me about it."

Well for Pete's sake, Ben thought, *I wasn't surprised by Rachel, but Mack, too?* "The reason I didn't was because I thought it'd be easier to tell you here at supper," he said, realizing that he just made the decision he and Rachel were going to think about. "Nate Castor wasn't in Lucas Blaine's class. Lucas cut him down so fast it woulda made your head spin if you'da seen it."

Mack stared at him for a few seconds, open-mouthed, his fork load of potato suspended several inches from his mouth. When speech returned, he shoved the fork full of potato into his mouth and chewed while he asked, "What are you talking about?"

"Lucas ain't dead, but Castor is. They fought and Lucas was so damn fast Castor didn't have a chance, even though he cheated and drew early. I just made that story up to give that family a chance to have a normal life with a new name. Sometimes dishonesty is the best policy." A wide grin spread all the way across Mack's face, so Ben said, "Now you know the true story, I know it, and Rachel knows it. I think it's best if we just keep it that way." He didn't mention Annie because he figured she didn't count. She never tells anybody anything.

Naturally, Mack wanted to hear the entire story, so Ben took him through it as it had happened, including the part when he dumped Nate Castor in a dry well. Mack was satisfied that Ben had done what he would have done in the same situation. "You're right about not tellin' anybody else about what really happened. The fewer that know, the better it is for Lucas and his family."

"Anything goin' on with your three guests while I was gone?" Ben asked.

"Nope, same ol' thing. Shorty and Jack just seem to be adjusting to jail life, and Reese gets crazier and crazier every day. He just might explode one of these days. And by the way, you ain't his favorite. He's pretty much convinced himself that you shot his brother. I've been tellin' him that it wasn't you. It was some vigilantes, but I don't think he believes me."

When they had finished eating and visited a while with Lacy and Cindy, most of the conversation centered on the tragedy of Lucas Blaine's death. Ben was glad when Myrtle came from the kitchen with supper plates for Mack's prisoners. He walked back up the street to the jail with Mack to give him a hand with the plates, so he wouldn't have to carry all four on the tray. When they reached the jail, Horace came out to help, but mostly to take his pick of the four plates. "Looks like the circus is back in town," Horace remarked and then nodded toward the Lost Coyote farther up the street.

"Harley Clackum," Ben announced. "He must be on his way back to San Antonio." Harley's colorful wagon was parked in front of the Lost Coyote. "I would like to go inside and visit with Reese while he's eatin' his supper, but I reckon I'll go on back to the Coyote."

"I'll tell Reese you thought about him," Mack japed.

When Ben walked back into the saloon, he saw Harley sitting at a table with Tuck and Ham Greeley, so he went over to the bar to talk to Tiny. "Harley's back," Tiny said, "and he's gettin' the whole story about Lucas from Tuck." He shook his head and remarked, "I swear, that's a pair, ain't it?" Harley saw Ben at that moment and got up from the table. "Uh-oh," Tiny said, "you've been spotted."

"Howdy, Harley," Ben greeted him when he walked

over to the bar. "You made a quick trip. I thought you were gonna be in Waco for a while."

"I was plannin' to," Harley said, "but I changed my mind when I ran into Nate Castor up at Hutto's Station."

"Oh, is that right?" Ben responded. "Was Nate Castor a friend of yours?"

"Hell, no," Harley said. "I seen him at Hutto's, actin' like he was the fastest gun in Texas. Feller over there," he said, referring to Tuck, "told me Castor killed Lucas Blaine, and that you saw him when he done it. Is that a fact?"

"That's right," Ben said.

"Something's wrong there somewhere," Harley insisted. "I've seen Lucas Blaine draw, and I can't see no way a clown like Nate Castor could beat him in a fair fight."

"I think you're right, Harley. He was faster than Castor. I told them how it happened. Tuck musta left out the part about Castor drawin' his gun before he really got to the spot where he was supposed to face Lucas. Lucas got a shot in him anyway, and he rode off to die I reckon 'cause he was hurt pretty bad. It was a gut shot."

"So Castor shot before he was supposed to?" Harley asked.

"That's right," Ben said. "Now, does that make more sense?"

"Makes a lot more sense," Harley replied. "I stayed at Hutto's an extra day 'cause I didn't wanna take a chance on ridin' with Castor. I was hopin', if they decided to face off, it wouldn't be until today or tomorrow. I wanted to see Blaine put him in the ground."

"I can tell you, it wasn't a fair fight," Ben said. He was already getting tired of patching up his story to suit each individual, so he changed the subject. "You gonna stick around town for a while?"

"I'm gonna park my wagon between the church and the post office again tonight. Then tomorrow I'll stay a while to see if I need to stay longer."

"Well, good luck," Ben said. "Now I reckon I'd better go see what Rachel wants." He knew that Tiny knew Rachel was not looking for him.

And Tiny was quick to back him. "Yeah, she was out here lookin' for you a few minutes ago." Ben nodded his appreciation and went to the kitchen where he found Rachel and Annie talking together.

"Speak of the devil," Rachel greeted him. "Are you able to keep your story straight?"

"Just barely," he answered. "Maybe I'd better write it down, so I can just read it to the next person that asks me how it happened. I need to tell you that Mack Bragg is in the secret circle. I told him the truth, but I ain't tellin' anybody else."

Not everyone who had experienced contact with Lucas Blaine was sad because of the news of his death. The following morning, the three prisoners in Mack Bragg's cell room overheard the sheriff telling Horace about Blaine's death at the hand of Nate Castor. "I never heard of Nate Castor," Reese Salter said. "But I'd like to thank him for doin' a job that needed doin'. I'm only sorry I didn't get to do it, myself." As each new day dawned, the thought that they were one day closer to the day when the U. S. Marshal Service would arrive with a jail wagon to transport the three of them to prison, weighed more heavily. "We've got to get out of this jail," Reese told Shorty and Jack. "Once they lock us in that jail wagon, we're as good as in prison. There ain't nobody left that can break us outta here. If we get out, it's gonna have to be us that comes up with a plan. I've been thinkin' about it and thinkin' about it. I believe I've got a plan that has a chance of workin'." He looked to see if he had the attention of both of them, and he felt satisfied that he did. The attitude of indifference they both had shown until now seemed to have disappeared with the passing of each day. "Our only chance of breaking out of here is when the sheriff is out of the office and there's nobody here but Horace."

He went on to tell them his plan, and although it seemed a simple plan, he believed it would work if they did their parts. Neither of his two partners were sold on the possibility of success of what he proposed. So he asked the question, "Do you want to go to prison for ten years?"

"No," Shorty Cobb answered. "But ain't nobody gonna bite on that plan."

"Are you tellin' me you don't wanna get outta here bad enough to even try it?" Reese demanded. "You rather just go on peacefully to prison instead of tryin' one little trick to get out? What if we try it and it don't work? Whadda they gonna do, lock us up? You ain't got nothin' to lose, but you've got a helluva lot to gain."

Jack Ramsey listened to Reese going back and forth with Shorty over his simple plan until he made a decision. "Count me in," he interrupted. "It might work."

Still not totally convinced, Shorty shrugged and said, "I reckon we're gonna try it."

"Our best time is after supper when Bragg goes out to make his rounds," Reese said. "I've been timin' him. He's usually gone for forty-five minutes to an hour, depending on how long he stops at the Lost Coyote."

"Are you talking about tonight?" Shorty asked, a little surprised.

"Yeah," Reese said. "Why? You got someplace you gotta go?"

Shorty looked at Ramsey, who met his look with a grin, then he looked back at Reese and answered him. "Yeah, outta here."

For the rest of the day, they talked about different things they could use to effect their escape and how best to present their decoy. When the sheriff told Horace to go up to the hotel and get the supper plates, Shorty turned to face Reese and Ramsey. "I hope we got something easy to chew with plenty of gravy," he said.

When Horace arrived with the supper plates, Mack stood by the cell with his shotgun and watched the prisoners as Horace handed out the plates. "Roast beef, fried potatoes and gravy, and kidney beans," Mack called it out as Horace passed it into the cell. "I'm gonna go down to the dinin' room and get myself some of that."

"You can have mine, Sheriff, and I'll walk down to the hotel," Shorty cracked. It was good for a chuckle out of Mack. He noticed that it also brought a grin to Reese's face, which he thought most unusual.

Horace came out of the cell after he brought coffee to them, and Mack locked the cell again. "Enjoy your supper, boys. You won't be havin' many more like the food you're gettin' from the hotel."

Sooner than you think, Reese thought, the thin smile still in place. He stabbed a bite of beef, stuck it in his mouth and started chewing. After a few seconds, he pulled the wad of meat back out of his mouth and looked it over. "I swear, I believe that meat is beginning to turn. It tastes funny."

"That's most likely your breath you're smellin'," Mack said. "The hotel ain't gonna serve any meat that's bad."

"That's what you say, but I'm smellin' this rotten meat." He held the half-chewed hunk of meat in the palm of his hand and held it out toward the sheriff. "Here, you smell it and tell me it ain't rotten." He looked around at his two partners. "How 'bout you boys? That meat smell all right to you?" They both hesitated to try it.

Mack had wasted all the time he intended to. "I don't know what kind of game you're playing, but there ain't nothin' wrong with the food. Is there, Horace?" Horace took a bite of the meat on his plate, then shook his head in answer. "So eat it, or go hungry, that's up to you." He and Horace walked out of the cell room and locked the door.

"I swear, that's good meat, though," Ramsey commented after they walked out.

"Don't eat it all," Reese reminded them. "You can chew it, but don't swallow it. Mash those beans and potatoes up all together. You gotta make it look like you already ate it. Stir some of your coffee up in it, too."

Shorty mixed his whole plate into one big mess, then sat there staring at it. "It just looks like my supper all mixed up," he said. "It don't look nasty. It just looks like I stirred it all up."

"That's because you know what you did," Reese said. "If somebody told you they puked it up outta their belly, it would look pretty nasty. You don't have to save all of it. Go ahead and eat a little bit of it if you're hungry."

Shorty stared at the mess he'd made of his plate. "I ain't so sure I'm hungry, anymore."

"What are we waitin' for?" Ramsey asked. "Why don't we go ahead and do it now while Bragg is down at the hotel?"

"'Cause it'll be hard dark when he comes back from

eatin' and goes out to make his rounds. There won't hardly be nobody on the street to see us leave. That fellow at the stable will be gone home, so we can get our horses without anybody seein' us. And Horace gets a lot shakier at night by hisself. It'll be better to wait till he makes his rounds."

"Won't we run a lot more risk of runnin' into Bragg when he's out on the street lookin' for anything that ain't right?" Ramsey asked.

"We will have to keep a sharp eye out for him, and if we see him checkin' the stores, we'll just hide until he moves on outta our way. Chances are, he'll make a longer stop in the Lost Coyote or the Golden Rail, because that's where anybody would be." He shrugged and said, "Even if he was to see the three of us walking on the street, he'd have to catch up to us to see who it was. And that would just be his tough luck when he found out."

So they sat there in the cell, resolved to bide their time over their full supper plates, waiting for the sheriff to return from the dining room. Then Reese had what he thought might be a better idea. "Clean most of that food off your plate and dump it in the water bucket. Let 'em think we ate most of it, but we still got a little bit to finish."

"Ain't that gonna foul up our drinkin' water?" Shorty asked.

"That's the idea, genius," Reese answered sarcastically, "but don't let on until Bragg leaves again."

"Right, I get it," Shorty said, even though he didn't really.

When Mack came back from supper, he asked Horace if the prisoners were causing any trouble, just as he always did. Horace answered, "I don't reckon. I ain't been back in there since you left. I ain't heard nothin' out of 'em."

Mack decided to take a look at them before he went out

to make his rounds. He picked up the cell room key from his desk and went into the cell room, where he found his three prisoners sitting on their cots, still working on their supper. "You boys ain't finished eatin' yet?"

"Almost," Reese answered him. "This stuff still has a rancid taste to it. It's takin' a while to get it down. But it's either that or go hungry till breakfast."

Mack shook his head, disgusted. "I swear, you're like a bunch of little girls. You get a crazy notion in your head and nothin' can change it. I just had the same thing for supper you did, and there wasn't anything wrong with what I ate."

"I expect there mighta been a difference in the meat they put on your plate and what they put on our plates," Reese claimed. "They got a little meat that's turned, why waste it? Give it to the prisoners in the jail. Right?"

Mack was rapidly finding it too exasperating to try to talk sensibly with him. "We don't work that way here. Eat it or leave it. If we find you dead in the mornin', we'll apologize and give you a respectable burial." He did an about face and left the cell room. As soon as the door closed behind him, Shorty and Ramsey looked at once to Reese for instructions.

"Just set tight and listen till we hear him leavin' the office," Reese told them. "We gotta make sure there ain't nobody here but Horace." They continued to sit and listen until they were sure they heard Mack leave. Then they continued to sit and wait a little while longer, just to be sure. Finally, Reese decided it was time enough. "Dump that stuff you've got left on your plate on the floor, so he can see it." He demonstrated with his plate then dropped the plate on the floor. Then he pulled the water bucket over closer to the door and splashed some of it on the floor as well, making a sizable mess. "You ready?" They said they were.

"Now, be actin' like you're sick when he comes in here." He yelled then. "Horace! Help!" Over and over, he yelled, louder and louder, until they heard the lock turn on the office door. "Get ready to do some actin'," he whispered.

Startled by the sudden onslaught of yelling for help, Horace's first reaction was to run to the front door to look for Mack. But Mack was nowhere in sight. The moaning and yelling from the cell room continued, so he knew he had to see what it was. He grabbed the cell room key and unlocked the door, then gradually eased it open to take a peek inside. What he saw almost floored him. The prisoners were off their cots, on the floor on hands and knees, moaning and calling for help. He didn't know what to do. He started to close the door again, but he saw Reese looking at him. "Horace," Reese called to him as pitifully as he could affect. "For God's sake, help us. We're sick as dogs. We've puked up about everything we ate and now our guts are on fire. Just give us some fresh water, please. Jack puked in the water bucket. Please get us some water."

Horace found himself living a nightmare. He pushed the door open and took a few steps into the room. He saw what looked like vomit in several spots on the floor. It caused a queasy feeling in his stomach. "I can't give you no water," he said. "Sheriff Bragg told me not to unlock that cell when he's gone. Can't you wait till he comes back?"

"Please, Horace," Shorty contributed. "My gut's on fire. Have mercy. Just give us a bucket of water."

"I'd have to unlock the cell to put a bucket in there, and I can't do that," Horace insisted. "Maybe, if you set your cups outside the bars, I can fill them with fresh water."

"Ah, Horace," Reese moaned. "We don't need cups of water, we need buckets of water. If you can't just swap out our water bucket, I'd druther you just take that shotgun of yours and put me outta this misery inside my gut."

Horace's nightmare only got worse. He didn't know what he should do. He could see the water bucket inside the cell now that it had been dragged closer to the door of the cell. He could see just enough to determine that there appeared to be vomit floating on the water. He fought back an urge to vomit himself. He made a decision. They didn't look to be in any shape to cause any trouble, and they were obviously suffering. "Just leave that bucket where it is. I'll get the bucket out of the cell next to yours and fill it with fresh water, and I'll put that one in there." He went back just outside the cell-room door where the cell keys were hanging on a hook. Then he returned to the cell room, went into the other cell and got the water bucket.

"Hurry," Reese begged, his tone more pitiful by the minute.

Horace went to the pump and filled the bucket. On his way back, he picked up the shotgun. He failed to notice that Jack Ramsey had crawled a little closer to Reese. "I'm gonna open this cell door just wide enough to get this bucket in, then I'm closin' it right away. If you try anythin' I'll have to shoot you."

"I ain't got the strength to try anything," Reese moaned. "Bless you for doin' this."

"Stay back," Horace said. "Gimme enough room to open the door." Reese made a motion as if he was trying to push back, but actually stayed where he was. All three hearts inside the cell began beating wildly with the sound of the key in the cell door. Horace opened the door just wide enough to set the bucket of water inside on the floor, and the trap was sprung. Reese lunged up from the floor to drive Horace backward, using the cell door to jam his arms against his body. Shorty and Ramsey were right behind him to wrestle the shotgun away from Horace before he could get his finger on the trigger to fire it. He ended up on the floor with Ramsey and Shorty holding him down.

"Oh, Lordy, Lordy," Horace moaned. "What have I done?"

"You messed up, Horace. That's what you did."

"There wasn't nothin' wrong with the meat, was there?"

"Not a thing," Reese answered. "I'm just sorry we had to waste it just to get your attention."

"Whaddaya gonna do with me? You might as well shoot me 'cause Mack's gonna do it when he comes back here and finds this cell empty. Lordy, Lordy."

"Well, I'll tell you the truth, Horace, I'd be glad to shoot you, but I ain't ready to have anybody hear a gunshot go off in the sheriff's office. And I ain't got time to waste here stabbin' you to death. So we're just gonna lock you up in our cell. Just make yourself at home, and Bragg will be back before long."

They locked Horace in the cell and went into the office where they broke into the gun cabinet and found their weapons and extra ammunition. Ready to leave then, they waited while Reese stepped outside and knelt on the small front porch and looked up and down the darkened street for sign of Mack Bragg. After a few moments, he thought he saw something moving down near the south end of the street, approaching the church. He kept his eye on the figure until he was sure it was the sheriff. "Come on," he said and went down the steps. Ramsey and Shorty followed at once. They hurried to the north end of the street, at a fast walk, to the stable. As they expected, Henry had locked up and gone home for the night, leaving them free access to the stock and the tack. What they were not aware of, however, was the fact that home for Henry was a one-room dwelling built on the side of the barn.

With a boost from Reese, Shorty got up on Ramsey's shoulders, and from there, he reached the floor of the hayloft and pulled himself up. Then he went down the ladder to the floor of the barn and came back to the door and opened it. Reese and Ramsey came inside, and they dropped the bar on the door, locking it again. "Let's find our horses and get outta here as quick as we can," Reese said.

"Hell, I'm gonna improve my ridin' stock while I'm at it," Ramsey said.

"I'm partial to that bay I've been ridin'," Reese said. "But we ain't gonna find a blame thing without some light."

"There's a lantern over here on this post," Shorty said. "I'll light it up and we'll get outta here a lot quicker. Who's got a match?" None of them did.

"Look on the post where you found it," Reese said. "There ought to be a piece of lumber bracin' the post from the beam above it."

Shorty went back and felt around the top of the post and, sure enough, there was a box of matches sitting in the joint between the brace and the post. He struck a match and lit the lantern. He turned the wick up and the lantern provided a large circle of light that lit up some of the stable area, including Henry Barnes, standing beside one of the stalls, his rifle ready to fire. All four individuals were stunned. Henry pulled the trigger, hitting Shorty in the chest, sending him staggering backward several steps before he stared down in disbelief at the hole in his shirt. He started to say something, but dropped to his knees, then fell over on his side. Henry, as shocked as they were, thought to crank another round into the chamber of his

Winchester rifle. It served to break Reese and Ramsey out of their shock, and both drew their six-guns and cut Henry down. Ramsey hurried to pick up the lantern Shorty dropped and began stamping out the small patch of hay that had caught fire, cursing in disbelief at what had just happened.

"Where the hell did he come from?" Reese asked.

"He was in here when we broke in," Jack Ramsey answered. "He never went home. He just stayed right here. Now we've really gotta move. Bragg is likely already on his way. How bad is Shorty?"

"He's done for," Reese answered, "and we're gonna be trapped in this stable if we don't get some horses saddled and get outta here." He was fighting to control the frustration of the explosion of his escape plan. Moments before, he was planning to find their packs and their packhorses as well and leave Buzzard's Bluff with the supplies they needed to live on while they put this hard-luck town behind them.

In front of the hotel, and starting back up the street, Mack was stopped when he heard the shots, one from a rifle, followed by two pistol shots. From the sound, he had to guess they came from the stable. He started for that end of the street at a trot. When he got to the Lost Coyote, he met Ben coming out the door. "The stable?" Ben yelled.

"That's what it sounded like to me," Mack answered.

"I'll go with you," Ben said. He didn't usually investigate gunshots in the town. That was Mack's job. But these shots came from the stable, and his horse was in that stable.

CHAPTER 24

When they approached the stable, they saw that the doors were open and there was a light inside, and Mack said there had been no light showing in there a short time before when he walked past. They both drew their weapons as they entered the barn. "Henry!" Mack called out. "You in here?" There was no answer, so they advanced cautiously back toward the stable when they came upon the bodies. Mack knelt beside the first one. "Oh, my God," he gasped. "It's Shorty Cobb! Ben, they broke out! Horace!" He looked frantically at Ben, who was bending over the other body. "They mighta killed Horace. I've gotta get back to the jail!" Then he saw the look on Ben's face. "Henry?"

Ben nodded. "But he's still breathing, if only barely. I'm gonna take him to Doc's." He reached down, feeling for a pulse. "He's still got a heartbeat. Henry, can you hear me? I'm gonna take you to the doctor. You hang on." He picked the slight man up in his arms and started to Doc Tatum's office, which was at the other end of the street, across from the church.

"Do you need help?" Mack asked as he closed the barn doors.

Ben knew he was concerned about Horace, so he said,

"I don't need any help, you go on ahead. I'll be back at the stable after I take Henry."

"Right," Mack said and hurried on ahead of him. He found his office door unlocked, and so was the cell-room door. Dreading what he expected to find next, he was relieved to see Horace alive, apparently unharmed as he sat patiently waiting for Mack to find him. He didn't say anything when Mack walked into the cell room. He just continued to sit there with his head hanging down, staring at the floor. "Are you all right?" Mack asked.

Without looking up, he said, "I messed up, Mack."

"Yeah, I reckon you did," Mack replied, "but I'm glad you're all right." He looked at the mess on the floor of the cell. "You wanna tell me what happened?"

While Horace related his horrible experience at the hands of Reese and his partners to Mack, Ben was at the south end of the street, knocking at the door of Dr. John Tatum. He knew the doctor and his wife had not gone to bed because there were lights on all over the house. When the door finally opened, it was Nancy, Doc's wife, who opened it. When she saw the big man standing on her front porch carrying a smaller man like a child, she was given a start. "Ben," she exclaimed, "who is it?"

"It's Henry Barnes, Miz Tatum, and he's been shot twice. He's in a bad way. I hate to call on Doc this late, but it just happened a few minutes ago. And he's still breathing."

"Oh, poor Henry," she reacted. "Bring him on inside, Ben." She held the door for him and called out, "John! It's Henry Barnes! He's been shot."

Doc Tatum came in from the living quarters of the house where he had been sitting in his favorite chair, enjoying his pipe. "Take him on into my surgery and lay him on the table, Ben."

"I appreciate you takin' a look at him, Doc. I'm sorry it's such a late hour to come callin'."

"No problem at all," Doc said. "Especially when it's a friend like Henry. I'd rather you came now, than wait till morning." He started pulling Henry's clothes apart so he could see the damage. "How'd it happen?"

"Those three fellows broke out of jail while Mack was making his rounds. They were after their horses in the stable, and I reckon Henry caught 'em. He shot one of 'em, and they shot him. So there's two of 'em on the run."

"I expect you'll be pinning on your ranger badge again and going after them with Sheriff Bragg and a posse," Doc assumed as he examined the two wounds.

"I suppose so," Ben answered. "I'm willin' to help if I can, and I reckon it's more of a personal thing when they shot Henry." He didn't say it to Doc, but he couldn't help wondering if maybe Henry caused himself to get shot when he shot Shorty. "Whaddaya think, Doc? Is he gonna make it?"

"I don't know yet," Doc answered. "The wound up in his chest is the critical one, and I'm gonna have to go in there to see just how much damage has been done. The other wound, lower down in his side isn't that serious. It's the chest wound we'll have to see about, and then it's going to depend on how strong Henry is to fight it." Even as he said it, Henry moved his head slightly to one side and mumbled something they could not understand. "That's a good sign," Doc said. "You go along and do whatever you and Mack have to do. I'll keep Henry here and do what I can for him."

"Thanks, Doc," Ben said, nodded politely to Nancy,

then went out the front door, wasting no time to get back to the stable to check on Cousin. Much to his relief, he found the big dun gelding standing quietly in his stall.

He was at the stable only a few minutes before Mack returned from the jail. "Horace?" Ben asked.

"He's all right," Mack said. "Just shook up for lettin' those three put one over on him." He told Ben how they had pulled the trick on poor Horace. "I shoulda suspected they were up to something when they started talkin' about the meat smellin' funny before I left there to go eat." Mack shook his head slowly when he said, "It didn't help his feelin's none when I told him Henry got shot. He was pretty sure I was gonna fire him, but I told him he just found out why I tell him not to open that cell for any reason when I'm gone." He paused only a moment, then asked, "What about Henry?"

Ben told him what Doc Tatum had said about the wounds and that he was going to keep Henry there to take care of him. "We're gonna have to get somebody to take care of the stable while Henry's gone. Too bad he ain't got any family livin' with him."

"We can ask Jim Bowden to take care of it till we find somebody to take it on until Henry's well enough to come back," Mack suggested. "Jim's shop is right across the street. It would be easy for him to keep an eye on the stable. 'Course, that's if Henry does come back. If he doesn't, then we've got a bigger problem. We'll have to figure all that out. We'll close the stable tonight, and the horses will be all right till mornin'."

"Are we goin' after them?" Ben asked.

"We sure as hell are," Mack answered. "And I'm glad you said, *we*. 'Cause I sure welcome your help with these two."

"Are you thinkin' about a posse?" Ben asked.

"Well, I was, until you said *we*," Mack said. "Now I ain't sure. I ain't had the experience of chasin' outlaws like you have, riding for the rangers for so long. Whadda you think?"

"I think we'll have a better chance of catchin' up to those two without a posse," Ben said.

"Too bad I ain't got a deputy to watch the town while I'm gone," Mack said.

"I'll be your deputy," Jim Bowden said as he walked out of the darkness to join them.

"I was gonna ask you to watch the stable," Mack told him.

"Why?" Jim asked. "Is something wrong with Henry?" He was shocked when Mack told him what had happened at the stable, and that he was surprised he didn't hear it, since his cabin was right behind his shop across the street. "I weren't there," Jim said. "I was at the Lost Coyote. Wasn't I, Ben?"

"That's right, you were, come to think of it," Ben said, "playin' cards with Merle Baker and that bunch."

"We heard the shots," Jim said, "and Merle said he wondered if Mack was gonna be lookin' for him to pick up a body. We saw Ben go out the door, but he never came back, so we just kept playin' cards. I swear, if I'd been home, I mighta coulda helped Henry."

"Or you mighta got shot too," Mack said. "Well, there is a body here for Merle to pick up. Ben and I are gonna see if we can pick up a trail to follow, but it's gonna have to wait till mornin'. We ain't gonna see much in the dark. We'll be lucky if we can pick out their tracks right here in front of the stable. There are so many, it'll be hard to tell if any of 'em are fresher than the others."

"You might be right about that," Ben said. "Let me take that lantern for a minute. I wanna check the back stable door. They mighta thought they'd be seen comin' out the front." Mack and Jim went with him when he went to the back of the stable. They found the door open and two distinct sets of hoofprints leading away toward the river.

"I'da thought they would have struck out on the north road toward Waco," Mack said.

Ben stood there a few seconds longer, looking at the tracks while he thought about the two men in their situation. He imagined Reese and Ramsey would assume the same thing Mack just said. They might think the sheriff would be leading a posse after them, up the road to Waco. But that might not necessarily be the case, he thought. The tracks he was staring at were tracks of only two horses. That told him that their situation was desperate, and they had only enough time to saddle two horses and ride. That meant they had no supplies at all, no food, no cooking utensils or pots. And yet, all their packs were stacked right there in the barn when they were captured. They didn't have time to look through them or to rig up their packsaddles on a couple of horses. They needed their packs because there was no place to get what they needed within a couple of days. Maybe they may be thinking about coming back to the stable tonight to get what they needed? They would assume that Henry was dead, and there would be no one in the stable for the rest of the night.

He shared his thoughts with Mack, and Mack was receptive to the idea. "It'd be a pretty gutsy move to come back here after you got away clean the first time," Mack said. "But I reckon there ain't nobody gutsier than Reese Salter."

"That's a fact," Ben said. "So I'm thinkin' that maybe I'll stay here tonight. If nothin' happens, we'll start out following those tracks out the back door as soon as it's daylight. Whaddaya think?"

"It's worth a try," Mack replied. "But I think maybe it ought to be me settin' up all night, waitin' for them to come sneakin' back in here, or at least the two of us doin' it."

"I thought maybe you might want to make sure Horace doesn't cut his throat or something tonight," Ben said, half serious. "From what you said, it sounds like he's let his mind get pretty messed up with his part in their jail break." Then he got down to his real concern. "Tell you the truth, Mack, I'm gonna sit here in this stable tonight, anyway. You might remember that I've already had my horse stolen out of this stable once before, and it cost me a helluva lot of trouble to go after him. I'll just feel a lot easier when mornin' comes if Cousin is still here."

Mack had to laugh because he remembered the adventure that occasion turned out to be for Ben. "That settles it," he said, "we'll both set up an ambush for them, if they ain't got any more sense than to come back here. Then in the mornin', we'll follow the tracks they left outta here." He turned toward Jim then and said, "You'll be in charge till we get back, Deputy Bowden. You can operate outta my office, if you want to. I'll explain to Horace what's goin' on."

"I've gotta go back to the Coyote to let Rachel and Tiny know where I'll be," Ben said. "If we have to get an early start out of here in the mornin', I know I've got enough basic supplies in my packs to take care of both of us for several days before we have to buy more."

"We can take a look in Henry's room on the back of the barn," Mack suggested. "He might have a side of bacon or something we could use." So they split up then, after agreeing to meet back at the stable later.

* * *

Ben had to give Rachel and Tiny, as well as Clarice and Ruby, a full report on what had happened to cause the gunshots that were heard, and why he didn't come back to tell them where he was going. He explained that he didn't come back right after he went out the door because he thought the shots came from the stable, and he was worried about his horse. They were shocked to hear about the jail break and concerned for poor Henry Barnes. Rachel wanted to know if there was anything they could do for Henry, and Ben explained that, at this point, he didn't know if Henry was going to live or die. "If he makes it back, he's gonna be stove up for quite some time before he'll be able to take care of that stable. We're gonna have to find somebody to take care of it until he's well, and right now, I don't have any idea who that would be."

"I know who could take care of it for him," Rachel said, "Johnny Grey. Annie says he works with animals all the time. You can ask her when she comes in in the morning."

"You may be right," Ben said. He hadn't even thought about Annie's husband. He'd most likely be a good substitute for Henry. "You'll have to ask her, though," he said to Rachel. "I won't be here when she comes in."

"Where are you going to be?" Rachel asked.

"I'm gonna be with Mack. We're gonna sleep in the stable tonight, just on the possibility we have another visit from Reese and Jack. Then, if we don't, we'll try to track 'em in the mornin'."

Rachel frowned. "Ben Savage, why do you think you always have to help the sheriff do his job. Hasn't anyone told you that you're in the saloon business, not the sheriff's department?"

"I swear, Tiny," Ben teased, "ain't Rachel got the cutest little frown you ever saw? You oughta frown more often, Rachel."

Down the street at the jail, Mack was explaining to Horace why Jim Bowden was going to bunk in the sheriff's office that night. He was having a tough time convincing Horace that Jim's presence there had nothing to do with Horace's having been skunked by Reese Salter, Jack Ramsey, and Shorty Cobb. Without having been told to do so, Horace was busy cleaning up the floor, which was left a mess by the outlaws' performance with their supper. "I'm gonna be in the stable tonight in case we get a return visit. I'm sure you'll most likely hear about it. But you'll just do your regular job. Jim will take care of anything goin' on in town, and he knows to come get me if he needs to." He looked at Jim then and said, "I'd be mighty surprised if you'll have anybody lookin' for the sheriff this late at night, but you know where I'll be if you need me."

"Right," Jim said. "Me and Horace will hold the fort, won't we, Horace?" Horace, still wallowing in his humility made no response. Mack shrugged at Jim and went out the door and headed back to the stable.

When he got there, he found that Ben had built a fire in the stove in Henry's living quarters and had set a pot of coffee on to boil. "I don't know about you," Ben said when Mack found him, "but I'm gonna need a little coffee to help me stay awake tonight."

"Damn good idea," Mack responded. "I knew there was a good reason I wanted you here tonight." He thought about it for a minute before asking, "You reckon we oughta be worried about somebody seein' the smoke from that stove?"

"I thought about that, myself," Ben answered, "so I went out back to find the stovepipe. You see how he's got an elbow in it that takes it to the wall? Well, outside it just went straight out with an elbow turned up. I turned it down, so the smoke goes toward the ground. It's on the opposite side of this room from the back barn door. So, I don't think anybody would notice it."

"I reckon you're right," Mack said. "We ain't gonna keep that fire up, anyway, so it ought not to be makin' much smoke."

"I can see right now, if they don't show up here tonight, you're gonna blame it on my smoke," Ben joked. "You oughta know, if they smell my coffee makin', it'll draw 'em here, quicker'n before."

"I reckon we'd best pick out our spots to hide and wait for 'em before it gets much later," Mack suggested, ignoring Ben's attempt at humor.

It stood to reason that they would come back through the door they went out when they left before. So it was nothing more than finding a position on each side of that door and catch them in a crossfire. It could be over in a split second with just the squeeze of two trigger fingers. And that would surely be the most satisfying solution to the problem. It was not that easy, however. There was the question of morality. Ben had many years of experience as a Texas Ranger, and he had taken an oath to give the guilty the right to surrender. He found himself reluctant to extend that right to these two individuals. He felt sure that Mack had never taken any such oath, but he had taken the responsibility to deliver three convicted outlaws to the U. S. Marshal Service. Ben wondered just how important that was to Mack. He had already lost one of the three. Was it his hope to turn the other two over to the marshals? Ben decided he'd better find out. "What have you got in mind, Mack," he finally asked. "If they come walking through that door, they're sittin' ducks. Are we shootin' to kill? Or do we give them the chance to surrender?"

Mack didn't answer for a long time. He had obviously been laboring over the same thoughts as Ben. Finally, he confessed his indecision concerning the issue. "Ben, I feel like shootin' the ruthless trash down and ridding the world of them. But I wonder if we recaptured them, it would look better on my record. I don't know if I even have to worry about my record. I may be the sheriff here till they turn me out to pasture. What do you think we ought to do?"

"Tell 'em they're under arrest," Ben answered. "If they resist, shoot 'em. If they try to run, shoot 'em in the leg."

"All right," Mack said, "I'm satisfied with that. It'll be them makin' the choice to take the easy way or the hard way."

"Good," Ben said. "I'm glad we got that settled. It's gettin' late, so I'm goin' to move Cousin to a stall in the front of the stable, away from this door. I'm goin' to throw my saddle on him just in case things don't go as planned and I wished I had. Then I'm goin' back by Henry's room and get one more cup of coffee. You want one?" Mack handed him his empty cup, then he took his position in an empty stall to the right of the back door. When Ben returned, he gave Mack his coffee, then he took his position in an empty stall on the left side of the back door. The door opened on the alleyway that ran between the stalls, all the way to the front of the stable. When Reese and Jack pulled that door open, they would step into the alleyway unprotected. But only if Ben and Mack guessed right.

Ben dropped his empty coffee cup in the hay that covered the floor of the stall. He took out his watch and squinted in an effort to read the time. He still couldn't see, so he held it up to catch a glimmer of light from a vent window. He could barely make out the time, two-thirty. He would have thought that surely they would have come by now, if he and Mack had guessed right. Maybe he had guessed wrong, and they were getting farther and farther away while his watch ticked off the seconds. Those thoughts were interrupted when he heard a sound behind him from the front of the stable. Unable to identify it at first, he suddenly realized it was the sound of the front barn door opening. They were coming in the front! The barn was where all the packs were stored. Either they wanted to see what supplies were there, or Reese was smart enough to guess, if anyone was set up in ambush, they would be watching the back door. And at two-thirty in the morning, no one was going to notice them coming in the front of the barn. All those thoughts shot through his mind in only a second before his natural reflexes took over. Inside the stall, he still had some protection, so he reversed his position and hustled to the opposite side of the stall. He looked across the alleyway between the stalls and saw that Mack had done the same.

They had no choice now. If they came out of the stalls, they would be advancing up an empty corridor unprotected. They would have to wait for them to come into the stable. He looked across at Mack and tried to signal him to be patient. They still had the advantage of surprise, and the two outlaws would have to come down this alleyway to get to the horses they would choose to carry their packs. After what seemed like a long time, he saw Jack Ramsey appear in the alleyway at the front of the stable. He started down the line of stalls, looking at the horses inside them. There were at least a dozen horses in the corral, his and Reese's packhorses included. But the better horses were in the stalls. Ben struggled to keep from acting when Ramsey stopped at the stall where he had put Cousin, in his effort to get him far away from any danger. "Hey, Reese," Ramsey said as Reese stepped into the alley, "this one's got a saddle on him."

Mack could hold it no longer. "Put up your hands!" he shouted. "You're under arrest!" Startled, their first reaction was to run, and run they did. Mack fired a shot that hit Ramsey in the back of his leg, but Reese was too quick to present another target, and was out of sight before another shot could be fired.

Ben came out of the stall and sprinted up the alleyway to the front of the stable, ready to fire if Reese was waiting for him to show. But Reese's only thought was to escape. He ran out the front door of the barn, jumped on his horse and fled. Ben ran past Ramsey lying flat on his belly. "Watch him!" He yelled to Mack, who was coming right behind him. Then he got to the door in time to see Reese galloping away up the road to Waco. He immediately holstered his pistol and ran back inside to get Cousin out of the stall. "Is he dead?" he asked Mack, who had removed Ramsey's gun from his holster. Mack said he wasn't. He was shot in the thigh. "Can you take care of him? I'm going after Reese."

"I've got this one," Mack said. "You watch out for that one!"

Chapter 25

Ben let Cousin gallop for about a minute just to keep Reese from getting too big a lead on him before he reined him back to a lope. He couldn't be sure how long this chase was going to be before it turned into an ambush. The road was dark, and he had no desire to end the chase by riding blindly into one. It was hard to tell what a man like Reese Salter was likely to do. He knew that Reese was convinced that he had killed his brother, so that alone was reason to believe an ambush was the most likely occurrence. He was convinced that Reese, if he was waiting in ambush, could not see any better than he could. But he would still have the advantage, knowing that Ben was coming up the road after him. When he closed the distance to the point where they could see each other, he would still be in the middle of the road, and Reese could be anywhere. He didn't care much for that option. He looked up at the moonless sky and wondered, why tonight? He figured it was just his imagination, but he felt like Reese was not that far ahead of him. As if to answer his question, he heard Reese's horse whinny up ahead, and Cousin answered. How far? He wondered. It was still hard to tell. He dismounted. "That does it for you, big boy," he said to the big dun gelding. "You had to answer and tell him where we are. You can stay here." He dropped the reins on the ground and started walking. Judging the distance from the sound of Reese's horse, he only walked a short distance before he went off the side of the road into the trees and bushes. Moving as quietly as he could, he continued making his way beside the road until he came to a stream. *This has to be it,* he thought. So he knelt and strained in an effort to see along the stream bed.

Lying on the gentle slope of the stream bank, his rifle aimed at the dark road from which he had just come, Reese Salter was ready to settle the one debt he was anxious to collect. He was sure it was Ben Savage who had come after him when he fled the barn. And now, he prayed Savage would keep coming. He stared hard at the middle of the road, ready to pull the trigger the second the horse and rider appeared. He froze, stunned, when he heard the voice. "Your choice, Salter. Drop the rifle or pay the consequences." Reese cried out like a wolf with its paw caught in a trap, moaning in his frustration, but he did not drop the rifle. "Drop that rifle, Salter, and I mean now, or I'll blow you away."

In a fit of anger now, Reese threw the rifle away from him and got to his feet. "Like you blew my brother away, right?" He snarled.

"Yeah," Ben answered, "just like that, just before he started to murder the sheriff. But I'm givin' you the choice of dyin' or goin' back to jail."

"If you were half the man you make out to be, you'd face me man to man and we'd let our six-guns decide who deserves to die," Reese challenged.

"I'm standin' here with a gun already aimed at you and my finger on the trigger, so I figure the only thing that would prove would be that I was dumber than you. So come on up outta that stream and put your hands behind your back."

"I didn't think you had guts enough to face me," Reese said and walked up from the stream. He made a pretense of dropping his hands behind his back, but his right hand immediately came back up with his six-gun in it. He was struck in the chest by the .45 slug from Ben's Colt.

"I figured you were gonna do that," Ben said as he bent over the dying man and took his gun out of his hand. "So that proves you're dumber than me." He picked up Reese's rifle and walked back up the stream a little way where he found his horse tied to a tree limb. He dropped the rifle back in the saddle scabbard and put the pistol in the saddlebag. Then he muscled Reese up to lay across the saddle, walked back to Cousin, and rode back to town.

When he got back to Buzzard's Bluff, he rode straight over to Merle Baker's establishment and unloaded Reese's body onto Merle's handcart and covered it with the canvas left there for the purpose. Then he went to the jail to report Reese's death to Mack and tell him he gave Reese the chance to surrender, but he chose to follow his brother. He went back into the cell room with Mack to take a look at Jack Ramsey's leg wound and agreed with Mack that it would be all right to wait till morning to get Doc Tatum to treat it. By that time, it was getting on to about five-thirty, so he decided to go on back to the Lost Coyote and build a fire in Annie's stove and get a pot of coffee started.

"Good morning, Ben," Annie Grey sang out when she walked into the kitchen to find him sitting there as usual, with her stove hot and the coffee made.

To Ben, she seemed unusually cheerful this morning for

some reason. "Good mornin', Annie," he returned. "There were some things that happened here in town last night, and the worst thing was those three prisoners broke outta jail and shot Henry Barnes." Her cheerful face faded into a look of despair. "I don't know if Henry's gonna make it or not, but I'll find out later on this mornin'. Even if he does make it all right, it'll be a while before he can take care of his stable. Rachel said I oughta ask you if Johnny might be interested in doin' that. I thought I'd ask him when he comes in this morning. Do you think he'd be interested?"

She nodded vigorously. "I know he would," she said. About half an hour later, Johnny came in to eat breakfast and confirmed what Annie said.

"Good," Ben said. "I'll give Doc time to get started this morning, then I'll go down to his office and see how Henry is doin'. I know it'll take a load off Henry's mind to know somebody's lookin' after his stable."

When Annie was rolling out some biscuits, Johnny asked Ben a question. "Was you havin' any trouble sleepin' or anything last night? Annie was havin' one of her worryin' spells, and last night it was about you."

"No, no trouble with me," Ben assured him. *I swear,* he thought, *one of her blame feelings. I hope Rachel doesn't hear about it.*

Later that morning, Ben went to the sheriff's office to see if Mack had been to Doc Tatum's office yet. "I was about to go down there right now," Mack said. "You wanna go with me?" Ben said he wasn't doing anything else, so why not.

Doc was pleased to tell them that Henry had fared the night pretty well, and he expected a full recovery. "It's not going to be overnight by any means. I need to keep him here for another day, but then he's gonna be laid up for quite a spell."

"Rachel and I were talkin' about that this mornin'," Ben said. "Henry ain't got anybody to take care of him while he's healin' from those wounds. We've got a room upstairs in the Coyote we could put him in. Clarice and Ruby are both willing to help take care of him, Rachel and Annie, too. I expect they'll most likely spoil him rotten. We won't bother him now, but you can tell him that when he's wide awake and feels like talkin'. And tell him Johnny Grey is gonna take care of the stable till he's ready to come back."

"I think that's going to do more for him than any medicine I could give him," Doc said.

"I've got another patient for you, Doc," Mack said and told him about Jack Ramsey's thigh wound. "I bandaged it up and stopped it from bleedin', but it didn't look bad enough to bother you with it last night. I'd 'preciate it if you could take a look at it." Doc said he'd stop by the jail before noon.

It was two more days before two deputy marshals showed up in Buzzard's Bluff with a jail wagon to transport three prisoners to Huntsville Unit, to find only Jack Ramsey available to return with them. Ben stood alone on the boardwalk in front of the Lost Coyote, watching the jail wagon roll out of town. Taking a deep breath and enjoying the pleasant morning, he felt a gentle tap on his shoulder. He turned to find a troubled Marva Gillespie looking up at him.

"Uh-oh," Ben said.

CHAPTER 1

"There's hell in Thunder Canyon!"

The excited shout made everyone in Fiddler's Green turn their head toward the entrance, where a man had just slapped the batwings aside and rushed into the saloon.

"What the devil is that rannihan going on about?" asked Biff Johnson, the former cavalryman who owned Fiddler's Green. Biff had named the place after an old cavalry legend that said every man who had answered the call of "Boots and Saddles" would journey after death to an idyllic meadow with a tree-lined creek on one side, where he would be able to sit in the shade and visit with all his former comrades. Biff had made his Fiddler's Green into something of an idyllic spot, itself, seeing as it was the finest saloon in the town of Chugwater, Wyoming.

"Why dinnae ye ask him what he's on about?" suggested Duff MacCallister, who was sitting at a table with Biff, Elmer Gleason, and Wang Chow. The latter two worked for Duff on his vast ranch, Sky Meadow, at least technically speaking. In reality, Elmer and Wang were more like members of the family.

Biff nodded. "I'll do that." He pushed to his feet and

started toward the agitated newcomer. Several men had gathered around to ask him questions.

Biff's powerful voice cut through the hubbub. "Pinky Jenkins, what do you mean by bursting in here and yelling like that? Can't folks enjoy a peaceful drink in the middle of the day without having their ears assaulted by your cater-wauling?"

Jenkins stared wide-eyed at him. "But Biff, there's hell in Thunder Canyon!"

"Yes, you said that. But what are you talking about?"

"Avalanche!"

That raised even more of a ruckus in the saloon. Duff stood up, went over to join Biff, and asked, "Was anyone hurt in this rockslide, d' ye ken?"

Jenkins turned his bug-eyed expression toward Duff. "It was more 'n a rockslide, Mr. MacCallister. The whole derned mountainside came down on the canyon! Closed it up, clear from one side to the other!"

"How do you know that?" asked Biff.

"I seen it with my own eyes!"

Biff grunted. "Then you can give us more details, or at least you should be able to."

"I reckon I can," Jenkins said. His tongue came out and swiped across his lips. "But the ride into town sure made me dry, Biff. I could prob'ly talk a whole heap better if my speakin' apparatus was lubricated some."

Biff glared, but it was all Duff could do not to laugh. Pinky was a decent wrangler and ranch hand, when he rattled his hocks long enough to actually work any. He had an inordinate fondness for Who-Hit-John, too, which meant that he had worked for most of the spreads around Chug-water at one time or another, sticking for a spell before he got drunk and did something to get himself fired. He was a colorful but amiable local character. Duff wasn't surprised Pinky would try to cadge a drink or two before he spilled whatever news he happened to have.

"Come on over to the bar," Duff told him. "'Tis happy I'll be to buy you a drink."

"I'm much obliged to you, Mr. MacCallister."

Duff put a hand on Jenkins' shoulder and steered him over to the hardwood. He nodded for the bartender to pour a drink. As the men pressed around him, Jenkins picked up the glass, threw back the whiskey, and licked his lips again.

"That helped a mite," he said, "but—"

"Tell the story first," Duff interrupted in a firm voice. "Perhaps then 'twill be time for another drink."

Jenkins nodded. "Yeah, sure, I reckon that makes sense. I was ridin' close to Thunder Canyon, thinkin' I might mosey up to Longshot Basin and take a look around. But thank goodness I wasn't in any hurry, because if I'd been in the canyon when that avalanche came down, I'd be dead now, sure as hell! I'd be on the bottom of thousands and thousands o' tons of rock."

Longshot Basin was an isolated valley some twenty miles northwest of Chugwater, Duff recalled. Although it was a large stretch of range with decent but not outstanding graze, no ranches were located there. The land was still open to be claimed because the basin was surrounded by sheer cliffs and there was only one way in or out: the trail through Thunder Canyon, a narrow slash in the rugged landscape.

Now, according to Pinky Jenkins, that trail was closed, meaning Longshot Basin was cut off completely from the rest of the world.

Elmer and Wang had joined the crowd gathered around Jenkins.

Elmer asked, "What started the avalanche? Rocks don't usually go to slidin' for no reason."

"That is not necessarily correct," said Wang. "A stone can be in perilous equilibrium and on the verge of falling for a lengthy period of time before it finally does so under the impetus of some force too miniscule for human senses to perceive."

Elmer squinted at him. "If you're sayin' what I think you're sayin', there still has to be *somethin'* that starts the ball rollin' . . . or the rock, in this case . . . even if it's too puny for us to feel it."

"Oh, I felt it, all right," Jenkins declared. "It was an earthquake, boys! Are you tellin' me you didn't feel it here in town?"

"I didn't feel any earthquake," Biff insisted. "In fact, I'm starting to wonder if maybe you were drunk and imagined the whole thing, Pinky."

"No, sir!" Jenkins looked and sounded offended at the very idea. "I was sober as a judge. More sober than some judges I've seen. Until the one Mr. MacCallister just bought me, I hadn't had a drink in three days." He looked a little shame-faced as he added, "Couldn't afford one. I'm stone-cold broke. That's the reason I was headin' up to Longshot Basin. I thought I might comb through those breaks and maybe turn up a few strays I could drive back to their home ranches. Figured I might get me a little, what do you call it, finder's fee that way."

What Jenkins said made sense. Even though no ranches— not even any little greasy-sack outfits—were located in the basin, from time to time a few cows wandered up through

Thunder Canyon and got lost in the rugged breaks that filled the basin. Rumor had it a sizable number of wild critters lived there, descendants of stock that had gone in but never came back out.

"I still don't think there was any earthquake," said Biff, shaking his head. "They have them up in the northwest part of the state, around what they've started calling Yellowstone Park, but there aren't any around here."

"Dinnae be so fast to think that, Biff," spoke up Duff. "Now that Pinky mentions it, earlier this morning when we were loading supplies onto the wagon, I thought I felt the earth shiver just a wee bit under me boots." Duff's broad shoulders rose and fell in a shrug. "I said nothing about it because I was nae sure I felt it or not."

"You did," declared Wang. "I felt the same faint motion of the earth."

Elmer frowned at them. "Well, I sure didn't. How come you never mentioned it, Wang?"

"It seemed of little importance at the time. Simply an inconsequential geological . . . hiccup."

"Not so inconsequential, to hear Pinky tell it," Duff said. "An avalanche big enough to close off Thunder Canyon is pretty major."

One of the townsmen said, "Aw, nobody lives up there. What does it matter whether anybody can get in or out of Longshot Basin? Nobody gives a damn about that place."

Duff shrugged again. "Perhaps not. Go on with your story, Pinky."

Jenkins licked his lips again, but when Duff didn't offer him another drink and neither did anyone else, he continued. "The ground shook and scared the bejabbers outta me, and then I heard this big ol' roar. Thunder Canyon sure lived up to its name! It was like the biggest, loudest peal of thunder anybody ever heard. When I glanced up at Buzzard's Roost, it looked like half the mountain was comin' down. I never seen anything quite as . . . as awe-inspirin' as all that rock tumblin' down into the canyon and throwin' up a cloud of dust higher than I could even see! I tell you what, the ground shook some more when all that rock landed in the canyon. It sure as blazes did! And then . . ."

Jenkins' voice trailed off as he licked his lips again.

Elmer exclaimed, "Oh, hell, give him another shot o' whiskey!" He dug a coin out of his pocket and tossed it on the bar. "I'll pay for it this time." He waited until Jenkins had downed the whiskey, then growled, "Now get on with the story."

"Sure, Elmer. Don't rush me. As I was sayin', that avalanche made a terrible racket and kicked up the biggest cloud of dust you'd ever hope to lay eyes on, and the whole thing spooked my horse so bad, it was all I could do to keep it from runnin' away with me. But I was far enough off that I knew I was safe, and I wanted to see what things looked like when the dust cleared.

"Well, sir, what I saw was a wall of rock a good twenty feet high, stretchin' all the way from one side of the canyon to the other! Ain't no tellin' how far up the canyon it runs, neither. But it plugged that canyon up just like a cork in the neck of a bottle, ain't no doubt about that!"

Duff, in his explorations of the countryside after he had come to Wyoming and started his ranch, had ridden through Thunder Canyon and into Longshot Basin a couple of times. He recalled that the canyon was approximately forty yards wide. It would take an enormous amount of rock to close off the passage, but from the way Pinky Jenkins described the avalanche, he supposed it was possible.

"Anyway," Jenkins went on, "once I'd seen what had happened, I lit a shuck for town. Figured folks here would want to know about it."

"And you figured the story was worth a few drinks," said Biff. He shook his head and chuckled. "I suppose you were right about that."

"I'd just as soon never see anything like that again," Jenkins intoned solemnly. "For a minute there, it was like the world was comin' to an end." He closed his eyes and shuddered. When he opened them again, he continued. "And witnessin' somethin' like that . . . it sure does leave a man with a powerful thirst!"

Pinky Jenkins continued repeating the story as long as the men standing at the bar with him kept buying drinks. Duff, Elmer, and Wang went back to the table where they had been sitting with Biff when Jenkins came bursting in to Fiddler's Green. Biff remained at the bar, keeping an eye on Jenkins.

Duff and his two companions had come to Chugwater earlier in the day to stock up on supplies. Their loaded wagon was parked down the street in front of the general store, ready to be driven back to the ranch. Because most folks around there knew the vehicle belonged to Duff, it was unlikely anybody would bother the wagon or the goods in the back of it.

And Duff MacCallister, for all of his mild, pleasant demeanor, was *not* a man anyone who knew him set out to get crossways with.

Tragic circumstances in his Scottish homeland had prompted him to immigrate to America. After spending some time in New York, he had headed west, eventually winding up in Chugwater and buying a ranch not far from the town. He had named the spread Sky Meadow, after Skye McGregor, the beautiful young woman he had loved and planned to marry, before she met her death at the brutal hands of Duff's enemies. Duff had avenged that murder, but vengeance didn't return Skye to him, so he had put that part of his life behind him and established a new life on the American frontier.

A tall, brawny, powerful man with a shock of tawny hair, Duff was a formidable opponent in any hand-to-hand battle, whether with fists or knives. He was a crack shot with pistol or rifle. But the quality that really made him deadly was an icy-nerved calmness in the face of danger. He never panicked, never lost his head and acted rashly. And if forced into a fight, he never quit until his opponent was vanquished, one way or another.

Because of all that, Duff had a reputation as a man not to tangle with. But he was also known as the staunchest, most loyal friend anyone could ever have. In times of trouble, he never turned his back on someone who needed his help.

As it turned out, after leaving Scotland under those heartbreaking circumstances, he had made quite a success of his new life in America. The newly acquired ranch had a gold mine on it, a mine no one had known about except Elmer Gleason, the colorful old-timer who had been hiding in the mine and working it in secret when Duff bought the place. Duff had befriended Elmer, and even though legally the mine belonged to him since it was on his range, he had made Elmer an equal partner in it. Elmer also worked for him as the foreman of his crew of ranch hands.

That crew had grown as Duff expanded the operation into raising Black Angus cattle, the first stockman in the area to do so. The effort had been successful and quite lucrative. Duff shipped Black Angus not only back east to market but also to other ranchers who wanted to try raising them.

The other man sitting with Duff in Fiddler's Green was Wang Chow, a former Shaolin priest in China who had been forced to flee his homeland, much like Duff. In Wang's case, the Chinese emperor had put a bounty on his head after he killed the men responsible for murdering his family. Duff had "rescued" him from a potential lynching, although it was likely that Wang, with his almost supernatural martial arts skills, could have fought his way free from the would-be lynchers. Just as in Elmer's case, that encounter had led to a fast friendship with Duff. They were a nigh-inseparable trio.

When they had finished their beers, they left Fiddler's Green, with Duff giving Biff a casual wave as they headed out. Biff just nodded, looked at the crowd still surrounding Pinky Jenkins, and sighed.

"Biff's a mite aggravated," commented Elmer, who had noticed the same thing.

"Aye, but as long as those fellows are buying drinks, I think he has little to complain about," Duff said. "Still on the same subject, I thought I might take a ride up to Thunder Canyon so I can have a look at this natural disaster with me own eyes." He had ridden his horse Sky into Chugwater today, so there was no reason he had to return to the ranch with Elmer and Wang.

"You reckon it's as bad as ol' Pinky made out it is?" asked Elmer.

"I dinnae ken. That's why I wish to have a look for meself."

"Thunder Canyon and Longshot Basin are a considerable distance from Sky Meadow," Wang pointed out. "Even if Mr. Jenkins' claims are correct, they have no bearing on our lives."

"Nae, 'tis true they do not," agreed Duff. "Just mark it up to curiosity."

"Sure, I don't blame you for that," Elmer said. "We'll see you later, Duff."

As Elmer and Wang climbed onto the wagon seat, Duff untied the team from the hitch rack in front of the store. Skillfully, Elmer took up the reins, turned the team and the wagon, and headed for home.

Duff was about to untie his horse so he could swing up into the saddle, when a voice said from behind him, "Not so fast there, Duff MacCallister."

CHAPTER 2

Duff turned his head and looked over his shoulder. A very pretty young woman with blond hair tumbling around her head and shoulders stood on the boardwalk and regarded him with a stern expression on her face.

Duff saw the good humor lurking in her blue eyes, though, so he wasn't surprised when a smile suddenly appeared on her lips.

"Did you really think you could come into Chugwater and then leave again without even saying hello to me?" she asked. The smile took any sting out of the question, which could have been taken as a reprimand.

"Sure, and I planned on stopping at the dress shop on me way out of town," Duff told her.

"Well, we'll never know, will we," said Meagan Parker, "since I spotted your wagon earlier and knew you were in town."

"Been keeping an eye out for me, have ye?"

She laughed. "Don't get a swelled head. Yes, I looked out the shop's front window every now and then to see if the wagon was still here, but I had other things to do, too, you know. My world wouldn't have come to an end if I'd missed a chance to see the great Duff MacCallister."

"But ye *are* glad to see me?"

"Of course, I am," she said, her voice softening. "You know that."

"Aye, 'n 'tis pleased I am to lay eyes on ye, too. Were we not in the middle of town, in broad daylight, I might lay a kiss on ye, as well."

Meagan sighed dramatically. "I suppose we should maintain some sort of decorum."

"I suppose," Duff said, "but 'tis not easy."

The romance between Duff and Meagan had begun pretty much at first sight, even though that moment had been in the middle of a gunfight and Meagan had been warning him of some lurking killers about to open fire on him. Since then, they had gotten to know each other very well, developing a relationship built on passion, trust, and genuine affection.

Meagan operated a successful dress shop in Chugwater, sewing dresses of such beauty and elegance that ladies from all over the territory hired her to add to their wardrobes.

She was also a partner in Duff's ranch, Sky Meadow, having loaned him some money when he was in financial straits. He could have paid back the amount many times over since then, but Meagan preferred to leave things the way they were, with her having a percentage interest in the herd of Black Angus.

Duff suspected that was because the arrangement gave her an excuse to visit the ranch from time to time, and also to accompany him when he delivered stock elsewhere. She was a partner, after all, so why not go along on those trips?

Most folks who knew them figured they would get married

someday, but for now, they were both happy with the way things were and saw no reason to change the easy-going relationship.

An idea occurred to Duff. "Did ye finish those other things ye were working on at your shop?"

"As a matter of fact, I did."

"Then ye have no pressing business at the moment?"

Meagan shook her head. "No, I suppose not. I mean, there are always things that need to be done . . ."

"I'm taking a ride up to Thunder Canyon. Why dinnae ye come with me?"

"Thunder Canyon?" Meagan repeated. "Why are you going all the way up there?"

"Dinnae ye hear the commotion earlier when Pinky Jenkins came riding into town?"

"No, I didn't. Pinky Jenkins is a pretty disreputable character, isn't he?"

"He's known to be, at times," admitted Duff. "But he brought a very interesting tale with him today." He filled her in on the story Jenkins had told about the avalanche closing off Thunder Canyon.

"My goodness, it sounds like quite a catastrophe," Meagan said. "Do you think he was telling the truth?"

"He seemed mighty sincere, and he insisted he was nae drunk when it happened." Duff shrugged. "So I thought I would go and take a look for meself, and now I'm for inviting you to come along."

"Could we ride up there and be back before nightfall?"

"Oh, I think 'tis likely."

"Would I have time to pack a little food? I've been busy today and didn't stop for lunch, but I have a loaf of bread and some roast beef I could bring along, as well as a bottle of wine."

"'A jug of wine, a loaf of bread, and thou'," Duff quoted. "To my way of thinking, Omar Khayyam had it right, but I'll not pass up a chance to put that old saying to the test!"

Meagan wanted to change into more suitable clothes for riding, so while she was doing that, Duff rode to the livery stable and had the hostler bring out the horse she kept there. Duff saddled the mount himself to make sure everything was the way it should be. Where Meagan's safety was concerned, he took no chances.

He mounted up and rode to the dress shop, leading her horse. Carrying a small wicker basket with a clean white cloth draped over its contents, she was just coming outside when he got there. Even her denim trousers and a man's shirt made the clothes look good on her. Her blond hair was tucked up under the brown hat she wore.

They rode for about an hour and then stopped on a grassy, tree-shaded hill to enjoy the simple but delicious picnic lunch Meagan had packed. Duff enjoyed the wine, too, although he preferred coffee, tea, beer, or a good Scotch whiskey, for the most part. But not surprisingly, the company made everything better, as when they stretched out on the grass and lingered in each other's arms for a while, sharing kisses.

Then they rode on, following a faint trail Duff knew led to Thunder Canyon and beyond that to Longshot Basin.

Buzzard's Roost, the mountain that reared its ugly peak just southwest of the canyon, was visible for quite a few miles before they got there. Even though they rode steadily, it didn't seem as if they got any closer to the mountain. It still loomed ahead of them, tantalizingly out of reach.

To the northeast lay a vast, high tableland bordered by sheer cliffs that formed the other side of the canyon. Those cliffs curved around to merge with the lower slopes of Buzzard's Roost and completely enclose Longshot Basin. It was an impressive geographical barrier. A man might be able to climb the cliffs in a few spots, but a horse couldn't, and getting a wagon over them was downright impossible. Duff had never been atop that sprawling mesa and didn't know anyone who had.

Finally drawing close enough to see they were approaching Buzzard's Roost and an even more obscure trail veering off to the left, they reined in at that spot to allow the horses to rest for a few minutes.

As they dismounted, Meagan pointed to the path, which would have been easy to overlook, and asked, "Where does that go?"

"I could nae tell ye, lass," Duff replied with a shake of his head. "I remember it from the last time I rode up this way, but I did nae follow it. From the looks of it, it either leads up onto Buzzard's Roost or, more likely, peters out somewhere betwixt here 'n there."

"It must go *somewhere*," said Meagan, "or else no one would have come along here to make such a trail."

"Aye, what ye say is reasonable. I'll ask Elmer about it. He'll ken the answer if anyone in these parts does."

They rode on, their route curving around the base of Buzzard's Roost until they came in sight of Thunder Canyon.

Or rather, where Thunder Canyon had been. Duff pulled

back on Sky's reins as he saw that the excitable wrangler had been right. The mouth of Thunder Canyon was completely blocked by a jumbled mass of rock—a pile of boulders that ranged in size from a few feet in diameter to huge slabs of stone the size of a house. Meagan came to a stop beside him, and they both sat there, staring at the impassable barrier.

"That's incredible," she said in a hushed, awed tone. "I'm not sure how far it goes up the canyon, but it would take weeks to dig through that."

Duff shook his head. "Ye could nae dig through it. Ye would have to blast a path with dynamite, which might cause even more rockslides. 'Twould be a job requiring months of hard labor. Maybe even years."

"And what's on the other side? Just an empty basin?"

"Aye. And you're looking at the reason why 'tis empty. Everyone in these parts knew that if such a thing ever happened as has occurred today, Longshot Basin would be cut off from the rest of the world."

A little shiver went through Meagan. "I'm glad I'm not on the other side of that."

"That goes for me as well, lass."

"What do you think caused it?"

Duff tilted his head back and stared up at the rugged slopes of Buzzard's Roost rising above them. He could see the long, fresh scar in the mountainside where hundreds of tons of rock had pulled loose and roared down into the canyon.

"Pinky Jenkins claimed 'twas an earthquake, and Wang and I felt it, too, although in Chugwater the effect was small enough that I was nae sure I hadn't but imagined it. Wang agreed with Pinky, though, and I trust his senses."

Meagan gazed intently at the devastation and said, "It's magnificent, in a way, isn't it? And yet, at the same time, I hate to think about how small it makes me feel. Humanity is really insignificant in the face of nature, isn't it?"

"Nae," Duff answered without hesitation. "If 'twere no humans to appreciate and be impressed by nature, what good would it be, I ask ye? The tallest, most majestic mountain . . . more majestic than ol' Buzzard's Roost here . . . would be nothing without human eyes to gaze upon it. Does anything truly even exist without someone to take note of it?"

Meagan laughed. "Why, Duff, you're becoming quite the philosopher. You must have been sitting out there at the ranch thinking deep thoughts."

"Nae, not really. But a man's mind *does* take strange turns now 'n then, when he's out riding the range alone."

They sat in their saddles for a few more minutes, drinking in the awe-inspiring sight in front of them, then turned their mounts and headed away from Thunder Canyon. The aftermath of the huge avalanche was impressive, but once you'd seen it, you'd seen it, Duff mused.

"You don't have to ride all the way back to town with me," Meagan said. "It would be out of your way. You should just cut back across country to the ranch."

"I would nae do that, leave ye to ride all the way back to Chugwater unaccompanied."

"Really, Duff, I'm not a helpless little child." Meagan patted the smooth wooden stock of a Winchester carbine that stuck up from a saddle sheath strapped under the right stirrup fender. "I'm not unarmed, either, and you know I'm a good shot."

"'Tis true," Duff admitted. "But ye would nae rob me of the chance to spend more time with ye, would ye?"

Meagan smiled. "Well, when you put it that way . . ."

Duff would have continued the enjoyable banter, but at that moment, from the corner of his eye, he spied movement off to their right. Turning his head to take a better look, he saw two riders angling toward them. After a moment, he realized the horsebackers were following the trail he and Meagan had seen earlier.

Meagan was to his right, between him and the pair of riders. Quietly, he said, "Move around here on the other side of me, lass."

"What? Is something wrong, Duff?"

"Nae, not that I ken, but yonder are a couple of strangers, and I'd be more comfortable if 'twas between you and them I was."

"Oh." For a second Meagan looked as if she might argue the matter, but then she slowed her mount, let Duff pull ahead of her, and swung around to his left.

"'Tis glad I am now that I dinnae let ye go on to Chugwater by yourself," he commented.

"You don't know those men mean us any harm."

"I dinnae ken they *don't.*"

It was entirely possible those riders were as wary of Duff and Meagan as Duff and Meagan were of them. As they drew closer, Duff got the impression the men hadn't been stalking them since the strangers were making no effort to conceal their presence. They had been following the other trail, and it could well be coincidence their route was going to intercept that of Duff and Meagan.

However, he could also tell the men had noticed them. One of them drew a rifle from its sheath and rested the weapon across the saddle in front of him. Duff did likewise, his movements casual and unhurried to show that he wasn't afraid, merely cautious.

Neither party slowed until they were about thirty feet apart. Then all four riders reined in.

Now that he could get a good look at them, Duff confirmed the two men were strangers to him, but at the same time, something about them seemed vaguely familiar. Since they were riding in the direction of Chugwater, the same as Duff and Meagan, he thought maybe he had seen them in town before. He had a good memory for faces.

And these two faces were memorable, in their way. The man who edged his mount slightly ahead of the other horse and rider was lean, with dark beard stubble covering the cheeks and chin of his lantern-jawed face. His eyes had what seemed to be a perpetual squint so pronounced Duff wondered how he could see through those narrow slits.

Duff knew the man could see him, though. He could feel the cold regard of that stare, almost like a snake was watching him, ready to coil and strike.

The man wore black trousers and a black coat over a white, collarless shirt buttoned up to the throat. His black hat had a flat brim and a slightly rounded crown. Duff spotted the walnut grips of a revolver under the man's coat, worn on the left side in a cross-draw rig with the butt forward. He was the member of the duo who had pulled his rifle out and had it balanced across the saddle in front of him.

The other man was much larger, with ax-handle shoulders, a barrel chest, and a head like a block of wood that seemed to sit directly on his shoulders with no neck. Dark, shaggy hair hung out from under a shapeless hat with a ragged brim. His bulk stretched the fabric of a patched, homespun shirt. His whipcord trousers were stuffed down in the tops of well-worn boots. He didn't have a rifle, but what looked like an old cap-and-ball revolver was holstered on his right hip.

Duff moved his horse a little to put himself more squarely between them and Meagan then nodded and said, "Good afternoon to ye, gents."

Neither returned the greeting. The man in black said in a flat voice, "What are you doing out here?"

Before Duff could say anything, the other man asked in a rather high-pitched voice, "Hey, Cole, is that little fella a woman? Look at the way his shirt sticks out in the front."

"Shut up, Benjy," the man in black snapped without looking around at his companion. He kept his reptilian gaze fixed on Duff and went on. "I asked you a question, mister. What are you doing out here?"

"'Tis open range hereabout, is it not?" Duff responded. "My friend and I are in the habit of riding where we please, as long as we're not trespassing."

The big man called Benjy got even louder as he said, "Damn it, Cole, that's a woman ridin' that other horse, I tell you. She's wearin' pants like a man, but she ain't no man."

"Benjy—"

"I'm gonna get her and take her home with me!" Benjy dug his boot heels into the flanks of the big horse on which he was mounted. The animal sprang forward. Meagan let out an involuntary cry of alarm and pulled her horse to the side. Duff jerked his horse to the right as Benjy started around him, trying to get in the big man's way.

The man in black whipped his rifle to his shoulder and fired, the sharp crack of the shot echoing over the rolling landscape.

Visit our website at
KensingtonBooks.com
to sign up for our newsletters, read
more from your favorite authors, see
books by series, view reading group
guides, and more!

BOOK CLUB
BETWEEN THE CHAPTERS

Become a Part of Our
Between the Chapters Book Club
Community and Join the Conversation

Betweenthechapters.net